After Midnight
Michael Geraghty

Hold Fast Publishing

Chapter 1

Caleb

As soon as I had walked through the office door, I was hit with that all-too-familiar smell. It didn't seem to matter what kind of doctor it was that I was seeing. Each office had that same sterile flavor to it, the same chairs in the waiting room, maybe even the same carpeting on the floors. Even the receptionists behind the plate glass sliding window started to seem the same to me. They all had a similar smile, condescending at times, as they nodded at me, handed me a stack of forms to fill out, and gave the sigh or eye roll when something was wrong, or you asked what they thought was an obvious question.

I certainly didn't relish being in any doctor's office, but this doctor always made me the most uneasy. Physically, I was in good shape. There was nothing wrong with me other than the bumps and bruises that would heal and the scars that were reminders of events that had been. It was the mental aspect that everyone always worries about, more so now than in the past. I admit I have a lot to deal with, but I never felt like I needed to see a psychiatrist at all.

When I was in the military, we did see shrinks after certain missions if the Army felt like what had happened was something we might need to talk about. The truth was I never wanted to talk much about what I saw or did. It was hard enough to deal with it the first time around, never mind bringing it up time after time with some doctor that didn't know you or the situation at all. I usually brushed them off, gave them gruff or standard answers, and they just sent me on my way. Now that I was out of the Army and trying to deal with life, it all was different.

My sister Linda kept pushing me, telling me I needed to talk to someone and get things sorted out. I know she only wants what's best for me, or at least what she thinks is best for me, but I just can't see how it is going to help me, my son, her, or anyone else for that matter, other than the doctor who gets to send a nice bill. I explained to her that there was no point and that the Army would insist on me seeing a doctor at the VA or at Womack Medical Center in Fort Bragg, but she was adamant I come to see Dr. Weber here in Swanson and that she would pay the bill.

So, I sat in Dr. Weber's waiting room, a small room with just a few chairs and the receptionist sitting there behind her glass wall, occasionally glancing up at me, trying not to be obvious about looking me over. I could feel myself tapping my left foot, a nervous tic I had picked up years ago, as I just sat there listening to the low tones of whatever soothing music was coming out over the speakers in the ceiling.

I could hear my leather jacket squeak against the back of the chair every time I shifted a little in my seat. The longer I waited, the more I felt that this wasn't right, and that I should bolt out of there. The smell of the office was starting to choke me, and I could feel sickness in my throat. Suddenly it was much hotter in the room than it had been just minutes ago, and I didn't know how much more I could take.

I stood up and walked over to the receptionist window and rapped on the pane of glass. The woman glanced up at me from her keyboard, sighed, and slid the glass open.

"Will it be much longer?" I said to her, trying to be as polite as I could under the circumstances. "My appointment was thirty minutes ago."

"I'm sorry, Mr. Wilson," the receptionist told me as she drummed her fingers on her desk. "Dr. Weber is a bit backed up today. He'll be with you as soon as he can."

"I'll just come back some other time," I told her, feeling sick and frustrated.

"You'll still get charged for this visit if you leave now," she told me in a scolding tone.

"Of course I will," I said with aggravation. I turned and walked out of the office anyway, rushing across the hall into the men's room that was there. I felt like I would get sick and hovered right around the sink, hoping no one else would try to come in. After a few dry heaves, the moment passed. I looked into the mirror and could see my face was red, so I turned on the faucet and splashed some water on myself, hoping it would help cool me down.

After a few deep breaths, I left the bathroom and exited the small office building and was back out on the street. Feeling the light breeze and the warmth of the sun on my face made me feel better right away, and I began to walk slowly along the sidewalk. I paid little attention to the storefronts I was passing, and even less attention to the people going by me. I was just glad to be outside.

My sister Linda's place was about a mile away, just off Oak Street, which is the main part of Swanson. Linda complained that ever since I had been home, I had been walking everywhere, leaving my practically brand-new Jeep under the car cover untouched. To be honest, I didn't mind the walking at all. I was used to walking much further than the mile or so roundtrip I was doing here, and I really had no desire to get into the Jeep.

It was only near the beginning of April, but the temperature here in Swanson was already warm in the early afternoon. The town was busy, even if the town itself had a small population. Swanson proper had just a few thousand people, but when Swanson College was in session just a couple of miles up the road, the population nearly doubled, filling the streets with teenagers and young adults looking to kill time, have fun, or who knows what else. College students were out enjoying the spring weather, laughing, smiling, skipping class and going about life without a care in the world.

I turned off Oak Street and headed up Carson Court where Linda's house was. The house was up a steep hill towards the end of the street. Linda had done well for herself, something I always knew she would do even when we were kids. She had gone off to law school, graduating from Duke with her degree, passed the bar and spent a few years practicing with a big firm in Raleigh before deciding to go into practice for herself. After some time in Raleigh, she decided to come closer to where I sort of was some of the time in Swanson, not far from Fort Bragg. She would be close to family since we only had each other at this point, and she kept an eye out on Adam, my son, and Ella.

Ella. Every time she crossed my mind, it made me stop in my tracks. I could see her face in my head, her blonde curly hair bouncing around her shoulders as she smiled and laughed. She always had that smile on, and that one dimple on her left cheek that showed when she did, the first thing I noticed about her when we met all those years ago. That image of her is forever burned into my brain and closing my eyes and seeing her like that helped get me through some harrowing times over the years. Now there are times where that image haunts me.

I shook my head back and forth, hoping to clear everything out of my skull, and walked up the long driveway towards the house. Since my return to Swanson about six weeks ago, I have been living in the apartment above the garage at Linda's home. She had told me to come and live in the house with her, that there was plenty of room there, but I said no. I preferred the apartment she had there, space she no longer rented out so that I could have a space that was mine and my own entrance so I could come and go when I wanted.

My son Adam was living in the main house, space he had been in for the last couple of years. Linda agreed to take Adam in while I was stationed overseas, allowing him to stay in the high school in Swanson without disruption. I didn't want to disrupt Adam's life and routine, especially since this was his senior year. The last thing he needed was a father in the house with him stirring around and keeping him off-balanced and worried. He needed stability, something I had never really been able to provide for him, and even less so since his mother passed away.

I climbed the steps to my apartment and let myself in. No sooner had I tossed my keys on the counter when my cell phone was ringing. I didn't even have to glance at it to know it was Linda. I sighed and pressed answer, knowing what was coming.

"Hey," I spoke to her before she could start in.

"What's going on, Caleb?" she said in an irked tone. "Arnold Weber just called me and said you walked out before even seeing him."

"I waited around for thirty minutes, Linda. The guy obviously had more important things to do."

"You know he's seeing you as a favor to me, Caleb. The least you could do is try to be a little accommodating."

"I don't need to see anyone. Everything is fine." I knew as soon as I said it that this was going to open another can of worms.

"Everything is not fine," Linda said in a hushed tone. I could tell she was trying to control herself and not raise her voice in her office. "Caleb, it's been six weeks since you have been home. You know how you have been acting, not just with me, but with Adam and with yourself. If you're dealing with PTSD..."

I cut Linda off right there. "I don't have PTSD," I yelled into the phone. "Why does everyone assume every vet that comes back has PTSD? It's not imprinted on everyone when we come home. I've had a lot on my plate Linda; it just is taking me some time to adjust to everything."

"I'm sorry," Linda said. I could hear the sincerity in her voice. "You know I'm just... I'm just trying to help is all. I'm worried about you, Caleb, and so is Adam. Arnold is willing to reschedule with you. He's making time to see you tomorrow at 6 PM. He doesn't even take appointments after 5, so you'll be the only one there. There won't be any delays or waiting. Please say you'll go."

I was silent on the phone for a bit as I contemplated what to do. I didn't want to go see him. I never wanted to go see him, but I knew it would make Linda feel better if I made an effort. I could go see the guy once, go through the usual routine, tell her it wasn't going to work, and that would be it.

"Caleb?" Linda questioned. "Will you go?"

"Fine," I muttered into the phone.

"Thank you," she replied with a sigh. "I'll call Arnold back right now. I'll see you later when I get home."

I hung up and tossed the phone back on the counter and sat at one of the barstools that were there. I rubbed my forehead and closed my eyes, feeling tense again just about going back to Dr. Weber's office. I needed something else to occupy my time so I wouldn't think so much about it but finding that thing to keep me busy was proving to be difficult and elusive.

After spending the last twenty years in the military with plenty to do nearly every hour of the day, all this downtime was starting to get to me. The first few weeks I was home I spent getting affairs in order, taking care of paperwork with the Army, meetings at Fort Bragg and so on. Even after that, some things needed my attention around here, things that I had put off or never had the time to deal with before. Linda spent a lot of time bringing me up to speed on everything, even letting me know what was going on with Adam with school, college applications, college visits and so on. She had taken on the burden after Ella died and I had gone back overseas, and she kept life running perfectly. Linda was always good at that, ever since we were kids.

I glanced at the clock on the wall and saw it was nearly three, meaning Adam was probably already home from school. I left the apartment and walked over to the back entrance to the house that led into the kitchen downstairs. I could hear music blaring from upstairs, signaling Adam was indeed there. I entered the kitchen and saw him rooting in the fridge, grabbing a bottle of water. He turned and looked at me, startled to see me there, and dropped his closed bottle on the floor. It bounced in a frenzy before spinning to a stop.

"Geez Dad," Adam said as he reached down to grab the bottle. "You scared the hell out of me."

"Sorry," I told him as I walked passed him to get my own bottle of water from the fridge. "How was school?" I asked, hoping to strike up a conversation with him.

"Fine, the usual stuff," he answered casually, twisting open his bottle of water and taking a sip.

Since I had returned, I tried to find different ways to connect with Adam. I was never much of a talker myself, and because I was not around much, I honestly knew very little about Adam other than what his mother used to tell me or what Linda said to me. Trying to learn his interests, what he liked, what he didn't, and who he was had become something of a necessity for me, but I hadn't found my way in yet.

We stood staring at each other for a moment, neither one of us sure of what to do next.

"Well, I've got homework," Adam said as he pointed his bottle of water towards the stairway.

"Yeah, sure," I said to him, taking a drink. "I'll see you at dinner."

Adam strode off towards the stairs, taking long leaps. He had the long, tall frame that my father had, the kind basketball coaches drool over. Adam played on the high school team and was getting close to finishing up the season with Swanson High School. He was good enough that he had scouts coming around from colleges asking about him and Linda said he had gotten some pretty good offers from a few schools, which made me proud. He was smart, athletic, friendly, and caring – everything a parent could want in a child. Now only if I knew something about him.

I took my bottle of water with me, left Adam to do his homework or whatever he was going to do, and went back over to the apartment. I sat on the sofa, flipping the channels on the TV with little to no interest in what was going on. The temptation was always there to switch over to one of the cable news channels and see what was going on overseas or with the military but looking at those things just reminded me of how I wasn't part of that anymore, for good or bad.

I turned the TV off and just sat on the couch, hearing nothing but the sounds of the birds outside. Even the quiet moments were not as relaxing as they should be. I always seemed to be listening for the less obvious, for what may not get noticed by everyone, so I was ready to react when it was needed. It was never going to be easy to get that feeling out of my system. Worse than that, the quiet left me alone in my own thoughts. Lately, nothing good ever came out of that. I turned the TV back on just to drown out the thoughts in my head. I let my mind get filled with infomercials, talk shows, reality shows and whatever else would fill the time between now and dinner with Linda and Adam.

There must be more to life than this, I wondered, laying back on the sofa.

Chapter 2

Sarah

It was 2 PM, and while most of the world was just hitting the wall at work, waiting for the day to end, or kids were getting ready to end the school day, I was just getting up for the day. My alarm went off, and I sluggishly hit the snooze button, giving myself another 8 minutes of restful bliss before the alarm went off again. My record for hitting snooze was six, but I knew today I was going to have to pry myself out of bed before that could happen.

I rolled onto my back and stared at the ceiling, blinking the sleep from my eyes. I adjusted my eyes to the blurry patterns on the ceiling, and then reached over and grabbed my glasses and put them on so I could see things a bit more clearly. I propped some pillows behind me and sat up in bed, grabbing my phone, so I could check for any messages, read my email and basically kill time until I felt like getting out of bed.

None of the messages were pressing, other than the reminder that I had to turn a paper in for one of my classes today. One of the great things about taking all online classes is that most of the time you have the flexibility of when you can listen to lectures, do assignments and get your reading done. This class on data security was fascinating to me, and I always jumped ahead, taking in as much information as I could and getting assignments done before they were due.

After spending some time catching up on the latest happenings in the world of online news, I heard loud footsteps thundering up the stairs near my room. The footsteps were followed by a rapid knock on my bedroom door. It was a clear sign that my niece Elizabeth was home from school.

"Come in, Lizzie," I yelled. The door pushed open, and Lizzie came in. She leaped on the bed next to me, bouncing the mattress up. She had a big smile on her face like she couldn't wait to tell me how her day at high school had gone.

"Sarah," Lizzie said anxiously, "guess what happened today?" Lizzie never bothered with the "Aunt Sarah" thing unless her parents were around. Since I was twenty-six and Lizzie was fifteen, there never seemed like there was much of a difference between us in age. We always acted more like sisters than aunt and niece, and I was okay with that.

"I'm thinking it was something good for you the way you are bouncing around in here," I said to her with a smile. "Did you get a high grade on that math test?"

"I did well on the test, but that's not it," she said, looking at me, giddy with excitement.

"Okay, so what is it?"

"Becky and Terri told me they heard that Aaron told Victor that he liked me." Lizzie rolled on the bed back and forth, kicking her feet in the air.

"Well that is big news," I told her as I got up out of bed. I remembered the days when hearing something like that third or fourth-hand was a big deal to me too.

"When we were walking to the buses, I saw Aaron looking over at me as I got on the bus, and then he turned away real fast, so I wouldn't notice. Oh, he's so cute!" Lizzie reached over and grabbed one of my pillows and hugged it.

"I'm happy for you Lizzie," I told her as I started to get my uniform clothes out for work tonight. I always liked to have everything laid out ahead of time, so I didn't have to rush around and try to find my work clothes, though the work clothes for me weren't much more than a black pair of pants and a white blouse.

"Do you think he's going to ask you out?" I asked Lizzie as I organized everything.

Lizzie sat up on the bed. "I hadn't thought about that," she said to me. "What if he does ask me out? Mom and Dad will never let me go out on a date with him, or any boy," she said with a pout. "They want to keep me locked up until I got to college."

"I don't think that's quite true," I told her, sitting down on the bed next to her. "They are just careful is all. They want to make sure you make good decisions. My parents were the same way with me."

Thinking back on it, my parents were much stricter than what James and Denise are like with Lizzie. I was raised in a rigid Catholic household with very little flexibility anywhere. I never had much interest in boys back in high school, but the few that I did like and showed interest in me were quickly discouraged once they found out my parents didn't want me to date anyone or even do much socializing. Lizzie didn't know how well she had it.

"Do you think they would let me go on a group date?" she asked me. "A group is getting together after the basketball game on Friday, and I know Aaron is going to be one of them. If we just happened to be in the same place at the same time..." she said with a grin.

"They might go for it if you told them it was a group. You know your Mom and Dad, though. They are going to want details."

"I know, that's the problem," she said with a huff. "I'm going to bring it up at dinner tonight. Will you back me up?"

"Lizzie, I don't know. You know I don't get in between what goes on with you and your parents."

"Oh, please Sarah," she begged. "I just need a little support here. If you say you think it's okay they might be more likely to let me go." Lizzie looked at me with her pleading face and eyes.

"How could I say no to that face," I said, grabbing her cheeks in my hand. "I'll support you, but I am not guaranteeing anything, okay?"

Lizzie threw her arms around me and gave me a hug. "Thanks, Sarah!" She sprang up off the bed with even more bounce in her step now. "I have some homework to do, and I have to talk to Becky and Terri!"

Lizzie darted out of the room, closing the door behind her. I laughed and shook my head, wondering how I was going to help her out with James and Denise. My brother James could be a little more reasonable and flexible, but Denise was inflexible when it came to Lizzie, and she really didn't like it when she thought I was butting in on family matters between the three of them.

Denise and I have always had a tense relationship at best. I was just a teenager when they first got together and then got married quickly after. They used me as a babysitter occasionally when they wanted to go out, but even then, she never really trusted me that much and always seemed wary of when I was around. Things got even worse once I asked James if

I could come and live with them in Swanson, and no matter how I have tried I have never been able to thaw that relationship at all.

James, on the other hand, has turned into the big brother that anyone would be proud to have. James is almost twelve years older than me, and we never had much of a relationship when we were growing up. We didn't spend much time together, and then he was off to college, met Denise, had a child and moved to Swanson all within a few years. He had established his own life and business and was doing well while I was working my way through high school and then starting college. It wasn't until I ran into some trouble in my early college days that James stepped in and was there for me. He took me in, gave me a place to live, and gave me the structure and support I needed most and still treasure.

I put on a pair of jeans and a t-shirt, my usual wear before I had to start getting ready for work, and then sat down at my desk and turned on my laptop. Once it was all booted up, I made sure to send my paper off to my professor and to check in on the two other classes I was taking to see if there was anything new that I had to pay attention to. There were no new lectures or assignments, and my analytics class was online tomorrow so I could listen to the lecture for that one. I did my reading online for my classes, so I could stay ahead of everything and keep myself organized.

By the time I was done with everything it was nearly five, so I went down to the kitchen to start dinner. Part of my responsibility in the household was to take care of dinner most nights since I was the one who was home. Denise worked in the Development and fundraising department at Swanson College and typically didn't get home until after six, and James had his own plumbing business and very often got home at six or later, depending on how things were going that day. I worked the graveyard shift at the Moonlight Diner, the local diner in Swanson, so I had a lot more flexibility when it came to dinner since my workday didn't start until 10 PM. It made things easier for everyone if I could get dinner on the table for when they were home so at the very least Lizzie had her meal before it was too late at night.

I put together a simple dish for dinner tonight, making baked pork chops that were marinated with some cumin, brown sugar and cayenne pepper, along with some Brussels sprouts and roasted potatoes. Even though I worked as a waitress, I had picked up some good cooking tips and skills from Justin, the cook at the diner on the nights I worked. When things were slow, he would take time to show me how to prep things, so I knew just what went into the dishes we were serving. It gave me a pretty good appreciation for the work he did and made me a better waitress.

I was just getting dinner out of the oven, and Lizzie had finished setting the table, when Denise walked through the door. She had a harried look on her face, something that she had most nights when she came home. She dropped her bag just inside the door and hung her coat on the coat pegs and immediately walked over to the fridge and grabbed the bottle of white wine that was in there and opened from last night. She plucked a glass from the overhead glass rack above the kitchen island, poured some wine, took a gulp, sighed, and took the bottle and her glass over to the table, all without even saying hello to Lizzie or me.

"What's for dinner tonight?" she asked without even turning around to face me.

"Pork chops and roasted potatoes," I said to her, trying to sound cheerful. I brought the plates of pork chops and potatoes over to the table and set them down. Lizzie came around with the Brussels sprouts and sat in her seat to the left of her mother. I returned with some iced tea and poured a glass for Lizzie and then myself, and then sat down to the right of Denise. She took another sip of her wine and then looked over at Lizzie.

"What are those?" she asked Lizzie, staring at the plate of roasted Brussels sprouts.

"Brussels sprouts," Lizzie told her, holding the plate up to Denise to take.

"Ugh, no thanks," Denise said, scrunching her face. "They smell awful."

I had learned long ago not to take everything Denise said personally. Even if she meant that she didn't think my cooking was good, I chose not to take it that way. I passed her the plate of pork chops, and she placed one on her plate and handed the plate to Lizzie. Denise then piled potatoes onto her plate as well and began to cut into the pork chop as Lizzie and I served ourselves.

"Where's Dad?" Lizzie asked, looking around hoping that he might be there soon so she could put her plan in motion.

"I haven't heard from him since this morning," Denise said as she put a piece of pork in her mouth and started chewing. "What is on this?" she asked, turning to me as she made a face and swallowed.

"Just some cumin, and brown sugar and cayenne pepper," I told her. "It's a recipe Justin taught me at the diner."

"Too spicy," she said to me. She grabbed her plate off the table, walked into the kitchen, and dumped it into the trash. Denise then proceeded to grab a frozen lasagna dinner out of the freezer and placed it in the microwave, pressing the buttons with aggravation to get the microwave going.

I looked over at Lizzie and saw the look on her face. She knew that today was probably not the best one to ask about going on a group date. Just then, James came rushing through the door. He tossed his leather case onto the floor and raced over towards his seat at the far head of the table, giving Lizzie a kiss on the top of her head as he went by her.

"Sorry I'm late," James said as he reached for the plate of pork chops. "Crazy day today. The phone rang non-stop, we had trouble with one of the vans, getting deliveries, you name it – everything seemed to go wrong at once."

After James finished filling his plate with food, he held it up to his nose and took a whiff.

"Wow, smells great," he said with a smile as he looked at me. He then looked down to the other end of the table as he saw Denise sit down with her plate of lasagna, the cheese oozing and sauce bubbling over the side of the paper container it was in. He knew better than to ask anything and set about eating his dinner.

Everyone ate quietly for a few minutes, with Lizzie glancing over at me now and then. I mouthed a "no" to her when it looked like she was going to make her move, but she didn't heed my warning.

"So, Dad," she started, turning to the one she thought might be her best shot at an ally, "a bunch of kids are getting together Friday night after the basketball game to hang out. Would it be okay if I went?"

James looked up as he swallowed a bit of pork chop, licking his lips from the bit of heat in the bite.

"Who's going? And where?" He popped a piece of potato onto his fork and looked at Lizzie, waiting for an answer.

"Well, Becky and Terri will be there, and I think Tori is coming too... and there might be a couple of other people there. We aren't sure where we want to go just yet."

"Who are a couple of other people?" Denise chimed in as she took the last sip of her glass of wine.

"Uhm... probably Victor, Peter, and Aaron," she said hurriedly, looking back down at her plate to eat some food. I tried to look like I was not paying close attention, casually eating but more pushing my food around my plate, feeling nervous for Lizzie.

"No," Denise said without a second thought.

"Come on, Mom," Lizzie spoke, trying not to whine. "It's just friends hanging out. We're not going to do anything."

"The fact that you felt like you had to say that to me means you thought about doing something," Denise replied. "The answer is no." Denise looked across the table to James and saw he was just eating his dinner, letting Denise have her say.

Lizzie looked down at her father, seeing that he wasn't ready to do anything just yet. She then shot a pleading look to me for some help.

"How about if they came to the diner after the game?" I said, not really looking up at anyone while I made my statement. After I said it, I looked up to see all eyes on me. "They could come and hang out, and I could keep an eye on them, and then Lizzie can walk home from there, or James could come down and meet her."

I looked over at Lizzie, letting her know that was the best I could do. Lizzie looked at her mother and saw that she was not going to budge, so she looked at her Dad. James put down his fork, looked at Lizzie, and then looked over to Denise.

"I think that would be okay, honey," James said to Denise, pushing his empty plate forward. "Sarah will make sure they are alright, and then I can walk down and meet her at say, 11?"

Denise rolled her eyes at James. "Really, James?" Denise pointed at me. "She's going to be working. She can't watch them the whole time, and Friday will be busy in there. Who's to say she doesn't just let Lizzie do whatever she wants anyway?"

"I... I wouldn't do that Denise, honestly," I said to her, trying not to sound confrontational.

"Hmmph," Denise grunted, paying little attention to what I was saying. "I know how Lizzie is with you," she said directing her statement to me.

"Denise, I think you're blowing this way out of proportion," James said, trying to get control of the situation. "Lizzie will be fine. We're only a few blocks away from the diner anyway."

Denise looked quite angry, as she often does, and glared at me and then down at James. "Well I was planning a night out with the girls Friday, James, so this is all on you." Denise grabbed her plate of half-eaten lasagna and tossed it into the trash, storming off towards her bedroom. The three of us just sat at the table, not sure what to do next.

Lizzie finally broke the silence. "So, does that mean I can go?" she asked timidly.

"Yes," James replied. "But I am telling you, Lizzie, you've got a pretty short amount of rope here. Don't make me regret saying yes."

Lizzie leaped up from her seat and wrapped her arms around James' neck, giving him a hug. "Thanks, Dad!" she exclaimed. "I'm going to call Becky and let her know. "

Lizzie came around to me at the table and gave me a hug as well.

"Thank you," she whispered into my ear.

James and I sat at the table quietly for a moment.

"Did you have anything to do with that?" James asked quietly.

"James," I said to him. "Lizzie asked me if I would help her out and I said yes. She's fifteen; she has to be able to go out with her friends occasionally, and there are going to be boys around. I'll be there the whole time. I doubt there will be a problem."

"I hope you're right, for all our sakes," James said. He piled a few more potatoes on his plate and ate them quickly before he put his fork down. He then looked over at me again.

"What?" I asked.

"Mom called yesterday," he said to me.

"Oh?" I replied casually. "How's she doing?"

"Mom and Dad are doing fine, nothing exciting," James said as he picked up his plate and mine and walked towards the kitchen. "She asked how you were doing."

"And what did you tell her?"

"That you were fine, busy with school and work." James placed the dishes in the dishwasher. "It wouldn't hurt if you gave her a call you know."

"Do you think she and Dad are ready to apologize to me?" I answered curtly. "If they're not, I really have nothing to say to them."

James closed the door to the dishwasher and looked at me as I walked into the kitchen.

"Sarah, it's been years now. Maybe it's time to..."

I cut him off right there. "Don't tell me it's time to forget about it, James. They threw me out of the house. If you and Denise hadn't taken me in who knows what would have happened. They gave up on me, not the other way around. I'm not just sweeping it under the rug."

I began washing the few dishes that were left, trying not to get too wound up over what James wanted to talk about. James came over and shut the faucet off and turned me to face him.

"I'm not saying you should forget about it, Sarah. What they did was wrong, there's no doubt about it. But are you honestly going the rest of your life without talking to either of them? How can they apologize if you never give them a chance to?"

"Did Mom say she was going to apologize?" I stated, putting my hands on my hips.

"Well, not in so many words."

"You mean not in any words," I said as I tossed the dish towel down on the counter. "Forget about it, James. It's not worth arguing about. I need to go shower and start getting ready for work."

I walked out of the kitchen and made my way up the stairs to my room, closing the door and locking it behind me. I stood with my back to the door for a moment, trying not to let the angry and upset feelings I was having get the better of me.

They are not disrupting my life anymore, I said to myself firmly.

I walked over and checked my work clothes to see if the blouse or pants needed ironing, and I took out my ironing board and pressed them anyway, just to give myself something to do and hopefully take my mind off my parents. By the time I was done ironing, I had taken my frustrations out on my shirt and pants, and they looked like they had been pressed at the dry cleaner.

Taking my shower didn't help as much either, and I had a hard time shaking the thoughts of my parents and that day when we had our falling out. I aggressively brushed my hair in the mirror, getting it straightened out, and got myself dressed, checking myself in the mirror to make sure everything looked its best. I then tied my hair back into the ponytail I always wore to work, tying it with a black ribbon.

My shift at the diner didn't start until 10 PM, so I sat down at my desk, typed out some notes for one of my classes, gave one last check of my email, and that was it. I gathered up my purse, slipped into my comfortable shoes and left the bedroom. I walked down the stairs, catching the end of James and Denise having a heated "discussion."

"You always take their side, James," Denise spoke. "You know I don't think she's a good influence on Lizzie; I have said it all along. Maybe it's time for her to go. She's been here five years now. When is she moving on?"

"Denise," James said quietly. "She's my sister. I'm not going to tell her to leave the house. She has nowhere to go. She works hard, goes to school, helps around here constantly, and I think she's been great for Lizzie. You need to put whatever personal beef you have with her aside. You sound as bad as my parents."

"Did you ever think that maybe they were right?" Denise shot back.

I tried to get down the stairs as quickly and quietly as possible so I could sneak out the front door without being seen. The last step on the stairs groaned loudly as I stepped on it, and James and Denise both turned quickly to look towards the noise and saw me. Denise gave me a sneer and went back towards their bedroom while James walked over to me.

"Heading to work?" he said, trying to put the other discussion behind him.

"Yes," I said, trying not to let on that I had heard part of their discussion. "I guess I'll see you in the morning." I walked towards the front door, opening it before James grabbed the edge of the door and held it for a second.

"Sarah," he said to me. "I'm sorry if you heard that. You know I would never..."

"Don't worry about it, James," I said interrupting him. "I know how it is. I've kind of grown used to it. Have a good night."

I hurried out the door and down the steps of the porch so I could get to the street as quickly as possible. I took a quick glance at my old beat up Honda, the car I have had for years now, and thought for a second about climbing in and driving off to go somewhere, anywhere where nobody knew me or anything about me.

Instead, I kept walking down the street, pacing the short blocks until I made the left onto Oak Street. Most of the businesses were closed for the night, so the walk was generally quiet until I passed Whisper's, one of the bars located in a town that catered to the college kids. Whisper's name always struck me funny since it was anything but quiet at the place no matter when you seemed to go by. There was lots of noise and music, and a few people pushing their way out onto the street. Even for a Wednesday, the place had a good crowd.

It was just another block down until I came upon the Moonlight Diner, where I worked. I could see that there were a few cars parked in the lot since it was still early by the standards of a place open twenty-four hours.

I made my way up the stone steps to the glass doors, sighed, pulled the door open, and went inside, hoping to put what had been dredged up tonight behind me so I could have a good night at work.

Chapter 3

Caleb

Before I knew it, it was 6 PM and the headlights from Linda's car were passing their beams of light just as the car began its ascent into the driveway. The lights always startled me a bit when I saw them unexpectedly, making me think back to times when our battalion would be crouching low, looking to avoid potential searchlights and flashlights scanning for troops in the area. There were many times, even after I was home, where I felt like I had to squat down or lay low on the floor just out of instinct.

To be honest, when I saw the lights today, it snapped me out of something of a trance that I seem to fall into lately. I couldn't even recall what I did to pass the time between the moment I saw Adam in the kitchen and now. I knew I hadn't fallen asleep, and I was sitting on the couch, but for the life of me, I could not recall what I did for that time.

When I saw the headlights, I got up and headed out the door of the apartment to greet Linda downstairs. Most of the time Linda was bringing home some sort of takeout for us to eat for dinner, at least since I had been home. I can't say that I blame her for doing it. She's much too tired to get involved in cooking anything after she had worked all day, and, to be honest, I simply did not have the cooking skills. When I was home, Ella always did all the cooking. In the military, we either had our meals in the mess area, ate our MREs when we were out in the field, or sometimes ate nothing at all because we were too busy doing whatever it was we needed to get done.

I felt like I needed to pitch in more around the house while I was here, but I wasn't even sure where to start when it came to the meals. Even in my apartment, where there was a small galley kitchen, I barely had anything in there other than some beverages, a couple snacks, and a few frozen entrees in the freezer.

I met Linda in the driveway as she was getting out of her car. She smiled when she saw me standing there, and I opened the back door of the car and took the bags out she had there. There were a couple of bags from the local Chinese restaurant, one of her favorite stops since it was right near her office.

"Hey little brother," she said to me as she slammed the car door shut. Even though I was a good five or six inches taller than her, I had always been the little brother to Linda, and I think I always will be. Linda reached in and grabbed her briefcase and waited for me to secure the packages of food before we walked together up the walkway towards the house.

We walked up the stone path to the front porch in silence. The sun was pretty much set in the sky at this point, and a light breeze blew the just-budding branches of the trees on the front lawn as we walked up to the porch. I held the door open for Linda and let her walk in ahead of me, and she gave me a quick, tired smile as she entered the house. Linda set her bag down just next to the stairs and turned to me.

"I'm going to run up and get changed," she said to me, tossing her brown hair back out of her eyes. "Can you get dinner set up? I'll roust Adam out and bring him down with me."

"Sure, no problem," I told her as I carried the bags down the hallway into the kitchen. I flipped the light switch, and the overhead lights in the kitchen bolted to life, making the room seem very bright suddenly. My eyes squinted as I adjusted to the brightness after the darkness in my apartment and the relative dark outside.

I placed the bags on the table and turned to the cabinets to grab some plates and silverware. After setting the three places, I pulled the familiar white cartons out of the bags. The smell of sweet and salty sauces immediately hit me, and I put everything out on the table so each person could just grab what they wanted. By the time I was done, Adam was coming into the kitchen, with Linda not far behind him.

We each slid into our customary spots at the table, with Adam already breaking open a couple of the cartons so he could grab some of the sesame chicken he wanted and some fried rice. Linda and I just glanced over at Adam, watching him dig in right away so he could devour his meal. His plate was practically empty by the time Linda and I had even put some food on ours, and he was already going back in for seconds.

"No practice tonight?" Linda said to Adam as she bit into an egg roll.

"No," Adam answered. "Coach gave us the night off. We'll practice hard tomorrow before the game on Friday."

"Oh, that's right," Linda offered. "It's the big game against Union on Friday."

I was feeling a bit lost in the conversation since I didn't know that much about Adam's playing beyond that he was good. I hadn't been to any of the games since I had been home. I knew I should go, but I always felt like I was out of place there.

"Yep," Adam said to us. "Coach said he thinks there will be a few college scouts there. It's a big deal for a few of us."

"You feel like you're ready?" I asked, trying to say something and add to the conversation. I looked over at Adam, and he locked eyes with me for a moment before looking back at his plate.

"Yeah, of course," he told me assertively. I wasn't sure if he was saying it to me with confidence or if it was like I was crazy for even asking him the question to start with. I went back to pushing around the pepper steak I had on my plate, spearing one of the green peppers covered in brown sauce onto my fork and bringing it up to my mouth.

Adam finished scarfing down the rest of his meal as we sat quietly. He then looked up at Linda and me. "I've got some homework to finish up," he said to us as he got up and carried his plate over to the sink.

"Okay, I'll talk to you later," Linda told him as he walked by and headed back upstairs. Adam had spent all of about 8 minutes sitting at the table with us and directed three words at me.

"That was fun," I said to Linda as I took another helping of pepper steak.

"You weren't exactly jumping in with things to say, Caleb," Linda expressed.

"What am I supposed to talk about?"

"There are lots of topics you could talk about, Caleb. The trick is you actually have to say something to him for a conversation to start. You have plenty you can ask him about. You haven't been around much for all seventeen years of life. Pretty much any topic will provide new information for you."

"I know," I told her. "I just can't seem to find anywhere to start. Ella was so much better at this than I was."

Linda sighed and patted my hand as she got up and brought her dish over to the sink.

"I know she was better at it, Caleb, but it's time for you to step up and start doing the parenting you need to do. She's been gone for two years now. I was more than happy to step in and help, you know that, and Adam needed it. But you're here now, and he needs you to take on that role."

I sat silently staring at my plate, looking at the patterns the trail of sauce had left at the empty pockets of my plate. Even just looking at that made me think back to looking at maps and a GPS for locations. My army life and my outside life were so closely tied together still that it was hard to shake.

"Did you hear me, Caleb?" Linda said as she came over and sat back down at the table, facing me in her chair.

"I'm sorry, Linda," I said, turning my face away from the plate and back up to her. "I guess I kind of zoned out there."

"I said I wanted to talk to you about Ella," she said to me. "The civil case looks like it is going to come to a close. Now that there is finally a trial date, they are getting worried that the story will get out, there will be a court case, and what not. They want to settle it. Their lawyer is supposed to send me the proposal in the morning."

I hadn't even thought about the civil case since it was filed. It was Linda who had pushed for it last year, saying there was a strong case and that the statute of limitations was only two years so that if we wanted to file something, we should do it soon. Personally, I didn't care about it. We didn't need the money if we would get any. Ella and I had always made sure to carry appropriate life insurance policies, just in case something were to happen to either of us based on what I did for a living. After she died in the accident, a lot was going on, and I was only allowed a brief time to come back from overseas to attend to everything. Linda, thankfully, picked up the slack once again and made sure all the legal matters were attended to. After the young man who caused the accident got away without getting charged for anything, Linda felt justice had to be done in some way and went after this suit with a vengeance.

"Whatever you think is best, Linda," I told her. "You know how I feel about it."

"I know you just want it over with, but I think it's important, from a legal standpoint and for you, Adam and for me for some closure."

"Money isn't going to change what happened, or the fact that he got away with it," I said with a hint of contempt in my voice.

"No it won't," Linda said, "but even if it is just money, it makes a difference. It won't change the experience or the pain, but it is a bit of justice getting served, and we have to take some solace in that."

"I suppose so." I stood up and brought my plate over to the sink, rinsing it off and watching the map on my plate got washed down the sink before I placed the plate in the dishwasher. I turned as if to leave and go back to my apartment.

"Caleb, wait," Linda called to me. I turned around and saw her sitting at the table. She had that look in her eyes that she used to get when we were younger, and she was worried about me.

"Sit and talk to me for a few minutes, please," she pleaded.

I sat back down in the chair and looked over at her. I could see the wheels spinning behind her eyes as she tried to figure things out and what to say.

"You know that I am here for you, no matter what, right?" she said to me.

"You always have been Linda, ever since we were kids. I know I can always count on you."

"Then don't be afraid to let me in and let me know what is going on with you. It kills me to see you like this."

"Like what? I'm the same that I have always been."

"No, you're not, Caleb, not even close. When we were younger, you were the scared little kid that I took care of when Mom and Dad were going at it. Once you went to the military that fear went away and you were strong, proud, capable of handling anything. You were the one everyone turned to for guidance and protection. But now... I don't know who you are now."

Linda clearly had a worried look on her face, and she waited for me to answer her, but there was no good answer right there for me.

"I'm... I'm just a little lost right now, Linda. I'm trying to figure it all out."

"You don't have to figure it out on your own, Caleb. I'm here for you, and Adam is too, but you have to let us in for that to happen." Linda reached over and took my hand. I could see she was tearing and fearful.

"I'll be okay, Linda, I promise," I said to her quietly. "I just need some time."

"I can't tell you that I can understand everything you have gone through, Caleb, or what you are still going through. I'm sure you have seen things that would change anyone for the rest of their lives. But that doesn't mean I can't be here to help you. Maybe seeing Dr. Weber will change that for you."

I had forgotten about Dr. Weber until Linda just brought it up. I was going to have to go and see him tomorrow to appease her.

"Maybe," I told her. "We'll see how it goes."

"Caleb, at least make an effort with him," Linda said. "I can tell by the tone of your voice how you think it is going to go already. It's the same tone you used to take with me when we were kids. Promise me you will make an effort. Arnold Weber is a good guy. He's worked with other clients of mine in the past that have gone through trauma and has always been a big help."

"Linda, I've talked with enough psych guys in my life to know how it is going to go. I told you I would go see him and I will. What happens after that, well, I can't make any promises."

"Fair enough," she replied, smiling at me. "Do you want some coffee? I'm making a cup; I've got some briefs to read that will keep me up for a while."

"No, thanks," I said to her. "I have a hard enough time getting sleep or finding any type of sleep schedule. Coffee at night probably wouldn't help that much."

"Your doctor... or Arnold could probably prescribe something for you to help you sleep," Linda said, trying not to sound too overprotective.

"Linda, I don't want any drugs or medicines," I said, trying to control my temper. "I think I just need to get some type of routine in my life again. Maybe I'll start running again in the mornings. I need more exercise."

"Good idea," Linda said as she finished making coffee in her coffee maker. "I think that will be a big help to you. Exercise, burn off some energy, stay in good shape, and maybe you'll feel more tired at night."

Running sounded like a great idea to me. Even though the activity still left me alone in my head for a while, I needed to get my blood pumping and my body moving again. I missed the activity that I got every day in the Army, even if it was an activity I wasn't always anxious to do. It always kept me razor sharp mentally and physically, and getting back to that would be a big help.

Coming to that resolution made me feel good about things for the first time in weeks. I could even feel a small smile creep across my face, and my body felt less tense and anxious.

Linda poured out her cup of coffee and stood next to me. "I need to go to my office upstairs to work."

"Sure, no problem," I said to her, standing up and giving her a kiss on the cheek. "I'll go back to the apartment."

"You can stay in here you know, Caleb," Linda said to me. "This is your home now too. You can hang out in the living room, watch TV, go down to the basement and do some laundry if you need to, go upstairs and talk to your son..."

"He's got stuff to do, and you have stuff to do," I told her waving my hand as I walked towards the door. "I'll see you tomorrow. Go do your work."

I walked out the back door and into the darkness of the backyard. The motion light flipped on as soon as I moved on the back steps to light my way back to the apartment over the garage. The night air was noticeably cooler now, and you could hear the signs of the springtime nightlife starting to come forward, with frogs, insects, and birds all making their noises.

I made my way up the steps and went back to my apartment. I casually went through the bit of mail that I had picked up from the house and didn't see anything of interest or note there. I opened up the laptop I had sitting on the counter and logged in to check my email. I have had the laptop for a while but rarely take the time to use it for anything. While everyone else seems to spend hours playing games and using social media, I just never bothered with it, even though I had the time and ability to do it now.

Email proved to be less than interesting for me as well. There was just the usual junk mail and spam and not much else. I rarely heard from the people I worked with in the Army beyond the occasional hello. The lack of communication from the world I once knew so well distanced me even more and left me feeling like I was caught between two realms without really fitting into either one.

I decided to bring the laptop over to the couch with me in front of the TV and do a double-dip of being a vegetable. I turned on one of the movie channels and just left on whatever happened to be there, whether it was some screwball comedy or action movie. I then also did a little bit of surfing the web, checking out some websites of all kinds, just looking to kill time until I started to feel tired. The problem was I wasn't feeling tired at all.

I ended up working to clean the computer up a little bit, getting rid of old files and consolidating things down. I wandered over to the Pictures folder, not thinking there would be anything on there, but I saw hundreds and hundreds of files there. I clicked on some and saw that the pictures were all family pictures, things Ella must have transferred over to my laptop at one point.

I wasn't in a lot of the pictures since many were taken while I was away from home, but there were some that have the three of us in there, including many from when Adam was pretty young. Pictures of us having fun at the beach, at a party at Ella's parents, of one Halloween where I was home on leave, and even a few of an early Christmas. The pictures were a mixed blessing for me. I loved seeing them, remembering those happy times, and seeing Ella there, whether it was dressed in her favorite Christmas dress, in her t-shirt and jeans at the park with Adam, or in her bikini on our trip to the Outer Banks one year.

It was also incredibly painful for me to see the pictures. It made me realize how much I missed Ella, and how much of her life and Adam's life that I had missed out on while I was away. Finally, after looking through many folders and files, I had to slam the computer closed because my heart and my head couldn't take it anymore. I rubbed my eyes, which were red from sadness and from a bit of exhaustion.

I looked down at my watch and saw it was 2 AM. All that time had passed quickly, and here I was still awake, with my emotions all churned up. I should have been tired at this point, but I wasn't, and staying here in the apartment like this was not going to benefit me at all.

I put my sneakers on, grabbed a sweatshirt, and walked outside. The late evening/early morning was quieter than I had expected. I thought about heading over to the house, but I didn't want to disturb Adam or Linda and have them worry. Instead, I decided that a walk might clear my head some.

I made my way down Carson Court and over to Oak Street, the main street here in Swanson. Naturally, most everything was quiet. Even the bars in town were already closed or just shutting down for the night, with just a few stragglers on the streets trying to figure out how to get home. I paced up the street, just letting the cool air hit my face and hoping to clear my head.

It was then I saw the lights up ahead for the diner in town – the Moonlight Diner. It was a place I had not been to in many years, perhaps since Ella and I first lived in Swanson and would go with Adam for breakfast on the occasions I was home. It was one of the few 24-hour diners left that you might find, taking advantage of having a college nearby that always had hungry young people.

The diner was as good a place as any for me to kill some time, get away from home, and maybe get out of my head for a little bit. I walked up the steps, pulled the door open and headed inside, not quite knowing what to expect in there, but not really expecting all that much.

Chapter 4

Sarah

For some people, starting your workday at 10 PM might feel like torture. For me, it was the ideal solution. I have always been something of a night owl and loved to be up late at night. The evenings held much more for me, gave me the time to enjoy the quiet, and let my imagination and thoughts run wild for a change. Daytime jobs just seemed to put me in the same rut that everyone else was caught up in. I was miserable along with them, dreading going to school, to work, or doing much of anything. At night, it was all different, and I came alive.

Walking through the door at the Moonlight Diner to start my shift at work always brought different feelings and adventures. You never quite knew what to expect from the graveyard shift, who was going to come along, and what might happen. Some people feared working this late at night because of the potential dangers that might be there. It's true that you never knew who would walk through that door and what they might try to do, but I always felt the same was true during the daylight hours.

As I walked in to start work, there wasn't much going on at the diner. It was typical for Wednesday night, not one of the busier nights of the week, and working Wednesday through Sunday gave me the chance to work the days where it was usually busiest here late in the evenings and early in the mornings. I avoided the dreaded Mondays and Tuesdays when the place would be dead aside from a couple of regulars. Working the busier nights made it so that the work went by pretty quickly.

The Moonlight had been around for many years and has long been one of the staples here in Swanson. The current owner, Doug Robinson, has owned the place for about ten years now. He had worked at the diner from the time he was going to college at Swanson College and kept right on working through school and beyond until he bought the place from the Devlin family, who had owned the diner for about sixty years before that.

The diner itself looked like many of the diners you might see all over the country. We had the classic counter with stainless steel stools topped with red vinyl cushions, the usual booths of wood and red vinyl, and tables scattered throughout the three rooms. Doug always made sure that everything shined and looked its best day and night so no matter what time someone came in they could expect the place to look its best.

To keep things looking as good as they do meant having a larger crew on at night than many other places that were open twenty-four hours. There were only two of us here to wait tables and the counter, myself and Francesca lately, and Justin was the graveyard cook in the kitchen. But, we typically had a couple of busboys working the night with us as well, helping to keep everything at its best. I've been in some late-night places where it was just one waitress and the cook all night, and it seemed to me that it would be hard to make it work well that way.

Working graveyard at the diner means more than just waiting tables though when you are on the wait staff. There is never much downtime if you want the place to look nice, and very often when things were slow I would find myself washing down tables, filling salt, pepper and ketchup bottles, vacuuming one of the rooms we close off when things are slow, or anything else that might help out so that the diner is ready to go when it gets busier come breakfast time, and the daytime crew shows up.

On the rare occasions where I've even done all those extra jobs, , I get the chance to work with Justin in the kitchen and pick up some extra cooking skills. Justin has been cooking for years and cooked in the Army when he was in the military. While he may not have gone to a fancy culinary school, his ambition to learn and real-life cooking experience made him a better cook than what you would find at many other diners. Some of the dishes he put together look amazing, and how he remembers how to cook and prepare fifteen or twenty pages of items on our menu astounds me.

Tonight didn't look like it was going to be a busy night. When I got there at 10 there were only a few tables and booths occupied, and it looked like they were all students from the college. Doug knew the diner was a gold mine because it was so close to the college and college kids with free time that are looking for food that is better than the cafeteria or what they can cook up in their dorm room, the Moonlight is the ideal answer. Doug purposely kept the prices on the menu low, knowing most college kids may not have a ton of money to spend on food, so they knew they would always have a place to go to get something when they wanted it.

I worked my way back behind the counter, and through the kitchen, to the small staff area we had with a few lockers, a beat-up couch many people used for napping, and an old coffee table one of the staff had salvaged and brought in so we could keep magazines and stuff in the back for breaks. I slipped my purse into one of the lockers, grabbed my black apron and tied it around my waist, and then clocked in to begin my work.

I walked out to the front, saying hi to Justin in the kitchen before I went. Justin just nodded and smiled as he worked over the flattop grill, getting a burger going on one end while heating up some onions on the other. He also had a grilled cheese going on the stove, stock and soup simmering, and probably ten other things I didn't notice him doing all at once.

I went behind the counter and surveyed the room. Francesca, the waitress who had been working with me for most of this year, was out in the dining room already taking an order from some guests. She gave me a quick smile before she darted over to the computer to enter the order she just took into the system.

"Pretty slow tonight so far?" I asked her as she tapped away at the screen with one of her long red fingernails.

"Yeah, I don't think we are going to see too much tonight," she told me in her New York accent. Francesca had come down to Swanson to go to school a few years ago and, through fits and spurts, was still working on her degree here. Her family stopped paying for her schooling about a year ago, telling her at twenty-five she should be done by now, so she took a job here at the Moonlight to help pay her way for what she hopes is her last year.

Francesca is like a lot of the women and men I have seen come through the Moonlight in the last few years that I have worked here. Many of them were students at the college looking for part-time work to help them get through school. They thought that working graveyard would be an easy way to make some cash because they didn't think they would have to work hard. Once they saw how much we needed to do at night, many fell by the wayside. Francesca had stuck it out for a while now, and I was glad she had. She is one of the few people I could call a friend here in Swanson.

Francesca was working the one dining room that would be open for the night, which meant I would work the counter area and the few booths we had over near the entrance. I liked nights like this since it usually was the diner regulars that I would deal with primarily, making it more comfortable for me. It also would mean more time doing chored work, making sure the counter was stocked, that the cases were filled, and all the other tasks I would have to take care of for the night.

Right now, no one was sitting in my area, so I went about pulling items out of the dessert display to see what needed replacing. Every once in a while, Francesca would come over and ask me to get her a soda or other beverage from the fountain area or mix up a milkshake for her. We did have a small liquor area and some beer in one of the lower coolers, but we didn't get too many requests for things like this. It was usually only kids under twenty-one hoping they could score an alcoholic drink late at night that might try, but once we would ask for ID, they would get shot down and go back to drinking Coke or iced tea.

I watched Francesca as she flirted with a couple of truck drivers sitting at a booth just outside of my area. Francesca had the dark hair, dark eyes, and curves that would get attention, and she had no problem flaunting and flirting a bit if she thought it might get her better tips. She always made sure to wear the black skirt as her uniform instead of the pants I wore each day so she could show off her legs, and she often wore stockings, tights, or pantyhose with eye-catching designs or patterns to them.

She sauntered back over towards me as she was ringing up the truckers and printing out their check.

"Did they watch me walk away?" she said to me casually as she punched in the ticket number into the computer.

"Of course they did," I told her with a smile.

"Oh, good. They'll be good tippers then. I keep telling you that you should start wearing the skirts, Sarah. You've got the long legs that guys like. Your tips would skyrocket."

"No thanks," I answered. "I don't want to invite any more attention than needed."

"Suit yourself," Francesca replied. She started to walk back towards the truckers' table, adding some extra wiggle to her walk as she went over, gently bent down to place the check holder on the table, and made sure to give the truckers just a quick peek at the cleavage she was showing.

Francesca was right – they did tip her well, giving her a ten dollar tip on a twenty-five dollar check. I handled the register as part of working the front, something I had gotten used to over my time here. When I first started, we used to have an assistant manager here overnight, or Doug would be here himself. Since I have been here a few years now, and have earned his trust, Doug only comes in on Friday and Saturday nights since those are the days we are busiest. Other than that, I take care of the register, keeping the receipts and everything that needs to be done before the morning crew arrives.

The hours can go by pretty quickly when you occupy yourself with things to do. Once midnight rolled around, the guests in the diner became fewer, giving us the time to do prep work that made things easier for the day crew. A big part of what we do overnight is to support the people that work during the day when it is the busiest, something many of the people I have worked with at night fail to understand or grow to resent. They would feel like we did all the hard work to make things easier for them, but the truth is working the day is much more taxing than at night. When I first started , I worked day shifts to train and get used to everything, and I hated it. I was constantly on the go, the rush is more hectic at lunch and dinner, and, to be honest, I found the guests were ruder and tougher to deal with. You get more of the "I am entitled" type of guest that demand everything instead of asking. They are unkind towards the staff, and don't appreciate the hard work that goes on beyond the scenes. I was happy to jump to nights and dove into the atmosphere with more energy and gusto, and it has paid off for me. I am one of the few full-time employees Doug has, and other than Justin, I am the only full-timer on the graveyard. It means I get benefits like insurance and vacation and a lot more stability with hours.

It was a little past two when things really started to slow down. There was just a couple in the one corner booth, nursing coffees and cheesecake, and that was it. Francesca had vacuumed and cleaned the closed dining area, so it was ready for the next day. Justin was hard at work getting things prepped for the morning rush, and the busboys were lending a hand in the back with the late night deliveries that came in with supplies. I polished down the counter one more time, checked to see if the coffee was old and needed to be refreshed, and then gazed out the front windows into the night, wondering what was going on in the world beyond Swanson.

I had my back turned to the front door as I refilled some napkin holders when I heard the door open and close. There stood a man with short brown hair and a nicely-trimmed beard in a sweatshirt and jeans, looking around at the place. I didn't recognize him as a regular, and figured it may just be someone passing by that wanted to see what we had to offer.

I put on my smile and walked over to greet him at the front by the register.

"Good..." I took a quick look at my watch, " well, morning, I guess," I said with a laugh. The man just looked at me without cracking a smile.

So much for your sense of humor, Sarah, I thought to myself.

"Just yourself?" I asked him as I picked up one of our menus.

"Yes," he replied, still looking around at the place. "Is it okay if I sit at the counter?" he asked me quietly.

"Sure, no problem," I told him and led him over to the counter, placing the menu down in front of the seat right in the middle of it. He tried to make himself a little more comfortable, unzipping his sweatshirt slightly so you could see an olive green t-shirt on underneath. He sat straight and tall, and he looked like he was acutely aware of everything that was going on around him. The way he watched my movements almost made me feel a little uncomfortable, like he was studying me and trying to anticipate my moves.

"Can I get you something to drink?" I asked him as he slowly picked up the menu and ran his gaze over it.

"I'll have a cup of coffee, please," he offered, looking the menu over.

I placed one of our white ceramic mugs in front of him and poured him a cup.

"It should be good, I just made the pot," I said, trying to engage him in conversation. "Milk and sugar?"

"No, just black, thanks," he replied.

"I'll give you a minute to look over the menu," I said, taking the creamer and placing it back in the refrigerator behind me. I could see him studying the menu again, his piercing brown eyes working rapidly overly the pages like he was quickly processing everything on the page. He turned his face up from the pages and closed the menu.

"What do you recommend for someone at this time of the morning, Sarah?" he said to me as he caught the nametag on my blouse. It caught me by surprise since most guests never used my name even though my nametag was clearly in view.

"Well, it depends on how hungry you are," I said to him. "Usually at 2 AM, we see college kids looking for burgers and snacks, or a late night driver that needs a cup of coffee and maybe a piece of pie. You don't look like you fall into either of those categories so the choice might be tougher."

"What category do you think I fall into?" he said to me, now looking on with some greater interest in me.

I looked him up and down, pursing my lips as I studied him.

"You're clearly a local," I said to him confidently, "which is unusual because we get pretty few locals in here at this time of day."

"How do you know I'm local?"

"The way you're dressed, for one. Locals know it's cooler around here at night this time of year, and you probably walked here based on the jeans, sneakers, and sweatshirt. Also, the way you were looking around leads me to believe you have been here before but not in a while and you're wondering how much the place has changed since the last time you stepped in here."

"You're pretty perceptive," he said to me, impressed by my observations.

"Working this late at night often enough you start to learn how to read people pretty well," I said, smiling lightly while I unconsciously wiped the counter near him with a dishrag I grabbed. A quick look at his hands revealed that they looked strong and hardworking, and there were no signs of any rings.

"So, back to what you would order," I said to him. "I would recommend if you're up to it, the BLT with some home fries. Since it's not quite breakfast but way past dinner, it gives you a little of both without being too filling. Justin makes a good BLT and some mean home fries."

I saw my guest crack a bit of a smile and chuckle lightly.

"Something funny?" I asked him, standing in front of him.

"BLT has always been one of my favorites, and I probably haven't had one in ten years. I think that would be perfect." He held the menu back up for me to take and I reached for it, our fingertips lightly touching as he held the menu for a moment. I gazed back at him and saw him still smiling lightly, and I smiled back at him.

"Great," I answered softly, shaking my head and snapping to as I pulled the menu back from him.

"What kind of bread would you like?"

"You mean you don't know that?" he said with a hint of sarcasm.

"Oh, I do," I said confidently, "I just wanted to see if you would say something different."

"Go with your gut then, Sarah," he told me.

I turned to the computer and put the order in for a BLT on white, lightly toasted, and home fries. I then noticed a young couple walk in the front door, more college kids up late. I walked over to them and led them to one of the booths towards the back where Francesca was working. She was just on her way back towards the couple she was already serving in the corner with a piece of carrot cake when she stopped me.

"There's a couple at table 11," I said to her, walking back towards the counter. Francesca stopped me for a second.

"Who's the guy at the counter?" she asked me, peering over at him. He was lightly drumming his fingers on the countertop while he scanned his phone.

"I don't know, I've never seen him before," I said to her. "He's a local."

"I looked at him while I was getting the cake," Francesca said to me. "He's hot. Rugged good looks, not like the soft college boys around here. I shot him a smile when I was over there, he barely flinched."

"Really?" I said to her. "He's been pretty chatty with me."

"Flirt him up Sarah," Francesca said as she whisked her way over to deliver the carrot cake.

Flirting was never my strong suit no matter where I was, who I was with, or what age I was at. It's just something that never clicked well with me, and I wasn't really that interested in drawing the attention of too many of the guys around here anyway. I preferred to just be myself, go about my life, and whatever happens, happens.

I walked back over to the counter and saw half of the cup of coffee in front of my guest was gone. I picked up the pot and brought it back over to where he was sitting.

"Freshen it up for you?" I asked, pulling him away from his attention from his phone. He looked up at me, and then glanced down at his mug.

"Please," he said.

I was just about to start up a conversation with him again when I heard the bell ding in the kitchen.

"That's probably your sandwich," I told him and went off into the kitchen. I saw his plate sitting there on the staging station and turned it towards me to get a good look at it. It looked good, which seemed like it would matter to this guest, so I grabbed the plate, yelled out a "Thanks, Justin!" and bumped the swinging 'Out' door open with my rump.

I walked over and placed the plate down in front of him, displaying the BLT with its fresh tomato, crispy lettuce, and perfectly-cooked bacon and bread that had the golden touch to give it just the right crunch.

"Here you go," I said to him. "I think you'll enjoy it."

He looked down at the plate and then looked up at me and gave that wry smile again.

"White toast," he said softly. "You were spot on." He looked up at me, and I could feel myself feeling a little flush from his gaze. I watched him pick up a piece of the sandwich and take a bite of one of the corners. The familiar crunch could be heard loudly in my quiet section of the diner, and he placed the sandwich down on his plate and picked up his napkin to wipe the dribble of the juicy tomato he had bitten into.

"You were right, Sarah," he said to me. "It's a very good BLT."

"I'm glad you like it," answered. "Our owner gets the bacon from one of the local farmers, so it's among the best you will get around here."

He turned back towards his sandwich and took another bite, and then a forkful of the crispy home fried potatoes with peppers and onions. I left him to his meal, feeling proud of myself that I got everything perfect for him, and Francesca came over and asked for a couple of refills of iced tea. I picked up the pitcher and walked over to her to fill the glasses.

"How's it going?" she said to me quietly, staring at the man at the counter.

"He's just eating his sandwich, Fran."

"Because you haven't given him any reason to look at anything else," Francesca said to me with a scowl. "You're all buttoned up like one of the Catholic school teachers I had back in Brooklyn." She started reaching for the buttons on my blouse.

"Forget it, Fran," I said, swatting her fingers away from me. "Go serve your iced tea, and it looks like the lovers in your booth are finally leaving."

Francesca turned to deliver her iced teas, and I went over to the register to ring up the couple that had been sitting there for hours. I took the check from the young man with just a hint of a beard on his chin and asked him how everything was, to which he just mumbled "fine" and he put his arm around the girl with him who looked like she was half-asleep at this point. He paid their check of ten dollars with a crumpled bill, and they quietly left.

I walked back over to the counter and saw my customer had polished off his sandwich, leaving just a hint of stray lettuce on the plate and a couple of overcooked bits of onion from the home fries.

"I guess you liked it," I said to him as I took his empty plate. "Can I get you anything else? There's not much in the dessert case right now, but I think there is some carrot cake and cheesecake. The fresh pies aren't quite done yet."

"No, thank you," he said to me. "I already had more than I should have at three in the morning. I should get going."

"Sure," I answered, clearing his plate away and going over to the computer to print out his check. I circled the amount due on the printout, wrote my name on the top and a 'thanks!' and passed it over to him. He took a quick look at it and went to grab his wallet.

"I can ring you up at the register," I told him, pointing over towards the front door. I walked ahead of him over to the register as he slid the check over to me and handed me a twenty dollar bill for his eight dollar check. I gave him his change, and he walked back over to the counter, presumably to leave me a tip. He then came back over to the register and looked at me.

"Thanks for stopping in," I said to him with a smile. "Enjoy the rest of your day."

"Thanks, Sarah," he said to me, looking me in the eyes and smiling. "You have a great day too."

" I will," I answered. "I only have a few more hours until 6 AM and then my day is done."

"Nice," he told me. I saw him reach over and pluck one of the wrapped peppermint candies from the bowl on the counter, unwrap it, and pop it into his mouth. He crumpled the wrapper loudly, sending a chill up my spine, and he laughed lightly when he saw me flinch at the sound.

"Sorry about that," he said to me, holding up the rolled piece of plastic. I held out my hand to take it from him.

"It's okay," I said to him. "I've always hated that sound, ever since I was little. I can take it for you."

He passed the wrapper over to my palm, and I felt his fingers slide slowly out of my hand over mine, causing me to feel a chill again.

"Bye, Sarah," he said to me.

"Bye," I said, almost feeling a bit mesmerized as I watched him walk out the door. My eyes followed him down the steps. He paused at the bottom to zip his sweatshirt up some more as I watched him walk off to the right and out into the night.

It was an odd feeling and connection I had made with this mystery guest. I walked over to the counter and saw that he had left me a ten dollar tip for his meal. I stood there holding the ten as Francesca walked over to me.

"He left you a ten for a BLT?" she said to me incredulously. "The carrot cake eaters in the corner for three hours left me a buck! Are you sure you didn't flirt with him at all?"

"Nope," I said to Francesca as I grabbed the ten. "I was just nice to him."

"Nice never works for me," Francesca said as she turned and walked back into the kitchen, responding to the bell that just rang.

It usually doesn't work well for me, either I thought to myself, wondering more and more just who this was and why we clicked.

Chapter 5

Caleb

My trip to the diner was not what I had expected. I figured I would go in, have a small something to eat or drink, kill some time, and then walk right home without it being a big deal. Instead, my experience was very different.

Sarah, the waitress who waited on me, grasped my interest from the moment I entered the Moonlight. It was more than just the way she looked, both strong and confident in her ability, but also the friendly, inviting smile that made even a guy like me feel comfortable around her. She had a presence about her that I found hard to explain, one that was intriguing and that I wanted to see more of so I could learn more about her.

She unusually connected with me, and I think she felt the same connection. It was more than just her being able to read me so she knew I would like a BLT. A waitress that is good at her job can likely figure things like that out and take an educated guess regarding what a customer might like. I got the impression that there was more to her, that we thought about and approached things in the same way. Even though I didn't know her at all, other than those brief interactions, she sparked an interest inside me that had not been there in a long time.

It was nearly 3:30 when I arrived back at my apartment, and even though I didn't feel very tired, I knew it was best to try to get some sleep. I kicked off my sneakers, took off my jeans and climbed into bed, hoping for a few hours of rest. Naturally, it didn't work out that way. I tossed and turned and while I did sleep for fits and spurts here and there, every time I fell asleep and started to dream, the dreams quickly turned into nightmares and forced me awake again. Images from days and nights during my tours in Afghanistan and North Africa kept filling my head, mixing with scenes and images of Ella along the way to bring all my nightmares together.

By the time 6 AM had rolled around, I was sitting up in bed, shirt off because it was soaked in sweat, and I knew it was best if I got out of bed and did something else. I pulled on a pair of gray running shorts, grabbed one of my compression shirts that had some reflective material in it, got my sneakers and went out the door. Running right now seemed like the best thing for me.

I used to run miles and miles when I was in training and even when I was stationed at different points around the world. If we weren't involved in a mission, I was out running somewhere. Running always helped me keep my thoughts focused, helped me keep my breathing in rhythm, and gave me the stamina I needed for those days when we were hiking through areas for hours on end. Ever since I had returned home, the drive to get out there and run just hadn't been there.

As soon as my feet hit the pavement, instinct took over, and my body got right back to where it knew it should have been. I made sure to pace myself properly since it had been six weeks since my last run and figured I would start out with a short one today and see how things went. I cruised up and over the streets in the area, trying to stick to what sidewalks there were to stay out of the street and away from the early morning drivers heading to work.

I headed up Connor Drive, which would take me out to Oak Street, and then I could run along the main strip for a mile or so before turning back towards home. Once I hit the corner of Connor and Oak, I made the right turn and saw the Moonlight Diner just up ahead of me two blocks over. I remembered what Sarah had said, that her shift ended at about 6. I glanced down at my watch and saw it was 6:15 and wondered if she would be nearby as I went past the diner.

I had no idea if she drove or walked to work, how close she lived, or even if she left already, but something drove me on to see if she would be around. I picked up my pace, going a bit faster than I normally would, so I could get near the diner and see how things were. As I got in front of the establishment, I took a quick peek up the stairs. I could see that more people were going in and out and more cars in the parking lot now, but I saw no immediate signs of her.

She's probably long gone home, I thought to myself and kept moving down the street, resuming my run.

I crossed another two blocks on Oak Street, dodging a few people coming out of the local coffee shop with their morning coffee, and I was just coming up on the corner near Adkins Road when I saw someone walking ahead of me. She was wearing a light gray sweater and black pants and seemed to have the same brown hair pulled back into a ponytail like Sarah had when I saw her. I moved a little quicker to catch up as she turned to walk down Adkins and was soon alongside her. A side glance at her revealed the familiar face, speckled with a pattern of freckles that were hard to forget. Sarah looked over at me without recognition at first and then did a double-take of surprise and gasped.

"Hi there," I said, slowing down a bit and then stopping as she took a step back in surprise.

"Hi," she said with some shock and bewilderment.

"I didn't mean to scare you, I'm sorry," I said apologetically. "I was just out for a run and thought it might be you."

"It's okay," she said, smiling a bit at me. "I was startled a bit to see someone come up next to me. It's not something that usually happens to me when I'm walking home."

"So, you live nearby then?" I asked her, realizing after I said it that I might be sounding a bit like a stalker at this point.

"I do," she said. "I'm a few blocks down and then over to Baldwin Court."

"That's not too far from me," I said to her as we started to walk along the sidewalk. "I'm over on Carson."

We walked a few more paces without saying anything, and only the sound of the bits of dirt grinding beneath our feet could be heard. I was having trouble coming up with something else to say and was getting ready to just break off and keep running. I didn't want Sarah to feel any more uncomfortable around me than she might already be.

"Do you run this way every morning?" Sarah asked, looking over at me and brushing a wisp of her hair away from her face.

"I do... I mean I try to," I corrected. "It's been a few weeks since I have been out running, but I really wanted to get back into it. It makes me feel better for the rest of the day."

"I haven't been running in a long time," Sarah told me. "I used to love to go for a run in the mornings. It's still quiet, the streets are pretty empty, and it does feel good."

"You should get back into it," I told her.

"It's hard now, working the shift I do," she told me as we crossed the street and then made the right towards Baldwin. "By the time I get off from work usually all I am thinking about is getting home and going to bed."

"I know, it can be tough to get into a routine when you don't keep regular hours. I remember when..." I cut myself short, not wanting to get into my time in the military and getting bogged down in all it might dredge up.

"When what?" Sarah asked me.

"Never mind," I told her. "I know finding time for exercise is not easy."

We came to a stop in front of a large home with an expansive lawn and long driveway.

"This is me," Sarah said casually, pointing to the house.

"Wow," I replied. "The owner must pay you really well at the diner."

Sarah smiled and laughed. "Not quite. It's my brother's house. I live with him and his family."

I felt awkward for saying what I had said and fumbled for words. "I'm sorry, that was kind of rude of me. I'm... I'm not very good at conversation sometimes."

"It's fine," Sarah said, looking into my face for the first time as we talked. "Thanks for the walk home. It was nice to have some company for a change."

"You're welcome," I said. I realized our conversation was coming to an end and Sarah was inching towards the driveway, waiting for me to make my exit. I didn't want to leave, but I couldn't think of anything else to say at this point either.

"Have a good day," I told her, turning to the right so I could begin my run back towards home.

"You too," she shouted to me as I moved away. I had gotten a few yards down the street, building up to a stronger run, when I turned behind me and saw Sarah watching me before she started moving down the driveway. I turned back to watch where I was going, took a deep breath, and picked myself up to a faster pace.

I felt energized again, striding down the blocks, thinking about how nice it was to talk to someone else, even if I sounded awkward and didn't have much to say. I reached Carson Court in no time at all and crossed into our driveway, putting my hands on my knees to catch my breath after sprinting much of the way. I looked up and saw Adam coming out the front door with his backpack, heading out for school.

"Hey," I said to him breathlessly, wiping some of the sweat I had worked up from sprinting the last part of the run.

"I didn't know you went out for runs this early," Adam said to me, adjusting his backpack on his back.

"I haven't for a while," I said to him, "and it shows with how worn out I am. I like running in the morning."

"I couldn't run at this time of day," Adam told me, glancing around and looking down at his phone.

"Heading out to school?" I asked, realizing it was a dumb question and another sorry attempt at conversation.

"Yeah," Adam replied, shifting his feet and looking past me up the driveway.

"Do you... do you need a ride?" I asked him. "I can get the Jeep and take you."

"No thanks," he told me, looking from side to side again. "Jack and Preston from the basketball team usually pick me up in the mornings."

Just then, I heard a car come to a stop at the top of the driveway. I turned to look and saw an expensive-looking white sports car there. The passenger window rolled down, and a voice yelled out: "Wilson, come on!"

"Gotta go, Dad," Adam said as he moved past me. I turned around to watch him head up the driveway and climb into the back seat of the car. The window quickly rolled up, and the car sped off down the street.

I made my way to the main house and walked into the kitchen to grab a bottle of water. Linda came in moments later, dressed impeccably in a navy-blue suit jacket and pants.

"I'm surprised to see you here," she said as she filled her travel mug with coffee.

"I just got back from a run," I said to her as I gulped some of the water from the bottle.

"I see," she said with a smirk. "I've got to head out now," she told me. "I have a meeting at nine that I need to prep for in the office. Don't forget, you have Dr. Weber at 6 tonight, Caleb."

"Linda, I won't forget," I said in an exasperated tone.

"I know you won't forget," she told me, patting me on the shoulder as she walked past me. "I just want you to actually show up there," she said as she went down the hall towards the front door. "See you tonight!" she yelled to me as I heard the front door slam shut.

I held the cold bottle of water up my forehead to help cool me down, took another sip, and then made my way out the back door and up towards my apartment. I polished off the water as I entered the apartment and made my way into the bedroom, collapsing on the bed.

I wonder how sore I will be after today, I thought to myself. I already felt my muscles on fire and it was not even a long run, at least by my old standards.

I had every intention of going right into the shower and letting the hot water work its magic on my muscles. But as I laid there on the bed, I suddenly felt comfortable and tired. I found myself wanting to go to sleep and felt better than I had in months. I closed my eyes and worked on relaxing, pushing the rough thoughts out, and concentrating on something else.

Sarah's face popped into my vision - the quick smile she gave, the freckles she wore – and it made me feel tranquil and gave me the good feelings that has been so elusive to me for so long.

Chapter 6

Sarah

The last thing I was expecting on my walk home from work was to run into my late-night diner guest again. He had only just left the diner at 3 AM, so to have him come across me while I was walking home just a few hours later completely caught me off guard. I was stunned to see him when he came up next to me as I walked, but I think I was more surprised in myself when I let him basically walk me home... well to the driveway of the house.

I have been very protective of my privacy for years now and am reluctant to let anyone in even in the smallest ways, like walking me home. I'm wary of people in general, thanks to what happened to me in the past, but there was something about this gentleman that overcame that feeling. Even though he was not very talkative and appeared as if from nowhere twice in the span of just a few hours, I didn't feel worried or scared around him. If anything, his behavior and attitude made me curious about him.

He was also quite easy on the eyes. While I noticed he was handsome when he was sitting at the diner, seeing him in just a t-shirt and running shorts gave me a more complete picture. He was in fantastic shape, without an ounce of fat on him, and he had clear muscle definition all over... so much so that I could make out his firm abs beneath his tight-fitting t-shirt. It made me wonder what he did for a living that allowed him to stay in such great shape. Perhaps he was a physical trainer of some sort or a professional athlete, but whatever he was, he looked great, even if he said he hadn't been running for weeks.

After our brief conversation on the walk home, when he left me at the top of my driveway, I allowed my eyes to follow him as he ran away. I could see the strong definition in his calves and thighs, and I even found myself peeking at his firm backside. It had been a while since I allowed myself to be physically attracted to someone, but I could feel in the pit of my stomach that familiar feeling of seeing a handsome man for the first time.

I made my way down the driveway and into the house and saw Lizzie walking down the hallway to the kitchen to grab something to eat before she left for school. Denise was in the kitchen as well, pouring herself a cup of coffee and putting the finishing touches on the brown bag lunch she made for Lizzie for school.

"Good morning," Lizzie said to me in her usual chipper manner.

"Good morning," I said as I sat down at the table, glad to be off my feet for the first time in hours. I looked over at Denise, but she quickly turned away from me and went back to getting things ready so that she and Lizzie could leave for the day.

"How was work?" Lizzie asked as she munched on a bagel.

"Nothing exciting," I said to her, somewhat honestly.

"Who were you talking to at the end of the driveway?" Lizzie asked me. I froze, unsure of just how I should answer her.

"What?" I asked her, taking my hair out of my ponytail and brushing it out with my fingers.

"I saw you out the window before I came down," she said, taking another bagel bite. "Some guy in running shorts."

Denise was suddenly paying attention to our conversation as well, peering over from the counter to see what I would say.

"It was just someone who came into the diner last night," I said, trying to remain calm. "He was running as I was walking home and we talked for a minute."

"You let some stranger follow you to the house?" Denise chimed in as she walked over and stuffed the brown bag into Lizzie's backpack. "That doesn't sound very smart."

"He wasn't following me or stalking me," I protested, but to be honest, I really didn't know if he was or not. I didn't get the usual red flags and bells going off in my head that I got when I meet certain guys at the diner that were trying to pick me up. "He was out for a run and saw me, so we talked. He said he lives over on Carson Court."

"What's his name?" Denise asked, trying to get information now.

It was then I realized I had no idea what his name was.

"I... I don't know his name," I said, feeling a little embarrassed. "We just met at the diner. I don't get the names of everyone that comes and talks to me." I knew that last statement was said with some intensity and was defensive, but I felt like I was being interrogated now by Denise.

"But you have no problem bringing strangers back to the house, is that it?" Denise said in an accusing tone.

James came walking into the kitchen just as things were getting heated.

"What's going on?" James said, knowing there was some tension in the room.

"Your sister is bringing strange men back to the house is what," Denise spat out.

I stood up from the table. "That's not true," I said in my defense. "I was talking to someone at the top of the driveway. He had walked with me a little bit. I didn't do anything wrong."

"No one said you did," James interjected.

"I said she did," Denise added, now standing in front of me, next to James. "I don't like the idea of you bringing someone we don't know to the house, especially with a young girl here. I won't abide by it."

"That's not what I did, and I would never do anything that would hurt or endanger Lizzie. You know I'm not like that James," I said turning to my brother.

"Is this going to turn into an episode like you had in the past?" Denise yelled. "Because if it is, you can start looking for another place to live!"

I stood in stunned silence. I looked at Denise, trying to control my rage, and then looked back at James, hoping he would say something to stand up for me. When he didn't answer right away, I could feel my heart sink.

"Maybe I should do that anyway," I said to Denise, moving quickly past her and heading up the stairs to my room.

I could hear James and Denise arguing through the floor, with Lizzie jumping in every now and then. While their argument was muffled, their voices were clearly raised. A moment later I could hear the front door slam, shaking the walls even up to my room.

I was just finishing putting my plaid lounge pants and t-shirt on so I could get to bed and try to sleep when there was a soft knock on my door. I quietly said, "come in," and James entered the room.

I sat down on my bed and looked up at him. James came over and sat down next to me on the bed.

"Sarah, what the hell happened?"

"Nothing happened James," I said looking at him. "A customer from last night ran into me as I was walking home. He was out for a run and just walked with me for a bit until I got to the house. He then left, and I came in. Denise is making it into something it isn't. I didn't bring anyone home or anything like that."

"Do you know this guy?" James asked me.

"I just met him last night. I didn't even really meet him. It's just someone local who came in. Why does that matter? I'm not twelve-years-old, James; I'm twenty-six. If I want to talk to somebody, it shouldn't be a problem, and I shouldn't get interrogated about it. I did nothing wrong."

"I know, but Denise is all bent out of shape over it."

"Well, she's just looking for an excuse to get rid of me. Maybe she's right; I think I might have worn out my welcome here. If I'm just going to be the source of arguments for you two and she is going to make life uncomfortable for me, I might be better off going somewhere else."

I turned and looked at James, and I could see he was feeling embarrassed about what had happened.

"I would never ask you to leave, Sarah. You know that. I think having you here has been good for Lizzie. We just have to try to figure this all out and make it work."

"It's not easy to do that if she keeps bringing up the past. What happened to me years ago was not my fault. I don't know why she thinks it is, or why Mom and Dad think it is, or why anyone thinks it's some kind of reflection on them instead of on me."

I got up from the bed and sat in my desk chair. I could feel myself getting worked up again and tears starting to form.

"No one thinks that Sarah," James said to me.

"Stop, James," I told him angrily. "Denise, Mom, Dad... they all think that it is an embarrassing mark on them because some guy posted pictures of me online. I can't change what happened, and I'm the one who must live with it. Having it thrown in my face constantly like that doesn't make it better, or any easier to move past."

My face felt hot, and I had a lump in my throat and in my stomach. The last thing I wanted to do was to rehash all this again with James. He knew how much this episode had hurt me, destroyed my confidence and my relationship with my parents. When it had initially happened, and my parents were mortified to hear from friends and then see online pictures of me in various stages of undress that were taken without my knowledge, I didn't think things could ever be worse. Then, when my parents in all their religious zeal and fervor, decided that it was best if I didn't come live with them when I wanted to leave college, I had nowhere to turn except to James. I called him late at night, in tears and distress, asking if I could come stay with him. James never hesitated, coming to the college in the middle of the night to pick me up and bring me to his home. Even though we may not have had the best brother-sister relationship to that point, he came through for me when I needed him most.

But that was five years ago. A lot has changed in his family dynamic since then. Lizzie is older, Denise has become more resentful of me and, it seems to me, Lizzie too. Lizzie turns to me more when she needs help, has a question, or wants advice, and I know Denise has come to resent it. I'm sure she would be perfectly happy to hear me say I was moving out.

I could feel a headache coming on after all of this. I was tired from work, felt emotionally worn out from this episode, and was upset that the past was coming to haunt me again.

"I need to go to work," James said, standing up and coming over to me, putting his hand on my shoulder. "Are you going to be okay?"

"I'll be fine," I muttered. "I'm sorry for yelling. I just need to get some sleep I think. We can talk about this more tonight if you want."

"We'll see," James said. "I'll talk to Denise and see if I can calm her down some. We'll work this out, I promise."

James left my bedroom, shutting the door behind him as he went. I crawled up on the bed, pulled the blanket under my chin, and could feel myself starting to gently sob. I had higher hopes for this day from early morning on, but somehow things had deteriorated quickly.

I can never seem to get too comfortable or happy, I thought to myself, shutting my eyes tightly and hoping to wish all the hurt away.

Chapter 7

Caleb

I was grateful to get a good night/morning of sleep for a change instead of the restless nights of the last few weeks. I probably would have slept even longer if Linda hadn't called me on my cell phone and woke me up. When I heard the phone shrieking through the air with its ring, I jumped out of bed and gasped. Once I realized it was the phone, I reached over and grasped it to see it was Linda. Not only was she calling, but apparently I had missed the eight text messages she sent before the call.

"Hi Linda," I said groggily into the phone.

"Why haven't you returned my texts?" she asked me, sounding more than a little annoyed.

"Linda, I was sleeping," I said to her, wiping my eyes. "I got in late and then went for a run this morning, so I was pretty tired."

"Got in late? Where did you go?"

"I couldn't sleep last night and went for a walk and ended up in the Moonlight."

"Why would you go to the diner? You could have just come over to the house for something to eat." Linda sounded more annoyed by the minute.

"I didn't want to wake you guys up, and I really wasn't looking for any food. I just wanted to walk and saw they were open so I went in for a cup of coffee... Why do I have to explain this to you?" I was getting a little annoyed myself now.

"That doesn't matter," Linda said. "I was calling you because it's three o'clock. I wanted to make sure you remember..."

"Yes, I remember about the appointment with Dr. Weber at 6. Linda, you need to calm down about this. I am going to the appointment."

"Okay, I'm sorry," Linda said. "I was just checking, and you didn't answer my messages, so I figured you were avoiding me."

"Not avoiding, just sleeping. I'm going to go now and take a shower and get myself dressed. There's plenty of time for me to get there. Dr. Weber's office is just a few blocks away. Go back to work."

"Okay, I'll see you when you get home. I'll pick up a pizza," Linda told me, trying not to sound too motherly now.

I hung up the phone and sighed, wondering if there would ever be a day where Linda wasn't worried about me. She's been taking care of me in one way or another for such a long time now that I don't think she knows of any other way to act. I appreciate all she has done and keeps doing for me, and for Adam, but at times it can seem a bit smothering.

I went into the bathroom and turned on the shower, letting it get nice and hot before stepping in to wash off the sweat from my run that had dried onto my skin. I never realized how much of a luxury a shower was until after I got home from the military. There were times where we would go days without access to a shower, so it was a treat to have the ability to go in and feel hot water on you whenever you wanted.

As I washed, I could feel my hands glide gently over the areas where I had scars. Though both scars were from wounds from quite a while ago, they served as constant reminders of what life was during my time overseas. One scar went across my right shoulder, while I had another just above my left hip. Even just soaping over them brought back memories of when each happened.

After letting the hot water run on me for a while, I got out of the shower and toweled off. Looking at my reflection in the mirror, I contemplated getting rid of the beard I wore. I had never had a beard before I went into the army, but as part Special Forces we were encouraged to grow beards, unlike other parts of the military where facial hair is a no-no. The beards helped us in relations with those in our area, particularly in Afghanistan, where men are more trusting of other men that have beards like themselves.

Now that I was out of the Army, having the beard didn't seem to make much sense to me, but I was also reluctant to get rid of it. It had been such a part of my identity for so long, I would almost feel naked without it. Instead of shaving it off, I decided to just trim it up a bit, so it looked neater. I took out my handy beard trimmer, a gift from Ella and Adam one Father's Day... one I hadn't used much since I was rarely home, and used it to get rid of some of the stray and unruly hairs so that the beard looked neater.

Once I was satisfied with how I looked, I went and got dressed. I needed to make sure I had something comfortable on for the doctor visit. The last thing I wanted was to sit there fidgeting because of my clothes. The experience alone was going to be uncomfortable enough for me; there was no need to make things worse. I decided a t-shirt and jeans would be good enough, and put them on, along with a pair of sneakers.

I put my watch on and saw it was after four, so I still had plenty of time. Grabbing my wallet, keys and my sweatshirt, I decided to go over to the house and see what Adam was up to and ask him about his day. When I walked into the house, there was nothing but dead silence. I didn't even hear any of his music playing. I called out, but there was no answer. Figuring he had his headphones on while doing homework or playing on his computer, I took a walk up the stairs and went to his bedroom.

I knocked on the door, loud enough so that he might hear me with his headphones on, but there was still no answer. I slowly opened the door, hearing it creak as I did. I didn't want to surprise or interrupt him, but as I opened the door, I saw his room was empty. It was then I remembered that he was at basketball practice for the game tomorrow night.

I took a quick glance around his room, not wanting to pry or invade his space, but just to see what it was like. There was still so much I felt I didn't know about Adam that I thought if I saw what he was interested in that maybe I could get a little closer to him. Without opening any drawers or disturbing anything, I looked around at his room and desk. It was sparse, with not much on the walls other than a couple of basketball pennants. He had shelves that held some of his basketball trophies and sports awards from years past, reminding of all the games and awards ceremonies that I had missed along the way.

I didn't want to touch anything on his desk, but I did notice a picture of Adam standing with his arm around a cheerleader from the team while she was giving him a kiss on the cheek. Adam never indicated to me that he had a girlfriend, and I didn't know for sure that he did, but the picture did seem to indicate something. It made me wish we were close enough where he could talk about things like that with me, or even give an indication that he was going out on a date or had someone special in his life.

I put the picture back down on his desk and left his room, closing the door, and made my way back down the stairs. I grabbed a bottle of water from the refrigerator and sat at the kitchen table, eyeing the clock on the wall and my watch, alternating between one and the other, hoping to see the time pass by so I could get this appointment over with. I still had about 45 minutes before I needed to be there, and the walk to his office would only take about ten minutes or so, leaving me to stress over the meeting until then.

I always worried about what doctors like this were going to ask. I never felt comfortable revealing a lot of aspects of my life to anyone. I did open up to Ella, and she seemed to be the only one that could understand me when I was feeling anxious, stressed, sad, lonely or any other emotion. I always had doubts that psychiatrists could help you get to the heart of things and provide you with any assistance at all. On the other hand, I did know, deep down, that I was not having an easy time handling a lot of things in my life right now. Gaining some insight from someone with some outside objective might be just what I needed at this moment.

The ticking sound of the kitchen clock seemed to be the only noise echoing throughout the house, and the more I focused on it, the louder it seemed to get. I was going to drive myself mad listening to that sound, and I knew I had to get out of the house. I walked out the back door into the fresh air.

The sun was starting to get lower in the sky as evening approached. As I walked along, I could see kids heading inside to get their dinners, running off their lawns as parents called them in. More cars came down the streets as people started heading home from work. I decided to take a longer route since I had so much time to kill and found myself wandering over towards Baldwin and passing in front of Sarah's house. I walked slowly past the driveway, looking up at the house to see the finely manicured lawn and long driveway. I wondered which window was hers and suddenly felt like a teenager who was enamored with the girl at school and just wanted to see where she lived. I stood just to the right driveway on the sidewalk outside the picket fence that surrounded the yard. A car pulled into the driveway as I stood there, and the driver and I locked eyes for a moment. The woman gazed at me through the car window as she eased into the driveway, giving me a stern look as she saw me there. I thought it best to be on my way before she got the wrong idea and turned up the street to head towards Oak Street.

Once I was on Oak Street, I worked my way back over to where Dr. Weber's office was. I could feel myself starting to tense before I even reached the front of the building. When I arrived at the small brick building, I stood in front of the door for a minute or two, trying to decide if I was really going to go in. I had made a promise to Linda and needed to follow through this time, so I sucked it up, swung the door open, and went inside.

I opened the wooden door to my right and was in Dr. Weber's waiting room. There was no one in there this time, not even the receptionist. I peered through the receptionist window to see if I could see anyone in the back but saw no sign of anyone. I gave a light rap on the glass window there, hoping to get someone's attention. My real hope was that no one came out so I could go back home, tell Linda I was here, and no one appeared, and just forget about the whole thing.

I guess I wasn't that lucky. The door to the inner office swung open, and there stood a tall, thin man with round-rim glasses and a smile on his face.

"Caleb?" he asked, having a stronger Southern drawl than I had expected him to.

"Yes?" I answered hesitantly.

"Hi, I'm Dr. Weber," he said to me as he thrust his right hand out towards me to shake hands. I shook his hand and felt his grip in mind. His hands were soft, and his grip was relaxed, much more relaxed than mine was.

"Come on in," Dr. Weber told me as he held the door open. I walked through the office door and a short distance down a small hallway into his office. His office was not what I had expected to find. I had seen several Army psychiatrists' offices, and they looked nothing like what Dr. Weber had. Sure, he had his diploma on the wall, a bookcase filled with books, and the obligatory desk with chairs. I didn't see the "couch" you might expect to see in the usual office, but I did notice that the chairs he had were stressless recliners to help you feel more comfortable.

"Have a seat," Dr. Weber said to me, pointing to the chairs in front of his desk.

"No couch?" I said to him sarcastically.

Dr. Weber let out a light laugh. "I used to have a couch in here, but I found people felt really self-conscious when they came in and saw it. The chairs made them more comfortable."

I sat down in one of the black leather chairs as Dr. Weber went behind his desk. He grabbed a folder he had and a leather portfolio and then came around and sat in the chair across from me.

"I'm glad you could come in," he said to me, adjusting his glasses slightly. His tall frame seemed too tall for the chair he was in, and he moved around a bit to find a comfortable location for his body.

"Well, I promised my sister I would come," I said begrudgingly.

"Linda's a great person," Dr. Weber told me. "She and I went to undergrad together at Duke, and then she went to the law school while I went to medical school. We've known each other for a long time. It was funny we both ended up in Swanson. I hadn't seen her in years until she started her practice here."

"Yes, she is a great sister." I kept crossing and uncrossing my legs, trying not to fidget too much.

"So, tell me a little about yourself Caleb," Dr. Weber said as he sat back in his chair.

"What do you want to know?" I said, trying to anticipate the direction he was seeking to go.

"Whatever you want to tell me. I know you were in the Army and recently retired. What was your military career like?"

"It was good, I spent twenty years in the Army."

"What did you do in the service?" he asked, jotting down something on his notepad. I kept a keen eye every time he started writing, wondering what he was putting down.

"I was in Special Forces."

"Wow," he said raising his eyebrows. "That's pretty impressive. It takes a special kind of person to do those jobs. Where were you based?"

"I was in the 3rd SF Group, 2nd Battalion, Alpha Company. I was based out of Fort Bragg but didn't spend much time there."

"I imagine not," Dr. Weber noted. "Where did you travel?"

"Afghanistan, North Africa, places around there. I'm not really supposed to talk about a lot of details about what I did. It's classified stuff in many cases."

"I understand," he said with a nod. "Don't worry – whatever you say to me is confidential. We don't have to get into specifics about where you went or what you did. I would think you saw some pretty intense things while you served."

"You could say that," I told him, sitting back in the chair now.

"It's a big change for you then, being in Swanson instead of somewhere in Afghanistan."

"It's certainly a lot slower paced," I said as I sighed.

"Are you glad you're home, Caleb?"

"Why would you ask that?" I said, sitting up and feeling defensive now. "Of course I am glad to be home. No one likes the idea of getting shot at every day or having people trying to kill you all the time for twenty years."

"Of course," Dr. Weber replied, sitting straight up in his chair. "All I meant was many veterans like yourself, after spending most of their lives in the military, find it difficult to adjust once they are out of the Army. Many exhibit signs of depression, anxiety, sleeplessness – some the symptoms I know Linda had indicated you were struggling with when she first talked to me about you. You may find that..."

"Let me stop you right there Doc," I interrupted. "If you are going tell me about PTSD and the medications I can take we can end this session now. I don't have PTSD, and I don't want to take any medications."

"PTSD is not the only issue that returning veterans face, Caleb," he answered calmly. "And I would never suggest you take any medication that I didn't think would help you. If you prefer not to take anything, that's fine. We can talk about whether I think you need anything as we go on and talk more. My goal is to help you feel comfortable with yourself, your surroundings, and your family. It seems to me that those are things you would want to work on."

I was glad to hear he wasn't trying to force a diagnosis on me and push medication that might make me a zombie all the time.

"Thanks," I said to him. "I appreciate that." I let out another deep sigh.

"You're welcome. Now that we have that established, have you had any trouble adjusting to being at home?"

I thought hard about how to answer this. The easy thing to do would be to lie and just say everything was fine, but deep down I knew that approaching things that way would not benefit me at all. I knew I should be honest, but I just didn't know how much I wanted to open up about just yet.

"Sure, I have," I told Dr. Weber. "When you spend that much of your life having everything regimented, and then you live on a heightened state of alert all the time, always expecting the worst, it's tough to come back and be expected to just pick up and live a normal life again. I've had trouble sleeping, felt anxious and yes... it's been tough to talk to and interact not just with my son and Linda, but with people in general."

"Do you have any friends in the area, outside of your family?"

"Not really," I said as I sank back in the chair. "The people I would call friends are all either still in the military or scattered around the country, living their own lives. I never knew anyone that lived in Swanson. My wife chose to live here because she liked the small town feel and it wasn't too far from Fort Bragg."

"Right," Dr. Weber said. He flipped through his folder and notes. "Your wife was Ella. I'm sorry for your loss. I didn't know her personally, but I know Linda has spoken of her. I'm sure all that makes it difficult for you to adjust around here as well."

"Doc, can we not talk about... about her. It's not something I want to get into." I felt myself fidgeting in the chair again and then glancing down at my watch to see how much longer this was going to go on.

"Sure, no problem," Dr. Weber said to me, closing his folder. "Tell me about what you like to do. Do you have interests outside of the military? Have you thought about looking for different work now that you are retired? It might give you a chance to meet some new people, try something interesting to you."

"I haven't thought much about another job just yet," I told him honestly. "My pension is fine for me to live on right now, and it's hard for me to envision another job that I would get as much from as I did in the military. I never had any hobbies or outside interests. The Army was pretty much my life."

"But I'm sure you have a lot of skills that can be applied in different jobs, especially if you were Special Forces trained. You must know how to do a lot of things that people can't even imagine."

"What I can do doesn't seem any more than what the other soldiers in Special Forces can do. We're cross-trained in a lot of areas so that we can cover different things and take on tasks as the assignment develops. Can I do a lot? Maybe, but I don't know how practical being a weapons specialist is in the real world. And maybe I don't want the job where those skills are an asset."

"Fair enough," Dr. Weber said with a smile. I noticed he glanced at the clock on his desk. "We're just about out of time for today, Caleb. I would like it if you would be willing to come back and see me. Maybe we can get together and talk once or twice a week?"

I considered what he was asking. I did feel more at ease with him than I had with any of the Army doctors I had spoken with, and he wasn't trying to push me in a direction I wasn't comfortable with, which was a big plus for me.

"I can give it a try," I told him.

"Great," he said, standing up from his chair. "How about we plan to meet on Monday and Wednesday next week? You can come during normal business hours if you want, or I'd be happy to meet you at 6 PM again, your choice."

"Evenings work fine for me," I answered.

"Okay, I'll put you down for 6 PM. One more thing – I would like your permission to get your records from the Army, at least what they are willing to send me. I think if I know some of your background it might be helpful moving forward until we get to know each other better."

Dr. Weber handed me a form to sign granting him permission to get my files. I took the pen from him and scribbled my name on the signature line. "I don't know how much you will get but knock yourself out."

"Thanks, Caleb, and thank you for coming in. Can I ask you one more thing?" he said as he opened his office door.

"You're getting a little pushy Doc," I said to him.

Dr. Weber laughed again. "I know, but this is a simple thing. Before you come in on Monday, I want you to take the time to try and meet one person in town, someone you can talk to, that you think could be a friend to you. Just do that, and we'll talk about how it went on Monday, okay?"

"I'll try," I said as I shook his hand. Dr. Weber walked me towards the reception room door.

"Perfect," he said with a smile. "Enjoy your weekend."

"Thanks, you too," I replied as I walked out of the office. I walked out of the building and out onto the street. Darkness had set in now since it was after seven, and I began my walk back to the house, moving past the people on the street. The visit had gone better than I had hoped, and Dr. Weber was not nearly as difficult to deal with as I thought he might be. I even surprised myself by agreeing so readily to see him again.

When I got back to the house, I could see Linda's car in the driveway. I knew she would be waiting anxiously for me to come walking through the door to see what my mood was like and how things went. I opened the front door and went in, trying not close the door loudly. No sooner had the door closed when I heard Linda's voice yell out to me.

"We're in the kitchen, Caleb!"

I walked down the hall and into the kitchen and saw Adam biting into a slice of pizza. I patted him on the back and made my way over to one of the empty chairs on the other side of the table and sat down. I reached into the pizza box and pulled out a slice of sausage and mushrooms, guiding it onto my plate. I took a bite out of the tip of the slice and started chewing and noticed Adam and Linda both staring at me.

"What?" I said as I tried not to spit pizza out while talking.

"How did it go?" Linda said to me as she sipped a glass of iced tea.

"It was fine," I told her as I took another bite.

"Did you like Dr. Weber?" Linda asked, hoping for some details.

"He seems like a nice guy. Very tall, weak handshake." I looked over at Adam and gave him a little smile. I think he was surprised to see I had a sense of humor.

"Caleb, stop it," Linda scolded. "How was he... as a doctor?"

"I guess he was alright," I said. "Better than any of the Army doctors I talked to over the years. He at least seems open to listening to what I actually have to say."

"Do you feel any better?" Linda asked, picking up her slice of pizza.

"Linda, it was one session. We didn't have any major breakthroughs or anything if that is what you mean. I think he just wanted to see what I am like and get some information. I'm seeing him again on Monday."

"Oh, good," Linda said, sounding relieved. "I really think he can help, Caleb. I'm glad you are giving him a chance."

I looked over at Adam, unsure as to how much Linda had filled him on me seeing a psychiatrist. He was casually going about eating his meal, working on his second slice of pizza already.

"How was practice?" I said to him as I poured myself a glass of iced tea from the pitcher.

Adam looked up at me, surprised I remembered he had practice today. "It was good. I think we're ready for the game."

"Great," I told him. "I'm looking forward to seeing you play."

"You're coming to the game?" Adam said, sounding shocked. Linda looked over at me, seeming just as surprised.

"Sure, why not?" I told him. "I never got to see you play for the first three years of school. I thought it might be fun to go. It's alright if I come, right?"

"Yeah, I just didn't think you would want to go and sit in the gym. You know, uncomfortable bleachers, screaming teenagers, all that stuff." It almost seemed like he was trying to talk me out of going.

"I know, I've never been in uncomfortable, loud places before. It will be tough, but I think I can manage."

"That works out perfectly," Linda said with a smile. "I have a dinner function to go to tomorrow night, so you can give Adam a ride."

"Oh, I don't need a ride to the game," Adam said quickly. "Preston was going to pick me up."

"Not a problem," I answered. "I can give you a ride home after and maybe we can grab some dinner after the game."

"Yeah, okay, I guess so," Adam answered, finishing his pizza.

"Unless you had other plans after?" Suddenly I felt like I was encroaching on his life again.

"No... no, it's fine Dad," he said, wiping the sauce from his chin with a napkin. "I've got some homework to get to, so I'm heading up. Good night," he said. Adam gave Linda a hug before he went upstairs, then looked over at me, stopped for a second, and then left to go upstairs.

I heard him go up the stairs and close his bedroom door.

"Well that wasn't too uncomfortable," I said to Linda.

"What?" Linda said to me, grabbing the empty plates off the table and putting them in the dishwasher.

"The way Adam reacted when I said I wanted to go to the game and take him to dinner. It was like I had leprosy or something."

"He said it was fine, Caleb," Linda answered. "I think you're reading way too much into it."

"It was the way he said it was fine, Linda," I told her. "It was like he was embarrassed to have me go to the game."

"I don't think that was it at all. I think he was surprised you wanted to go. You've been more than a little withdrawn since you came home, Caleb. Maybe he was beginning to wonder about whether you wanted to be around him or not."

"I know," I said, feeling guilty about the way I have been towards Adam, and towards Linda. "I'm trying, Linda, I really am. It's just not so easy for me right now."

Linda came over and gave me a hug, just like she used to when we were younger.

"I understand it's been tough for you, little brother," she said to me. "I'm glad to see that you're trying to change things. I think you're headed in the right direction."

"Thanks," I said to her, breaking the hug.

"Hey, want to play some cards tonight?" I asked Linda.

"Cards? Really?" she said. Now she was the one sounding shocked.

"Sure," I said to her. "You and I used to play rummy all the time when we were kids. It will be fun."

Linda smiled over at me. "I don't know Caleb. It's already 8:30."

"Seriously? It's 8:30 is your excuse? Now you sound like an old lady," I teased.

"Old lady?" she yelled. She reached into one of the kitchen drawers and rummaged around a bit before she found a deck of cards.

"Sit down, little brother," Linda said as she started shuffling the cards. She reached over and grabbed a pad of paper and a pen off the far side of the table.

"I'm going to kick your butt like I did when we were kids," Linda said with a grin.

Chapter 8

Sarah

As tired as I was after working all day and then a gut-wrenching argument right after walking through the door, I couldn't get myself to sleep right away. Every part of my body ached and seemed filled with anxiety. Whenever I closed my eyes to try to sleep, I would get flashbacks to that incident of years ago, something I desperately tried to put behind me. I could see myself waking up in the morning and checking my email and social media only to see pictures of me plastered everywhere, pictures that I still don't know who took or how they were able to get onto my social media pages so my friends and family would see them.

Someone had obviously placed cameras in my dorm room and in the shower room in my dorm suite and was able to take pictures and video of me getting undressed, showering, and getting dressed. My roommate at the time, Andrea, a junior like me, swore up and down that she didn't know anything about it. Campus security was finally able to find the cameras hidden in different places, but they never found out who placed them there. To make matters worse, this person or persons had hacked into my social media accounts, posted the pictures and video, sent emails to everyone on my contacts list, and made life miserable for me. Everyone I knew, including my parents, ended up seeing these pictures, and I was mortified. It took some effort to get the pictures removed, and even with the investigation, they were never able to track who got into my accounts and put them there.

At the time, I was just starting to come out of my shell and into my own at Swanson College. I was making friends, doing well in classes, and I thought I had people around me I could trust and count on. All that changed in an instant, with people looking at me everywhere I went, talking behind my back or coming right up to me, saying crude and hurtful things. After a week or two of dealing with it constantly, day and night, I couldn't take it anymore and broke down. I called my parents, hoping I could leave school and just come home. It had taken a lot to convince them I could live on campus and be my own person without trouble in the first place, even though the college wasn't more than an hour from their home.

Unfortunately, they were not there for me like parents should be for their children. My parents were always strict, religious people that thought highly of their reputation in their social circles. When the pictures got around, and word got out about them, they didn't know how to react. They both blamed me for "allowing" this to happen to me, not believing me when I insisted I had not posed for or consented to the pictures, even though I had never given them any reason to question me or my behavior in the past. My mother insisted it would be too much if I came home and lived with them, and that people in the church and the town would never be able to accept and handle having me there. My father refused to even talk to me about it, and while I begged and pleaded to come home, the answer was clearly a no.

The shock as my mother hung up the phone left me stunned. I began to believe what they said and felt – that this somehow was my fault, that I should be ashamed of how I could let this happen to me, and I felt that way for a long time afterward. It took me years to overcome those feelings, to build my self-confidence back up to where I felt good about myself, even to the point where last year I finally started taking college classes again, although all the classes I took were online classes that Swanson offered. I still could not bring myself to set foot on that campus again, even if most of the people I knew or were aware of the incident were long graduated or gone. I changed my major so that I focused on computer analytics and security. I was determined to not let something like this happen to me again and to have a way to help others prevent it from happening as well and threw myself into my coursework.

The whole mess also kept me from having a social life as I withdrew and became reluctant to let people in, keeping most people at a distance. That is why working the graveyard shift seemed so inviting to me and has worked well. I don't have to deal with a lot of people all the time. Most of the people I have worked with over the years I have been at the Moonlight have come and gone, staying for a short time while they worked through school or until the work became too much for them. Other than Justin, the cook, no one I started with was still there. Francesca was the first person I have allowed myself to get friendly with, even to the point where I told her privately about what had happened, which was a big step for me.

Now all the strides I thought I had taken to move forward and past everything have fallen by the wayside, and I felt like I was right back in that same position, curled up in my bed, blanket tucked under my chin, crying because it was all my fault. Even the ally I thought I had in James felt like he was slipping away now, and I wasn't sure just what I was going to do.

It was plain to me that Denise didn't want me here anymore. When I first came to live with them five years ago, Denise was more helpful and receptive to the idea. She had wanted to go back to work at that point in her life and having me here afforded her the opportunity to do so and still have someone at home to take care of Lizzie afterschool, help with chores and meals, and so on. I was more than happy to take on the role, feeling grateful just to have a place to live, and I relished getting to spend time with Lizzie and James, neither of which I had gotten to know very well.

Lizzie and I clicked right away, and I was able to help her with school, teach her some skills, and be an aunt, friend, confidante, and sister all rolled into one. I think Denise began to resent our relationship as time went on, but she liked having the flexibility to go out to parties, work late, spend time with friends or go away for trips without having to worry about her daughter. I don't think she liked that Lizzie started to come to me more and more for what she needed in life. All of that was coming to a head now, and she saw this as the ideal opportunity to get me to leave.

My mind spent hours spinning over and over the past and the present, and then it settled on all this occurring because of an innocent walk home. I never thought in a million years that a quick walk home and some conversation with someone I didn't know at all could turn on me so quickly. It made me feel like it wasn't worth it to seek out any type of friendship or anything else with anyone, let alone with a man.

Thinking about it more, I couldn't even remember the last time I had what you could call a boyfriend. I was shy and withdrawn in high school and barely dated at all, and I certainly didn't see anyone to the length you could say was a boyfriend. Once I got to college and began to open some more, I did socialize and date. I had a boyfriend, Paul, in my junior year, that I really liked. We had dated for a few months and I even allowed myself to give up my virginity to him just a few weeks before the whole mess with the pictures broke. Once all that happened, though, he turned his back on me, telling me he couldn't deal with all the talk and what it was doing to me. That may have been the final straw for me as I felt crushed and alone. I hadn't dated anyone since then, though I have had plenty of flirts and offers come in through the diner.

None of that made a difference right now. I did finally manage to get a little bit of sleep in, and it wasn't until I heard a gentle rap at my door that startled me out of sleep that I woke up. I looked at the clock and saw it was past three, and I knew it had to be Lizzie knocking at my door. At first, I was reluctant to even acknowledge it and hoped she might leave me be, thinking I was still asleep.

Through the silence in my room where all you could hear was the light breeze from outside gently brushing the curtains of my window, the light knock came again. I sat up in my bed and let out a "Come in," trying to clear my voice and keep it from cracking.

Lizzie timidly pushed the door open, peering in to see me sitting in bed. She quickly closed the door behind her and came over and sat at the foot of the bed.

"Hi," she offered shyly, looking down at her feet and not making much eye contact with me.

"Hi Lizzie," I said, sitting up straighter in bed. "How was school?" I was trying to make conversation with her as normally as possible.

"It was fine. Everyone is all excited about tomorrow night."

"Great," I told her. "It should be fun for you and your friends."

"Are... are you still okay with me coming to the diner?" she said with hesitation.

"Of course. Why wouldn't I be?"

"I thought... I thought maybe you were mad at me for everything that happened this morning."

"Why would I be mad at you, Lizzie?" I asked her. "You didn't do anything."

"I was the one who brought up seeing you talking to that guy," Lizzie blurted. Her face quickly turned, and I could see tears running down her cheeks. "If I hadn't said anything, Mom wouldn't have exploded like that, there would have been no argument between you and her, you and Dad, her and Dad... it's all my fault."

"None of that is your fault, Lizzie," I said to her, scooting closer to her on the bed so I could put my arm around her. "Your Mom has issues with me that go back further than that."

"I know," she said to me. "She and Dad were yelling back and forth about something that happened years ago. I... I kept trying to ask questions, but they didn't even want me in the room anymore. Why would Mom say those things about you?"

Lizzie's statement made me wonder just what Denise had to say and what Lizzie heard. I could only imagine that they included words like "slut" and so on, just like I heard from countless other people.

"I don't know what your Mom said, but I can tell you that it more than likely is not what is true."

"Can I... I ask you what happened?" Lizzie said, almost afraid to ask the question in the first place.

I took a deep sigh and shook my head.

"Lizzie, I don't know if I should get into the whole thing with you."

"Sarah, I'm fifteen. I know a lot more than everyone around here gives me credit for."

"You're right, I'm sorry. Back before I moved in here with you guys, there was an incident at college. Someone took some pictures and video of me while I was changing and showering and spread it all over the place – on campus, the Internet, to my friends and family, everywhere. It made life... very difficult for me."

I looked at Lizzie's face to see how she was reacting. I could see that she had questions forming in her mind already.

"But it's not like you posed for the pictures or anything, right? They weren't your fault, so why would people say those things about you and think you had something to do with it?"

"Because people make judgments without knowing the whole story, or just assume that something like that is your fault, even if you are the victim, unfortunately."

"Is that why you don't see Grandma and Grandpa?"

That question was one I wasn't really prepared to answer, but she deserved to know how I felt about it.

"Yes, that's a big part of it. But that shouldn't affect your relationship with Grandma and Grandpa. That's between them and me, not anyone else. Please don't bring it up to them when you talk to them. I don't want you to get involved in all that."

"Okay," Lizzie answered. "Are you going to leave?" she then asked me, turning towards me and showing the worry on her face. "Because I don't want you to go. I need you here."

I put my arms around Lizzie and held her tightly as she cried into my shoulder.

"I don't want to leave, Lizzie," I said to her. "But it may reach a point where that is what is best for me, your Mom and your Dad. Even if I stopped living here, that doesn't mean I wouldn't be there for you. I'm always here for you."

Lizzie cried on my shoulder for a few more minutes, and I kept reassuring her that everything would be okay, but in my heart, I didn't know if they would be or not. Finally, I pulled back a bit and looked at her.

"I should get up and start thinking about what to make for dinner," I told her. "You want to help me? We can make whatever you want tonight."

Lizzie looked at my face, her eyes puffy from crying, and got a sad look again.

"Oh," she said to me as if she were searching for words. "Mom sent me a text before, telling me to meet her in the driveway at six, that she and I were meeting Dad at Marino's for pizza tonight."

"Okay," I said to her. She looked like she was going to start crying again, and I put up a brave front to try to see her through it.

"It's not a big deal, Lizzie, really," I said to her.

"But I don't want to have dinner with them without you," she said. "She's just doing it to be mean to you."

"Lizzie, go to dinner with them and just enjoy a night out. Don't make it about me, okay? You have to promise me that. I don't want to be a problem between you and your Mom. Enough is going on there already. Putting you into it will just make it worse for all of us."

I looked Lizzie in the eyes and waited for her to answer me. She nodded her head and sniffled, wiping the tears from her face with the back of her hand.

"You should go do your homework before dinner," I said to her, trying to restore some order to our lives for the moment. "I know I have homework to do, too. Enjoy your pizza tonight. I'll see you in the morning."

Lizzie stood up from the bed and looked at me sitting there.

"Are you going to be okay?" she asked.

"I'll be fine," I told her, telling her a white lie. I didn't think I would be fine anytime soon.

Lizzie left the room, shutting the door behind her, and I breathed out a big breath while letting a few tears stream down my face. I worked to regain my composure, concentrate on doing some of the schoolwork I had to do and hoped it would take my mind off everything else for a bit.

I threw myself into the schoolwork I needed to accomplish: watching the lectures I needed to watch for the week, tackling reading, and even working on the projects I had to turn in for classes at the end of the semester, so I could stay ahead of everything. I did whatever I could to help keep my mind off the troubles swirling around me, and I didn't even remember hearing Lizzie go down the stairs or close the front door when it came time for her to leave.

By the time I pried myself away from my computer, it was dark outside and was 7:00. I had plowed through over a week's worth of work, turned in assignments, posted to class bulletin boards, and even contacted professors about assignments. I headed in to take a shower and wash the day away, get myself ready for work and try to push the unpleasantness aside.

I got myself ready for work in record time and decided to leave early, giving myself a chance to perhaps grab something to eat at the diner before my shift started. I grabbed my purse and a sweater and got out the door to leave the house before there was any chance of James and Denise getting home before I left. I even found myself hurrying up the driveway and down the street so I could get onto Oak Street before they had a chance to see me.

I hustled to the diner and dashed inside, going right to the back to store my things without even saying hello to Doug, the owner, who was finishing up his day. I pulled my hair into a ponytail, put my apron on, and walked into the kitchen to see what Justin was up to tonight.

I found him working on searing a salmon fillet in a pan, flipping burgers on the flat top, and stirring a sauce.

"Hey, Sarah," he said to me in his husky voice. "Would you mind pulling the fry baskets up for me before I burn them?"

"Sure, no problem," I told him as I went over and lifted the baskets carefully, seeing the fries at the perfect golden color they should be. I dumped the fries into the large stainless-steel bowl next to the fryer, sprinkled on some salt, and tossed them lightly to coat all the fries evenly, just as Justin taught me. I brought the bowl over to the plates he had for the burgers, snapped on some gloves, and shared the fries out onto the plates for him while he plated the burgers.

"Thanks, hon," Justin said to me with a smile. "What are you doing here so early?"

"Oh, the family went out for dinner, so I was by myself for the night. I did some homework and thought I would come see if you have anything good for dinner."

"Go grab a seat," he said with a smile. "I'll whip up something for you in a minute."

I went and sat in the breakroom, putting my feet up on the rickety coffee table while I sat on the couch. I gazed at the silent TV that was on, watching some game show without really watching it as I got a chance to give my mind a break for the moment.

Before I knew it, Justin came walking in with a plate and handed it to me.

"I had just made a batch of chicken salad," he said to me as I took the plate. "I tried a new recipe. I hope it's okay."

I looked down at the plate and saw the white toast stuffed with creamy chicken salad. There were celery and bits of grape scattered through the salad.

"Looks delicious," I told Justin with a smile. "Thanks, Justin."

I reached onto the plate and picked up a slice and took a bite. Justin never walked away until he saw your initial reaction to what he made. The bite was a wonderful combination, and I ate it happily.

"Is that tarragon in the chicken salad?" I said to him as I wiped my face with a napkin I grabbed off the table.

"You're getting good, Miss Sarah," Justin said with a smile as he walked back into the kitchen.

I finished eating my sandwich, putting the last morsel in my mouth before Doug walked into the back room. He stood over me as I licked my lips and murmured out a "hello" in between chewing and swallowing.

"You're early tonight," Doug said to me. "I don't usually get to see you except on the weekends. How's everything going?"

"Fine," I lied, putting my plate down on the table and standing up. "Anything I need to know about for tonight?" I figured if I started talking about work Doug wouldn't pry too much into my personal life.

Doug was a good, honest man that had worked hard to build up a great business here at the Moonlight. He wasn't really prying when he asked you questions about your personal life. He was genuinely concerned about his employees, and took good care of everyone, no matter what your job was, how many hours you worked, or how long you had worked at the diner.

"Nah, it's been a pretty normal Thursday," he told me. "Just keep an eye on the soda machine behind the counter," he told me. "It's been a little temperamental today. I put a call into the repair company, but they won't have someone out here until tomorrow afternoon at the earliest. Hopefully, they get it fixed before tomorrow night when we get busy."

"No problem, Boss," I said to him, giving him a salute.

Doug smiled down at me, showing off his perfectly white teeth and giving the hearty laugh he had. He glanced down at his watch and then looked back at me.

"Since you're here, I am going to head out early and leave the place in your capable hands. Is that okay? It will be nice to get home and relax and maybe watch some baseball before I fall asleep."

"Go home, Doug, I got this," I told him confidently.

"I know you do," he said to me. "Have a good night. Call me if you need anything."

He always said that before he left, but I never had anything come up that I couldn't handle, either by myself or with a little help from the other staff.

I walked out into the diner and saw that there were still some tables filled with people from the late dinner crowd. The day shift crew was still on, so I positioned myself at the register to handle hostess duties and ring up guests until ten rolled around.

I did whatever I could to occupy my time, refilling the mint jar at the register, putting a new tape in, and even dusting some of the liquor bottles in the small bar area that rarely gets used. I was determined to keep the negative thoughts out, work through this, and maybe, just maybe, turn the bad day into a good night.

Chapter 9

Caleb

I had more fun staying up and playing cards with Linda than I had in a very long time. She was right – she kicked my ass at rummy that night as I tried to fumble through, remembering the rules of the game and how to play. It certainly brought back some good memories for me, like the nights we spent as kids playing cards into the late hours, or the times where I would play cards with the other guys in the battalion to pass the slow times we had when we were stationed somewhere.

Linda and I played, laughed, and talked like we had not done in many years. I was able to forget about the things that had been troubling me lately and get back to some semblance of a normal life for a change. Before we knew it, it was well after 1 AM. Linda looked at the clock on the wall and was horrified by what she saw.

"Shit, Caleb, it's 1 AM," Linda said, scrambling to get out of her chair.

"So what? "I said to her.

"I have a meeting scheduled at 8:30. I need to get some sleep."

"Linda, it's your practice, you're the boss," I said to her. "Is it something really important? A life or death meeting?"

"Well, no," she admitted. "It's just Jack Collins. He wants to talk about some stuff for his business, but nothing critical."

"Why don't you give yourself a break?" I told her. "You have been in fifth gear moving along for years now. It's okay to take things slower, go in late now and then, or even take a day off if you think you need one."

"A day off?" she laughed. "What's that? It's been so long since I have had one. Getting the practice going and keeping it moving took a long time, and then everything with Ella..." Linda stopped herself short as she was talking and looked at me.

"Caleb, I'm sorry, I didn't mean it that way, you know that," she said apologetically.

"Linda, it's okay," I said to her as I sat back in my chair. "You took on a lot for Adam and for me. I don't know how I could have done anything without your help. I know it meant your time and big sacrifices for you."

Linda looked at me and smiled. "You would have done the same thing for me if things were reversed. I just did what was right and what needed to be done."

Linda got up from her chair, stretched and yawned, and came over and gave me a kiss on the head.

"You're getting some gray up here, little brother," she said teasingly.

I ran my hand through my hair. "Gee, thanks."

"It's okay, she said to me. "It happens to the best of us. I just color mine to hide it better. Good night, Caleb. Thanks for the fun night. I needed it."

"I did, too. Good night," I told her.

Linda retired upstairs to her bedroom while I cleaned up the glasses and other items we had left out in the kitchen. I picked up my sweatshirt and walked outside into the cool night air. The sky was very clear tonight, and it seemed like there were more stars than ever dotting the night sky. Between the stars and the moon shining brightly, you didn't need any kind of artificial light at all to guide your way.

I glanced at my watch, saw it was 1:30, and still didn't feel tired. My internal clock was well out of whack at this point, and I never knew when I was supposed to be tired anymore. I didn't feel like just holing up in my apartment again, and soon I found myself walking towards the Moonlight Diner and thinking about Sarah.

I remembered what Dr. Weber had said to me earlier today about going out and finding a new friend. Finding someone like that at this hour of the night meant either going to a bar and talking with someone that was likely drunk and wouldn't remember you or heading over to the diner to see who was there. I already knew there was a friendly face there that I would like to see again, so the decision was easy for me.

When I arrived at the diner and made my way up the steps and inside, the place looked empty. There was no one at the counter or the register, and when I peered inside, all I could see was one person sitting at a booth, nursing a drink. They gazed up at me as I looked in, met my eyes for a moment, and decided that their drink was more interesting than me.

Maybe she isn't working tonight, I thought to myself, disappointed that she might not be here.

It was then that the doors to the kitchen swung open and I saw Sarah come walking out. She stopped when she saw me, with a mix of surprise and discomfort on her face. She walked over to where I was near the entrance and met me.

"Hi," Sarah stated.

"Hello, again," I told her with a smile. We stood awkwardly for a moment before Sarah picked up a menu.

"Is it okay if I sit at the counter?" I asked her, unsure of what she wanted to do.

"Sure," she said, leading me back to the same spot I sat in yesterday.

"Something to drink?" she asked matter-of-factly. I was wondering if she was purposely standoffish with me.

"Could I get a coffee, please? Just black," I offered.

"I remember," she said with a hint of a smile.

Sarah placed the coffee down in front of me. I hadn't even bothered to pick up the menu to see what I might want to have.

"What can I get you?" Sarah said, taking out her pad.

"Well, you did so well with the BLT last night, maybe I should just let you pick something out for me."

Sarah stood back and placed the tip of her pen near her mouth, giving some thought.

"I think I have just the thing for you," she told me. "Let me put your order in." She then headed off to the kitchen, back through the swinging doors.

As I sat at the counter, I saw the other waitress from last night come walking over near to where I was sitting.

"Hello again," she said to me with a big smile. Her dark hair framed her face nicely, and she seemed to be friendly, maybe even a bit too friendly. The white blouse she wore was unbuttoned down to reveal cleavage that she hoped people would notice.

"Hi," I said politely.

She seemed disappointed that I didn't engage her more in conversation and quickly turned her back to me to operate the soda fountain and get some drinks. She placed a glass underneath the Coke dispenser, but nothing came out. I saw her try it a couple of times, pressing the button, but the dispenser did not seem to be working.

"Damn," she said loudly. "This thing isn't working again." She was frustrated, and her face was getting red. Just then, Sarah came walking out.

"What's the matter, Fran?" she asked the waitress.

"The stupid fountain isn't working. Nothing is coming out."

"Doug told me there was something wrong with it. The repair guy is supposed to show up sometime today," Sarah told her as she tried the buttons to see if anything was working.

"That doesn't help much now, or later once breakfast and lunch roll around," Fran said to her.

I could see that it was a problem for both of them right now, and they couldn't solve it.

"I can look at it if you want," I offered.

Sarah and Fran both turned and looked at me, unsure of how to respond.

"You know how to fix these things?" Fran asked me bluntly.

"I've never worked on one, no," I said honestly, "but I'm pretty handy. I might be able to figure it out for you."

Sarah seemed reluctant about it.

"I don't know," she said. "Doug's pretty protective about this stuff, and if something else goes wrong with it, he'll freak out."

"Sarah," Fran said to her, "it's not like it can get any worse than it is now. It's not working at all. Let him at least look at it."

I sat on the stool looking at Sarah. She stared back at me as if she was trying to read me and get a better idea about me. Finally, she shrugged her shoulders.

"Sure, go ahead," she said, waving her arm towards the soda fountain.

I climbed off my stool and walked behind the counter, moving past the two waitresses. I didn't know the first thing about these soda fountains, but to be honest, I thought it would be something easy to fix. To me, it seemed like there was either a clog in a line somewhere, or perhaps it was a power problem.

"Do you guys have a pair of rubber gloves I can wear? And maybe a screwdriver to use?" I asked Sarah.

"I'll get them!" Fran exclaimed as she ran into the kitchen for the gloves. Sarah stood close to me since there wasn't much room behind the counter itself. I saw her look down quickly as I looked over at her, shuffling her feet lightly before crossing her arms and leaning against the back counter.

Fran appeared with the gloves and a few different screwdrivers she had retrieved from the back. She handed them to me with a smile, and I nodded in thanks.

I snapped the gloves onto my hands, wanting to do my best to keep the system sanitized if possible. Before doing anything, I asked where the power was to the machine. Sarah indicated it was right behind the machine, and I bent down a little and moved the machine slightly so I could reach the plug and remove it from the wall. As soon as I put my hand back there, I could feel that the plug was not all the way in. I pulled it out completely and then pushed it back into the outlet.

"I think that will solve your problem," I said to the ladies. "The plug wasn't connected all the way. Maybe it just came loose when someone was cleaning it. Give it a try and see if it is working now."

I got out of the way, and Fran placed a glass under the Coke dispenser, after sputtering a bit, the pressure was fine, and the soda came out without a problem.

"Thanks, sweetie," Fran said to me with a big smile. "You're our hero of the night." She walked away with her sodas, and I went back to my stool and sat down.

Sarah looked over at me and refilled my coffee mug.

"Thank you for your help," Sarah said to me. "You probably saved Doug $100 in a service call we didn't need."

"You're welcome," I replied. "It was no big deal. I didn't really do anything." I took off the rubber gloves and placed them to the side.

Just then, I heard the familiar sound of the bell ringing, and Sarah disappeared back into the kitchen. She came out with a plate and placed it in front of me. It was a sandwich with some French fries, but I wasn't sure what the sandwich was.

"What have we got?" I asked her, picking up the toasted bread and inspecting it.

"it's a new recipe our cook is trying," Sarah said to me. "It's chicken salad with some bacon on rye toast. I think you'll like it."

I leaned in and took a bite of the sandwich. There was a loud crunch of the toast and bacon, and I got a good helping of the chicken salad. I looked at Sarah and tried to smile through my eating.

"It's good, I like it," I told her as I took another bite. "Thanks for choosing it."

I sat there eating while Sarah did some straightening up on the counters, wiping things down. I tried to think of things to say to her, to work on it like Dr. Weber had asked, but nothing was coming to mind for me. Luckily, Sarah broke the ice.

"You know, if you're going to be a regular around here I should probably at least get your name," Sarah said, looking down at the counter instead of looking at me, wiping away with her towel.

"Oh, I guess you're right," I said to her. "I'm Caleb... Caleb Wilson."

Sarah finally looked up from the counter to meet my gaze. "Nice to meet you, Caleb," she said to me. "I'm Sarah Miller."

I took another bite of the chicken salad, not expecting Sarah to ask me another question right away.

"So Caleb, what do you do for a living that allows you to be awake at two in the morning every day?"

I swallowed and wiped my mouth with my napkin before answering her.

"Right now, not much," I told her. "I just retired from the Army after twenty years," I said to her.

"Wow," she said with surprise. "You don't look old enough to have been in the Army for twenty years."

"Thanks for the compliment," I chuckled. "I enlisted when I was eighteen."

"I guess you have seen a lot of the world," Sarah remarked.

"I have," I told her, munching on a French fry. "Maybe more of it than I ever thought I would... or wanted to."

"Did you like it... the Army, I mean?" Sarah asked. "Well, of course, you did if you stayed in for twenty years."

"I did like it," I told her. "I learned to do a lot of things, met some great people, and learned a lot about life. It was a great experience."

"So, how come you retired? You look like you're in good shape, and you liked it."

I hesitated before answering. I didn't know if this was something I wanted to get into, but I also knew if I wanted to let people into my life, I had to be more open about things.

"I had put my twenty years in, and since my son is in his last year of high school, I wanted to spend time with him while I had the chance. It just felt like it was time to go."

"It's nice that you get to be with your son and see him graduate," Sarah said. "It must have been tough on him and your wife with you being away in the Army so often."

I felt a pang in my heart when I heard Sarah say that, and I think she saw something on my face and regretted the statement.

"My wife... my wife passed away two years ago," I said quietly. I picked at my French fries with my index finger for a few seconds before looking up at Sarah. She was staring at me, and I could see the sympathy in her face.

"I'm so sorry," she said to me, coming closer to me. "I didn't know. I would never have said..."

"It's okay," I said, putting my hand up. "There was no way you could know. She died in a car accident while I was overseas."

I took a deep breath and pushed away my empty plate, hoping to break the difficult silence that hung in the air between us.

"That was a fantastic sandwich, Sarah. Thanks so much for recommending it," I told her, wiping my face one more time to make sure no food was caught in my beard.

Sarah stood up and took the plate from in front of me, still looking closely at me, before she shook her head as if to break the spell that was there between us.

"I'm glad you liked it," she said, whisking the plate away from me and bringing into the kitchen. She reappeared a moment later, pausing to go and ring up the only other customer that was in the diner at the time. Once he was taken care of, she came back over to me and smiled at me.

"Is there anything else I can get you? Let me get you a piece of pie, on the house, as a thank you for your help." She made a move to go towards the pie case before I stopped her.

"No, thank you, that's not necessary," I said to her. "I didn't do anything except plug the thing in. Besides, that sandwich has filled me up. I should probably get going."

"Oh, okay," Sarah said, seeming a little disappointed. She passed the check over to me, and I tucked a tip for her under the ketchup bottle still on the counter.

I walked over to the register to pay, and Sarah took the check from me. I decided then that the time was right to try to put Dr. Weber's suggestion into motion. I handed a twenty over to Sarah to pay for the meal, and she rang it up for me.

"You know," I said to her quietly, "instead of dessert, if you want to thank me, maybe you could do a favor for me." I was suddenly feeling quite nervous.

"Sure," Sarah said, "what do you need?"

"I thought maybe, if it was okay with you, that I could maybe stop by on my morning run and walk you home again after work if you're comfortable with that." It took a lot for me to get that out, and I could feel my eyes looking up and down, avoiding direct eye contact with her, while she contemplated what I had said.

When I finally looked up, Sarah brushed a stray hair away from her eyes and looked over at me. I could tell she was considering it and was unsure what to do. Waiting for an answer from her seemed like torture.

"Don't feel obligated to say yes," I said quickly. "I just thought since I come this way anyway, maybe you wouldn't mind a bit of company for your walk home." I stuffed the change she handed me into my jeans pocket and turned to walk away.

"Caleb," Sarah said to me, getting me to turn around. "I get off at 6. I'll meet you out in front of the steps?"

I smiled broadly back at her. "Okay, great. I'll see you then."

I pushed the door open with some gusto and bounded down the steps, pacing my way down the empty streets. I felt a tingle throughout my body and like a big weight had been lifted off my shoulders.

I turned off Oak Street and headed back towards home, moving along at a quick pace, and I got to my apartment in no time at all. I looked at my watch and saw that it was close to three, leaving me three hours before I would have to meet Sarah.

There was no way I was getting any sleep now. I felt a burst of energy and was overcome with a giddy feeling. It was then that I realized something – for the first time in a long time I felt like I had a good day, a day I could be proud of, and I was happy.

I also realized something else – this whole situation, asking if I could walk Sarah home, also felt a lot like a date. That notion paralyzed me for a moment. I hadn't been alone with a woman in a social situation since Ella, and the last time it was with a woman other than Ella I was about sixteen years old.

Was this a date? Does Sarah think of it like a date? What have I gotten into? Am I ready for this?

I was pretty sure my time from now until I left for my run my brain was going to be racing with these thoughts as I tried to come up with answers and figure out how this was going to go.

Chapter 10

Sarah

So, he does have a name, I thought to myself after our conversation and after Caleb had left the diner. I smiled to myself as I watched him walk out the door. It gave me a good feeling to have someone want to spend time with me, even if it was only for the brief walk home from the diner. There was something about Caleb that sparked an interest in me, maybe something even beyond just wanting to have him as a friend.

There was no denying he was an attractive man. Seeing him run from the driveway the other day, watching him move, made that clear to me. He had the physical attributes that any woman would notice and find attractive. While I felt drawn to him physically, there seemed to be more to him than what many people may even realize. I got the impression from our conversations that he did not let many people in and kept most at arm's length. Perhaps it was because of his military background that he was that way. Or maybe it was because of the tragic circumstances of his marriage, and he did not want anyone close to him. Even with that, it appeared to me that he was not only willing to talk to me, but it was something he sought out and wanted. Let's face it – no one seeks out coming to the diner at 2 AM several days in a row for nothing, even if the food is good. It seemed to me he was looking for something in his life, and maybe there was a glint of that here – with me.

Caleb occupied my mind for the rest of my shift, no matter what I seemed to do. I told Francesca about my conversation with him, getting his name, finding out a little about him, including the loss of his wife, and how he had asked if he could walk me home after my shift.

"Seems very sweet," Fran said to me, "but a little corny too."

"Come on Fran," I said to her, crossing my arms. "I think he's looking for a friend, and besides... I do find it a little romantic. Guys don't ask to do stuff like that at all anymore."

Francesca looked over at me and smiled.

"You're so smitten with him right now," she said to me.

"No, I'm..." I interrupted myself and stopped being defensive. "Okay, maybe I am a little bit. He seems very nice, he's polite, a gentleman..."

Fran stepped on my words right there.

"And he's hot as hell," Fran said to me as she put a coffee roll on a plate for a customer.

I did get a little flush at the thought.

"Yes, he's attractive, there's nothing wrong with that either."

"I never said there was, Sarah," Fran told me as she turned to walk away. She turned back to me and said: "It sounds like you're the one trying to convince yourself about him."

Fran was right. It had been so long since I had anyone that showed interest in me that I was interested in as well. I was to the point in my life where I was suspicious of anyone that displayed even a hint of interest that I had forgotten what it was like to find someone attractive.

I also wanted to make sure to temper my expectations with Caleb. After all, it was just a walk home and nothing more. If he is just looking for a friend and wanted someone to talk to and hang out with, I could certainly be that person. Goodness knows I could use more friends in my life as well.

As the clock got closer to 6 AM, I found myself going to the break room to gather my things and get ready to leave. Fran walked into the back as well to gather her belongings from her locker. I was just putting my bag on my shoulder and getting ready to walk out when she stopped me.

"You're going to meet him like that?" she said with surprise.

"What are you talking about?' I replied.

"You don't want to fix your hair or put on some makeup or something? Dress yourself up a little bit?"

"Fran, he's seen me here working the last two nights. I don't think I need to pretend I look like something I'm not just for a walk home. That seems a bit ridiculous. He can like me or not just the way he sees me.

I'll see you later tonight." I stood straight, smiled at her, and headed out towards the front door.

I walked out the front door with my cardigan on, but the temperature outside was feeling higher than it had in recent days. Spring weather was settling in nicely, and it looked to be much warmer today. I looked around as I waited outside the steps, but I didn't have to wait long. Within moments, Caleb was turning the corner and coming up on the diner, moving at a pretty good clip. He was wearing a gray t-shirt and black running shorts, and as he came up to me, he stopped short, catching his breath for a second and placing his hands on his knees.

"Sorry I'm late," he said breathlessly. I could see a hint of sweat on his forehead. I could also see that his arms were strong and muscular, matching the strength that showed in his legs. "I hope you weren't waiting long," he said to me, wiping his forehead with the back of his hand.

"I just got out here myself," I told him. "Do you need a minute to catch your breath?"

"No, I'm okay," he said, standing up straight again. I could see a hint of sweat marking the collar of his shirt, and the shirt clung closely to his body, giving definition to his abs and pecs that I hadn't seen before. "When I saw I was starting a little late I ran a little harder to make sure I got here on time. It's going to take me some time to get back into shape."

If this is out of shape, I can't imagine what he looks like when he's in his best condition, I thought to myself.

I shook my head a little to get these thoughts out of my head so I could carry on a conversation with Caleb without getting caught up in what I found myself feeling now.

"I wouldn't worry about it, Caleb," I said to him. "You are far from out of shape."

We started walking slowly in the direction of home for me.

"How was the rest of your night, or morning?" Caleb asked me.

"Oh, not very exciting," I said to him. "We had a few customers, but usually that time of the morning I spend the rest of my time cleaning, getting the place ready for the morning crowd and morning shift. It makes things easier for the staff that way when we get crowded."

"It sounds like you're a pretty big piece of the puzzle for that place," Caleb told me.

"Nah, not really," I told him. "I'm just more accustomed to it I guess."

"How long have you worked at the diner?" Caleb asked as we walked.

"Oh, it's been about four years I guess," I told him. I hadn't realized it had been that long since I started there. It was longer than I had ever anticipated.

I looked over at Caleb and saw him watching my face. I felt a blush come over me.

"So, you'll be running the place before long then," Caleb said, looking forward again as we walked.

"I don't think that will ever happen," I told him. "Doug, the owner, is there during the days and takes care of everything. I just help where I can. Besides, I don't plan to stay there forever."

"Oh?" Caleb questioned. "What do you plan to do?"

"I'm trying to finish up my degree," I told him.

"What are you studying?"

"Analytics and security, computer stuff," I said in passing. Most people's eyes glaze over when I say what I am studying, thinking of it as techie, nerd stuff. Caleb though showed some interest.

"Good for you," he told me. "That's a good field, lots of growth potential. If you're good, you can go anywhere and have an excellent career."

I felt a sense of pride wash over me when Caleb said this.

"Do you know a lot about computers and technology?" I asked him. We had turned the corner off Oak Street and were heading down Baldwin towards my house, much faster than I thought we would get there, and faster than I wanted to.

"I know a little," he told me. "Just some basic stuff I learned in the Army, but nothing to the level that someone like you will be able to do."

"I'll bet you learned a lot of different things in the Army," I said to him, seeing if I could get him to talk freely a little bit.

"Oh yeah," he told me. "But that's boring stuff. Most of it is not very practical for what you do in the civilian world."

"I'd love to hear more about it," I encouraged.

Caleb didn't really answer me about that question, and we walked a bit more without saying anything. I could see my house looming ahead, just down the street, and I was sure Caleb saw it as well. I tried to walk a little slower and extend our time.

"So, what do you do with the rest of your day now?" Caleb asked me.

"Generally, I sleep until about two, get up, do my schoolwork, make dinner, and then get ready for work."

"That doesn't leave you much free time to enjoy life. Do you ever get a break?"

"I have Mondays and Tuesdays off at the diner, so those are free days, but it's hard to live a normal life when you are used to being up all-night long. I try to stick to my routine and end up staying up late on those days too."

We reached the top of the driveway all too soon. I positioned myself on the driveway so that we were shaded from the windows of the house, over by a couple of trees up near the fence.

"That means you'll be working tonight then," Caleb said to me. He was shuffling his feet a little bit as he talked.

"Oh yes, Friday is always a busy day for us," I told him. "We get all the kids from the college and the high school coming in at all hours. Will you... you are coming in tonight?"

Caleb looked at me as he considered the question. It then looked as if an idea hit him and he smiled.

"I can actually come in a little earlier tonight," he said to me. "My son, Adam, plays on the high school basketball team. I'm going to watch his game tonight, so I can come by after the game ends, probably between ten and eleven."

"We'll be pretty busy," I told him, but I didn't want to discourage him from coming. "It would be nice to see you though. I can use seeing a friendly face when things get hectic."

Caleb smiled a little wider when I said this.

"Okay, then," he said to me. "I'll make sure to come by after the game. It will be fun to see you in action," he said and laughed.

"Thank you again for your help tonight," I told him, "and thank you for walking me home. It was very nice."

"You're welcome, it was my pleasure, in both instances."

Caleb started to jog lightly in place to get himself moving again.

"Are you heading right home now?" I asked him before we parted.

"No, I'll run a bit longer," he said to me. "I need to stretch myself out and get back up to my usual length."

"I wish I had your energy," I told him.

"You know," he said, coming closer to me again, "if you want, tomorrow morning, we could both go for a run... together, I mean. I could meet you at the diner when you finish work, and we can go for a run then if you feel up to it."

Part of me worried about going for a run since I hadn't done it so long, but another part of me loved the thought of getting to spend more time with Caleb.

"That would be great," I heard myself saying before I could think about it any further. "I'll bring some clothes to change into after my shift, and we can go."

Caleb seemed energized again.

"Fantastic," he said enthusiastically. "Okay, I'll let you go and get some rest. I'll see you tonight."

"See you later," I said to him as I watched him turn and start his run again. I watched him move down the block and found it difficult not to notice how he looked as he moved away, his arms and legs pumping, and his shorts moving tightly against his backside. I felt a warmth come over me that I don't feel too often.

After I saw Caleb disappear down the block, I moved away from the shaded area and started down the driveway. I got to the middle of the driveway just in time to see Lizzie and Denise coming out of the house to leave for the day.

"Running a little late today?" Denise said to me curtly.

"Just extra prep work to get things in place for a busy Friday," I told her, trying to keep things as impersonal as possible.

Denise climbed into the driver's seat while Lizzie moved around to the passenger side.

"I'll see you at the diner tonight!" Lizzie said with excitement.

I had almost forgotten that Lizzie was coming with her friends tonight and I promised to keep an eye on them. I had been so caught up with everything else that it had slipped my mind.

"I'll be there," I said with a smile.

Once Lizzie was in the car, Denise quickly backed out of the driveway. I watched them drive away and went inside the house. I had planned to go right upstairs, but I heard James in the kitchen, and he apparently heard the front door close as I came in.

"That you, Sarah?" James called out.

"Yes," I said to him, feeling tense now and worrying about what he might want to talk about. I made my way slowly down the hall to the kitchen and saw him sitting at the table, dressed for work, and drinking a cup of coffee.

"How was work?" he said as he sipped his coffee.

"Fine," I told him. "Business as usual."

"Sit down, relax," he said to me, pointing to one of the chairs at the table.

"James, I'm pretty tired from work," I told him. "I just need to get some sleep. It's going to be a busy night tonight."

"Just sit for a minute, please," he asked me, pushing one of the chairs out with his foot.

I came over and slumped down into the chair.

"I just want to apologize for yesterday," James said to me. "Denise was out of line with all that stuff, including the going out to dinner thing."

"You don't have anything to apologize for, James," I told him. "You didn't do anything. Besides, you three are entitled to have time to your-selves. I don't have to be included in everything. That's your family. I get it."

I went to get up from the table, and James reached across and grabbed my hand.

"Hey," he said to me, holding me there, "You're my family too, and you're a part of this family. Don't forget that."

"I won't," I said to James.

James let go of my hand and sipped his coffee again.

"So, who's the guy you were with this morning?" he asked me. "Is it the same guy from yesterday?"

I stared at James with my mouth slightly open.

"It's okay, Sarah," James said to me. "I had walked out through the garage to grab something from my car, and I saw you two standing over by the trees. Is it the same guy?"

The only sound you could hear in the kitchen was the refrigerator motor running.

"Yes, it is," I said honestly. "Did... did anyone else see us?"

"I doubt it," James said to me. "Denise and Lizzie were already in the kitchen getting everything together to go. So, who is he? Someone you're dating?"

"No... I mean not really... I guess I'm not sure yet," I answered him. "His name is Caleb. He just moved back to Swanson. He was in the Army and just retired."

"Retired?" James said with surprise. "He doesn't look like he's an old man."

I laughed and smiled. "He's not. I think he's about your age. He has a son who's a senior in the high school."

James put down his coffee mug. "He's not married, is he Sarah? If he is, I don't want to see you getting..."

I cut James off there.

"Give me some credit, James. I wouldn't start hanging around a married man like that. His wife... she passed away a few years ago. He said it was a car accident."

"And you believe him?"

"Why would he lie about it? That would be a pretty horrible thing to do."

I had never considered that Caleb might be lying about his wife's death until just this moment. I'm usually so protective of myself that I was surprised I didn't think of that possibility, but Caleb didn't seem like a person who would lie about that.

"I'm not saying he is, Sarah," James answered. "I just think that you should be careful before you think about getting involved with someone. I don't... I don't want to see you get hurt."

"I appreciate your concern James, I really do," I told him as I stood up from the table. "I'm not involved with him. We're just friends. I... I need to get some sleep."

James got up from the table as well.

"Sarah, don't be mad," he pleaded. "I'm just looking out for you is all."

"I know you are," I told him. "But I'm a big girl now, James. I can look out for myself. Have a good day at work."

I walked down the hall and went upstairs to my room, shutting the door. I kicked off my sneakers and plopped down on the bed. I stared up at the ceiling for a few minutes, considering what James had said about Caleb. I didn't want to feel suspicious about Caleb, his motives, or his friendship, but the seed had been planted in my head. With my past experiences, that's all it took for me to start to worry.

I got up from the bed and went over to my desk. I sat and flipped my laptop open, letting the screen spring to life. I went on the Internet and to my search engine and typed in 'Caleb Wilson Army Swanson NC.' I hesitated for a second, worrying about what I might discover, but then I hit Enter.

I had results in seconds, with the top few being about an Ella Wilson. Her obituary and a story in the newspaper from two years ago were there. The article explained that she was killed in a suspected DWI accident in April of two years ago when she was only thirty-six. There was a picture of a mangled car on the side of the road, and based on the picture, she was hit head-on.

I scanned the article and found information about Caleb. The article noted that he was a Weapons Sergeant with the 3rd Special Forces Group, 2nd Battalion, Alpha Company, that was based out of Fort Bragg. At the time of the accident he was stationed overseas, and the article did not get specific as to where he was or what he was doing. The article also mentioned her son, Adam, who was at Swanson High School.

There weren't a lot of details about the accident, other than to say the other driver was Brandon Sterling, the son of Wesley Sterling, owner of Sterling Industries, a large textile company near Swanson. Apparently, Brandon was taken into custody, but the article mentioned nothing else.

I knew the Sterling name. Everyone in Swanson did because the family was from the area, donated a lot of money to the college, and had business all over the place. I also knew the name because Brandon was around Swanson College the same time I was going there. While he didn't attend, he was at some of the same parties I went to because his cousin, Jared, who I did know of, went to the school. I never particularly liked either one of them, and the interactions I had with either of them were few and usually not pleasant, ending with me getting hit on, rejecting them, and being called a name.

I did another search to see if I could find out more about the accident, and there was one other article a few weeks after the accident, indicating that the charges against Brandon had been dropped. Police said there was a problem with the way the evidence was collected, and they did not have a strong enough case to prosecute.

I went back to performing searches specifically about Caleb, but there was little to no information to be found other than the obituary and articles about the accident. There were no mentions about his service, what he did in the Army or anything beyond that he was part of Special Forces.

I admit, like most people, I had heard of Special Forces, but also like most people, I only heard the name in passing on the news or saw it in action movies. The guys in Special Forces were supposed to be highly-trained experts in many areas. If Caleb was a Weapons Sergeant, he clearly had expertise in fields that went beyond what the average soldier could do, and probably was involved in a lot of missions that were secret and confidential that the public knows nothing about.

I got up from the desk, stripped out of my work clothes, and put on a t-shirt and sleep shorts and climbed into bed, the whole time thinking about Caleb, his wife, his son, and the life he led and was leading now. There was obviously a lot more to him than I knew or realized, a lot that he probably was not ready to share with me.

With my head on my pillow, I stared at the ceiling again, watching a small spider work its way across the white surface, pausing now and then like it was considering what to do and where to go.

"I know how you feel," I said to the spider.

Chapter 11

Caleb

The walk home with Sarah was just what I had hoped for. We got to spend a little more time together, and I got a little glimpse into what her life is like beyond what I have seen of her at the diner. When she agreed to go for a run with me tomorrow morning, I was elated. I didn't know what her limitations would be for the run as far as distance, but I knew I could go at her pace with ease and make her comfortable.

To make sure I was in good shape for the run tomorrow, I lengthened my run for this morning and went a bit further than I had the previous day. When I was on active duty, I had no problem with stamina and running several miles without feeling exhausted. While I might not be able to reach that level again just yet, I felt confident that it was not far off.

I had reached a pretty good sweat by the time I finally made it home after my run. I looked at my watch that had been recording my distance for me and saw I was able to do six miles this morning, which was a good effort, in my opinion. Since my run had gone on a bit longer than usual this morning, I missed seeing Adam and Linda leave the house before they started their day. Instead of going into the house, I went straight up to my apartment.

I went right to the shower to wash off, and the hot water made me feel better right away. When I was done, I toweled off and went into the bedroom. I didn't even bother getting dressed and just laid down on the bed to rest. I hadn't slept at all last night, getting back from the diner and staying awake until I went for my run to meet up with Sarah. When I had returned from the diner, I had too much energy and excitement coursing through me to relax at all.

As I lay on the bed and closed my eyes, I found my thoughts not drifting to the usual things I would think of – experiences in the Army, things I had done in the military, or even thoughts and visions of Ella – but instead, I was thinking about Sarah. She had pervaded my thoughts in the last few days in a very big way, more than I had ever expected. I found myself thinking about her as more than just a friendly face I had seen at the diner. I had the pictures of her in my head, walking with me, the sunlight gently bouncing off her hair, the highlight of the freckles on her face, the wonderful smile that she shared and so much more.

I hadn't had any feelings like this in a very long time. I thought I would have difficulty handling it, but it made me feel good to think about Sarah, to be with her, and to talk with her. Seeing her, even at these odd hours, had added something to my life that had been lacking and that I sorely needed. I realized I relished the moments we were spending together and that they were spurring me on in the rest of my life to try to make things better. In a very simple way, Sarah had helped me turn a corner that I needed to turn.

Exhaustion finally got the better of me, and I drifted off to sleep. My sleep was peaceful, restful and serene. I had dreams of being with Sarah, not just on the walks home that I have enjoyed or the time we spent in the diner, but of being with her in a more romantic setting. I found myself dreaming of being with her. We were in a bedroom somewhere unfamiliar with a large king-size bed, dim lighting in the room, and Sarah dressed in a short green satin nightgown, her brown hair down to her shoulders, coming towards me. She put her arms around my shoulders, looked deep into my eyes, and we kissed. The kisses were short and sweet at first, but become more sensual, filled with longing and meaning. I finally scooped her up in my arms and took her over to the bed, lying next to her and gazing into her eyes.

The feelings I had for her were so intense, and I felt my hand gliding down her body as she lay on her side looking at me longingly. My hand slid over her nightgown, down to the hem just at the tops of her thigh, and then worked its way back up her body. I reached my arm behind her and pulled her close to me, pressing her body against mine. There was no disputing that each of us was aroused at this point, and I continued to kiss her before shifting my body, so I was over her.

As I looked down into her eyes, I could see that they seemed to be looking deep inside me, touching me in a unique way that made me feel warm, safe, and happy. Within moments we were both caught up in the throes of passion. I was holding her tightly against me again, moving in and out of her while she held herself close, moving with me. We were both covered with sweat, and I could hear her crying out, clutching me close, as she reached her climax, gripping me close to her. I was so close myself, I was panting, moving with her, and I knew I couldn't hold out much longer, and then...

The loud knocking on my door finally woke me up. I woke with a start, sitting up in the bed. I found myself covered in sweat again and realized that someone was knocking loudly on my apartment door. Getting out of bed, I saw I was still naked. I grabbed a nearby pair of shorts and pulled them on, hoping that they would cover up the arousal I was still fighting from the dream I had. Thankfully, by the time I reached the door, they had done their job.

I pulled the door open and saw Adam standing there. He was dressed in his pregame workout clothes for his game and stared at me like I had two heads.

"Dad, I've been knocking on the door for like five minutes," he said in a huff. "What the heck is going on? I have to leave to get to the school before the game."

He looked me over and saw I was shirtless.

"I guess you're not coming?" he asked with a hint of disappointment, but I sensed some relief as well.

"Adam, I'm sorry," I said to him. "I was up late last night into the morning and didn't fall asleep until the morning. What time is it?"

"it's five o'clock, Dad," he told me. "I have to be at the school by five-thirty."

"Just let me put a shirt on, and I can drive you over," I said, turning to go inside the apartment.

"Dad, it's fine. Preston is picking me up. I just wanted to see if you were going to the game or not. It's no big deal."

Adam turned to go and started walking down the steps.

I went out the door and yelled at him.

"Adam!"

Adam turned to look back at me.

"I will be at the game, I promise. What time does it start?"

"The game starts at 7:30. If you don't make it, it's fine. I can get someone to give me a ride home after."

"I said I'll be there, and I will," I told him with conviction. Adam looked back at me, and I saw him nod before he turned and went down the steps and then walked to the top of the driveway. A minute later, there was the car I had seen the other morning picking him up again, and he was off.

I couldn't believe I had slept so long. I must have slept for at least nine hours, something I had never done before. Not only did I get to sleep, but my sleep was filled with those intense visions of Sarah. The dreams were so intense that I knew I needed to take another shower before I would go over to the school for the game.

I showered as quickly as I could, trying to focus on making sure I got to the game on time so I could be there for Adam. I wasn't even sure if he really wanted me there or not, but I knew I needed to make an effort and show him that I do care, that I do take an interest in him and his life. It may have been more important to me than to him right now, but hopefully, it would show him that he matters to me.

I got dressed in a pair of jeans and a black t-shirt, put my sneakers on, grabbed my gray hooded sweatshirt, and was ready to go out the door. After putting my wallet in my pocket, I realized I was going to need my keys to drive over to the school. I had to do a little searching to find the keys to the Jeep, but I finally found them in a box on my dresser, alongside a few other things I had there. I had some of the medals I had received in the Army, but there were also two pictures in there. One was of Ella, Adam, and I just days after he was born, smiling as we stood outside Ella's parents' house. The other was just a picture of Ella, and it was my favorite picture of her. It was just a silly picture that was taken when we had a weekend together in Atlantic City years ago. She was dressed in a pair of jean shorts and a red tank top and had her picture taken with one of the characters dressed up and walking on the boardwalk. This one was of a giant Italian ice, and Ella had her arm around it, smiling and waving to the camera. She looked so happy, so sincere, and even though it seemed like a meaningless picture, it always showed me the beauty she had and made me realized how much in love with her I always was.

I slid the pictures back into my box and closed it, picking up the keys and getting out of the apartment before I got too caught up. I walked out of the apartment and down to the garage below, opening the garage door.

Inside was my Jeep, covered with a tarp just as it had been for most of the last six weeks since I had been back. I had taken the time to go down and start it occasionally just to check and make sure it was running. I had bought the jeep four years ago, to give myself a car of my own while Ella drove her Camry, which she thought was safer.

I pulled the tarp off and climbed into the Jeep, starting it up and listening to the engine roar to life. I pulled out of the garage and was on my way, being careful as I drove along since it had been a while since I was behind the wheel of a car. I tried to remember my way to the school, getting lost once when I made the wrong turn and ended up going the wrong way down a one-way street. I finally figured out where I was and how to get to the school and pulled into the lot and parked.

The high school lot was crowded since this was considered a rivalry game with Union High School, the school the next town over. Teenagers were streaming all over the parking lot, walking into the school with a lot of excitement and energy. I had never been to one of Adam's games before, and never had to even be in the school. Ella took care of all those things like parent-teacher conferences, calls from the school nurse, going to games and performances, and the like. After she died, I know Linda picked up the mantle and did many of those things herself. For me, this was a first.

I walked into the crowded gymnasium and found a seat on the bleachers on the home side of the gym. I picked a spot a few rows up, so I had a good position to watch the game. It wasn't long before the place was filled and raucous. Both teams came out to screams from the crowd for their warmups. Adam was easy to spot since he was one of the tallest people on the team, and I watched as he went through the warmup drills with the rest of the team. As the team finished their drills, they headed over to the sidelines for instructions from the coach. The Swanson High cheerleaders took the floor and riled up the crowd some more. I spotted the girl in the picture with Adam cheering with the team. She was a perky blonde, with her ponytail bobbing as she jumped up and down and seemed to be one of the leaders of the team, much like Adam was with the basketball players.

It was only a few minutes longer until the game started, and things did not get going well for Swanson from the start. They missed shots and played sloppy, almost like they were nervous facing their rivals at home.

The team fell behind by twelve points, and Adam seemed to be having trouble getting open to get shots off. The Union players were big, fast, and strong, and were outmuscling Swanson easily. Frustration showed on Adam's face as I watched the buzzer for the end of the first half sound and Swanson trailed by fourteen.

The teams went to the locker rooms, music blared throughout the gym, and some people filed out to grab snacks or just get out of the hot, noisy gym. I had unzipped my sweatshirt and taken it off to avoid sweating like crazy for the third time today. I looked around and saw parents of other players proudly wearing t-shirts or sweatshirts indicating they were parents of players and felt like an outsider for even being there to root for Adam.

When the second half started, Swanson again struggled to keep up. Adam was able to get open some more and take more shots, and he was getting more aggressive with his rebounding and moving on the opposing team. Swanson was able to close the gap to just six points with a little over two minutes left in the game. The Swanson coach called a timeout and pulled the team over, and I could hear Adam yelling in the team huddle, urging the team on to get them to the finish.

Swanson had the ball and took it right down the court and hit a three-point shot, getting the crowd on their feet as they closed to within three points. Union brought the ball down the court, worked the shot clock, and took a shot with one second before the shot clock expired and missed, giving our team the ball with just over a minute left. After working the ball around and down to Adam inside, he quickly kicked the ball out to a teammate behind the three-point line, and he sent a beautiful shot swishing through the basket to tie the game. The crowd went berserk, and I could feel the gym bleachers shaking violently beneath my feet as people stomped, screamed and jumped.

After a Union timeout, they inbounded the ball and moved it around, running the clock down to about twenty seconds before they took a shot. The shot clanged off the rim and Adam leaped high to grab the ball before anyone else, pulling it down with his elbows swinging to keep people away. He passed the ball quickly to the team's guard and ballhandler, who worked quickly down the court as everyone got into position. I could see Adam struggling for position on his man down low, and with six seconds on the clock, a Swanson player put up a jump shot that bounced off the back of the rim. Adam, moving with great instinct, got his hand on the ball, tipping it back up deftly with his fingers so that the ball tipped off the backboard and went right through the basket as time expired.

The crowd exploded in excitement, with high-pitched screams piercing the air as students stormed onto the court in celebration. I could see Adam get swept up in the frenzy as his teammates and friends surrounded him. He was beaming with pride, and so was I. It was a fantastic moment that I was so happy to get to share with him, even if he probably had no idea I was here.

I worked my way through the crowds and down to the court, where I saw Adam high-fiving teammates and friends. I was able to get over to him, and he finally noticed me standing there. I went over to him and gave him a hug, catching him by surprise.

"That was a great game, Adam," I said proudly. "Congratulations."

"Thanks, Dad," he said as we broke the hug. He smiled at me and seemed like he was glad that I was there to see this moment. More of his friends and teammates came back over to him, slapping him on the back.

"Do you want me to meet you outside?" I yelled to him, trying to get heard over the excitement.

"Yeah," he yelled back. "I'll meet you out front in about fifteen minutes or so."

I worked my way through the crowd to find a way out of the gym and outside. I was glad to get out of the stale air inside and get some fresh, cool air on my face. Teens and parents were all over the place outside, relishing in the Swanson victory with cheers. Even when I was back in high school myself, I never got caught up in school spirit or the teams we had, so it was different to see it from this side as the parent of a player. I could see how and why parents want to be a big part of this for their kids.

I stood off to the side outside the school, waiting for the crowds right by the doors to thin out a bit before I moved over that way so I could see when Adam came out. It was about twenty minutes of standing around, looking at my watch, checking my phone for a message from him, and just killing time before I saw him come out the school doors. He was with a couple of his friends and had his arm around the cheerleader when he spotted me standing there. I gave a casual wave to make sure he spotted me in the dim lighting. I saw him say something to the people he was with and he then broke free from them and walked over towards me.

"Got everything?" I said to him as I pulled my keys out of my pocket.

"Yeah, I do," Adam said, glancing back at his friends. "You know, if you wanted to just go home, it's fine. I can hang out with my friends and get a ride with them." He glanced back at the group standing over to the side.

I was torn in what to do. I could see that Adam probably would rather hang out with his friends than me to celebrate, but I wanted to try to make this a moment we could share together and maybe get a little closer.

"Look, Adam," I said to him, "if you would rather be with your friends, I totally understand that, and if that's what you really want than I will go my own way. I just thought it would be fun to go grab some dinner and spend some time together."

I didn't want to make him feel guilty about wanting to see his friends, but I wanted some time with him as well. He looked at my face and could see I was willing to give him space if he wanted it.

"How about this?" he offered to me. "They are all heading to the diner. Can we go there and eat together, and then I can go hang out with them after we are done eating? This way we get time together and then I can hang with them."

"Sounds fair to me," I said to him. Adam ran over to tell his friends the plan, and I felt great that Adam was open to having dinner with me. When he came back over to me, I patted him on the back, and we walked together to the Jeep.

We got in the car and worked our way over to the diner, fighting with the traffic that only existed in Swanson when an event like this was going on. Adam and I talked briefly in the car, with me telling him how great it was to watch him play and how impressed I was with him, and him giving me one-word answers to my questions and statements. I was hoping the conversation would progress beyond this once we got to the diner.

I was lucky enough to snatch a parking spot in the diner since the place was crowded. Even though the diner had a large parking lot, most of the spaces were filled already. Sarah wasn't kidding when she said they got busy on Friday nights. I glanced at my watch and saw it was nearly 10:30, so I knew Sarah would be working already. I was hoping she would have at least a second or two to say hello.

Adam and I walked up the steps to the diner and went inside. The diner was buzzing with people, and I saw that most of the booths and the counter to the right where I had been sitting were filled. I was disappointed, because this meant we would be sitting in the main dining room somewhere, and Sarah probably wouldn't see us.

We got up to the register and were greeted a tall, older gentleman who gave us a big smile as we came in.

"Good evening, gentlemen," he said to us as he picked up a couple of menus. "Two of you this evening?"

"Yes, just the two of us," I said to him as I saw him looking to the left and then to the right to see if he could find a spot for us. Just as he was about to decide, I saw Sarah come walking by with a tray of food in her hand. She caught my eye and smiled when she saw me and stopped to talk to the gentleman looking to seat us.

"Doug put them in my section," she said to him as she then whisked herself away into the dining room.

Doug nodded and waved to us to follow him. We made our way through a maze of tables and booths towards a back room I had not even seen the times I had come in. Tables were filling the center of the room, and booths along either wall on the side. Doug seated us at one of the booths to the left and handed us the menus as we sat down.

"Sarah will be right with you," Doug said to us with a smile. "Enjoy your meal."

Doug walked away, and a busboy appeared within seconds with two glasses of water for us. Adam grabbed his water and drank most of it down quickly before he picked up the menu to see what he wanted. I noticed he kept glancing up over the top of his menu to look into the other dining room. I took a quick turn around to see his friends sitting at a large booth along the far wall in the other room. I looked back at Adam and smiled.

"Well, at least you know where they are," I said to him as I picked up the menu. I looked to our right, and there was a table of teenage boys and girls sitting at the table, laughing and carrying on. One of the boys pointed over at Adam, recognizing him. He yelled out, "great shot, Wilson!"

I could see Adam blush a little and nod over to the table.

"Do you know that kid?" I asked Adam.

"Not really," he said casually. "They're all sophomores at that table, so I don't really know them well."

"I guess you're a celebrity now," I told him jokingly.

"Yeah, right," he answered.

A moment later, Sarah appeared next to our booth, greeting us with a smile.

"Whew, it's crazy in here tonight," Sarah said to us. "It's nice to see you, Caleb. And this must be your son. Hi, I'm Sarah."

Adam sat staring at Sarah with his mouth slightly open. He was looking back and forth between Sarah and me without saying anything. Finally, I nudged him with my foot under the table to break his spell.

"Yeah... Hi," he finally got out. "I'm Adam."

"It's nice to meet you, Adam," she told him with a smile. "Can I get you something to drink? I know your Dad wants black coffee, but how about you?"

Again, Adam looked caught off guard. "I'll just have a Coke, please," he answered.

"Great. I'll be back in a second with your drinks." Sarah walked away from the table, pausing at the table of kids just across from us to talk to them for a moment, before heading out to get our drinks. Once she was out of earshot, Adam, looked across the table at me with a stunned look.

"What's the matter?" I said to him.

"How does she know you?" Adam asked with surprise in his voice.

"I've been in here a few times at night when I couldn't sleep. She works late at night, so we've been talking."

Adam sat back and smiled at me and chuckled.

"What's so funny?"

"Nothing, Dad," Adam said to me, still chuckling. "But by the look on your face, I can tell you like her."

"What are you talking about it?" I said, mindlessly flipping through the menu.

"Dad, there's nothing wrong with that, you know. She seems nice, and she's pretty."

"I... I guess so," I stammered. "I hadn't noticed that closely."

Sarah came back to the table with my coffee and Adam's Coke, placing the drinks in front of us.

"So, what can I get you gentlemen tonight?" she asked, turning and giving me a smile.

Adam turned to Sarah to order. "I'll have a cheeseburger, medium, and fries, please."

"So polite," Sarah noted as she wrote down the order. "You've raised a nice boy, Caleb. What can I get you tonight? A BLT again? Or should I pick something else out for you?"

I could feel my body getting warm and saw Adam looking at me with a grin.

"I think I'll have the grilled chicken sandwich tonight, Sarah" I answered, closing the menu. "With French fries, please."

"You got it," Sarah noted. When she finished writing the order down, she turned to me and said, "It's probably a good idea to keep it light tonight anyway so you can be ready for our run in the morning. I'll go put this in for you guys."

Sarah walked off and turned the corner, and Adam's smile got even wider.

"You've been running with her in the mornings?" he asked with a raised voice.

"Keep it down, please, Adam," I begged him. "No, tomorrow is the first time we'll run together. But I have... walked her home a few times while I am out on my run."

"Way to go, Dad," he said to me, holding up his glass of Coke as a toast. "Are you going to ask her out?" he asked me after his sip.

"I... I don't know. I don't know if I should," I replied, suddenly feeling very sheepish about the whole conversation.

Adam's face turned serious for a moment.

"Dad, you know it's okay for you to want to see someone. Mom's been gone for two years now. You don't have to be by yourself all the time. She... she wouldn't have wanted that for you," Adam said solemnly.

I looked over at Adam and realized I was impressed by him in many ways that night. He had shown himself as a great athlete, a leader of his team, and as a smart, insightful, and caring young man.

"I know, Adam," I said to him quietly. "It's... it's just hard for me, I guess. We'll see how it goes. For now, we're just friends," I said, even though in my head I had already thought beyond friendship.

This was the best Adam and I had connected in a very long time, and I was relishing the moment. I wanted to try to do whatever I could to keep it going, but I could see Adam kept looking over at his friends or getting text messages from them so that he kept looking down at his phone.

"You know," I said to him, "It's okay if you want to go over and sit with your friends," I told him. "I know it's a big night for you."

"They can wait until after I finish my burger," he said to me, smiling up at me. I felt even better after he had said this to me, making it obvious that he wanted to spend time with me just as much as I wanted to be with him.

We continued to talk like we never had before, with him telling me all about school, basketball, how he was still deciding about colleges, what he hoped to do this summer, and more. We even talked about planning a trip in the summer, going up north or out west, so he could see parts of the country that he had heard about but never visited. I learned more about him in those ten minutes or so than I knew in the entire seventeen years before, which made me feel guilty that we had never done this before.

I think Adam could see the look on my face that I was feeling bad about it all.

"What's wrong?" he asked, polishing off the last of his Coke with a slurp.

I looked up at Adam and said, "Adam, I feel badly that... that I never got the chance to spend time with you growing up, to get to know you better. And then, even after what happened to your Mom, I wasn't there for you like I should have been. I'm sorry about that."

Adam peered back at me, unsure of how to react. He finally broke the silence.

"Dad, don't feel bad about it. Sure, there were always times where I wished you were around more. I even complained to Mom about it when I was younger – how you were never there to go on vacations with us, to show up at school stuff, family parties, or games – and she always explained to me that you would have wanted to be there if you could, but your job was important not just to us but to a lot of other people, people we would probably never meet. When I got older, I understood all of that better. There... there was a time after Mom died... that I was mad at you, mad that you were home and then you were gone, and we never got to talk about any of it, and I was left on my own to deal with it. That was hard for me. Aunt Linda made things a little easier, but if you were here..."

I could see Adam was getting teary-eyed, and he quickly wiped his eyes before he thought I or anyone else would notice.

"Adam, I know it was hard for you, and I'm sorry for that. I didn't know how to process it all myself, let alone how to help you with it too. I've been trained for so long to put emotions aside and focus on the tasks at hand, that I think part of me lost sight of how to do the things you needed – I mean, we needed – to cope. Your Mom was always that part of me, that part of our family that took care of that. When she was gone, I don't know, I just couldn't. But... I want things to be different now, okay? I am trying to do things differently, for you and for me."

Sarah came over to the table and put the plates down in front of us, breaking up the conversation some. We both sat back in the booth, trying to shake some of the emotion of the moment we had. Sarah must have noticed what was going on.

"I'm sorry to interrupt guys," she said as she delivered our food. "Can I get you guys some refills on drinks?"

"That would be great, Sarah, thanks," I said to her. I looked up at her, and I could see on her face she recognized what we were talking about.

"Okay, let me check on my other tables, and I'll be back in a few minutes," she told me, hoping to give us some space.

"Before we start eating, Dad," Adam said, "I just want to say I know you're trying Dad, and I know it's all been tough for you – with Mom, leaving the Army, working through what you need to work through. I was trying to give you space just like you were doing with me. I am glad that things are getting better."

We both smiled at each other.

"Okay, enough of that stuff," I said to him. "I'm starving, and this sandwich looks good."

Adam and I both tore into our food. Watching a seventeen-year-old in action when he is hungry is a sight to behold, and his hamburger and French fries seemed to be gone just as quickly as Sarah had placed the plate down. I still had more than half of my sandwich left when his plate was empty, and he started helping himself to some of the fries on my plate.

Once we were done with our meals, we both sat back and took a deep breath, almost simultaneously, causing us both to laugh. Sarah came over and saw the empty plates and began to clear them for us.

"Boy, I guess you guys didn't like the food," she said sarcastically. "Can I get you some dessert?"

I looked over at Adam to see if he wanted anything. I could tell by the look on his face that he wanted to go see his friends now, but he didn't want to disappoint me if I wanted to hang out more for dessert.

"I think Adam is going over to join his basketball buddies to celebrate their victory, but I would love to have a piece of cherry pie if you have any," I told Sarah.

Adam slid out of the booth and stood next to Sarah.

"It was nice to meet you," he said politely to her. He then gave me a quick wave and walked over to the booth where all his friends were located. I saw him slide in next to the girl from the picture, and everyone at the table started giving him high-fives and laughing as soon as he sat down.

"I'll go get your pie for you," Sarah said to me as she turned and walked back towards the kitchen.

I looked around the diner and saw that it seemed even busier than it was before. The noise level was higher than when we had walked in, and the tables and booths were filled with teenagers and college kids, all enjoying their Friday night of freedom. It seemed like most of them were all eating the same things as their were plates piled high with French fries, onion rings, burgers, nachos, chicken tenders and the like.

Sarah came back with a huge slab of cherry pie for me with a generous helping of whipped cream.

"I don't know how you deal with all this," I said to her, raising my voice a bit so she could hear me over all the loud conversations and laughing.

"You get used to it," she said to me. "I barely even notice it now, except when you hear some the shrieks the girls let out occasionally."

Almost on cue, there was an ear-piercing shriek from the table just to my right, and Sarah looked over to see what the commotion was. One young girl was shrieking and laughing with her friends as one boy had soda coming out of his nose.

Sarah turned back towards me, laughing.

"That's my niece, Lizzie," she said to me, pointing to one of the young girls who was laughing the loudest.

"You don't look old enough to have a niece that's a teenager," I said to her.

I could see that Sarah blushed a little. "Thank you for that," she said with a smile. "My older brother is a bit older. I was 11 when Lizzie was born."

"That's the brother you live with, I assume?" I asked.

"It is," she replied. "James owns Miller Plumbing here in Swanson. He's a good guy, and it's fun to live with Lizzie. James was out of the house as I got older, so I never had any siblings around. Lizzie is kind of like a little sister to me."

There was another shriek from the table as a glass of soda spilled this time.

"I better go," Sarah said to me, rushing over to the table to help clean the mess and try to calm the kids down before the mess got bigger.

I sat and enjoyed my piece of cherry pie. It had a nice brown sugar crumble topping to it, and it was cooked perfectly. I slowly savored each bite, looking around at all the commotion going on. Just as I was finishing up my piece of the pie, Sarah came back over to the table, this time with someone right behind her.

"Caleb, this is my brother James, and my niece Lizzie," she said to me.

I stood up from the table to shake James' hand. James was in good shape, fit and trim, and you could tell he took care of himself. He had a firm grip and calloused hands that obviously worked hard each day.

"Nice to meet you, James," I said to him. "And you as well, Lizzie," I said to the girl who hung a little bit to the back behind her father. She gave a sheepish wave hello.

"Nice to meet you too, Caleb," James said. I could tell by the way he was looking at me that he was sizing me up in the way any brother would when getting introduced to a man by their sister.

"Sarah said you are in the Army," James said to me as we stood facing each other.

"I was," I corrected. "I retired about six weeks ago."

"Were you out of Fort Bragg?" he asked. He was feeling me out to see what information he would get and if I were honest with his sister.

"I was, but I hardly spent any time there," I told him. "I spent a lot of time overseas."

We stared at each other for a minute, and he could see he wasn't going to get much more out of me.

"Well, thanks for your service," he said to me in a sincere tone. I just gave him a simple nod. James then turned to his daughter. "Okay, Lizzie, let's get out of here and let Sarah get back to work. Nice meeting you, Caleb. Sarah, I guess we'll see you in the morning."

"Yep," she said casually. "Oh, James, I'll be a little later getting home. Caleb and I are going for a run after I get off work."

James looked back at me, and then at his sister and gave her a smile. He nodded his head to her.

"Okay, well enjoy your run."

James put his arm around his daughter, and they started to walk out.

I sat back down in the booth and finished what was left of my coffee. Sarah looked down and grabbed the empty plate in front of me.

"Your brother and niece seem nice," I said to her.

"They are," she said to me. "I'm sorry about the interrogation. I think it's a big brother thing."

"It's okay. I do the same thing with anyone that my sister introduces to me, and she's older than me. It's just a protective brother thing when you meet a guy your sister…" I cut myself off before I let the word "likes" slip out of my mouth and assume something.

Sarah noticed and sensed what I might say and quickly changed the subject.

"Can I get you anything else?" she said, fumbling with her pad.

"I think I'm done," I said to her.

She reached into her apron and pulled out the check for me and handed it to me.

"Thanks," I said to her. "I guess I'll see you at six?"

"You bet," she said with a smile. "I've got my stuff, and I'll be ready. See you then."

I got up from the booth and started walking out, making sure to walk over to the booth where Adam was sitting. As soon as I walked over, everyone got quiet at the table.

"I'm taking off," I said to Adam.

Adam looked around the table and removed his arm around from the girl sitting next to him.

"Is it okay if one of the guys gives me a ride home?" Adam asked.

"Sure, no problem," I said to him. "You guys have a good time. I'll see you later."

"Thanks, Dad," Adam said. I gave him a wave, and as soon as I started walking away, the noise at the table started up again.

I got up to the counter to pay, and Doug was there to take my check.

"How was everything?" he asked me as he rang up the check.

"Great, as always," I said to him. "Sarah is fantastic," I said to him as I watched her walk by with a tray of sodas for a table.

My eyes followed her out into the dining room before turning back to Doug, who was standing there smiling at me.

"Yes, she is," he said to me. "Best employee I have had here in a long time."

I handed Doug the money for the tab. "Say, do you know what the check will be for that booth over there?" I said to him, pointing to the table where Adam and his friends were sitting.

"No, I don't know it, but knowing typical teens, it won't be too high."

I reached into my wallet and handed Doug $120. "Take this to cover their check," I said to him, "and whatever is left, please give to whoever their waitress is. She surely will have earned it."

Doug let out a hearty laugh. "I will do that, sir," he said to me. "That's very kind of you. Have a good night."

"Thank you, you too," I said to him as I walked out the door.

I had walked a few paces down the block before I realized I had driven to the diner and had to go back to get my Jeep. I took the quick ride home, pulling into the driveway and parking the car next to Linda's. I looked over to the house as I got out of the car and could see that the lights were off in her bedroom. She must have gotten home from her meeting and gone right to sleep. I decided to leave her be and just went up to my apartment.

I tossed my keys and wallet on the counter, my sweatshirt on the back of a chair, grabbed a bottle of water out of the fridge, and put myself down on the couch. A quick look at my watch showed it was 11:30, so I still had plenty of time to relax before I needed to get back to the diner to meet Sarah.

I flipped the TV on, putting on the sports channel so I could avoid the politics and world news that I likely didn't want to hear. I mindlessly watched while the anchor talked about some baseball player that had just retired after setting a record, but I was thinking more about how well the day had gone overall.

I was feeling good about myself, about Adam, about Linda and about life in general, and had something to look forward to in the morning with the time I would spend with Sarah. I made sure to set the alarm on my phone for 5 AM in case I fell asleep on the couch and went back to watching TV.

The sports anchor said the player had decided that he was at a good place in his life and now was the time to enjoy it the most.

"You said it, brother," I said aloud to the TV, holding up my bottle of water to the ballplayer's picture.

Chapter 12

Sarah

Friday nights are the perfect mix, for me at least. The nights are always busy with customers, pretty much from the time I arrive at 10 PM until about three or four in the morning. Even then, we still get more than usual in the wee hours of the morning, with college kids looking to come in to eat something greasy to help them get through the binge drinking they just did, or other kids looking for a jolt of coffee to keep them going for the night. There's also always the couples that come in just looking to get away and have a quiet place to go when they don't want the night to end just yet.

Sure, the work can be hectic for us as we run around filling orders, clearing tables, cleaning up messes and so on. But the busy times make the hours go that much faster for all of us that before we know it, our shift is over and we are ready to call it a day.

This Friday was just like that for me, with some added excitement thrown in because of Lizzie and her friends, Caleb coming in with his son, and the feeling of looking forward to going for a run with Caleb. It was wonderful to get to see him with his son, who was a nice young man, and see that they were having a good time. Couple that with the great time Lizzie had with her friends, and it was a nice night.

When it got closer to six and the morning crew had started to arrive, I was able to take a few minutes to go into the back and grab the clothing I wanted to change into for my run with Caleb. I pulled out a baby blue t-shirt and my black running shorts, some cotton socks, a sports bra and my sneakers and went off to the bathroom in the back that was for employees. I changed into my clothes quickly, pulling my ponytail a bit tighter so that it would stay out of my face while I ran. I kept adjusting the sports bra, one I hadn't worn in a while since I had given up running myself or going to the gym, hoping to get it to fit right, so it didn't look like I just had a uniboob under my shirt. I knew I shouldn't care so much about how I looked while going for a run, but something inside of me wanted me to make sure I looked good.

I stepped out of the bathroom and walked back over to the break room, grabbing the little backpack I had brought to put my purse and clothes in so I could run without too much getting in my way. Justin was just finishing up his shift in the kitchen, talking things over with the morning cook and asking about supplies he wanted to be left out for tonight when he saw me stroll out of the break room.

"Where are you off to this morning?" he said to me as he tossed his dirty apron into the hamper in the kitchen that would get taken to the laundry with the other linens.

"Oh, I'm going for a run this morning," I said to him, hoping not to draw too much attention or too many questions about it. We started walking towards the front door, giving Francesca a wave as we went out and she headed towards the back.

Justin and I walked down the steps together and stood outside as I waited for Caleb. Even though the sun had not come up quite yet, it was already feeling warm and a bit humid out. I knew the run was going to be a challenge for me if the weather stayed this way.

"Are you going running with that guy who's been walking with you?" Justin asked me.

I looked at him with surprise.

"Don't look so shocked, Sarah. I've seen him here the last few mornings walking with you. It's the same guy who has been coming into the diner at night to see you."

"I'm sure he hasn't been coming in just to see me," I said, crossing my arms in front of me and looking around to see if Caleb was coming soon.

"Come on, Sarah," Justin said to me with a smirk. "No one is coming in at 2 AM every night because they can't wait to try what I am cooking. He obviously comes in to see you."

Somewhere in the back of my mind I knew what Justin was saying was right, but I was reluctant to admit to that just yet.

"Okay, so maybe he has been coming in to see me," I told him. "He's a nice guy, and is friendly, and asked if I wanted to go for a run with him this morning."

"Good for you," Justin told me. "It's nice to see you doing something."

"I do things," I said defensively.

"Sarah, you come to work, go home and sleep, do your school work, and then come to work again. I haven't even heard you say you are doing something fun on one of your days off. It's great that you are going out, making friends, meeting people."

Just then, Caleb came running around the corner and met us in front of the diner. He had a little bit of a shine of sweat on his forehead, and I could see a bit of a ring around the gray t-shirt he was wearing.

"Hey," Caleb said to me as he came up, a little surprised to see me standing there with Justin.

"Hi, Caleb," I told him. "Caleb, this is Justin. Justin is our cook overnight."

I watched the two men shake hands and greet each other cordially.

"You're the guy that makes the awesome chicken salad," Caleb said to Justin.

"Among other things," Justin said with a laugh. "But thanks, I am glad you enjoyed it."

I saw Justin take a glance at the t-shirt Caleb was wearing.

"ODA 3211?" Justin said, pointing at Caleb's shirt. "I never got to Fort Bragg myself when I was in the Army."

"Oh yeah?" Caleb said, taking an interest. "Where were you?"

"Oh, I spent time in a lot of places. Fort Stewart, Fort Hood, overseas in Germany and Korea, some time in Afghanistan. I put in my twenty years and got out and retired down here. It's much quieter than leading the Army life."

"You said it," Caleb said with a smile. "I just retired myself. I'm still getting used to life outside."

"It takes a bit, but I'm sure you'll get the hang of it." Justin took a look at me and could see I was ready to get on with our run.

"Well, I'll leave you two to your run. I am going home to crash. I'll see you tonight, Sarah. It was nice to meet you, Caleb," Justin said, shaking Caleb's hand again. Justin winked at me as he turned and started walking towards his car.

"You all set?" Caleb said to me, looking me up and down.

"I think so," I said to him with some hesitation. "I haven't run in a while, so hopefully I won't hold you back too much."

"It will be fine," Caleb said to me. "We'll go at your pace, for as long or short as you want. I don't want you to hurt yourself."

"I'm not that fragile," I said to him with a smile. "I can hold my own."

"Great," he said, flashing his own confident smile. "Let's do it."

We started off at a light jog just to get things going. We worked our way down Oak Street for a bit before turning off down one of the side streets that I had not been down before. Munson Lane was a quiet, tree-lined street with just a few homes on it, and the houses were nicely spaced apart, so there was plenty of room between each place. We ran along quietly, and I kept myself in step with Caleb's pace so that we were running right next to each other. Every once in a while I would glance over at him and could see him concentrating on his stride and his breathing. He made the run look very effortless, and it was easy to see that he could go for many more miles than I could.

Munson Lane went down a lot further than I had ever known, and soon we were far off from Oak Street and away from other homes. I was starting to feel the running, with my calves burning a little and my feet asking me why I was torturing them like this after being on them for eight hours straight at work, but the run was making me feel good. Sweat built up quickly, and I could feel it starting to soak through my shirt, making me wish I had brought one of my wicking t-shirts with me instead of this blue one.

I had started to drop a little behind Caleb, who was still going strong without any sign of a struggle. He was probably about five yards ahead of me when he turned, didn't see me next to him, and stopped and turned around. I caught up with him, and we stood for a moment, me huffing hard.

"You okay?" he asked me, checking his watch to see how far we had gone so far.

"I'm alright," I said to him, though I could feel that my cheeks were red, and I was breathing hard.

"We can take a break for a bit if you want," he said to me. "I didn't realize it was going to be this warm this morning."

While I put my hands on my knees and worked to catch my breath, Caleb looked around at the area.

"You ever been down this way before?" he asked me.

"No, I haven't," I told him.

"Me either," he said to me. He walked a little way up the street to a house that had a sign just outside the driveway that it was for sale. Caleb stood at the top of the driveway, looking down at the house. He waved over to me to come where he was.

I slowly walked to his spot, glad to give my legs a break from the running. I looked down the driveway and saw a nice house sitting on a well-manicured piece of property. The house was smaller than many of the others that I had seen, especially in the neighborhood where James lived where big mansion-like homes were the norm.

"Looks like a nice house," I said to Caleb. I was finally catching my breath a bit as Caleb started walking down the driveway towards the house. "Caleb? Where are you going?" I said to him in a rushed tone.

"I just want to get a better look at the house."

"Caleb, we can't go down there."

"Why not?" he asked. "It's for sale. We're not doing anything wrong. Come on."

I followed Caleb down the driveway towards the house. I could see there was a separate garage at the end of the driveway in the same colored siding as the house, a light yellow that looked a little faded. The house itself was small, clearly older, and well-surrounded by large trees lining the front yard, the back, and the sides. There was a small front porch that gave the home a very quaint look to it.

As we got closer to the house, we noticed a woman come walking out wearing a gray suit jacket and matching skirt.

"Oh, hello," the woman said to us as we walked near the house.

"I didn't mean to disturb you," Caleb said. "I just saw the sign at the end of the driveway and wanted to see the house."

"No disturbance at all," the woman said to us. She was middle-aged, with her hair perfectly straight, and gave us a big smile you would expect to see from what was clearly a real estate agent.

"I was just setting everything up for the open house that starts later this morning," she told us. "I'd be glad to show you around if you two would like."

Caleb looked back at me and smiled. I was reluctant to do it, but I could see in his eyes that he was prodding me on, so I walked up next to him, and we followed the agent into the house.

"I'm Adrianne," she said, extending her hand to Caleb.

"I'm Caleb," he said, wiping his hand on his shorts before shaking Adrianne's hand. She then held her hand out to me.

"Sarah," I said to her.

I looked around the house and saw we were standing just inside the door and there was a small living room to our right.

"Well, it's not a very big place," she said to us. "This house was built in the 1960s when there weren't nearly as many people in the area as there are now. It was an older couple that lived here and raised their family. It's got two bedrooms, and an office space that could be another small bedroom if you wanted it to be. Do you two have any children?"

I could feel myself blush at the question and shot Caleb a look. He smiled at me and turned to Adrianne.

"Just one," he said as he put his right arm around me, pulling me closer to him. "He's seventeen and going to college next year."

"Then this house could be the perfect size for you," Adrianne said with enthusiasm.

She proceeded to walk us through the house, showing us the living room with its stone fireplace, the kitchen with new appliances, the bathroom downstairs, and then the rooms upstairs. It was a nice place and in good shape for an older home. Adrianne took us out to the backyard so we could see that there was a good deal of property and a stone patio perfect for outdoor entertaining.

We stood on the back patio viewing everything, and I could see Caleb liked what he saw.

"This would be a nice place," Caleb said to me quietly.

"What do you think?" Adrianne said to both of us hopefully.

"I am definitely interested, Adrianne," Caleb said to her. Adrianne's face lit up immediately.

"Oh, I think you two would be very happy here," she said. I had to do all I could do to keep from laughing as she and Caleb discussed particulars. I let the two of them wander back into the house while I stayed outside and looked around. I could see that this would be a very warm and inviting home for whoever lived here. I found my mind wondering what it would be like to sit out on the patio at night with a fire pit out here, cuddling up under a blanket, Caleb with his arm around me...

You're getting a little ahead of yourself, Sarah, I thought to myself, snapping back into reality.

I heard Caleb and Adrianne come back out the back door and turned around. Caleb was standing there with a stack of paperwork from Adrianne and then took another business card from her.

"Come here, honey," he said to me with a wink.

I walked up to him and put my arm around his waist while listening to the last of Adrianne's instructions about what she would need from "us" if we wanted to put in an offer on the house. Caleb then thanked her for her time, and she showed us out the front door.

"I hope to hear from you soon!" she shouted to us as we walked down the driveway.

When we got to the top of the driveway and started to walk away from the house, Caleb started laughing.

"I'm sorry to put you on the spot like that," he said to me.

"It's fine," I said to him. "It was fun for me."

"There's just something about this house that just... seems right." Caleb looked down at the folder of material he had. "Do you mind if I put this in your backpack while we finish our run?"

"Not at all," I told him. He unzipped the pack on my back and slid the folder inside and closed it back up.

We resumed our run, and I was grateful for the break as it gave me a chance to get my legs back under me to keep going. We worked our way around Munson Lane some more, which apparently looped all the way back towards Carson, where Caleb lived, going around the route that would take you back to my home. We were both sweating a bit at this point as the sun was out now and starting to get stronger.

Caleb came to a stop at the corner for Carson Court, and I stood next to him. I could see the sweat dripping off me at this point, and my shirt was completely soaked through and clinging to my body.

"If you want, we can walk over to my place and grab some water," Caleb said, pointing to the large house just down the street a bit.

"Sure, that's fine," I said to him as we walked slowly. I could feel my legs shaking a little underneath me and was glad the running was over.

Caleb looked down at his watch and noted that we had done just about four miles for the morning.

"Pretty good for someone who hasn't run in years," I said to him proudly.

"It is," he said to me. "You did great."

We stopped at the top of the driveway of a large home, and Caleb turned to walk down the driveway.

"You live here?" I said to him. "Why are we looking at that little house when you have this?"

Caleb laughed as we walked.

"The house," he said pointing to the big house, "belongs to my sister, Linda. My place is the apartment over the garage."

"You and Adam live in the apartment?"

"No, just me," Caleb said as we walked up the steps to the apartment door. "It's kind of a long story. Adam moved in with Linda after Ella... my wife... passed away."

Caleb paused briefly before continuing. He unlocked the apartment door and let me in.

"When I got home, I thought it would be easier if I just stayed here for now so I wasn't a disruption." Caleb went over to the fridge and grabbed two bottles of water, handing one to me.

I rubbed the cold bottle on my forehead and then on my neck, cooling myself down. I looked around and saw the apartment was sparsely decorated, with just a couch and a chair with a TV in the living room and a small counter surrounding the kitchen with stools.

"I thought that house might be a good place for Adam and me to have a place of our own. It's something... well, something I always thought about having when I retired." Caleb took a sip of water. I could see he was feeling a little melancholy about it all and was probably thinking about how he thought his life would be different right now.

"I think it's a beautiful place," I said to him quietly. "It will be perfect for... for you and Adam."

I pulled off my backpack and took out the folder for him and handed it to him.

"Thanks," he said to me. His hand overlapped mine on the folder, and he held it there for a moment. I could feel his index finger lightly rub on mine, and I felt a chill run through my body.

Caleb must have seen me shiver and took the folder from me.

"Your shirt is soaked," he said to me. "I... I can lend you a t-shirt if you want to put something dry on."

Before I could say anything to him, he was off down the small hallway to get a t-shirt. I glanced down at the shirt I was wearing and saw it covered in moisture, so much so that you could clearly see the outline of my sports bra underneath. I felt a bit embarrassed, thinking Caleb had seen me this way.

Caleb reappeared with a t-shirt in hand, a black t-shirt with the same print of ODA 3211 on the left chest.

"Thank you, Caleb," but you don't have to..."

"It's fine," he interrupted. "I have dozens of those t-shirts. I certainly won't miss one, and you don't want to wear a wet shirt any longer than you have to."

I held the shirt in my hand and looked at Caleb for a moment. I could see that we locked eyes and gazed at each other. I was looking deep into his eyes, and I could feel myself getting that chill again.

"The bathroom is just down the hall, on the left," Caleb said, breaking the spell between us.

I walked down the hall to the bathroom and shut the door behind me. I stripped out of the wet shirt and held the black t-shirt in my hands. It had a particular scent to it, one I noticed from the time I held it in my hands to when I pulled it over my head and onto my body. I inhaled deeply and felt that chill again. I could see the t-shirt was a bit form-fitting on me because of my figure, but I was glad to have it on, not just because it was dry, but because it reminded me of Caleb.

I came out of the bathroom and stuffed the blue t-shirt into my backpack. Caleb stared at me and watched me, fumbling with his bottle of water. I giggled slightly and could see he was a little flustered.

I went to put the backpack on and was having some trouble with one of the straps, so Caleb walked over to me to give me a hand. He helped slide the strap up my arm and onto my shoulder from behind. I turned around to thank him, and he was standing inches away from me. I could feel the electricity between us, and I could also see the strong definition of his abs and chest showing through his own sweat-soaked t-shirt. I looked up at Caleb as he slid his hands from my shoulders and down my arms.

In an instant, Caleb was leaning in and gave me a soft kiss. His kiss, and his actions caught me off guard, and while I gasped lightly at first, I quickly found myself kissing him back, putting my hands at his waist and holding him there while he kissed me. The kiss was long, slow, and amazing, and when he slowly moved his lips from mine, I felt a little woozy.

"I'm sorry," he said to me, stepping back a bit. "I didn't mean... I mean I wasn't planning that or anything," he said as he struggled for words.

I put my left hand on his right arm, touching him lightly.

"Caleb, it's okay," I said to him gently.

Without thinking, we found ourselves locked in another embrace, this time kissing more passionately and with more meaning. I felt myself pulling my body tightly to his, wanting to kiss Caleb deeper, and over and over. We just kept kissing, with slight breaks to catch our breath, before I finally stepped back to try to regain some control over myself.

I looked down at my watch and saw that it was well after eight.

"I really should go," I said to Caleb. I could see the disappointment on his face, and I felt it in my stomach as well.

"Yeah, I'm sorry, I know it's been a long night for you," Caleb said apologetically. I walked over to the apartment door, and Caleb walked with me, opening it for me. I stepped over the sill and turned back to face him.

"Thank you for the run, and for... for everything else today," I said to him with a wry smile. "I had fun."

"Me too," he said softly, looking down into my eyes again. Part of me wanted to just push my way back inside the apartment and push Caleb back onto the couch, but another part of me knew maybe that wasn't the best thing to do just now.

"Do you want me to walk you home?" Caleb asked.

"No, that's okay," I answered. "You're already home. It's not a far walk from here. I'll be there in a few minutes. Thank you though. You're such a gentleman." I leaned in and gave him a small kiss on the lips.

"I'll come by the diner later," he yelled to me as I walked down the steps and onto the driveway.

I stopped and looked back at him. "That will be great," I yelled back, and gave him a wave as I started on my way home.

Suddenly, I felt energized even though I knew my body was tired. The kisses were not something I had thought would happen, but I was so glad that they did. I felt so good about myself, and about Caleb that I was home before I knew it. I'm sure all the daydreaming I did along the way made all the difference. At one point I even felt like I was skipping.

It's great to feel happy, I told myself as I turned into our driveway and walked towards the front door.

Chapter 13

Caleb

Those kisses lingered with me all throughout the morning and well into my dreams once I fell asleep. I never planned on kissing Sarah like that. It wasn't something I had plotted out, waiting for just the right moment. The moment just came upon me as we stood there together in my apartment. There was something about the whole day – the run, the house visit, and her coming back to my place – that just made it feel right to do.

The guilt was there too after I did it. I didn't feel guilty about Sarah – she responded better than I could have hoped to it. I did feel guilty that I had, in some way, betrayed Ella by letting myself fall for someone else. I knew somewhere in my mind that there was no rational reason to feel this way, but I still did. All these years Ella had always been the only woman in my life, going back to when we started dating in high school.

There had been plenty of opportunities that came up over the years since we had been separated so often, but it never crossed my mind to do anything like that with anyone else. Ella was always first and last in my heart and mind. I saw plenty of other soldiers that didn't think twice about getting together with other women wherever we happened to be stationed or assigned at the time. To them, they never felt like they were doing anything wrong or betraying anyone. They just saw it as purely physical, something they needed to do, and then went back to their regular lives. I could never see it that way.

But now there was no reason for me to see it that way, and yet I still felt like there was something wrong with what I just did. It was a tough thing for me to reconcile in my brain, and in my heart. Part of me felt like I had to remain loyal to Ella, even if that didn't make sense, but another part of me was growing, and that was the part that wanted to get closer and closer to Sarah.

After a few hours of fitful sleep and then a shower, I got dressed and walked over to the house to see what Linda and Adam were up to. It was already early afternoon, so both were up and about, doing their own thing. I ran into Linda working out in the yard, doing some spring cleaning to get the property in shape for some planting she always said she was going to do but never seemed to have time for. Linda was loading up a wheelbarrow with weeds, fallen branches and other clutter from the yard.

"Hey there," she said to me, looking at me as she was pulling some weeds from one of the garden beds. Even though she was wearing sunglasses and a wide-brimmed hat, she still raised her hand to shade her eyes from the bright sun of the day.

"Need some help?" I asked her as I knelt with her.

"Thanks," she said, grabbing an extra pair of gloves she had in the straw bag she had at her side. "I'm just trying to get some of this weeding done while I have the time and energy."

I went about pulling up some of the obvious weeds around the flower bed.

"You know, Linda," I said to her as I tugged a weed out, "You could just hire a service to come in and do this for you instead of complaining about how the garden looks. You have had the house for years, and you never have time to do the garden the way you want it."

"I know," she said, sitting back on the grass. "I want to do it, I really do. I just can't find the time to do it all."

Linda went back to pulling some more weeds out.

"So how was last night?" she asked me casually.

"Oh, the game was great. Adam was the hero. I am glad I was there to see it. And we had a nice time afterward at the diner."

"I know, Adam told me all about it," Linda said. "I'm glad you two got some time together like that."

There was a long pause before she started up again.

"So, when were you going to tell me about Sarah?" she asked me without looking up from her chore.

I put down the small shovel I was using to dig out some weeds and stared at her.

Linda looked over at me and smiled.

"What? Did you think Adam wouldn't mention it to me? It was all he could talk about at breakfast. If you were awake, you could have joined us and answered everything then. Oh, that's right, you were out on your run... with Sarah."

I knew she was giving me a hard time, like the big sister she is. I sat back on the grass as well, facing her.

"What do you want to know?" I said bluntly.

Anything you want to share would be nice," she answered. "Apparently, you've been sneaking out for 2 AM feedings at the diner to see her, and today you went running together, so you obviously like her. Why wouldn't you tell me about her?"

"I don't know, Linda. I do like her. She is friendly and kind and smart, and I find her very attractive. I didn't tell you, well because I didn't want you to judge me for it."

Linda came closer to me.

"Caleb, I would never do that. You're a grown man, and you can do what you want and see who you want. I would never pass judgment on anything you do."

"I know that I guess. I just feel like... like I am betraying Ella in some way, and that you would feel that way too, even if you didn't say it to me."

I looked over at Linda, and she looked a bit hurt.

"Caleb, you know I loved Ella like a sister. While you were away, she was my connection to you. You, and Adam and Ella – you're the only family I really have. When she died, it devastated me the way it did you and Adam. No one can replace her in my heart – but that doesn't mean there shouldn't be someone else at some point for you. You're not betraying her by being happy and finding someone you like to spend time with. And goodness knows I would welcome someone else that can put up with you."

Linda smiled at me and gave me her big sister look.

"All I have ever wanted for you, Caleb, is that you are happy," Linda told me.

"I know," I told her. "You've made it your mission since we were kids."

"Someone had to look after you," she said to me. "Mom and Dad certainly didn't make it a priority to watch for either of us. Besides, you turned out okay," she said with a laugh.

"You did too," I said to her.

"So, when do I get to meet her?" Linda asked me pointedly.

"Linda, it's not like we're really dating or anything. I have seen her at the diner a bunch of times, and we went for a run this morning and..." I almost let it slip about the kiss, but I held back.

"And what?" Linda said, jumping up from the ground. "There's something more, Caleb. You're holding out on me. Spill it."

I stood up, brushing some of the dirt from my jeans and started walking towards the house. Linda followed quickly behind me as I opened the screen door and went into the kitchen.

Adam was sitting in the kitchen having a sandwich when he saw me walk in with Linda close behind me. I opened the fridge and stuck my head in hoping to kill some time, but Linda would not give up.

"What happened, Caleb?" Linda said relentlessly.

"What's going on?" Adam chimed in as he wiped sandwich crumbs from his face.

"Your Dad went for his run with Sarah this morning, and something happened," Linda said, standing with her hands on her hips.

I closed the refrigerator door, grabbing a bottle of water out first. I took a slow sip while Adam and Linda both watched me like hawks.

"What happened, Dad?" Adam said, now turning to face me.

"Great, now I have two of you," I said, sitting down in one of the chairs. Linda grabbed a seat next to Adam so they could both stare at me. "I'm sorry I ever mentioned anything," I said aloud.

"We're just curious, Caleb," Linda said to me. "It's not often we get any information about what's going on with you, you know. This is a real treat," she snickered.

"Look, we went for our run, had a good time, and we came back here for some water, and... well... we kissed a little... I can't believe I'm even telling you this. It's none of your business, either of you," I said pointing at the co-conspirators.

"You kissed?" Linda yelled. "Caleb, that's..." Linda then tempered her enthusiasm. "That's very nice. I'm happy for you."

"Can we be done with this now?" I asked, feeling exasperated.

"Are you going to ask her out now, Dad?" Adam asked me.

"Since you've kissed, it might be nice if you went out on an actual date," Linda added.

"We'll see," I told Linda and Adam. "It's not as easy as you guys seem to think it is. Her schedule is kind of crazy... she only has off on Mondays and Tuesdays... and I'm not sure she would even say yes. To be honest, the thought of asking her out... well, it scares me a little."

Linda had to hold in her laugh for a bit.

"I'm sorry, Caleb, I didn't mean to laugh," Linda said. "Just the thought of this woman making you nervous, knowing you have been in war zones and life-or-death situations before, is kind of funny, you have to admit."

"Linda, I haven't asked anyone out for over twenty years. Figuring it all out again is a little intimidating."

"I can give you some pointers if you want, Dad," Adam said. I could see the smirk on his face as he and Linda could barely contain themselves.

"You two are a real big help." I sipped some more of my water while Linda and Adam enjoyed the moment they were having giving me a good ribbing.

"Seriously, Dad," Adam said to me, "Just be yourself. You were fine last night. I could tell you were comfortable with Sarah. Just ask her to dinner, or for drinks, or coffee. Go somewhere where you can sit and talk. It will be fine."

"Yes, Caleb," Linda added, "Besides, she must like you too if you were kissing. She's obviously got some interest. "

"Maybe I'll ask her tonight," I said to them as they kept watching me. "I can meet her over at the diner and ask her to do something on Monday."

Linda sat back and clapped her hands together.

"This is so exciting," Linda said, putting her arm around Adam and pulling him to her. "We should do something together tonight to celebrate."

"Oh, I would Aunt Linda," Adam said, standing up from the table," but... I have a date tonight. Ashley and I are going to the movies with a few other people."

"So, she has a name," I said slyly, glad to have the spotlight off me for a change.

"I would have introduced you to her last night, Dad, but you left before I could do it. By the way, thanks for paying for us," Adam added.

"You're welcome," I said to him. "And I would like to meet her some-time."

"Maybe you two can double-date sometime," Linda said with a laugh so hard it caused her to snort.

"Maybe we can fix you up with someone, and all go out," I added.

"Me?" Linda said with shock. "I don't have time for dating. Besides, I have more fun living vicariously through you two."

"Well, since Adam is out, how about you and I do something, sis? Maybe another round of cards tonight?"

"I'll make you a deal," Linda said to me. "We'll play cards tonight. If I win, you take me to the diner tonight for a late dinner so I can meet Sarah."

"And if I win?" I asked her.

"You can think of something," Linda said, "but I'm not worried about it. No matter what you come up with, it doesn't matter. You haven't beaten me at rummy in thirty years. That's not likely to change now," she said with a challenge.

Somehow, I had a feeling I was going to have a guest with me at the diner tonight.

Chapter 14

Sarah

1 ⁴

I walked through the front door for the first time in days without any concern about Denise or any arguments that might erupt just from my presence. The morning I spent with Caleb had me riding on a high I didn't want to come down from. I walked down the hall into the kitchen and saw James and Lizzie both sitting there, chatting and smiling. They turned to me as soon as I entered the room and stopped their talking.

"Good morning," I said with a smile and with a lilt to my voice.

I took off my backpack and placed it on the floor next to me as I took a seat at the table. James and Lizzie looked at me, looked at each other, and then back at me.

"You're in a really good mood for having worked all night," James noted.

"I am," I stated boldly. "I had a great night at work, and then went for an invigorating run, and now I feel awesome. Tired, but awesome."

"Glad to hear it," James said, grabbing his empty glass off the table. "I'd love to stay and chat and hear all about your night, your run, and Caleb, but I need to run into the office for a bit this morning. Denise is out running a fundraiser this morning, so is it okay if Lizzie is here? I know you'll be sleeping, but at least if she needs something you're close by." James looked down at me, checking out the shirt I was wearing with a puzzled look on his face.

"It's fine," I said happily. "I'm happy to do it."

"Thanks," James said, peeling his gaze from my shirt. "Where did you get the shirt? That's a military issue shirt."

"Oh, Caleb lent it to me. The shirt I wore for our run was soaked in sweat, so he gave me a dry one to wear." I glanced down at the shirt again, happy to have it hugging my body.

"You went back to his place then?" James asked with some concern.

"We were running by there anyway, and we needed a break. We had been running for a while. I went in, had some water, changed my shirt, and left." James didn't need to know any more than that at this point.

"I'm just surprised you would go to his place is all," James said to me.

"James, you really need to stop being so suspicious. There's nothing sinister going on here. You know, I was in a good mood when I got back here. Why are you trying to take that away from me?" I shouted as I stood up from the table.

"Hey, calm down," James told me, putting his hand on my shoulder. "I didn't mean anything by it. I'm sorry. It's just... out of character for you is all, Sarah. You're always so guarded and cautious. I'm not used to seeing you like this."

"I'll try to tone down my happiness for you," I said as I grabbed my backpack off the floor and marched up the stairs to my room.

Why did everything have to be such a confrontation lately whenever I walked through the door? It was almost as if James and Denise didn't want to see me enjoying my life again. I was opening up a little more and acting different, and I think Caleb had a lot to do with that.

I sat on the edge of my bed and kicked my sneakers off. I pulled off my socks as well and then took off the running shorts, leaving me just in Caleb's t-shirt and my black cotton panties. I pulled the shirt over my head so I could take off the sports bra, and once I tugged it off, I was happy to pull Caleb's shirt back on. I reached over and flipped on the ceiling fan in my room to circulate some of the air around and cool things off. I got under the top sheet and put my head on my pillow, feeling the coolness against my face and the sheet on my bare legs.

My plans to try to drift off to sleep right away were interrupted by a knock on the door. I peeked my head up and saw Lizzie poke her head in.

"Can I come in?" she asked me.

"Sure," I said to her, sitting up in my bed.

Lizzie entered the room, closing the door behind her, and sat on the bed cross-legged right in front of me.

"Dad left for work," she told me. "I think he felt bad about making you upset."

"Don't worry about me and your Dad," I reassured her. "We'll be okay. Things just seem a little tense in the house lately I guess."

"I wanted to say thanks for letting me come to the diner last night," Lizzie offered. "I had a great time with everyone. Aaron even sat next to me at the table," she said with excitement.

"I saw that," I said to her. "Did he say anything to you?"

"Well, not directly, but Tori told me that he told Victor before they got there that he wanted to sit next to me. I guess that's something." Lizzie was twirling her hair looking at me.

"What?" I asked her.

"So, do you like Caleb?" she asked me, looking at the t-shirt.

I was caught a little off-guard by her question and hesitated to answer for a moment, worried that she might let something slip to James or Denise.

"I think I do like him," I said to her quietly. "He's very nice, and gentle, and sweet..."

"He's pretty handsome too," Lizzie said to me with a smile.

"Yes, he's definitely that too," I replied, letting out a little sigh afterward.

"Has he asked you out yet?" she asked, coming up to sit next to me.

"No, he hasn't," I told her. There was a tinge of disappointment in my voice. "But he..." I stopped myself from replying.

"He what?" Lizzie prodded. "He gave you this shirt. Did he do something else?"

"We did kiss a little," I told her. I was glad to have someone to share it with, but I did worry about her parents finding out. "Lizzie, don't mention that to your parents, please. I mean, I know I'm an adult and all, and it shouldn't matter, but things have been weird around here. I don't want to cause any more problems."

"I won't tell, I swear," Lizzie said. "So, what was it like? Was he a good kisser?"

"Oh yes," I said with a smile. Lizzie squealed a little when I said it. "He was very tender and gentle. It was wonderful."

"Sarah, you are so lucky," Lizzie told me. "I wish Aaron would at least try to hold my hand. Boys are so..." Lizzie struggled to find the right word.

"Dumb," I told her. "Boys are dumb, Lizzie," I said to her honestly. "Teenage boys are pretty awkward. They are slow to pick up on things, like when a girl likes them. You just have to give him time. He'll catch on eventually, and if he doesn't, well that's his loss."

Lizzie was looking at the shirt I had on again.

"What do those letters and numbers mean?" she asked me.

"I'm not really sure," I told her. "I think they have something to do with the unit he was in when he was in the Army."

"Are you going to keep the shirt?"

I hadn't really thought much about it, but I knew part of me certainly didn't want to give it back anytime soon.

"We'll see," I said to her with a grin. "Okay, I need to get some sleep," I said to Lizzie, shooing her off the bed.

"Okay, I'm going," Lizzie said as she got off the bed.

"If you need anything, come in and get me," I said to Lizzie as I let out a yawn. I laid back down on the pillow.

"I'll be in my room, probably talking to Tori and Becky, listening to music or something. I'll see you later." Lizzie left my room and shut the door.

I climbed out of bed to close the shades and make the room a little darker, keeping out the bright sunlight so I could get some sleep.

I would have thought that I would fall asleep as soon as my head hit the pillow, but I didn't. It wasn't for lack of trying to sleep, and my body was feeling tired, but my brain didn't want any part of sleep just yet. I kept flashing back to when Caleb kissed me, and then kissed me again and again, and how wonderful it felt to be in his arms, to be held like that, and to be kissed – really, sincerely kissed. Even the boys (and yes, they were boys) I had kissed in high school and in college never made me feel like this.

Every time I closed my eyes, there Caleb was again, standing in front of me with his tight t-shirt showing off his abs, gazing at me, and then moving closer to me. Each time I thought about it, I could feel him getting closer and closer to me, pressing his body against mine so that

I could feel the strength in his shoulders, his back, and everywhere on his body.

I hadn't felt this way about anyone in a very long time. I hadn't let myself feel this way or even wanted to, and I think I had forgotten what it was like and now I was reacting in a big way. Beyond that, I think my heart had been avoiding it even more, but now it didn't have a choice.

He may be just what you need in your life, my brain was telling me.

"I think you're right," I whispered as I snuggled under the sheet to try to sleep.

Chapter 15

Caleb

1 5

I tried hard, but just as it always was when we were kids, Linda beat me at rummy once again. We got down to playing just after Adam was picked up by his friends. Linda put some music on, we had some drinks and snacks and played cards. It came down to the last hand, and I really thought I had a chance, but somehow Linda always seemed to pull just the cards she needed to get the win. Of course, she emphasized her victory by doing a dance around the kitchen to celebrate.

While she was dancing and crowing about her win, I glanced down at my watch and saw it was nearly 11 PM. Sarah was already on her shift at the diner, and I wanted to get over to see her. I hoped that Linda would be too tired or would have forgotten that she promised to go with me tonight if she won. Much like the card game, I had no such luck there either.

"So, let's head over to the diner, little brother," Linda taunted, grabbing a light jacket to put on before we left.

"Okay," I said to her, sounding like a sore loser. "But you have to promise me you are not going to grill her or give her a hard time. She is at work after all."

"Caleb, of course, I wouldn't do that," Linda answered. "If anything, I am going to embarrass you and give you a hard time. Maybe I can bring one of the photo albums from when we were kids..."

"Let's go," I told her, taking her arm and leading her out the back door.

Linda headed for the driveway and over to her car while I kept walking up the driveway.

"What are you doing?" she asked as she reached into her purse for her car keys.

"I'm going to the diner," I told her. "What are you doing?"

"I was going there, too. Get in the car."

"Linda, the diner is a ten-minute walk at most," I told her. "It's ridiculous to take your car. Besides, this time of night on a Saturday you are never getting a parking spot there."

"Fine," Linda said, tossing her keys back into her purse. "But I'm counting on you to protect me."

"Protect you from what? A stray raccoon getting a late-night meal?"

"Do you really think there are any raccoons out there?" Linda said, hesitating at the top of the driveway.

"When did you get so soft?" I told her as I grabbed her arm and started to walk with her. "You used to beat up all the boys in the neighborhood without batting an eye."

"That was a long time ago now, Caleb. I'm a refined lady now," she said as she tossed her hair back and smiled.

We walked along up to Oak Street, with Linda getting skittish at every little sound she heard or thought she heard, along the streets. She was grateful when we got to Oak Street, and there were more street lights to light the way. The streets of Swanson were busy with college kids out and about, hitting all the spots that might offer food or drinks or both. When we got to the diner, we could see the parking lot was full, and there were even some people milling around in the lobby like they were waiting for tables.

I walked in and up to the front register, and there was Doug, smiling away, happy to see all the business in his place.

"Well hello there!" he said happily when he saw me. "It's nice to see you again. And who is this lovely lady you have with you?"

Linda blushed and smiled when Doug said this, running her hands through her hair.

"It's my sister," I told him. "I don't suppose you have room for the two of us? I can see you're pretty busy with people waiting outside."

"Oh, those are kids looking for the big tables to sit together. I can seat the two of you, no problem," Doug said as he picked up two menus and began to lead us to the back dining room. I scanned the room and didn't see Sarah anywhere.

Doug sat us at a booth, waiting for Linda to slide in before handing the menu to her and smiling.

"Let me know if I can get you anything," Doug said to us, though he was saying it more to Linda than to me.

Linda nodded and smiled as Doug walked away.

"Well he was certainly nice," Linda said to me as she opened the menu.

"He's the owner," I told her. "He's supposed to be nice to everyone."

"Don't spoil it for me, Caleb," Linda chided. "it's not often I get to hear a man say nice things to me."

I opened the menu, still taking time to look around to see if I saw Sarah anywhere. I hadn't come across her yet and decided to look at the menu to see if there is something I wanted.

Linda and I busied ourselves looking at the menus when suddenly someone appeared beside our table. I looked up with enthusiasm but was a little disappointed when I saw it was Francesca.

"Hey there, sweetie," she said to me, beaming. "It's great to see you here tonight."

"Hi, Francesca," I said to her politely, placing the menu down. Francesca could see I was looking past her. "Is Sarah here tonight?"

I could see the disappointment on her face when I asked about Sarah.

"Yeah, she is, but she's working the other room tonight, so I guess you're stuck with me," Francesca said, still trying to act flirty. "Can I get you two something to drink while you decide?"

I looked over at Linda so she could order first.

"I'll have sweet tea, please," she said as she went back to flipping through the menu pages.

"Unsweetened tea for me, please," I said to Francesca.

"Be back in a minute," she said as she sashayed away from the table.

"So, we're not going to see Sarah?" Linda said, looking saddened.

"Maybe not," I told her. "They are pretty busy tonight. Sorry about that," I told her, though part of me was glad that I wouldn't have to sit through an exchange between Sarah and Linda.

A moment later, Sarah appeared, walking over to our table with drinks and a smile.

"Hi," she said to me. She placed the one glass down in front of me and the other in front of Linda, making sure to smile at Linda.

"Hi. I didn't think I would get to see you tonight."

"We are crazy busy tonight,' Sarah said to me. "But Fran told me you were sitting over here with someone, so she switched off with me. I gave her one of my big tables. She'll like the tip."

Sarah glanced back over at Linda and then back at me.

"Sarah, this is my sister, Linda," I told her. "Linda, this is Sarah."

Sarah breathed a little sigh of relief and laughed.

"It's nice to meet you, Linda," she said and then turned back to me. "Fran told me you were sitting here with a woman and I..., well it doesn't matter. I was being silly I guess."

"Oh... well, I would have come by myself but Linda, she kind of..."

Linda cut me off.

"What my little brother means is that he lost at cards to me and had to take me out for dinner, so here we are."

"Lost at cards, huh?" Sarah giggled. "Caleb, I thought you were the master of everything."

"Ha!" Linda laughed loudly. "Hardly. I can tell you all kinds of stories about him. Why I remember when he was ten..."

"Okay, Linda," I interrupted, wanting to end this quickly. "There's no need to bore Sarah with stories about me. What would you like to eat? Get whatever you want so we can get some food in your mouth."

"Hmmm," Linda said, looking back over the menu again. "I think I'll have the turkey club sandwich on rye."

"Got it," Sarah said. "How about you, Caleb? My choice or yours tonight?"

I could feel Linda staring at me, and suddenly I felt flustered just trying to order something to eat.

"I'll have the BLT please," I said to her. I realized I had polished off my iced tea already from nervousness thanks to my sister.

"And a refill on your tea?" Sarah said, taking the glass from my hand so that our fingers touched.

"Please."

"Great. I'll be back in a bit." Sarah walked off to get my refill while I scowled across the table at Linda.

"Very smooth, little brother,' Linda said to me.

"I knew this was a bad idea," I muttered.

"You compose yourself while I go to the ladies' room," Linda said as she slid out of the booth and walked off.

Sarah came back with a tall glass of iced tea for me and placed it down on the table.

"Your sister seems like fun," Sarah told me.

"Yeah, she's a real hoot," I answered.

Sarah leaned down and whispered in my ear.

"I think it's cute the way you got all flustered," and then she gave me a quick peck on the cheek. I could feel my face get warm right away. Sarah grinned and walked away from the table to go back to work.

The kiss on the cheek made my night, and I was glad Linda wasn't here to see it. It took her a bit to get back to the table, and when she came back, I noticed she had a big smile on her face and was looking back towards the entrance.

"What took you so long?" I asked her.

"Oh, well there was a line at the bathroom. This place is crawling with college kids now. So, I was chatting with the owner while I waited. He is such a nice gentleman. He was asking about me, what I did, how I knew you, if I was seeing anyone..."

"He was hitting on you?"

"I wouldn't say it so crudely, Caleb," Linda replied. "We were having a nice, friendly conversation. Maybe a little flirting took place."

Linda took a long sip of her iced tea and smiled at me while I just shook my head.

"So, he wasn't scared off that you are a lawyer?"

"No, actually he was interested. He said he could use some good legal advice."

"I'll bet he can."

Sarah appeared again with our meals, placing Linda's sandwich, piled high with turkey, in front of her, and then sliding my BLT in front of me.

"Can I get you guys anything else?" Sarah asked me.

"I think we're good," I said, smiling at Sarah.

"Okay, if you need anything, track me down. Enjoy!" Sarah said as she raced off again.

Linda dove into her turkey club, eating it like a lion tears into a gazelle. There was no disputing that when she was hungry, there was no stopping her. I looked at her in amazement when most of the sandwich was gone, and I had barely taken a few bites of mine.

"What?" she said as she swallowed another bite. "I'm hungry! I'm not used to waiting to eat until this late at night. I get cranky if I don't get my meals at regular times, Caleb. You know that."

Linda polished off her sandwich, fries, coleslaw, and pickle and then helped herself to my coleslaw and what was left of my fries. I was glad my hands moved away from the plate fast enough before she took a bite out of me.

By the time Sarah came back to clear the plates, all the food was gone. Sarah grabbed the empty plates and asked if we wanted anything else. Before I could say no, Linda chimed in.

"Do you have any seven-layer cake?" she asked.

"Yes, we do," Sarah replied.

"Caleb, let's get some. It was always one of your favorites."

"Okay," I said resignedly. "Two pieces of seven-layer cake, Sarah, please, and coffee too."

Sarah laughed as she walked off to get the cake. She returned quickly with two big slices of cake and placed them down on the table along with our cups of coffee. No sooner had Sarah placed the forks down when Linda attacked her piece of cake, savoring every bite she took. I did manage to get one or two bites of cake before she decided to help herself to most of my piece as well. When Linda looked up at me, she had a long smear of chocolate just under her bottom lip. Naturally, I didn't tell her about it.

Sarah came back over with the check and slid it onto the table. Linda just looked at it and then looked at me, assuming I was paying since I had lost at rummy. I grabbed the check and smiled at Sarah.

"I'm sorry I didn't really have time to chat with you two," she said apologetically. "We're just so busy tonight I barely get ten seconds to breathe."

"It's okay," I said to her. "I think I am better off anyway. Goodness knows what might happen if Linda had time to talk to you."

Before Sarah could say anything else, we heard the familiar ding of the bell from the kitchen.

"I have to run, that's me," she said hurriedly. "Linda, it was nice to meet you!"

I grabbed the check and left a tip on the table and waved to Linda for her to get up. We walked over to the register, where Doug had just finished ringing up some teenagers. Linda smiled widely at him as we got up to the register.

"How was everything?" Doug asked Linda as I handed him the check.

"Just wonderful," she said coyly. "You have fantastic food here, Doug."

"Why thank you, Linda," Doug answered politely as he handed me my change. "I guess you liked our cake," he said smiling at Linda.

"I did," she replied. "How did you know we had cake?"

"Well, you have some here on your chin," Doug said. He whipped his handkerchief out of his jacket pocket and gently wiped the chocolate off Linda's chin for her.

Linda was mortified and looked at me, while I could barely contain my laughter.

Linda marched out the front door, with Doug yelling behind her that he hoped to see her soon. I saw Sarah walking by before I walked out and stopped her.

"Can I come by at six to walk you home?" I asked her.

"I was counting on it," she told me as she put her hand on my right forearm. "See you later," she said with a sly smile.

I nodded to Doug and walked out, finding Linda standing there on the sidewalk, tapping her left foot rapidly on the pavement.

I walked over to her, and she immediately punched me in the arm. Linda always threw a good punch, and it was probably harder than I had been hit in a long time.

"You jerk!" she said to me as I laughed. "You let me walk up to him with chocolate all over my face!"

"At least he knows you like the food," I told her as she hit me again.

We began our slow walk home without Linda saying much before she chimed in.

"I didn't get to talk to her much, but Sarah seems very nice, Caleb."

"I think she is too."

"She obviously likes you too if she was jealous enough to switch tables to see who you were sitting with," Linda said.

"I guess so."

"Does that mean you are going to ask her out?" Linda asked me.

I walked along a bit without answering, moving myself a little bit ahead of Linda, so she had to scurry to catch up to me.

"Are you going to answer me?" Linda said, pushing me with her shoulder.

"I would like to, yes," I finally said.

"Oh, that's so great Caleb. I am so happy for you! Where are you going to take her? There are some nice places you can go for dinner."

"I don't know. I think I'll ask her if there's anything she might like to do. She doesn't get much free time to herself."

"It would be better if you had a plan, Caleb. I'll see if I can come up with some choices for you," Linda said to me as we reached the driveway.

"Great, you can be my social director too," I answered.

"Geez, it's nearly 1 AM," Linda said, letting out a small yawn. "I don't know how you do this staying up late thing. I need to get to bed." Linda gave me a hug. "Thanks for dinner, little brother. And, really, I am glad that you found someone."

"Thanks, Linda," I said as we broke the hug.

"And if she can put up with you make sure you don't piss her off. We need to keep her around and happy, for all our sakes," Linda said as she walked towards the house.

"Go to bed, old lady," I yelled as I walked up to my apartment. I could see that Linda raised her hand and gave me the finger as she kept walking.

I made it up to my apartment, took off my sneakers and relaxed. I had five hours to kill before seeing Sarah again, so I set the alarm on my phone for 5 AM again to wake me up in case I fell asleep. I walked into the bedroom and lay down on the bed. I noticed the picture on my nightstand, a picture of me, Adam, and Ella taken about a year before she passed away.

I picked up the frame and held the picture for a moment, and it made me wonder if what I was doing right now was the right thing. I hadn't felt this happy at all in the last two years or so since she was gone. Part of me still felt guilty, but I think what Adam had said to me was right – Ella wouldn't want me to be sad about her forever.

I put the picture back down and blew her a kiss.

Chapter 16

Sarah

Saturday night turned out to be one of the most exhausting nights I have had in a while. There was a constant stream of customers from the time I arrived at 10 PM Saturday night until quitting time rolled around at 6 AM Sunday morning. I slumped onto the couch in the break room, pushing aside Francesca's legs on the couch so I could sit down. The push seemed to rouse her from the quick sleep she had fallen into.

"My feet are killing me," Francesca said with a grunt. She sat up next to me and put her head on my shoulder.

"Mine too," I added. "Today is one day where I wish I had my car, so I could drive home."

Justin had come into the breakroom, opening his locker and grabbing his jacket so he could head home.

"I can give you a ride home if you want Sarah," he said to me.

"Oh, thanks, Justin, that's sweet of you, but Caleb is coming by to walk me home this morning."

Justin looked over at me and smiled, and Francesca lifted her head off my shoulder to look at me.

"You two have something going?" Francesca asked me.

"No... I mean, I don't know, maybe," I told her, with Justin taking an interest in what I was saying. "We haven't gone out on a date or anything, but we've become... close."

I didn't really know how to put what it was I had with Caleb.

"What does that mean?" Francesca stated, giving me a sly smile. "Have you slept with him?"

I felt flush with embarrassment at the question.

"No!" I answered her immediately, standing up from the couch and feeling a little offended at the question. "Geez, Fran, how could you think that?"

Francesca stood up in front of me.

"I'm sorry, Sarah," she said sincerely. "I was just joking."

"It's okay," I told her. "I think I'm just tired and cranky."

"But if that's not it, what do you mean by close?" she questioned.

"We just like spending time with each other," I told her. "And... well... we kissed a little."

"I knew there was more to it!" she shouted. "You wouldn't have given up a table with a fifty-dollar tip to wait on two people if there wasn't something behind it!"

Francesca opened her locker to grab her things, putting her purse over her shoulder.

"So, do you like him? Well, I guess you do if you're making out with him," Francesca joked.

"I do like him," I told her honestly. "And I should probably get going if I am going to meet him outside. I'll see you tonight, Fran."

I grabbed my jacket and purse out of my locker and went to head out. Justin walked along with me as we walked out of the breakroom.

"How much do you know about this guy, Sarah?" Justin asked me.

"Not a lot just yet, Justin," I answered. "Don't tell me you're going to start on me too," I said with some frustration.

"No, it's not that," Justin said, stopping me as we got into the foyer.

"When I saw you two the other day he was wearing a t-shirt that had ODA 3211 on it," he told me.

"Yes, he gave me one of those t-shirts the other day," I told him.

"Do you know anything about his military life?" Justin asked. "I was in the Army, Sarah. Those guys in Special Forces, where he was, they've seen and done a lot of things, things that can get ugly. You don't get to choose that line of work in the Army; they choose you."

"So, he's done some Rambo stuff," I said to him. "That's not that big of a deal."

"Sarah, it's not Rambo stuff," Justin said with seriousness. "He's probably done stuff he's not allowed to talk about, stuff he won't want to talk about. Those units get called on to do some nasty things sometimes. They train rebels in other countries to learn how to use weapons and fight, but they do other missions -secret missions - too. He's not just some soldier like I was."

"What are you saying, Justin?" I asked him. "That I should be afraid of him? He hasn't shown any signs of anything I should worry about." I was starting to take offense to what Justin was saying.

"No, I'm not saying that," Justin replied. "All I am saying is that after twenty years of doing that kind of work, he may have a lot of baggage that he needs to deal with. You don't just bury the stuff you see in combat, and it goes away. I just want you to be aware is all. Look, I want you to be happy, you know that. But I don't want you to get hurt – emotionally. You've had enough of that. Just be careful, okay?"

I looked at Justin and could see he was serious about what he had just said.

"Thank you, Justin," I said, putting my hand on his. "I know you mean well, but I don't think there is anything to worry about. I want the chance to get to know him better, and then, if there's anything to worry about, I'll deal with it."

"Fair enough," he said to me. I saw Justin glance out the door and then turn back to me and smile.

"Your ride is here," he said with a grin.

I looked out the door and saw Caleb standing there in his t-shirt and running shorts, waiting patiently for me.

Justin and I walked out the door together and down the steps towards Caleb.

"Hey there," Caleb said to both of us. "Have a good night?"

"Super busy," I said to him. "I'm exhausted. I don't know how Justin here keeps up with it all in the kitchen."

"I just go on auto-pilot and start to make stuff and hope it comes out right," Justin said with a laugh. "You two have a good day. Nice to see you again, Caleb. I'll see you tonight, Sarah."

"Bye, Justin," I told him as he walked towards his car.

Caleb and I walked along on Oak Street a few paces.

"He seems like a good guy to work with," Caleb said to me. "Justin, I mean."

I looked over at Caleb and smiled at him.

"He is," I replied. "Justin's a real sweetheart, a big teddy bear."

I could see a look come over Caleb's face and I smiled.

"You don't have to be jealous," I said and reached over and gently took Caleb's hand in mine, holding it as we walked.

"What, me?" Caleb said, feeling defensive. "I'm not jealous, really," he said as he tried to cover himself. "I'm just glad you have a good guy to work with you. And if he's a vet, well I know you're safe in there all night." Caleb gave my hand a gentle squeeze as he smiled back at me.

"It was nice to meet your sister," I told Caleb as we turned the corner and walked down towards my house.

"Yeah, she's something alright," Caleb said sarcastically. "She's the typical big sister. She likes to give me a hard time about things, but she always thinks I need looking after, even after all these years. She wasn't going to let me get away with leaving the house last night to see you without coming with me so she could check you out."

"I guess that's what older siblings do," I said to Caleb. "I'm pretty sure that's why James made a point of coming over to you the other night too."

We walked on silently, holding hands until we reached the top of my driveway.

"So, did I pass the sister test?" I asked Caleb as I looked up into his eyes.

"Oh yeah," he said to me. "Linda told me...," Caleb hesitated a bit, and then continued, "well, she told me I should try to... to keep you around." Caleb looked at me, and I could see some real caring in his face.

"That's nice of her," I said softly, moving closer to him.

Caleb bent down and kissed me softly. I felt his lips press lightly against mine and I moved closer to him so we could kiss deeper. At first, I felt like I should hesitate, knowing we were probably in plain view of anyone that might be looking out the windows of the house, but then I decided I didn't care who was watching.

Let them watch, I thought defiantly. *This is my life, not theirs.*

Caleb slowly broke the kiss as he pulled away from my lips.

"You know, these walks home are not nearly long enough," he told me. "It feels like I only get to spend ten minutes alone with you."

"I know," I said to him. "I wish I had a normal schedule like other people, so you didn't have to get up in the middle of the night to watch me work. You must be tired like me."

"It's fine," he said as he ran his index finger along my cheek tracing down to my chin before lifting my chin back towards him for another kiss. I felt like I was going to melt right there on the spot.

"Maybe we need to figure out how we can spend some more time together," Caleb told me.

"What do you suggest?" I said coyly.

"I mean... well, you are off on Monday. Maybe we can get together and do something."

"You mean like a date?" I told him. I was just playing with him now to get a reaction out of him.

"Yes, like a date," he finally said.

"Where would you like to go?" I asked him, putting my arms around his shoulders and then leaning in to kiss him again, giving him a long, lingering kiss this time.

"It's hard to concentrate when you keep doing that," Caleb groaned. "We can go anywhere you like. You know the area better than I do, and we can do something that you would like. A movie, dinner, drinks, whatever."

"I'll tell you what," I said to him, reaching over to kiss him once again and then slowly prying myself from his lips. "I'll think about it today, and when you come to meet me tonight... you are coming to see me at work tonight, right?" I asked.

Caleb simply nodded, wanting to kiss me again. I put my hand up to playfully stop him.

"When you stop by tonight or walk me home tomorrow, I'll have a suggestion for you. Okay?"

"Sounds good," Caleb told me. He then quickly pulled me towards him and kissed me again, running his hands through the back of my hair and holding me there. When we broke this kiss, I could feel my legs were a little weak. This time, I wanted to go back for another one, and he playfully stopped me.

"You better go and get some rest," Caleb said softly to me as he slowly backed up. "If we spend any more time out here kissing your neighbors are going to call the police."

"Spoilsport," I said to him with a pout.

"I'll see you tonight," Caleb told me. He began to run backward down the street a bit, watching me as he ran before he turned around and broke into a jog for his run. I kept watching him, seeing his muscular legs move with machine-like precision as he went. I could feel myself audibly sigh and then break my gaze so I could head inside.

As I got closer to the door, I did feel a pang of anxiety come over me that someone might have been watching. I glanced at my watch and saw it was still very early and no one was likely to be awake in the house this early on a Sunday morning.

I quietly opened the door, trying my hardest to keep it from squeaking and groaning, and shut it without making much noise. I went straight up the stairs and to my room, quickly closing the door to my room to avoid any interaction with anyone who might be up.

I sat on the bed, kicking off my sneakers and taking my pants off, and then my white work blouse. I reached over and pulled on Caleb's t-shirt, which I had left on my bed from last night. I lifted the collar of the shirt and gave it a smell, picking up still a hint of his scent on the shirt. I loved having the shirt on, having him this close to me, even if it was just an old t-shirt.

I laid back on the bed, feeling the exhaustion from a night of hard work coming over me. As tired as I was, I had nothing but flashes of Caleb on my mind every time I tried to close my eyes. There he was, in front of me, wearing his t-shirt and shorts, kissing me and holding me. Suddenly, in a flash, we were back in his apartment.

This time I wasn't backing off or heading home. This time I wanted Caleb to keep kissing me and touching me, touching me like I hadn't been touched by a man in a very long time. We were no longer in the living room but now we were in his bedroom, and I was watching him strip out of his running clothes before he laid on the bed with me.

His hands and touch seemed to be everywhere, touching me tenderly, holding my cheeks as his kissed me. It wasn't long before I felt his hands working their way down my body, steadily gliding over my breasts, teasing my nipples, moving down to my hips, and then finding their way to the warmth between my legs. My breathing quickened with each touch as his fingers worked over me expertly like no one had ever done before.

It was all in a haze as he lifted himself over me and slowly pushed inside me. Chills were shooting through my body which each thrust and motion as I moved with him, wanting him closer and closer to me. I couldn't control myself any longer and felt my body tense up, push tightly against him, and I just wanted him to hold me at this point, to make this feeling last.

I pried my eyes open, barely opening them, feeling completely satisfied and relaxed. I could see the t-shirt bunched up to just under my breasts and felt that warm feeling coursing through my body that I hadn't felt in a long time.

I let out another big sigh as my heartbeat started to slow down to its natural rhythm again and rolled over onto my side on the pillow. My body was still feeling much too warm to pull even a top sheet on.

See what he is bringing out in you? I heard a voice in my head whisper.

I sure do, I answered back and felt myself smile.

Chapter 17

Sarah

1 ⁷

I slept soundly after a long night at work, sleeping right through until 3 PM. It felt good to get that much rest, and I might have slept longer if I hadn't heard the rumble of thunder outside my window that woke me up. I rolled over and made sure to hop out of bed to close the window before any of the just pattering raindrops could make their way in.

I stretched and yawned, and then sat myself down at my desk to take a quick look at my computer. There were a couple of emails from the instructors of my classes, compliments on the work I had done and the projects I had turned in. It always made me feel good to get remarks like that, and I knew I was getting closer to finally finishing up my degree and getting all the credits I needed. The time wouldn't be long off where I would have my diploma and could go out and get a good job with a tech company or security company. Then I could live out on my own, have my own space, and not worry about what other people thought.

I knew I had to get dressed and work my way downstairs since everyone typically ate dinner early on Sunday. Sunday was really the only day Denise cooked dinner anymore, and even then she very often didn't want to do it, and I picked up the chore, or James cooked something out on the grill. I wasn't quite sure what to expect today, but I knew if they wanted me to cook someone would have been up here to wake me up already to get things going.

I picked a simple blue tank top and a pair of shorts to put on so I could be comfortable. I made sure to fold up Caleb's t-shirt and tucked it under my pillow, knowing I would wear it to sleep in again when I got home from work early tomorrow morning. I slipped on a pair of flip-flops and headed downstairs, trying to remain as upbeat as possible.

I went down the hall and into the kitchen, where Lizzie and Denise both were working away. Lizzie was putting together some vegetables for a salad, tossing everything together in a large wooden bowl, while Denise was following a recipe on her tablet, looking back and forth to make sure she was getting the potato dish she was making just right.

"Hello," I said, working hard to sound cheery and nice. Denise gave me a quick look up and down and stretched her lips into a smile that seemed less-than-genuine. Lizzie, chirped a hello as well as she finished folding the greens together.

"Anything I can do to help," I offered.

"Everything is done already," Denise snapped, making sure to give the potatoes she had in the saute pan a quick stir. "James has some steaks on the grill."

"Would you like me to set the table?" I said, walking towards the cabinets where the plates were.

"Lizzie can take care of it," Denise answered curtly, shooting a glare over to Lizzie that indicated to her that she better go and get the plates and cutlery out.

Since I clearly wasn't needed in the kitchen, I worked my way out the back door and on the patio where James was manning the grill. He was standing with an umbrella, fighting off the sporadic raindrops, and had just flipped the lid of the grill open. Smoke billowed up, with some flames shooting up between the grates as fat from the steaks dripped through. He seemed a little taken aback by the flames, and I walked over and grabbed the tongs from the side of the grill and deftly moved the steak to a cooler side of the grill, turning the heat on the gas grill down.

"You don't want them covered in burn marks," I said to James. "Just nice grill marks."

"Sorry, chef," he said to me with a smirk as he took a sip of his beer. I just raised an eyebrow and looked back at him.

"Want a beer?" he asked me, flipping open a small cooler he had on the patio with him.

"Sure, why not," I said to him, grabbing a cold bottle out of the cooler and popping the bottle open using the opener James had drilled to the side of the grill. I took a swig of the beer, probably a little more than I had intended, and ended up coughing half of it back up. It had been a while since I had a beer and it tasted good, at least what I had managed to get down on the first try.

"Smooth move, sis," James said with a laugh.

"Smoother than you burning the steaks," I choked out. I took a slower sip this time and had a little more control as the beer went down nicely.

"You're right," James said to me, coming closer to me. "If you hadn't saved them and they burned, Denise would never have let me hear the end of it. We would end up ordering in instead."

"Is... is everything alright with you two?" I asked quietly. "Denise seems kind of curt and snappy lately... at least with me. Even more so than usual."

James sighed as he took another sip of his beer, this one a little longer than the last one.

"I know, and I'm sorry about that," James said to me. "I'm not really sure what's going on. We've been fighting more, she's been nasty to you, and even short with Lizzie. I think it's just all the long hours she's been working. I told her she didn't have to work so hard, or even at all if she didn't want to, and she really ripped into me when I said that, saying it was the only thing she really liked right now. I don't know what's going on lately."

"I'm trying to stay out of her way, James, I really am," I told him.

"I know, but you shouldn't have to walk around on eggshells every time you come through the door. It's not fair to you. Hopefully, it will all blow over soon."

Lizzie leaned her head out the back door and yelled at us.

"Dad, Mom wants to know if the steaks are done yet. Everything else is done."

James looked at me and shrugged. I pressed my index finger to the steaks to see how much give they had, another trick I had picked up from Justin to test the doneness of the steaks.

"Feels like medium to me," I told him. "I would say they are done."

"Good enough for me," James said as he picked up the tongs. "Tell Mom they're done," James said to Lizzie as he lifted the steaks onto the tray he had. After he had the steaks on the tray, James turned to close the lid to the grill and shut it off and juggled the tray. I reached over and snatched the tray from him, giving him a sigh as I did.

"You need to learn how to carry these things the right way," I scolded. "Put heavy items towards the middle of the tray. One hand underneath, palm under the center of the tray. It's not rocket science, James."

"You've had a lot more practice than I have," he said as he held the door open for me. "I use tool boxes and tool belts to carry stuff."

I placed the tray down on the center of the table and took my seat. Denise and Lizzie were already sitting in their places, passing the salad around. Lizzie politely passed the bowl over to me with a smile.

"How was work last night?" James asked me as he spooned potatoes onto his plate.

"Super busy pretty much non-stop until I left. Saturday nights get crazy as it creeps closer to the end of the school year. All the college and high school kids get antsy," I said as I looked over at Lizzie.

"Of course we're antsy," she said as she put a steak down on her plate. "Summer vacation is coming. We have all that lounging around to look forward to."

"I thought you were going to get a job this summer," Denise asked her. "I would prefer you weren't just laying around the house all summer long."

"I guess I could pick something up in town," Lizzie answered, looking disappointed at the idea of working. "Do you think there would be anything I could do at the diner?" she asked me.

Before I could even answer, Denise abruptly answered.

"Certainly not!" she exclaimed. "My daughter is not going to work at that place and be subjected to rude men and teenagers leering at her all day. It's not acceptable. No one should do that."

"I don't think Doug could hire you anyway, Lizzie," I answered, keeping my cool. "Waitresses have to be at least eighteen because we serve alcohol."

"Another reason not to work there," Denise mumbled as she took a bite of her steak.

"You could come to work in the office with me," James said to her.

"Yippee," Lizzie said in mock excitement. "Eight hours in a plumbing office."

"The pay is good, and the work isn't too hard," James replied. "Just answering phones and handling paperwork. I could use the help."

"Can I think about it, Dad?" Lizzie said, hoping to change the subject quickly.

James just nodded as he ate, shrugging his shoulders.

When dinner was over, I helped to clear the table and do the dishes, finishing up everything and cleaning the counters. As I finished wiping down the counter, I heard Denise's tablet buzzing and saw she had a video call coming in. Denise hurried over and grabbed the tablet and answered it.

"Hey, Denise," I heard the familiar country drawl let out. My body tensed immediately as I recognized my mother's voice. I worked to try to finish cleaning up quickly and quietly so I could go up to my room before I got pulled into anything. James and Lizzie just looked on from the table.

"Hi Mom," Denise said, suddenly sounding friendly and cheerful for the first time since I had been downstairs. "What's new?"

"Oh, nothing much around here, you know," she said loudly. "Retired life is pretty quiet most of the time. Bill is out on the back patio reading the paper, and I just finished clearing dinner, so I thought I would call and see how y'all were."

"We're doing pretty well," Denise answered. "Say hi everyone!" Denise yelled as she turned the tablet around and flashed it over to James and Lizzie. They both waved and shouted hello.

"Hi, Grandma!" Lizzie yelled.

"Hi, Mom," James said to her, giving a casual wave.

Denise then turned the tablet so the camera stayed on me as I wiped the counter. I looked into the screen and saw my mother looking back at me. I hadn't physically seen her in years. James had shown me a few pictures of her and Dad over the years, but she looked grayer now. She still had that same stern look I remember.

"Hello, Sarah," she said in a monotone voice.

I was quiet for a few seconds, not saying anything, and glared at Denise. I took a deep breath and tried to fight my way through the upset feeling welling up in my stomach.

"Hi, Mom," I said quietly, trying to get back to cleaning the already-cleaned counter.

"How are you?" she asked, not knowing what else to say.

"I'm fine," I replied, keeping the conversation short with the hope it would end quickly.

"James said you're working hard and going to school. Are you still working at that diner?"

"Yes, yes, I am," I told her. I could feel my voice starting to tremble a little because I knew where this conversation was going.

"Hmmm," she said, with a hint of disdain behind it. "I'm surprised you stayed with it so long. I would think there's something better suited for you."

"I like my job," I shot back. "There's nothing wrong with it. I work hard and do it well." I was ready to storm out of the room.

"Yes, and you meet all kinds of interesting men there, too," Denise said loudly and with a snicker.

"What the hell is that supposed to mean?" I said angrily. The control of my temper was gone now.

"Sarah Jane, there's no need to cuss," my mother scolded on video. I could see her face turning, reminding me of what it was like in my childhood when I swore. "And what men are you consorting with now?"

Denise turned the tablet back towards herself.

"Some man who keeps coming into the diner late at night to see her. She let this stranger follow her home. Goodness knows what they are up to. I told her I didn't like it, Mom."

"Denise!" James shouted from the table. I was standing there frozen, stunned at what she was saying. James stood up and came over towards where we both were standing. He could see my face was getting red with anger while Denise just smirked at me.

"I don't need to stand here and listen to this," I said just as James stepped between Denise and me.

"Learn to control yourself, Sarah," Denise told me tauntingly.

I pushed my way past James and raced up the stairs. I felt like I was going to hyperventilate by the time I reached my room. My head was spinning, and I reached over and grabbed one of the pillows off my bed and screamed loudly into it.

I went into the closet and pulled out some work clothes and stuffed them into my backpack. I kicked off the flip-flops and put on my sneakers, taking three times to try to tie them because I was so angry I couldn't see straight. I grabbed my phone, my backpack, and my purse and went

out of my room and headed for the stairs. James met me at the bottom of
the staircase, grabbing my arm before I could burst out the front door.

"Sarah, wait," he pleaded.

"James, I need to get out of here before I say or do something I'll
regret," I said. I could feel my face burning as I spoke to him.

James didn't want to let me go.

"Where are you going to go?" he asked me. "You don't have to be at
work for hours."

"Don't worry about it," I said in a huff. "I don't think anyone around
here cares."

"Hey, that's not fair," James said to me, holding my arm as I tried to
wrest it away from his grip.

"James, let go of me," I hissed. He released my arm, and I stormed out
the front door, slamming the door behind me. I marched over to where
my seldom-used car was parked in the driveway, thinking I could just hop
in and go somewhere, anywhere, maybe someplace far away and forget
all this nonsense. Of course, when I got in the car, all I could see parked
behind me was Denise's luxury car, blocking my path out.

"Fuck!" I yelled at the top of my lungs.

As tempting as it was to just throw the car into reverse and drive
through her car, I knew she would just call the police on me and have
me arrested at this point. I got out of the car, slamming the door so hard
I could see paint chips fly off.

I started marching up the block quickly, just wanting to get away from
the house as fast as I could. I knew I could go to the diner and hang out
there until it was time for my shift, but no one I was close with would be
there yet, and I would have no one to confide in or console me.

Instead of going all the way up to Oak Street, I turned myself around
and started walking back towards the house. When I reached the top of
the driveway, I made a right and kept walking in that direction, hoping it
would clear my head. The rain was falling lightly all around me. Once I
had walked a few blocks, I knew exactly what direction I wanted to head
in.

Chapter 18

Caleb

There's nothing better than getting some sound sleep, except for experiencing that good sleep a few days in a row. It had been so long since I felt like I was rested that I almost didn't know what it was like anymore. Sleep was fleeting for the twenty years I was in the Army, and there were times where I went days without getting any. Even after I was done, up until now, I had slept erratically at best. I had been feeling so good lately that I almost didn't want to wake up whenever I had to.

I thought today might be a good day to get a catnap in since I wanted to be rested to go see Sarah tonight, but I also wanted to be able to get some regular sleep so we could go out and do something over the next two days she had off. I also had to keep reminding myself that I had to go back to see Dr. Weber on Monday night. Really though, I didn't have to remind myself much since Linda did a good job of making sure I wouldn't forget the appointment.

After sleeping, walking Sarah home this morning and lingering over the good feelings it gave me to spend time with her and get to kiss her, I went into the house and had some lunch with Adam and Linda. I felt better about the three of us getting to spend more time together over the last few days, and it seemed to me that maybe I was finally getting more at ease with being back home.

I hadn't mentioned the house I had stopped to look at to Adam or to Linda, but I had gotten in touch with the real estate agent who showed the house and sent her my information. She had promised to get back to this week about putting in an offer once all my loan application work was done. With my background, she didn't think I would have any trouble getting the loan for the house, and I knew I had money set aside where I could take care of a good chunk of the payment upfront. Ella and I had been squirreling away money for years with the goal of one day buying our own place once I was out of the Army. It made me a little sad to think she wouldn't get to enjoy it with me, but I knew it was still the best thing to do for me, for Adam, and for Linda. It would give Linda a chance to live her life without having to worry about us all the time.

When I was done with lunch, I went back to the apartment to relax a bit more so I would be energized and ready to go to the diner late tonight to see Sarah. I sat on the couch mindlessly flipping channels for a while before settling on a John Wayne movie I saw on one of the channels. I found myself dozing and drifting off just as The Duke was getting ready to get involved in a gunfight.

It was one particularly loud explosion that I thought jolted me out of a haze. I sat straight up, working to catch my breath from the surprise. At first, I thought it was just the gunfight on TV, but it was then that I realized the noise was still there and it was a mixture of thunder outside and someone knocking rapidly on my door.

I stumbled up from the couch, making my way to the apartment door, thinking it was probably Linda or Adam with something they needed help with. I was more than a little surprised when I saw Sarah standing there in front of me.

Sarah had a frantic look on her face. She had clearly been crying and even seemed a little bit out of breath. She was also wet from the rain that was coming down. I rubbed my eyes to help clear my head and make sure what I was seeing was real and not just another dream.

"Sarah," I said to her. "What are you doing here? What's wrong?"

She burst out crying, pushing herself into my chest, and I wrapped my arms around her to hold her. I guided her into the apartment and took her hand and led her over to the couch to sit down. She was overcome with tears and had a hard time getting the words out she wanted to say.

"I had a fight... well, not really a fight... I don't know what it was... it all happened so fast... and it was so upsetting, and I didn't know where to go... and all I could think of was that I needed to see you."

She started sobbing again, and she put her head on my shoulder as she wept. I held her there, letting her get her feelings out before she started to get some control over herself. Sarah sat back on the couch, taking a few deep breaths, while I handed her some tissues from a box I had on the end table next to the couch.

"What happened?" I asked her quietly.

"it was crazy," Sarah said, sniffling as she dabbed her eyes with a tissue. "We had just finished dinner, and everything was fine. I was helping clean up when Denise's... Denise is my sister-in-law, James' wife – when her tablet started ringing like she was getting a call. She picked it up, and my mother was there on the screen. That's when things got ugly."

"I don't understand," I said to her. "Why is your mother calling a bad thing?"

Sarah looked at me and took another deep breath. I could tell already that whatever she was about to say was not going to be easy for her.

"There's a long story and a lot of history between my parents and me," Sarah started. "About five years ago I was going to Swanson College and working on my degree. I was going into my junior year, and everything was going great. I had friends and a steady boyfriend for the first time in my life. I thought it was going to be a great year. One morning I wake up in my dorm room, turn on my computer and open my email and there are all these messages with pictures... pictures of me getting dressed and undressed, in the shower, getting into bed... there were dozens of them flooding my email. I don't who sent them or where they came from. Then I started getting emails from friends and family, asking me about the pictures they got in their emails of me. Then I saw on my social media accounts that pictures of me were posted there too. They seemed to be everywhere I looked. I... I didn't know what to do or where to go for help. My roommate didn't know anything about them or how they got taken. I got in touch with campus security, and they investigated for a while and contacted the local police. They finally found tiny cameras... cameras hidden around my room, and in the shower. The police tried to find out about it. They interviewed me for hours, talked to my roommate, my friends, my boyfriend, anyone they thought might know something, but they never got anywhere."

"The pictures just kept circulating around and around. Even after I shut down my social media accounts, my email, changed cell phone numbers, everything – they would still pop up thanks to someone somewhere. Eventually, my boyfriend couldn't take it anymore and broke up with me. My friends started avoiding me, people started saying all kinds of things about me behind my back. I felt like I had no one to turn to that I could trust, Caleb. So, I called my parents and told them I was dropping out, and I wanted to come home."

Sarah took another deep breath before she continued.

"My parents are very conservative, very religious people. They never liked the idea of me going away to college, even though it wasn't that far from where they lived, and my brother was right here in town if I needed anything. They thought I would get into trouble. When all this happened, and they got the pictures in their email... well, it was more than they could take. They said they were embarrassed and ashamed, that people they knew had the pictures, people at church, and they thought my being home would be too much of a scandal for them."

I was stunned that parents would say that to a child.

"Are you serious?" I said to her, shocked at their reaction. "How could they do that to their own daughter?"

"I wondered the same thing, then and now," Sarah said to me. "I couldn't believe they didn't want me home and were just willing to strand me like that. So, I called James, and he came and got me right away. I started living with them, helping them out around the house and taking care of my niece while James and Denise worked. I was so grateful they took me in, and everything was fine for the first year or two. But as Lizzie started getting older and was spending more time with me, getting help with homework, with clothes, talking about boys – I think Denise came to resent me. Things have been getting more and more tense for a while."

"Then..." Sarah looked at me, "Then she saw you outside with me one morning a few days ago when you had walked me home. I didn't really know you... I didn't even know your name yet... and she freaked out about me letting someone follow me home."

"Sarah," I said to her, taking her hand, "I am so sorry. I never meant to cause any problems for you. I was just... just looking for a friend, is all."

"Oh, Caleb, you have nothing to be sorry about," she said to me, holding my fingers in hers. "Believe me, I was looking for a friend, too, and I am... I'm so grateful you came along to be my friend... and more," she said softly.

Sarah grabbed another tissue and gently dabbed her eyes dry again before continuing.

"Denise, though, I think she saw it as an opportunity, a chance to maybe force my hand to get me out of the house. This call from my mother to Denise... Denise never talked to my mother directly. It was only after my mother called James or he called her. I am sure she arranged for it to happen when she knew I would be there. I haven't talked to my parents in years since that all exploded. Denise took the opportunity to put me on the spot and then tell my mother about you in a way that made me look... well it made me look the whole thing from the past was my fault, and it made me feel like it was my fault all over again. I grabbed a few things, stormed out of the house, and then I didn't know where to go. Then I thought of you."

Sarah looked drained after explaining it all to me. I pulled her to me again to hold her close to me. I could feel her body shivering, partly from being damp from the rain and partly from how upset she was. I wanted to take the pain away from her so that she could feel better, feel happy again, but I knew all too well what it was like to carry around pain like that inside. It hurt to have it in there, but it was even more painful when you tried to share it with someone else. It made you have to relive it all over again, something I never wished on anyone.

"Is it okay if I stay here until I have to leave for work later? I don't have to be there for another four hours," Sarah asked me tearfully.

"Of course," I said to her, holding her. "As long as you don't mind the mess around here." I looked around the apartment and saw that there were some clothes strewn about and lots of folders and papers piled up on the counter by the kitchen.

Sarah laughed, seeming a bit more like the Sarah I knew when she did.

"This is hardly a mess, Caleb," she said to me. "You should see my niece's room. You can't even see the floor most of the time. Teenagers can be the worst."

"I don't know," I said to her. "Adam keeps his room neater than most hotel rooms I stayed in. I think his mother must have drilled it..." I cut myself off, not wanting to get melancholy about Ella, not when Sarah was feeling down already.

We both sat quietly for a moment before I got up and straightened up some of the papers and gathered up some of the dirty clothes.

Sarah stood up and came over to me, grabbing the stack of folders in my hands and placing them back down on the counter.

"Caleb, you don't have to do that," she said. "Come back and sit down with me, please."

We walked back over to the couch, and I sat next to her. I put my arm around her as she curled on the couch, pulling her legs up onto the cushions. Sarah placed her head against my chest. I am sure she could feel that my heart was beating a mile a minute. She tilted her head up at me and smiled.

"Your heart is racing," she said as she kept listening, snuggling closer to me and wrapping one of her arms around my waist. "Do I make you nervous?"

"More than a little," I said to her honestly.

Sarah sat back up next to me and brought her lips to mine. What started out as a soft kiss quickly turned to a more passionate one, and I could feel her mouth open slightly against mine. We held our kiss together, and I could feel my hands instinctually start to roam up and down her back. Somewhere in the back of mind, I knew it had been a long time since I had kissed or felt anyone like this, and I may have felt a little more tentative, and perhaps even a little scared about where things may go.

Even with this feeling deep in me though, I found myself wanting Sarah more and more. As we kept kissing, I could feel her hands roaming on me as well, over my shoulders, across my neck, and eventually down across my chest. It was as if neither of our hands knew exactly where else to go at this point as we waited for one of us to make the next move.

My brain and body finally started to coordinate things as we stopped our last kiss. I could see a familiar look in Sarah's eyes, one of hope and passion, one that I had only ever seen in one other woman in my life, until now. I took Sarah's hand and helped her up from the couch and led her down the hall to my bedroom.

My bedroom was hardly what I would call ready to entertain any guests, but at this point, I didn't think either of us really cared that much. Sarah and I walked over to the bed and sat down next to each other and resumed our kissing. Within moments our actions were getting more heated and eager. I found my hands moving from her back slowly around her waist and then moving up, gently cupping her breasts in my hands as we kissed. Our kissing stifled a light moan and sigh from Sarah as I touched her. Before long, my hands were at the hem of her shirt, lifting it up and over her head. Sarah quickly did the same to me so she could guide her hands over my bare chest.

I could feel myself leaning my body to Sarah's, getting closer to her as my arousal heightened. I moved closer to her, guiding her body back onto the bed, so we were lying next to each other. Our hands continued to explore, with my hands gliding over the front of her bra to the back clasp so that they could undo the hooks. Once undone, I began kissing Sarah's left shoulder, slowly pulling the strap of the bra down over her shoulder until I could easily free it from her arm. I did the same with her right shoulder, starting by kissing her lightly on the nape of her neck and working down. I could feel her breathing becoming more rapid, her skin getting hotter before I was finished kissing and taking her bra off completely.

At first, she seemed a little shy, moving her arms to lightly cover her bare breasts, but once I returned to kissing her neck, she relaxed again, letting her arms fall to her sides. I glanced up at her face and could see that her eyes were barely open and she was getting lost in the feelings she too was experiencing right now.

I continued with light touches from my lips across her shoulder and downward, planting kisses just over the top of her right breast as my right hand reached up and cupped her left breast. I felt her warmth fill my hand and gave a gentle squeeze, causing her to softly moan again. All the while Sarah's hands were freely roaming over the muscles in my chest and stomach, tracing the outlines of my pecs and abs with her fingertips and fingernails and sending chills throughout my body.

The tip of my thumb barely grazed across the tip of her nipple, eliciting electric excitement from her body as I heard her gasp. Sarah grasped her hand behind my head and kissed me deeply as my thumb circled her breast and nipple. I could feel that Sarah was starting to squirm a bit on the bed, looking to get her torso even closer to me.

I moved from our kiss and looked down into her eyes. Her eyes opened wider from the slits they had been so she could focus more on me. She could tell I was hesitating before I did anything else.

"Caleb," she said to me breathlessly, "You should know that... well, I haven't been with anyone in a long time... there's only ever been once, a long time ago, and I..."

I interrupted Sarah before she could say anything else.

"Sarah, it's fine," I reassured her, reaching down to gently move a stray wisp of hair in front of her face.

"The only woman I have ever been with was Ella," I said to her honestly. "I've never wanted to be with anyone else... until now."

I bent down and kissed her again, pressing my lips close to hers,
gripping her hands in mine. I broke the kiss and stood up as Sarah moved
further up on the bed to get more comfortable, laying her on one of the
pillows. I moved back on the bed and over her, kneeling between her
legs. I started kissing her stomach, putting my hands on her hips as I
did, kissing her lightly in different areas. My hands then moved down
and gripped the waistband of the cotton shorts she had on and slid them
down her legs and over her feet.

After tossing her shorts aside, I went back to her body, running my
fingers up the insides of her legs, from her calves up to the tops of
her thighs, watching as goosebumps formed on her legs. I then traced
my index finger over the waistband of her thin cotton panties, causing
her hips to arch lightly upward. I hooked both index fingers into the
waistband of the panties and inched them down as well, tossing them
on the floor next to the shorts.

I looked at Sarah's naked body on the bed laying beneath me and felt a
surge of yearning building up inside me. I tugged my own shorts down,
so I was naked as well, letting my arousal be seen by her for the first time.
I knelt between her legs once again, getting closer to her, leaning forward
so I could kiss her on the lips once again.

Our hands went into exploratory mode again, frantically searching
over each other's body to see how the other would react to touch here,
a kiss there. My left hand moved across Sarah's body, down to her waist,
and drifted down further between her legs. I could feel her warmth and
readiness before I even slipped my finger inside her. I let my index finger
linger just outside her, brushing against her, teasing her a bit as I moved
up and down. I dipped briefly into her with my finger, pressing the palm
of my hand on her mound while I did, and Sarah let out another groan.

"Oh, Caleb... please..."

I wanted her badly, and the nervousness I had felt inside at first was
long gone now and replaced by intense desire. I shifted my body quickly,
so I was hovering over her again before I slowly slipped inside her. I closed
my eyes at the feeling as I inched in, experiencing a force washing over me
that I had not felt in so long. I moved against Sarah tentatively at first,

not wanting to go too fast, working to make this encounter last for both of us.

Sarah pulled me close to her again, mashing her chest to mine, entwining her legs with mine as I slowly moved with her body. The slow movements did not last long as we both could feel excitement and power building and building. My breathing quickened with each thrust and motion, and I could feel Sarah's fingers digging into my shoulders. I looked down at her, and her eyes were closed, her breathing through her mouth occasionally interrupted by her teeth biting down on her lower lip to try to control herself more.

There was no controlling it anymore, for either of us. Sarah's body started to tighten and tense as our pace picked up, and she gripped my body tightly, her legs and arms trying to hold me in place as I thrust one more time, hearing myself groan loudly as I did. My body shuddered as Sarah held me tightly and she cried out in pleasure.

I collapsed my body against Sarah, both of us covered in a light sheen of sweat, and my lips found hers once again. I moved off to the right so I could lay next to her, and immediately took her in my arms, holding her close to me. We both lay there, panting and trying to calm our bodies down.

I kissed Sarah on her damp forehead, brushing her hair aside again before I smiled at her.

Sarah placed her right hand on my chest, pressing her palm against me.

"Boy, I thought your heart was racing before," she said with a laugh.

"I guess you have that effect on me," I told her as I placed my hand on her chest. "Yours is thumping pretty good right now too."

Sarah snuggled her buddy closer to me, giving me a light kiss on my chin and then my neck.

"I just want to be here," she said to me with a sigh as she hugged me.

"That's okay with me," I told her.

"I'm glad to hear that," she said, propping her head up on her hand. "But I have to go to work in a few hours."

"When was the last time you took a sick day?" I asked her.

"I don't think I've ever taken one," Sarah answered.

"I think if you ever needed a mental health day, today would be it," I told her. "Besides, how busy could they be on a Sunday night? Give yourself a break, Sarah. Sometimes we all need time to step away for a minute."

Sarah looked at me and smiled, and then quickly hopped out of bed and padded out of the room and down the hall. I sat up on the bed, waiting to see what she was doing. I could hear her talking and her voice got closer as she came down the hall.

"Are you sure it's okay, Doug?" she said into the phone as she stood in the doorway to the bedroom, still completely naked.

"Thanks so much," Sarah replied. "I'll see you on Wednesday. Bye, Doug."

Sarah pressed a button on her phone, slowly walked back towards the bed, and placed her phone down on my nightstand before climbing back into bed with me.

"Doug was more than happy to give me a day off," Sarah said as I wrapped my arms around her again as we both lay on our sides. I moved her hair aside so I could kiss her neck.

"Great," I told her in between kisses.

"I guess that means we have a few days together," she purred as I kept kissing her and ran my hand down her side to her bottom.

"We'll have to come up with things to do," I told her.

Sarah turned around, so she was facing me now.

"I'll bet if we think hard enough we can come up with something," she said with a grin, snaking her right hand down my body, letting it linger on the inside of my right thigh.

Chapter 19

Sarah

19

A day that started out as one of the worst of my life quickly morphed into one that I would never forget for good reasons. When I decided to come to Caleb's house after my argument at home, I was seeking to come here for comfort. I just knew he was the one person that could make me feel better and feel safe. With all that in mind, I hadn't expected to end up in bed with him. When Caleb and I started kissing, I knew if he wanted more I was willing. All my tentative feelings I had about men, and about people, just seemed to wash away when I was with him, and more than anything I wanted to be with him in that way.

As we lay together in bed and the day turned into night, I nestled my head against his chest, listening to the rhythm of his heartbeat, and all the worries that I had just a few hours ago seemed to melt away. I listened to each breath that he took as he slept, and I slipped my arm across his chest and abdomen to hold myself closer to him. His muscles were rock hard, and I could feel the definition of his body underneath my fingers. He was clearly a strong person, inside and out.

While my fingers were holding him, I could feel a defined scar on his left side, running around just under his ribcage. I let my index finger trace it lightly, touching it and fingering the slope and differences in it. I felt Caleb move slightly beneath my touch and I pulled my fingers back. I glanced up at him and saw his eyes open as he looked down at me.

"I'm sorry," I said to him gently. "I didn't mean to wake you. I was holding you, and I noticed... well, I noticed the scar."

Caleb sat up on the bed and turned to face me. I pulled myself up into a sitting position, letting the blanket fall from my body.

"It's okay," Caleb said to me. He took my right hand in his left and led it back to the scar. He held my hand as I traced it again, feeling it with my fingers and the palm of my hand.

"What is it from?" I asked him, holding my palm against his side.

"It's from a knife," he said to me, looking down at my hand as I held him. "We were on an early morning mission in Afghanistan. We had just entered a home where suspects were, and I thought we had cleared everyone. Someone jumped out from behind a stack of boxes and slashed me just under my vest. He got me pretty good. I spent a while in the hospital recouping from that one."

"Oh my God," I said to Caleb. "How did you survive after he slashed you? You must have gone to the ground."

Caleb got a serious look on his face.

"I stood up, took my knife out, and stabbed him in the chest."

We sat silently for a moment as I processed what he was saying.

"Situations like that, when you're facing someone that way and your life hangs in the balance, everything just sort of kicks in – instinct, training, adrenaline – it's all there. I did what I had to do to survive and keep him from killing anyone in my unit. That was my job."

Caleb said it all in a very matter-of-fact manner. It was almost like he was detached from himself when he was talking about it, like he was discussing another person or something you saw in a movie.

I wasn't quite sure what to say or how to respond to that. Part of me never really thought about what he might have done as a soldier. Before I could say anything, Caleb continued. It was like he needed to get this out and say it before it got shut away again.

"You don't set out with the goal of killing anyone, Sarah. Have I done it before? Yes, more times than I'd like, for sure. But I did what I had to do, and I'm glad I'll never have to do it again."

I placed my hand on his left cheek, cradling his face in my hand. I leaned in and kissed Caleb on the lips. It was then that I noticed the scar just below his shoulder, above his chest.

"That one is from getting shot. Sniper fire in Africa," Caleb said to me as I pressed my finger on the scar.

It was difficult to process for me, and I could only imagine how tough it was for him to process and go through.

"It must have been terrifying," I said to him. "How did you do it... living every day like that? Never knowing if someone is going to try to kill you?"

Caleb sighed, and I wasn't sure if that was a sign that he was uncomfortable talking about all this or not.

"You can't think of it like that, Sarah. You learn not to think like that because if you do, you get tentative, you make mistakes, and people die that way. The guys in your unit, they trust you more than anybody in the world – more than their parents, girlfriends, wives. It has to be that way. They needed to know I was watching out for them just like they were watching for me. "

I wrapped my arms around Caleb again and held him tightly.

"I don't know how..." I cut myself off before I could finish the sentence.

"Don't know how what?" Caleb asked as we lay back on the bed.

"I don't know how your wife... how she did it," I said somberly. "I don't know that I could have done it. The worrying, the not knowing where you are, what you're doing, if you are okay. I would have been a wreck."

Caleb was silent again. I hoped I hadn't hurt him by bringing up Ella. I knew her presence was strong in his home and his life, and if I wanted to be part of his life, I would have to deal with that.

"Sometimes I don't know how she did it, either," Caleb said to me quietly. "She was incredibly strong, strong enough for the both of us and for Adam. I am sure she had her moments – all Army spouses do. I know it was tough for her with me being in Special Forces, not being able to tell her where I was or talk to her as often as I would have liked to. Somehow, she shouldered it all."

Caleb turned to his side and looked at me, looking deep into my eyes.

"I think you're a lot stronger than you give yourself credit for, Sarah," he told me. "You've been through a lot and dealt with it. You should be proud of yourself for what you have done. You work hard, you're close to getting your degree, and that doesn't just happen."

"I'm not strong," I answered. "It took me a long time to get over all this, to finally get to a place where I felt like I could trust someone again, and the first sign of a problem, I ran away."

I was feeling dejected again, but Caleb wouldn't have any of it. He pulled me close to him, pressing his bare flesh against mine.

"It's not easy to... to deal with life all the time. There have been plenty of times where I have run and hid too, especially since I've been home. I think sometimes we just need the right person to come along in our lives at the right time to make a difference and turn things around. Maybe... maybe we're both at that point right now."

I smiled up at Caleb and realized I was feeling even stronger about him now. We kissed again and held each other for a long while before I heard Caleb's stomach rumble. I laughed as I looked over at him.

"Are you hungry?" I asked him.

"Well, since I'm not getting to the diner tonight for my late-night fix, I guess I could eat something. How about you?"

"I'm on a different eating schedule than most normal people," I told him. "I eat dinner by 5 or 6 at the latest, and then I'm good for the night. But I would love to make something for you."

"Hmmm, well I don't think I have much here in the fridge," he replied, getting up out of bed and putting a pair of black boxer briefs on. "I usually eat my meals with Adam and Linda at the house. Let's see what I've got around here."

Caleb walked out of the bedroom towards the kitchen. I reached over to the floor and grabbed my panties and put them on. I then noticed the t-shirt he had been wearing laying on the floor. I picked it up and slid it on and made my way to the kitchen.

Caleb was leaning over, peering into the fridge in his small kitchen. I sidled up alongside him, bumping my hip against his playfully as we looked in.

"You're right," I told him. "You don't have much going on here."

I noticed some eggs and bacon, and a few vegetables and knew I could make something from them.

"How about an omelet?" I said to him as I bent over and peered into the fridge. I looked back over my shoulder when he didn't answer and could see him peering at me.

"I didn't hear a word you said," he said to me with a smile.

I turned to face him, getting up close to his body.

"I asked you if you would like some eggs," I said softly and then gave him a quick kiss.

"Sure, that sounds good," he replied. "Is there anything I can do to help?"

"You can make some coffee if you have some," I told him as I gathered ingredients out of the refrigerator.

"You got it," Caleb said as he poured water from the tap into the coffee pot.

I went about getting everything I needed, like a cutting board and knife, and a frying pan from under the cabinet. Every time I bent over and could feel the t-shirt riding up on my body I knew Caleb would be staring at me. The last time, I made sure to give a little wiggle to grab his attention. After that, Caleb came up behind me, wrapping his arms around me while he kissed my neck.

"You're not playing fair," he whispered into my ear.

"Go sit down," I told him, "or I'll never get these eggs done."

"Yes Ma'am," he said with a mock salute. He walked out of the kitchen to the other side of the counter and sat on one of the stools so he could watch me cook.

Once I had all my supplies, I set to work, getting the bacon going in one frying pan. While the bacon sizzled, I chopped away at some red onion, tomato, and orange pepper to dice them nicely. I then grabbed a couple of eggs and cracked them into a big coffee mug and beat them gently with a fork. I let the other fry pan start to heat up while I took the bacon out and let it drain on some paper towels.

Following what Justin had taught me at the diner, I poured the eggs into the center of the heated pan and gave them a vigorous stir for a few seconds before lifting the pan and tilting it to spread the egg around the curds that were gently forming. After letting the eggs set and get a nice crust, I gave the pan a little shake to make sure the omelet was freed from the pan. I sprinkled in the veggies, made my folds, and slid the egg onto a plate. I tossed on the bacon and sprinkled some salt and pepper on. As a final touch, I added a little hot sauce I found in the cabinet to give it a kick.

"Here's your omelet," I told him, placing the plate down. I turned to grab the pot of coffee and poured each of us a mug, handing Caleb his mug.

"Wow, thanks," he said to me. He dipped his fork into the egg, grabbed a piece and ate it happily. "You're a good cook," Caleb said with his mouth full. "This is great."

"Thanks," I said with a blush. "Justin taught me a lot of cooking tricks when things would get slow. I like cooking anyway, and knowing some techniques makes it more fun."

"I feel bad," Caleb said to me as he picked up a piece of crispy bacon and munched on it. "You spend your life serving food. You shouldn't have to do it on your time off."

"Oh, it's not a big deal," I said to him.

"It is to me," he said. "Let's go out somewhere nice tomorrow night, anywhere you want to go. You deserve a night out where you don't have to worry about anything."

"We don't have to do that," I told Caleb as I snitched a piece of bacon off his plate.

"Yes, we do," he insisted as he polished off the last of the omelet. "You have a few days off. Let's try to make the most of them."

"That sounds good to me," I said with an upbeat smile. I walked around the counter and stood next to Caleb. He got up from his stool and took me in his arms.

"In the meantime," he said as he lifted me off the ground so that he cradled me in his arms, "I have something else we can do to make the most of our time."

Caleb carried me down the hall and into the bedroom, playfully tossing me onto the bed before climbing onto the bed with me. In no time at all, I was in his arms again as he kissed me over and over. Caleb looked over at me as we lay facing each other. I saw his gaze move up and down my body.

"What?" I said to him.

"I just noticed you're wearing my t-shirt," he said to me.

"I like it," I told him as I hugged myself. "I already stole your other one and have been wearing it to be every night," I admitted.

"Really?" he said with a smirk. "Well I don't think my t-shirt has ever looked better," Caleb remarked as he trailed his fingers down from the shoulders of the shirt across my hips until he reached the hem of the shirt.

"Actually," he told me, "there is one way it will look better." He quickly lifted the shirt over my head and tossed it on the floor, then turning back to me with a grin as we rolled on the bed.

Chapter 20

Caleb

T he entire day was a whirlwind experience for me. Opening the door and finding Sarah standing there, in obvious distress, and knowing that she turned to me to help her, to give her the safe place that she could count on, made me happy. The rest of how the day occurred was not something I had planned. I was easily swept up in the moment and didn't want to resist it in any way. Being with Sarah that way all day and night restored something that had been missing from my life for a long time.

Part of me thought I would feel guilty or should feel guilty about making love to Sarah. More than once I saw the picture of Ella on my nightstand during the night, and I thought for sure it would be pangs of emotion across my mind and heart, perhaps even enough to stop what I was doing. But that moment never came. Everything just felt so right to me throughout the night. Every movement, motion, reaction, and feeling were in the right place at the right time, and I didn't want it to end any time soon.

When I woke in the morning with Sarah in my arms and the sun lightly peering through the blinds on the window, life felt perfect for the first time in a long time. I managed to move out of bed without waking Sarah, and she curled up comfortably on my bed, burrowing further into the pillow, as I rose to go take a shower. By the time I got out of the bathroom with a towel wrapped around my waist, Sarah was propped up in the bed, blanket pulled up to just over the top of her chest, smiling at me.

"Good morning," I said to her as I went to my dresser for some clothes.

"Hmmm, good morning to you," Sarah purred. "That may have been the best night I have had in a very long time."

Sarah rolled onto her side as she watched me get dressed. She gave a wolf whistle when I tossed the towel to the ground to put my briefs on. I then grabbed a pair of jeans and tugged them on, and then sat on the bed next to her, bending down to kiss her. Sarah moved her face, so it was right under my chin and inhaled.

"I love the smell of a freshly showered, clean man," she growled as she snuck in a longer kiss this time.

"I'm glad to hear it," I said as I kissed her back, letting my hand wander down to the small of her back.

Sarah lay back on the bed, so I had more room to get next to her on the bed.

"So, what's the plan for today?" she asked me. "I'm usually just in bed for a little bit at this time on a Monday, so I have a lot of energy with a good night of sleep behind me."

"We can do whatever you want," I told her. "The only thing I have to take care of is an appointment I have at 6 tonight."

"What do you have to do so late in the day?" Sarah asked. At first, I felt a twinge of reluctance to tell her, but I wanted to be honest and upfront with her from the start of this relationship.

"I have a doctor's appointment," I said to her. "It's with a psychiatrist here in town." I did feel a little embarrassed about letting her know and wasn't sure what her reaction would be.

Sarah looked over at me, and the leaned her head against my chest.

"Okay," she said softly to me. "Do you think it helps you?"

"Well, I've only seen him one time so far, but yes I think it was a big help even just from the start. He convinced me to open up a bit, talk to people, and make new friends." I put my arm around her and kissed the top of her head.

"I'm glad that you listened to him," she said, looking up at me.

"After my appointment today, we can go out. Or even before the appointment if you want. It's your choice."

Sarah sat up next to me and lightly kissed my neck as her left hand gently brushed against my chest.

"Let's go out after your appointment," she said to me with a smile. "I'll have to go back to the house so I can grab some clothes and things for tonight."

Sarah hopped off the bed and went over and grabbed the t-shirt of mine she wore for part of last night. She put the t-shirt on and her panties, and then went over to the nightstand and grabbed her phone. She looked down at it and grimaced.

"What's wrong?" I said to her.

"Nothing, really," she said to me. "My brother sent me a bunch of messages and called several times looking for me."

"You should let him know you're okay," I told her. "He's probably pretty worried about you."

Sarah sighed and then began typing on her phone, obviously crafting some reply to her brother. Within seconds of her sending it, her phone was vibrating, indicating a call.

"I should answer this I guess," she said to me as she walked out of the bedroom and into the living room. I closed the bedroom door to give her some privacy and then finished getting dressed. I sat on the bed, pulling my sneakers on, and could hear Sarah's muffled voice get raised a bit at times. I knew if it was my sister that had disappeared during the night I would be worried sick about her and would want to know she was safe, so I was sure her brother felt the same way.

I finished making the bed and Sarah came in the bedroom, her face a little red.

"Everything okay?" I asked her.

"I guess," she said as she slumped down onto the bed. "I told James I was fine and that I was with you. He was a little upset that I never returned his messages or calls, especially after he went to the diner last night and they told him I took the night off. I'm surprised he didn't track down where you were and come pounding on the door."

"Sarah," I said to her, taking her hand, "if you need to go back home then go. I understand completely. You need to work things out with your family."

"Caleb, I don't want to go back home just yet," she said. I could see the sadness in her eyes about the thought of going home and what it might hold for her. "Is it... is it okay if I stay with you... just for a few days... until I can figure out what I'm doing?"

"Sure, of course," I told her.

"Thank you," she said quietly. "Would you go over to the house with me? I know there shouldn't be anyone there right now, but just in case... I don't know if I could handle it by myself right now."

"I'll drive you over," I told her, standing up from the bed. "If you see a car there and are worried about it, we can just drive along and go somewhere else."

Sarah stood up and grabbed the shorts she was wearing last night and put them on, and then grabbed her purse, and we headed out the door. The warmth of the sun hit us both right away as we made our way down the steps to my Jeep. I saw that Linda's car was gone, which was no surprise since it was after nine, and I climbed into my car as Sarah got in the passenger's side.

As we made the short ride over to Sarah's house, I could see her starting to get tense as we got closer to the location. She was biting her bottom lip as she turned to look out the window as we got close to the driveway. When we pulled in and she didn't see any cars there but her own, she let out a big sigh. She reached into her purse and grabbed her keys.

"I'll just be a few minutes," she said as she got out of the car.

"No problem," I answered and watched her walk quickly to the front door. She slipped inside and closed the door behind her. I looked down at my own phone to see if there was anything for me and saw a message from Linda from this morning.

Everything okay? I didn't see you at breakfast before we left. Don't forget your appointment with Dr. Weber tonight. See you later.

"Forever the big sister," I said out loud to myself. I typed a message back to her, letting her know I was fine, that I was spending the day with Sarah, and that I would not miss my meeting tonight. Linda simply sent back a smiling face emoji to me.

It wasn't long before Sarah came darting out of the house, slamming the door behind her. She was carrying two small bags with her as she rushed over to the Jeep and got inside. She smiled over at me as she pulled her seatbelt on.

"I grabbed my laptop, and some clothes and stuff for a couple of days. I hope it's not too much," Sarah said to me. "Are you sure you're okay with this? I am sure I could stay with Fran for a couple of days."

"Sarah, it's fine," I reassured her. "If anything, you're the one that will have to put up with me and my quirks. Maybe we should run out to the store and grab a few things for my apartment. I'm sure I need some supplies to satisfy more than me."

I drove over to the local supermarket, pulling into the small parking lot, and we both got out and walked into the store. I grabbed a shopping cart, and we worked our way around the store, picking up some basics that I never had in my refrigerator or cabinets but normal people probably had all the time in their homes. I also made sure Sarah picked out things that would make her more comfortable in my home. While most people may find the ritual of going to the supermarket mundane, this trip for me was a good one. It had been a long time since I had been out to do something like this with anyone and brought back memories of what it had been like to go shopping with Ella when I would be on leave. Just shopping with Sarah like this was helping to make me feel whole again.

We went through the store and got what we needed, and then headed back to the apartment so that we could put everything away. Sarah took over right away, working diligently to make sure the groceries got put away where I could find them and use them. She even picked up a few things like fresh fruit and vegetables and some meat for meals.

"You know, Sarah," I said to her as I was helping to put things away, "I eat most of my meals with Linda and Adam at the house. I probably don't need all this stuff here." I looked at the fresh broccoli she bought and handed it to her to put in their fridge.

"And I bet you guys get takeout all the time, don't you?" Sarah said with a smile.

"Well, yeah, usually," I admitted. "Linda works hard all day, and Adam has school work to do and practice, and, well... I don't really know how to cook much myself. I ate Army meals for twenty years unless I was home, and then Ella always did all the cooking."

Sarah closed the fridge as she finished storing the goods. She came over to me and put her arms around my waist.

"I can teach you to cook a few things so you can make dinner for everyone," she told me. "I'm not an expert, but I'm pretty good."

"I'd say you were an expert," I told her, giving her a sly grin as I slid my hand from around her back to her hip, gently guiding it under the t-shirt she wore so I could feel her bare flesh tingle under my fingers.

Sarah sighed lightly and closed her eyes as my hand worked across her stomach and inched its way upward towards her breasts.

"Caleb," Sarah gasped as my hands grazed across her nipples, "What are you doing?"

"I was feeling a little hungry myself," I told her, eagerly kissing her neck as my hands continued to explore her body.

I took a step back from Sarah to look at her, and she opened her eyes to peer back at me.

"What?" she asked me, as she stood with her body lightly shaking.

"I think I'd like to have lunch in bed today," I told her as I quickly grabbed her hand and raced with her towards the bedroom as she squealed and giggled.

Chapter 21

Caleb

2^1

Sarah and I spent most of the afternoon together, getting to know each other more and more on different levels. There was certainly the physical aspect of it as we explored and learned the subtle nuances of each other, finding the spots that elicited the blissful reactions we each wanted. We also got to know one another more on a personal level, asking questions about our pasts, our presents, and our futures. Sarah gave me insight into what it was like for her to grow up in a strict, religious family, while I gave her a glimpse of the life Linda and I had as kids, where she spent more time protecting me from my parents than them worrying about what was going on in our lives.

Sarah let me know she wanted much more from life than what working as a waitress had to offer, and she felt confident that the education she was getting from Swanson College, even with its fits and starts, was going to give her the opportunities that she dreamed about. It made me think back to when I first started with the Army, looking for new chances to do different things, to learn, and to forge a life and career that I would be happy with and proud of.

The afternoon wore on, and I finally was able to get an answer out of Sarah about what she might want to do for the evening. She settled on going to Peter's, an upscale restaurant in Swanson that all the locals rave about. I knew Linda had entertained clients and other lawyers there before and gave her a quick call to see if she could finagle a reservation for this evening there for me. She was more than happy to help, feeling glad I was going out and spending time out of my apartment. She also made sure to remind me, once again, about seeing Dr. Weber tonight.

"I know you're feeling better, Caleb," Linda said to me, "but it's still important that you go to see him. I think you need this in your life right now."

"Linda, don't worry. I'm going, I promise you. We'll go to dinner after I am done, so if you could make the reservation for 7:30, that would be great."

"I'll take care of it for you," she said confidently. "Have a good time little brother."

"Thanks, big sister."

After that phone call, I went back to snuggling with Sarah in bed, until it got to be about five o'clock. It was then I knew I had to start getting myself ready since I would have to go right from Dr. Weber to dinner.

I opened my closet and saw I only had two choices for a suit and chose my black suit to wear. I started looking through my small selection of shirts to wear with the suit when Sarah came over to the closet to join me.

"Let me pick something for you," she said to me as she flipped through my shirts. "There's not much in here, Caleb. You need to add some color to your life."

"I never had much of a need to wear suits. It was either my military clothing or t-shirts for me."

"This one will work," Sarah said as she pulled a light blue-colored shirt from the back of the closet. "Now you need a dark blue tie to go with it. Where are your ties?"

I pulled the tie rack over from the edge of the closet, and Sarah looked through to find a tie that would match. Sarah scanned over the selection before she found what she was looking for.

"Perfect," she said as she grabbed the navy-colored tie.

I got dressed in my suit, and I could spy Sarah watching me in the mirror as she looked at me tying my tie. I saw her rise off the bed and come up behind me as I put the finishing touch on the tie and centered the knot perfectly.

"Hmmm," she purred as she peered over my shoulder. "I just love watching you do that. It just seems so... manly." She crept in front of me and kissed me, and then looked me up and down in my suit. "You clean up very nicely," she said to me with a laugh. "I've only ever seen you in jeans or running clothes. This is quite a turn on."

Sarah snaked her hands under my suit jacket and wrapped them around my waist, bringing her body right up against mine. My body was steadily reacting to her touches, especially when I felt her right hand moving beneath my waist.

"Sarah...," I groaned. "As much as I would love to, I have to go to this appointment."

"I know," she pouted. "Okay, you get going. I have to get myself ready anyway. I'll walk over and meet you at the restaurant."

"You don't have to walk," I said to her. "Take my Jeep over, and I'll walk over and meet you. It will be easier."

"Are you sure? I don't mind the walk."

"Take the car," I told her, handing her the keys. "You don't want to walk all that way in whatever shoes you are going to wear, I am sure. The doctor's office isn't that far from Peter's. It will take me ten minutes, tops."

"If you insist," Sarah said, planting a kiss on my cheek. "I'll see you at the restaurant then."

I grabbed my wallet and headed out the door, going down the steps and walking up the driveway. As I was moving up the driveway, I heard a noise behind me. I saw Adam wheeling the garbage can up to the driveway for pickup in the morning.

"What are you all dressed up for?" Adam questioned as he rolled the cans.

"Oh... well, I... I'm having dinner tonight... with Sarah."

Adam got the can to the top of the driveway and stopped there.

"Wow, that's great Dad," he said to me.

"Are you sure you're okay with it?" I was worried if he would be accepting of the idea now.

"Dad, I'm fine with it, really. There's no reason why you shouldn't go out and have a good time. Have fun."

"Thanks, bud," I said, putting my arm on his shoulder.

"Just so you know," I said, feeling a bit sheepish, "Sarah is up in my apartment. She's going to take the Jeep over to the restaurant. Just let Aunt Linda know so she doesn't freak out when the car is gone."

Adam glanced up at the apartment and then back at me. He smiled at me and nodded.

"I'll let her know. See you later."

I watched Adam walk down the driveway towards the house before I went up the street and made the trek over to Dr. Weber's office. I arrived right on time, entering the office building right at six and opening the door to his office.

"Nice to see you, Caleb," Dr. Weber said, standing in his waiting room as if he was waiting for me. "You really didn't have to get dressed up to come over here today," Dr. Weber joked as we entered and sat down on the chairs in his office.

"Oh, this," I said, looking down at my suit. "No, I'm going to dinner after this, and needed to look nice."

"Oh, where are you going?" he asked me.

"Peter's."

"Wow, nice place. I love going there. Get the ribeye, it's fantastic."

"I'll keep that in mind," I told him.

"Going with anyone particular?" Dr. Weber asked as he sat back in his chair.

"Well... yes... a woman I met last week." Suddenly I was feeling uncomfortable about talking about it.

"Great," Dr. Weber replied enthusiastically. "I'm glad to see you met someone. How do you feel about going out like that?"

"I'm excited about it, but I also feel a bit nervous."

"Why do you feel nervous?" I saw Dr. Weber lean forward a bit in his chair.

"I don't know. I haven't been on a date in almost twenty years, at least not with someone who wasn't... wasn't my wife." I heard my voice trail off a bit as I answered him.

"Are you nervous that you won't know how to act, or are you nervous because you feel like you're doing something you shouldn't be doing?"

I shifted in the chair a bit, hearing the fabric of my suit rustle against the chair.

"I think part of me still feels like... like I am betraying Ella in some way. Even though I know I shouldn't feel this way, I do feel a twinge of guilt. I really like Sarah... she's the woman I have been seeing... and we have connected well, better than I ever thought I could with a woman again. I look forward to every moment I get to spend with her, but somewhere in the back of my mind, Ella is still there."

"Caleb," Dr. Weber said to me, "have you ever grieved about Ella?"

I almost felt offended by the question.

"Of course I have," I said indignantly. "Hearing about her death, the funeral, and afterward... I felt terrible. And then dealing with Adam, the details, and just life without her... I think about her every day."

"That's not exactly what I meant," Dr. Weber said to me. "Have you ever given yourself the opportunity to cry about it, let the emotion out beyond just thinking about her?"

I sat back in the chair and looked at Dr. Weber.

"I... I haven't... and I don't know that I could. Right after the funeral, I didn't have much time to process everything. I had to get right back to overseas, and then I was so caught up in what I was doing, I couldn't take time to do something like that. After I got home, it just seemed like it was so long ago, I just didn't."

"Do you think it's because you didn't feel you needed to, or because you didn't want to deal with it?"

I wasn't sure how to answer that.

"I think it's probably a little of both," I said honestly. "Part of me thought I was through grieving about it, but another part of me never wants to face it."

"Properly grieving about it can be a big help to you, Caleb. Whether that's talking about it with your sister, your son, with me, or with this new person in your life. You have a lot of emotion you have been holding in for a long time, not just about what happened to Ella, but what has gone on in your life. You've been through a lot, Caleb. More than what the average person must deal with. Having an outlet for all of that building inside you is necessary."

I stood up from the chair and considered leaving the office. Even though I knew Dr. Weber was right about all of it, facing all of what was inside... from what I went through as a kid, to what I saw in the Army, to Ella – it all seemed too much to deal with.

"I can't," I said to Dr. Weber. "I can't take all that on at once. It's too much."

"I'm not asking you to do that," Dr. Weber told me as he stood up next to me. "I think we can take it a piece at a time, talk about things, figure out how you can best cope with them, and move from there. Does that sound good?"

I sat back down in the chair and looked at him, feeling a lump forming in my throat.

"Okay," I said to him, trying to remain calm. "Where do we start?"

"That's up to you," he said, moving over from the chair behind his desk to the one right in front of me. "Let's start where you feel most comfortable. We can talk about your childhood, your marriage, the Army, whatever you want."

"Let's talk about the Army," I told him, feeling that was a topic I was most in control of.

"Okay," Dr. Weber said. He went back to his desk and grabbed a folder he had. "I got some of your records from the Army like I said I would. You were right. They made sure to redact a lot of what you did, but from what I read I think it gives us a good place to start. Why did you go into Special Forces?"

"It wasn't a goal of mine when I joined the Army," I answered. "I went into the military because I saw it as a good way out of where I was. Linda was already out of the house and in college, and I had started to spend as little time as possible at home anyway. My parents were not the ideal people to be around, and when the Army recruiter came around talking to seniors in high school, it sounded like it had everything I wanted, so I enlisted. It was while I was at basic training that they approached me about it, and I thought, cool, that sounds like it would be for me, and it was. Even though the training was grueling, it was all worth it. I learned things during training that most of the world might never know how to do. I can speak different languages, swim and run long distances, assemble weapons with ease, and even diffuse volatile situations when needed. I also formed some of the strongest friendships I'll ever have working with my battalion for so long."

"So why did you give it up?" Dr. Weber asked me. "I'm sure you could have stayed in if you wanted to. You're still a young man, still, fit and capable. What made you want to leave that behind?"

"There were a lot of reasons, I think. I knew Adam was in his last year of high school and that this might be my last chance to spend any time with him. He'll be going to college, forging a life of his own, and I have hardly played a part in his life up to now at all. Another part of it was that I think my concentration wasn't what it needed to be anymore. After Ella died, I threw myself into work, giving it my all, focusing on what we were doing stronger than ever because... because I didn't want to think about all the other stuff in my life. After doing that for two years, I think my commitment started to wane. Also, we were no longer in Afghanistan. We had gone back to Northern Africa and were still doing important work, but it wasn't the same for me anymore. I knew if I wasn't concentrating the way I should be that I didn't want to chance making a mistake that could cost lives. When the time came and my twenty years rolled around, I put in my papers, and that was it."

"Do you miss it?"

"I miss the camaraderie, the men I worked with, and yes, there are parts of the job I do miss. But there are a lot of things about it that I don't miss, too."

"Like what?"

"Watching people you care about die comes to mind. Killing other people is something I don't miss either."

"I imagine that is a difficult thing to resolve for you," Dr. Weber said as he sat back, removed his glasses, and wiped them on his shirt.

"That's being mild about it, Doc," I told him. "Too many people today are so anesthetized to things like that. You see video games, and movies and TV shows all the time with people getting shot, blown up, stabbed or whatever, and they don't think about what it's really like when you experience a situation like that. You can't take a second to decide whether it's the right thing, to hit the pause button on the game or reset it. You just have to do it, or the people you care about get hurt or die."

"It sounds like you dealt with situations like that a lot."

"Are you asking me if I killed many people?"

"Did you?'

I took a deep breath. I could feel my hands gripping the sides of the chair tightly.

"More than I probably know of directly over the years. There were times when I knew directly, and others where I fired long-range weapons that likely killed people as well. It was my job to do that. What I was doing was saving more lives and keeping my men, my country safe."

"No one is questioning that, Caleb," Dr. Weber reassured. "You were among the chosen elite to do that job and protect everyone – your men, other soldiers and civilians in the area, me, your family, your country, and yourself. That doesn't mean you don't feel anything about having to do that. It's perfectly natural to feel the emotion in that situation, whether it is anger, guilt, or sorrow. And it's okay for you to deal with those feelings."

"It doesn't feel like it should be okay," I said. "I think that is one of the things I have struggled with the most since I have been home. That and…" I cut myself off again.

"And what, Caleb?"

"And the fact that I feel like I have no direction here," I said abruptly. "I don't know who I am at home. In the Army, I knew exactly who I was, what I was doing, what my purpose was. For the last six weeks, I haven't had any sense of who I am or what my purpose is here. I mean, I know I'm here to be a father to Adam, but outside of that, I can't seem to find any meaning for what I am supposed to be doing here. I feel like a big part of my identity has been stripped away, and I don't know how to find out what I should be doing. In a few months, Adam will be away at school, and that scares me because I feel like I'll really have nothing here anymore. The goal was always to retire and spend time with Ella, find what makes me happy, and grow old together. Once that got all fucked up, the rest fell apart, and it seems even harder to figure things out now."

"What you're going through isn't uncommon for veterans, Caleb," Dr. Weber stated. "You spent twenty years with the Army, with them telling you that everything you did had a purpose and was meaningful, and it was. Now, without anyone telling you that or giving you direction, you aren't sure where to go. Feeling that way affects all the avenues of your life – your relationships with your sister and son, with making friends, connecting with anyone, your behavior and more."

"So, what do I do to fix this?" I asked. "I don't want to go through life this way anymore."

"I think you're making strides already, even if you don't see it," Dr. Weber said to me. "Your growing relationship with Sarah is an important first step for you. Working on the importance of your relationships with Linda and Adam are big too. How do we fix this? I wish I could tell you there was an easy answer to it but coming here to talk with me is one way to help yourself. I think through our talks you can understand more about the difficulties you're facing, how to manage them, and manage your relationships."

I sat silently for a moment and then nodded my head in agreement with Dr. Weber.

"Yes," I said with affirmation. "That's what I want."

"I do have another suggestion that I want you to consider," Dr. Weber said to me. "Have you consider looking for a support group for veterans? A group that may address some of the issues you face?"

"All those groups deal with PTSD, and I don't..."

Dr. Weber cut me off.

"I know you don't think it's PTSD, Caleb, and to be honest, I don't think that's the issue with you either. Do I think you've been through trauma and experience stress? Absolutely. But I think you're dealing more with transition stress than PTSD. Dealing with the grief of losing your wife is an added issue for you, but you are struggling more with finding your way after your military life. I think speaking with a group of vets that have that same experience can be helpful to you, help you reintegrate yourself to civilian life better and talk to people facing the same challenges you do. Just consider it, okay?"

What Dr. Weber was saying did make sense, and maybe talking with other vets might help me see with some clarity what's going on with me and how I can deal with it better.

"I'll consider it."

"Fair enough," Dr. Weber said as he rose from his chair. "I think we had a good session today, Caleb. Can you come back on Thursday so we can talk some more? Same time?"

"Yeah, I'll be here," I told him as I got up. "Thanks, Doc. I appreciate your help."

"I'm glad you see it as help, Caleb."

We walked out into the front office, and he opened the door for me.

"Enjoy your date tonight," Dr. Weber told me. "I am anxious to hear how things go for you."

"Me, too," I told him with a smile. "See you Thursday."

I walked out of the office and the building and into the dusk. Streetlights were on as I made my way up the street, taking a deep breath and exhaling as I went. The talk with Dr. Weber was stressful, painful in some ways, but it did make me feel like some of the weight was lifting from me. I felt like I was headed in the right direction for the first time not just since I had been home, but for the first time since before Ella died.

I made my way up the street, looking at my watch to see it was already 7:30 and I was running late. I hadn't realized we had been talking so long in our session, but I had gotten caught up in everything and didn't really want to stop.

I picked up my pace walking up Oak Street, knowing I still had at least five minutes before I would get to Peter's. I was walking past the local florist and saw they were just getting ready to close shop, but I jumped in quickly.

"I'm sorry to catch you before you are closing," I said apologetically to the woman behind the counter. "I was hoping I could just get a single red rose from you. I'm on my way to a date, and I thought... well, I thought she might like it."

"Aww, that's so sweet," the woman said to me with a smile. "Sure, I can fix something up for you."

She went behind the counter to the case where she had the roses, selected a single rose that looked perfect, and surrounded it with some baby's breath. She wrapped it nicely for me and put a cap of water on the end of the stem to help keep it fresh.

"Here you go," she said to me, handing me the flower in its floral paper.

"Thank you so much," I said to her, handing her the money for the flower and then heading towards the door.

"I hope your date goes well!" she shouted to me as I walked outside, the bells of the door jingling behind me as they closed.

I hope so too, I thought to myself as I continued my walk up the street towards where Sarah was waiting for me.

Chapter 22

Sarah

2^2

In a way, I couldn't wait for Caleb to leave for his appointment. I was enrapt in every moment we have had to spend together over the last day, but the time before we would go on our first official "date" gave me a chance to treat myself a bit. I had so few occasions where I got the chance to dress up and wear something nice that this was special for me. I had made sure to grab what I thought my best dress was out of my closet when I had packed quickly when Caleb took me home, and I even grabbed my favorite heels to match the dress.

Being alone in Caleb's apartment felt a little weird to me at first. It was almost like it was a place of my own, something I had never experienced before. Before I took the time to get dressed, I found myself going around and straightening up the apartment, making things look neat. When I went into the bathroom to take my shower, I even made sure to fix things up in there, so they looked their best when I was done.

After my shower, I pulled out the clothes I wanted to wear for the night. I took some time in the mirror first, drying my hair and brushing it, so I had some nice body to it. I even put some makeup on, something rarely did at all, but I figured if I was going all out tonight I might as well give it a shot. It had been such a long time since I had put on anything like blush or mascara that I had to try to remember how to do it correctly, but I was happy with the results and used just a little bit to give me a look I wanted.

I had plucked a black bra and matching panties from my drawer and remembered to snatch the only pair of black stockings I had in my dresser, hoping they didn't have a run in them so I could wear them tonight. After getting the undergarments on, I slid into the black dress, a sleeveless, A-line dress with a little bit of flare that came down to just above my knees. The dress had just the slightest v-neck so that it showed just a bit of cleavage. I had bought the dress a few years ago, thinking I might never wear it since it showed more leg and cleavage than I ever did in my life. I loved the dress though, and it made me feel good to know I had something like in the closet that I could pull out for a special occasion, and this was the perfect opportunity.

I slid into my black heels, making me just a bit taller so I would be even with Caleb. I reached into my handbag and pulled out my perfume, giving myself just a quick spritz so I would have that faint smell of flowers around me. I had a black shawl I grabbed to throw over my shoulders, put it on, and I looked in the mirror. I felt I was at my best, picked up my purse and the keys to Caleb's car, and headed out the door.

I gingerly made my way down the wooden steps, trying to make sure I had my balance in heels that I almost never wore. The last thing I wanted was to slip down the steps and have an accident and be laying there, splayed out in my dress, calling for help. I made it down the steps with a little work and walked over to Caleb's Jeep. I saw there was another car in the driveway at this point, figuring it belonged to Caleb's sister and hoped they wouldn't think it was too weird that I was coming from Caleb's apartment and taking his car.

As I was unlocking the car, I heard a voice come up from behind me.

"Hi, Sarah," cut through the air, and I turned around and saw Caleb's sister standing there, dressed in her business suit and holding her briefcase. I assumed she had just gotten home and out of her car when she saw me there. I could feel myself blushing profusely, trying to figure out in my head what I was going to say.

"Oh, hello…" my mind raced trying to remember her name.

It's Linda! My brain screamed at me.

"Hello, Linda," I said to her, feeling more embarrassed now.

"Wow, you look great," Linda said to me as she looks over my dress.

"Thank you," I said to her, trying not to feel self-conscious.

"Caleb said to take his car, I hope it's okay," I told Linda, though I was not sure why I felt the need to explain it to her.

"Of course!" she said to me. "You should take his car. Goodness knows he hardly ever drives it. He's always walking everywhere. I think all those years in the Army convinced him he needs to march to every location."

We both let out a little laugh. I took a quick look down at my watch and said to Linda nervously, "I should get going. I don't want to be late to the restaurant."

"Oh sure," Linda said to me. "I didn't mean to hold you up."

I climbed into the front seat of the car, moving the seat up close enough so my feet could reach the pedals. I started up the car and was getting ready to pull out when Linda startled me by knocking on the window. I found the control to roll down the window and looked out at her.

"Sarah, I just wanted to let you know... well, to let you know that I think it's wonderful that you and Caleb are seeing each other. I know it means a lot to him and it has made a big difference, even just in a few days."

"Thank you, Linda," I said to her. "It's made a big difference to me, too."

"Okay, get going," Linda said. "I already held you up long enough. Have a nice time." Linda patted the car and stepped back and waved. I gave her a quick wave and backed out of the driveway so I could head out.

It was funny to drive a car that was not only a lot nicer than what I was accustomed to driving but even to drive at all. I realized I was probably a lot like Caleb in this way. I walked everywhere I had to go, and my car had been out of the driveway as infrequently as it seemed Caleb's was.

I made my way over to Peter's, which was up towards the end of Oak Street that led to the college. I didn't get up this way very often anymore as I tried to stay away from the campus if I could. I could see some of the college kids that milled about on this side of town, hitting the local bars and cheaper places to eat. Peter's stood out from all those places, giving the feel of class and expense that none of those other places carried. Peter's was the place that you find a lot of the professional staff and the wealthy older folks in town that shunned the pizza, beer, and burgers joints.

I pulled into the parking area and quickly realized that Peter's had valet parking. I stopped near the podium where a couple of young men in red jackets, black bow ties, and black pants where standing around. As soon as I pulled up, they seemed to snap to attention, and one opened the door for me so I could get out.

"Thank you," I said as the young man gave me his hand so I could step down and out of the Jeep without trouble. He smiled and nodded to me and handed me a valet ticket. I walked towards the front door and had it pulled open by another young man in red so I could walk through with ease.

I had never set foot in Peter's before, but I had certainly heard about plenty. The restaurant had been around in Swanson for many years, and I knew that James and Denise had come here several times for dinner. The place screamed refinement and class from the moment you stepped inside, with beautiful chandeliers decorating the lobby area, a coat room just inside so you could check your coats, and quiet, classical music playing in the background.

I walked up to the host area and was greeted by an older gentleman dressed in a black tuxedo. His hair was slicked back, and he bared a friendly smile as soon as he saw me.

"Good evening, miss," he said to me politely.

"Good evening," I answered. "I'm meeting a gentleman here tonight. We have reservations at 7:30."

"The name?" the maitre'd asked me.

I had to think back quickly to what Caleb's last name was, and finally was able to pull it out of my memory.

"Oh, Wilson... Caleb Wilson," I said quickly.

"Oh, yes, here it is, 7:30," he said as he checked it off. "Mr. Wilson has not arrived yet. I can seat you at the table, or you can sit in the bar, whichever you prefer."

"The table would be fine, thank you," I said politely. The man nodded to me and led me through the dining room, over to a quiet area that featured several tables for two, along with some small booths. We stopped at one of the tables that looked out over the back garden the restaurant had that featured a small pond and waterfall.

"I hope this table is satisfactory," he said to me as he pulled the chair out for me.

"It's perfect," I said to him as I took off my shawl and placed it on the back of the chair, sat and looked out the window.

"Your server, Eric, will be out shortly. When Mr. Wilson arrives, I'll bring him over. Enjoy your meal, miss."

"Thank you," I said to him as he bowed lightly and walked away.

This was easily the fanciest restaurant I had ever been in, a far cry from most of the places I would eat at. There were some other couples at tables nearby, and a couple tucked into the corners where the booths were, giving them a little more privacy. As I gazed out the window, watching the waterfall gently cascade and ripple into the pond below, our server appeared at our table.

Eric wore a black tuxedo like everyone else. He was clearly a young college student, with his short black hair nicely combed and gelled into place. He smiled at me and bent down to light the candle on the table.

"Good evening," he said to me as he stood back up. "I'm Eric, and I'll be your server this evening. I see you're still waiting for another guest. Can I get you something to drink while you wait?"

I almost never had any alcohol to drink, and my immediate thought went to order an iced tea, but I wanted to feel more like a grownup today.

"I'd like a gin and tonic, please," I offered.

"Of course," Eric replied. "Any gin you would prefer?"

I couldn't think of any gins off the top of my head since it had been so long since I had gin.

"To be honest, Eric, it's been a long time since I had one. Is there one you recommend?"

"Well, Bombay Sapphire is quite nice. I would recommend that," he said confidently.

"I trust you, Eric," I said smiling at him.

"Very good," he said and walked off to get my drink.

I sat nervously and could feel myself tapping my feet under the table, anxiously awaiting Caleb so I could feel more comfortable. I knew it might take him a bit to get here since he was walking up Oak Street and hoped he wouldn't be too much longer.

I watched a few other couples get seated and looked around the room at the nicely decorated walls, with pieces of artwork from local artists. I could see that there were many older couples, some sitting casually like coming to a fine restaurant was a daily experience and others that were clearly on a special date and wanted the evening to be memorable. Seeing couples like that made me think about how special this night was for me.

It was then that I saw the maitre'd coming towards me with Caleb walking tall behind him. I smiled broadly when I saw him, and the maitre'd guided him to the seat across from me.

"Enjoy your meal, folks," he said kindly as he bowed once again and moved away.

"Hi there," I said to Caleb, as he got into his seat and got comfortable.

"I'm sorry I'm late," Caleb replied. "The walk was a little further than I thought, and I stopped along the way to get this." He reached over to me and handed me a single red rose wrapped nicely in paper.

"Oh, Caleb, that's so sweet." I held the flower up and sniffed it, taking in the lovely scent. I couldn't remember the last time anyone had given me any flowers, or if anyone ever had for that matter.

"I know, it probably seems a little corny," he said to me. "The last time I was dating it seemed like a nice thing to do."

"It's still a nice thing to do," I said to him, reaching over and taking his hand in mine. "Thank you very much. It's lovely."

I gazed over at him across the table and met his eyes.

"Speaking of lovely," he said to me, giving my hand a squeeze. "You look amazing."

I looked down and could feel a surge of warmth come over me.

"Thank you," I said softly. "I bought this dress years ago and never had a chance to wear it."

"Well, I'm glad you wore it tonight, and that you have a special occasion to wear it."

Eric appeared next to our table with my drink and placed it down in front of me. He then handed menus to Caleb and me and asked Caleb if he wanted a drink.

"Do you have Macallan?" he asked Eric.

"Of course, sir," Eric said, equally surprised at the question and that Caleb might even ask.

"I'll have Macallan and water, please," Caleb said politely. "And I'd like to see the wine list as well."

"Right away, sir," Eric said as he went off to grab the wine list.

Caleb smiled at me as I took a sip of my drink.

"I think you caught him off guard with your drink order," I said with a smile.

"I'm not much of a drinker, to be honest," Caleb told me. "I acquired a taste for Macallan from one of our captains along the way and like to indulge every now and then. I did learn a lot about wine over the years though. Sometimes knowing stuff like that helps you connect better with people."

Eric quickly returned with Caleb's drink and the wine list and then proceeded to let us know about the specials for today. He then moved off to another table while we decided on what we wanted.

Upon my first look at the menu, the thing that jumped out at me the most was the prices on the menu. I was used to seeing our hamburgers and entrees at the diner for no more than fifteen dollars, twenty at the most. Here, the cheapest entrée seemed to be almost twice that.

"Caleb," I said quietly, "this place is very expensive."

"I know," he said back to me. "Ella and I came here once years ago and were floored by the prices. We almost walked out but managed to stick it out and ordered cheaply. We're not doing that tonight. Get whatever you want, Sarah. You're entitled to indulge every now and then you know. Tonight, you get to feel special."

I tried to relax some and took a quick sip of my drink. I still felt bad about ordering something that would cost forty or fifty dollars, but everything on the menu sounded decadent and delicious.

Eric came back and took our order, with me ordering a roast duck dish and Caleb opting for a surf and turf dinner. Caleb insisted we each order first courses as well, so I went for a simple Caesar salad, while he decided on a tuna sashimi appetizer. Caleb also ordered our wine, selecting a bottle of wine I had never heard of or knew about. Just from the name it alone it sounded expensive, and from the reaction of our waiter, he was both surprised and impressed at the same time.

The entire meal from start to finish felt like a whirlwind and left my head spinning. Between the drinks, the wine, and the richness of the meal I had, I was completely full and didn't think I could have one more morsel.

"Would either of you care for dessert?" Eric said to us as he cleared the dishes. Caleb looked over at me and could see that I was feeling full.

"Perhaps something we could share, Eric? Do you have any suggestions?' Caleb asked him.

"We offer a Bananas Foster tonight that I think is excellent," he said proudly.

"That sounds perfect," Caleb told him. "And I would like a cup of coffee. How about you, Sarah?"

I decided if we were going all-out tonight I might as well get the chance to order something that I never get that chance to have in my everyday life.

"Can I get a cappuccino, Eric, please?" I asked him.

"Of course," he said with a smile and went to get our drinks.

"Caleb, I am so full," I told him. "I don't know if I can eat anything else."

"I'm pretty full myself, but this is a once in a blue moon dinner," he said to me, reaching over and taking my hand. "We may as well make the most of it."

Eric came back with coffee and cappuccino, and just the smell of the cappuccino told me it was much better than anything we crafted at the diner that passed as cappuccino. Eric then came back with a tray and made the Bananas Foster right in front of us, creating the sauce with the butter, sugar, and bananas, and then adding the dark rum and lighting it to create a dazzling burst of flame that made me jump a bit in my seat. He let the flames die down and then expertly served the sauce over vanilla ice cream and placed the bowl on the table for us, along with two spoons. Caleb and I both gave Eric a round of applause for his performance, and he smiled and took a quick bow before leaving us to eat our dessert.

"Oh, this is so good," I said to Caleb as I spooned another bite into my mouth.

Caleb just took a bite or two along the way, and I found myself devouring most of the ice cream and bananas. Finally, when the dessert was done, I had to push my chair away from the table to give myself room. I felt like I would explode if I had to eat anything else.

"That meal was amazing," I said to Caleb.

"It sure was," he answered. "I almost want to walk home because it will take me miles of walking to work all that off."

I decided now was a good time to excuse myself to the restroom and stood up and walked from the table. I had walked just a few steps and turned around and could see Caleb watching me as I walked. I smiled

back at him, feeling fantastic that this handsome man was treating me so
well and that his eyes were following me wherever I went.

I ran into Eric and asked him to direct me to where the ladies' room
was, and he pointed me in the direction to go. I worked my way to
the opposite end of the dining room and was passing the last booth
tucked into the corner when a face caught my eye. I slowed down as I
was walking to make sure I wasn't making a mistake, but there was no
denying that there was Denise, dressed in one of the business suits she
often wore to work. At first, I thought maybe it was just a business dinner
for her, but she was there holding hands with a blond gentleman that
was certainly not my brother. I saw the man lean in and start kissing her
neck, and while Denise craned her neck to allow for the kisses, her head
turned in my direction, and our eyes locked briefly.

I quickly turned and headed back to our table, where Caleb was
looking over the bill. I sat down quickly and had a panicked look on my
face. Caleb took notice of my distress right away.

"What's wrong?" he said as he folded money into the check holder to
pay the bill.

"We need to leave, now," I said to him, standing up from the table.

Caleb placed the check down on the table and took my hand, and I
moved ahead of him, leading him out of the restaurant and away from
the side of the room where I had seen Denise. We got outside fast and
stood just outside the front door at the valet desk.

"Are you okay?" Caleb said to me with a worried look on his face.
"What's going on?"

It was then I realized I had left my shawl back at the table.

"Damn," I said. "I left my shawl inside..." I said with panic as I looked
back at the restaurant.

"I'll go get it," Caleb said calmly. "You get the car, and I'll meet you
out here."

"Forget it, Caleb," I said to him, not wanting to delay our leaving any
further. "It's not important." I fumbled to open my purse to find the
valet ticket.

"Sarah, don't be silly," Caleb said to me. "It will just take a minute."
With that, Caleb was back through the restaurant door to go back to the
table.

I finally found the valet ticket and handed it to the valet, hoping they could have the car here as fast as possible. I could feel nervousness building in my stomach the longer it seemed to take. I felt a hand touch my shoulder and felt relaxed that Caleb had gotten back so quickly, but when I turned around, I didn't see Caleb standing there. There was the blonde man I had seen at the table, standing in front of me and grinning. It was then it dawned on me that I knew this face from somewhere. It was Jared Sterling, and he had that same smug grin he always had when I would see him at parties.

"Hello, Sarah," he said to me as he rubbed his chin. "I haven't seen you in a long time."

"Hello, Jared," I said to him and then turned to see if the car had been brought up yet.

"What are you doing here? I thought you only spent time at the diner now." Jared allowed himself a little laugh, expecting me to join in with him. I just turned and shot him a look.

"I'm here with someone," I told him coldly. "I'm expecting the car any second, Jared..."

"Oh, I'm expecting mine, too," he said to me. "They're always slow out here, but it gives us time to chat."

Jared moved from behind me to in front of me. I could see his eyes scanning over my body, looking me up and down, and his vision settled right on my cleavage for several seconds before his eyes came back up to meet mine.

"You're looking better than ever, Sarah. I don't think I've ever seen you look this good."

I crossed my arms over my chest and turned my head to the side, hoping beyond hope that the car, Caleb, something would come along to end this.

Jared leaned in close to me, gripping my right arm inside his left hand just above my elbow.

"I don't know what you think you saw inside before, but I'm pretty sure it was nothing, right?" I felt his grip on my arm tighten slightly.

"I don't know what you're talking about," I told him as I tried to free my arm.

"Good answer," he said to me. "You know, I had always hoped we would hook up when we were in school, but you always shot me down. Even before I saw those nice pictures of you..."

I felt a big lump in my throat and tried to push myself away from Jared, but he wouldn't let go. Just then, I felt two hands behind me pull me away.

"Is there a problem here?" Caleb said, as he stood in front of me and faced Jared. Caleb towered over him, making Jared back up right away.

"No problem at all," Jared said as he stepped back, surveying Caleb and realizing he was someone he probably didn't want to mess with. The valet appeared with the Jeep and Caleb took my hand, leading me to the car while making sure to stare down Jared. Jared wouldn't even look at him, and instead kept his eyes on me until Caleb had helped me into the car and closed the door. Caleb came back around, handed the valet a couple of bills, gave Jared another cold look, and got in the car. As Caleb started to pull away, I saw Denise come out of the restaurant and stand next to Jared. I could see her watching the Jeep as we pulled out of the parking lot.

"Who was that clown?" Caleb asked me. "Are you alright? Did he hurt you?" I felt Caleb step on the brakes before the car got out of the parking lot as if he was ready to go back and confront Jared again.

"Caleb, no, let's just go home, please," I said. I was clearly shaken and frightened, but Caleb relented and drove on. I sat there silently for the ride until we got back to Caleb's driveway. He parked the car and came around and helped me out of the car. He put his arm around me and let me go up the steps to his apartment ahead of him. Once we were inside, I finally felt safe again and sat down on the couch.

"Sarah, what's going on? Something happened back at the restaurant. Please, tell me what went on so I can help."

Caleb was sitting next to me on the couch now, his hand on my bare knee. I turned to him and could felt tears forming in my eyes. Before I knew it, I found myself shaking and fell into his arms. Caleb held me for a bit, and then slowly pulled back so he could look at me.

"Sarah," he said softly, "You can trust me. I'm not going to let anyone hurt you. Let me know what happened."

"I saw my sister-in-law, Denise, at a table when I got up to go to the restroom," I told him as I tried to control myself. "She was there with some guy holding her and kissing her neck... someone who wasn't my brother. I was pretty sure she had seen me, that's why I rushed back to the table to get you so we could leave. I didn't want to confront her. Then, when you went back in to get my stupid shawl, that man... Jared, someone I knew from college... came up to me. He's the one I saw with her. He was...he always scared me, Caleb. There's something about him I don't like. I think he was threatening me."

I put myself back into Caleb's arms and Caleb held me tightly, trying to comfort me in any way he could.

"Don't worry," Caleb said to me, stroking my hair as he held me. "You don't have anyone to be afraid of, not while I'm around."

I wanted what Caleb said to be true, but in the back of my mind, I feared what may be just ahead for me, and for us.

Chapter 23

Caleb

Sarah spent the night in my arms, first on the couch as she recounted what she had gone through at the restaurant, and then when we went to bed. I held her all night, keeping her close to me and promising to protect her and give her the help she needed. No matter how I tried to reassure her, she still felt worried. It wasn't until we woke the next morning that she started to show some signs of feeling better.

I had gotten out of bed before her and made us some coffee and toasted a couple of bagels. I put everything on a bed tray and brought it into the bedroom, where Sarah was curled up wearing one of my t-shirts that she had become accustomed to having on at night. I saw her start to pop her eyes open as she got a smell of the aroma of the coffee.

"Hmmm, that smells good," she said to me as she sat up and stretched her arms straight above her head, causing her t-shirt to ride up slightly and expose her stomach. I placed the tray at the foot of the bed and passed a cup of coffee to her, and she took a quick sip. I then offered her a bagel, and she took a small bite.

"I feel like I'm still full from dinner last night," Sarah said as she took another small bite. Sarah sipped her coffee again and then put her mug down on the nightstand and looked at me.

"I'm sorry if I ruined the date last night." Sarah had a sad look on her face.

"Hey," I said to her, putting the tray down on the floor and then placing my hand under her chin, so she had to turn her eyes up to look at me. "You didn't ruin anything. I had an amazing time with you last night. It was great to get out and see you enjoy yourself. Don't let what happened at the end of the night stand in your way."

"That's easy for you to say, Caleb," Sarah replied. "I can't get any of it out of my head. The thought that Denise is betraying my brother, and their daughter, makes me angry, but then everything that happened afterward with Jared... it just frightens me to think about it. What's going to happen when I go back to the house? What am I going to say to my brother? How am I going to deal with Denise?"

"You don't have to think about that right now," I told her. I moved closer to Sarah and kissed her. "You can stay here until you have to go to work tomorrow. We can figure out the rest after all that."

"Thank you, Caleb," Sarah said to me, bringing her hand to my cheek. "I don't know what I would do without you right now." Sarah leaned in and kissed me, deeper than the first kiss we had today. She put her hands on my sides, pulling me closer to her. I moved my lips down from her mouth, kissing her chin and then softly kissing her neck, planting small kisses all over her neck and causing her to flinch and giggle. I looked her in the eyes and was happy to see her smiling again.

I went back to lightly kissing her neck as she lay her head back into the pillows. My kisses worked their way down her body, across her shoulders, until I was lightly kissing her breasts, first through the t-shirt she had on, and then after I helped her lift the t-shirt over her head, on the bare flesh of her breasts. Sarah held my head in the palms of her hands as I kissed her soft skin. I could hear her mewling lightly as I kissed her, moving from one breast to the other. I then kissed her stomach, moving down to her hips.

My fingers hooked into the lace waistband of the black panties she was wearing, and I pulled them down her legs, over her calves and feet, until they were free of her. I then kissed my way back up her left leg, taking my time to go over the contours of the muscles in her calves, the curve and bend of her knee, and the soft skin of her thigh until I reached the top of her thigh.

Sarah was breathing a bit harder now and had instinctually parted her legs. After reaching the top of her thigh, I slowly moved over to her right leg, passing over the warmth radiating from her body, and then worked my way down and then back up her right leg, kissing and caressing her until I was back to the top of her thigh. I looked up at Sarah and saw her eyes were closed and she was getting lost in the moment.

I lowered my head so my lips could meet her where she wanted me the most. Her hips thrust up to meet me almost immediately and when she first felt my lips and tongue graze her, she gasped and moaned. I continued to lightly brush my fingertips on the insides of her thighs, sending chills up and down her body, as I kissed, nibbled and licked at her most intimate spots. My tongue gently probed a little deeper with each upward and involuntary thrust Sarah seemed to make, allowing me to taste more and more of her.

Another glance up at Sarah saw that her eyes were shut tight, her head further down into the pillow, and while her left hand was gripping the headboard of the bed, her right hand had moved down to guide my head so that I was kissing and touching her with my mouth just where it would please her the most. The first time my tongue made the slightest contact with her clitoris, she moaned deeply and held my head tightly.

I knew just where she wanted me and what she wanted me to do as I felt her bend her knees slightly, opening herself up to me more. My tongue made long, slow strokes up and down, coming to a stop just short of her clitoris time and again until she couldn't take it anymore. Sarah forced my head down, so my mouth was pressed deep against her, probing in and out of her. Her thighs tightened around me, holding me in place as I felt her hand release from my head so that she could hold on herself as her body tensed and then released the orgasm building inside her.

I looked up at Sarah, her hands clenched on the headboard, her chest moving rapidly as her breathing had quickened and then started to slow. As her blissful feelings started to subside, her eyes slowly opened and peered down at me. She gave me a crooked smile as she lifted her head to look at me.

"No one had ever done... oh man..." Sarah said to me as her head buried back into the pillow.

"I hope that doesn't mean you're too tired," I said to her as I moved my body up and over her so that I could kiss her deeply. I pressed my body closer to her, and I could feel her hands slipping down the shorts I was wearing to get them off me. Once my shorts were down enough, she used her feet to remove them the rest of the way, smiling and giggling at me as she did this. I then easily slipped inside her, feeling her body envelop me right away.

Sarah's hands gripped my backside pulling me as close to her as possible with each movement I made up and down. I kissed her hard on her right shoulder and then her neck, feeling my own breathing getting faster and more deliberate in no time at all. I started to try to slow things down, to make it so that I could last longer, but Sarah would not have any of it.

"Don't," Sarah said breathlessly as I thrust more slowly. "Please, I want to feel you."

I resumed my faster pace, pushing us both closer and closer. Sarah's body's rhythm was meeting mine with every movement, and finally, I couldn't hold back any longer. One final thrust, feeling the warmth and wetness of her, was too much for me to take. I groaned as I felt my body release, and Sarah tightened herself on me once again, holding herself against me. We both tried to keep still, to feel the intensity each other was experiencing as well, but the feelings coursing through me were too good to just hold still. I pressed my lips tightly against hers, kissing her deeply repeatedly until our orgasms started to subside.

I was sweaty, spent, and feeling a deep sense of euphoria. I moved down onto the bed and lay next to Sarah, watching her catch her breath. She turned her head and smiled at me, reaching her right hand over to gently stroke my cheek. She pulled my face to hers so we could kiss again and again.

I was looking deep into her eyes, her smile, and I whispered to her.

"I'm falling in love with you," I said to her softly.

Sarah seemed surprised and maybe even taken a little aback at first. I could see her eyes clouding with tears.

"Oh, Caleb..." Sarah said, and she looked like she wanted to continue talking, but I interrupted.

"Before you say anything else," I said to her, "please let me finish. I realize we haven't known each other for very long. And I know I have... I have issues and baggage that some women may not want to deal with, I get that. But I want you to know that I'm working to change that, and you make me want to be a better person, for myself, my family, and for you. I understand if you think it is too soon to say something like this, but I wanted to tell you. You don't have to..."

Sarah put her fingers up to my lips to stop me.

"Will you give me a chance to say something?" she said to me with a smile. "I know you have issues you are dealing with. Goodness knows, you know I have issues of my own I'm facing too. But I have never felt better about anything or anyone in my life. Caleb, you make me feel things I never thought I would get the chance to feel in my life. Hearing you say you're falling in love with me… it brings happiness to me that I can't even put into words. And it makes me glad to say that I'm in love with you, too."

Sarah kissed me before I had the chance to say anything else and rested her head on my shoulder. We just lay there quietly with each other for a long while until I could hear Sarah breathing softly and slowly. I knew she was asleep in my arms, and I didn't want to move at all to disturb her peacefulness.

I thought that I would feel nervous about saying I was falling in love with Sarah, but the words came easily to me. I didn't experience any guilty feelings, and I knew I wasn't betraying Ella in any way. I knew that this was the right thing for me, to live a happy life, and do the things that would make my life fulfilled. It was just like what I had talked about with Ella if anything were to ever happen to me while I was in combat. She understood it much easier than I did back then, and I think it just took meeting the right person in my life for me to comprehend it.

After some late morning sleep and early afternoon lovemaking, I decided to get out of bed and shower, and Sarah wanted to do the same. I let her shower first while I straightened up and made the bed. When she came out with a towel wrapped around, it took all I could to keep my hands off her. I tried to tempt her into tossing the towel aside and getting back into bed, but stronger heads prevailed, and she ushered me off to the shower to clean myself up.

By the time I got out of the shower, Sarah had dressed in a pair of black shorts and another of my t-shirts that she had taken from my dresser.

"You know if you keep taking my t-shirts I'm not going to have any left," I said to her as I got clothes out for myself.

"I can't help it," she said to me, coming over and kissing me as she slowly unwrapped the towel from around my waist. "I just love the thought of wrapping myself up in them. And they feel good, too," she told me as she pressed her body in the t-shirt against my naked body.

"Keep that up, and I'll be taking that one off you right now," I growled into her ear.

"Get dressed," she said, tossing the towel into my hamper and walking out of the room, smiling.

I hastily put on a t-shirt and shorts myself and went out into the living room to see what Sarah was doing. She had her head in the refrigerator, looking over what we had bought at the store.

"What are you doing?" I asked her as I sat on one of the barstools.

"I thought I would make some dinner tonight," she said to me.

"Well, I usually eat with Linda and Adam," I said to her. It had seemed like it was so long since I had seen them. I didn't want them to think I was shutting them out of my life.

"Okay," Sarah said with a smile. "We can cook dinner for them over at the house."

Sarah gathered up the supplies she needed from my kitchen, tossed them into a couple of bags and was ready to head out the door. I dutifully followed her down the stairs and across the lawn to the back door of the house so we could go right into the kitchen.

"This kitchen is much nicer than yours," Sarah said teasingly.

"That's why I don't cook anything myself," I told her.

"Well, today you get to be the sous chef."

"I think it's much easier if I just watch you do the cooking," I told her, sitting down at the table.

"I'll bet it is," Sarah said to me as she came over and pulled me out of the chair.

"Come on," she said to me. "Think of how impressed your son and sister will be when you say you made dinner tonight."

"They might not be so impressed when they see and taste the results if I am cooking."

"Oh, stop it," Sarah said playfully. "Come over here and start chopping some vegetables. We'll keep it simple."

Sarah handed me a knife and a cutting board, and I went to work on the carrots and broccoli, making sure to cut them just as she instructed. She then put me to work on peeling potatoes for mashed potatoes, while she went ahead and took care of the main part of the meal, the meatloaf she was making.

"How's this?" I asked as I finished slicing the potatoes. Sarah took a quick glance at them and nodded in approval.

As I was rinsing off the potatoes and putting them in the pot, Adam came walking into the kitchen. He had a surprised look on his face, not so much because Sarah was there, but because we were working in the kitchen, or I should say that I was working in the kitchen.

"What's going on?" he asked, looking at me with a grin on his face.

"Your Dad and I are making dinner tonight," Sarah said proudly.

"No kidding?" Adam said with a shocked look on his face. "You know how to cook, Dad? I can only ever remember you making pancakes when I was little, and those were from a box mix."

"Thanks for your show of support," I said to Adam. "Sarah is insisting I can do this, so I am giving it a try."

Adam held up his phone and snapped a picture of me at the counter pouring potatoes into a pot.

"What are you doing?" I said to him.

"I had to get a picture to document this," he said with a laugh. "I need to send this to Aunt Linda so that she knows not to pick up dinner on the way home."

"Great, thanks," I said to Adam.

Sarah had put the meatloaf in the oven already, and I got the potatoes boiling on the stove. Sarah then had me toss the carrots and broccoli with some oil, garlic, and spices and we put them in a roasting pan and slid them into the oven as well. In no time at all, I had to admit that the kitchen smelled pretty good.

I went about setting the table while Sarah put a quick salad together and checked on everything in the oven and on the stove. She then walked me through what to do with the potatoes, how to mash them properly with the masher and how and when to add the milk and butter. She also made sure I didn't overdo it with the potatoes and turn them into wallpaper paste.

Just as I completed my tasks with the potatoes, Linda came walking in the front door and came straight to the kitchen. She giggled and smiled as soon as she saw me in the kitchen.

"I had to make sure I left the office early so I could get here and see this for myself," she said with a laugh.

"I'm glad I am such a source of entertainment for everyone," I told her.

Linda came over and hugged me from behind.

"Relax little brother, I'm impressed that you were able to do this. Who knew you had it in you!"

"Sarah did all the hard work," I told her as I plated the mashed potatoes and put the bowl on the table. "She took care of the meat and told me everything else to do."

"Sarah, I don't know how you did it," Linda said to her, "but if you somehow could get him to cook dinner, you are a miracle worker."

Sarah just smiled as she placed the sliced meatloaf on a platter and put it on the table. Adam came back into the room and sat down at the table with the rest of us so he could take part in the meal.

Everyone filled their plates with food and dove right into the meal. The way Adam and Linda ate you would have thought they never had a meal quite so good. I guess when you were eating takeout as often as we do a home-cooked meal is quite a treat. I had to admit that everything tasted great, and I was proud of the compliments I received for the work that I did.

"Sarah, this is awesome," Adam said as he went back for seconds on everything.

"You've done it now, Sarah," I said to her with a smile. "Once you feed him like this, he's going to expect it all the time."

"I'm sure you can do the cooking just as well, Caleb," she said to me.

"No, he can't," Linda and Adam both said together.

"What a nice vote of confidence," I told my family.

"We're just kidding, Dad," Adam told me. "You did a great job." Adam wiped his face with his napkin and tossed it onto his empty plate.

"Thanks, buddy," I told him. "Now you can clear the table and put things away."

"Sorry, Dad," Adam said to me. "I've got a test to study for tonight." Adam sprinted up from the table and headed upstairs.

"You better really have a test!" I shouted after him as I heard him race up the steps.

"It's okay," Linda said to me. "I can take care of the cleanup."

"Don't be silly," Sarah said to her as she stood up and pulled me out of the chair. "We can help, too." Sarah looked over at me and smiled her pretty smile, and I could feel myself melting.

"Yeah, of course we can," I said with mock excitement. I grabbed some plates off the table and started loading them into the dishwasher.

Sarah went to washing the pots and pans while Linda put away the little leftovers that there were, making sure to make herself a little something to take to the office for lunch the next day. Sarah tossed me a dish towel, indicating I should start drying the dishes.

"I can dry," Linda said, coming over to take the towel from me.

"Caleb can do it," Sarah said to her. "You worked hard all day. You can relax while we finish up."

Linda leaned in between Sarah and me and smiled at me.

"Make sure you keep her," Linda said to me. "I'm going to get changed, and I'll be right back down."

Linda went off to change while Sarah and I finished up the dishes and put everything away. I started a pot of coffee, and it was just ready when Linda came back, dressed in a tank top and shorts. She sat down at the table, and I handed her a cup of coffee and then poured one for Sarah before getting one for myself.

"What did you two do today?" Linda said to us as she sipped her coffee.

I looked over at Sarah and smiled, and then picked up my mug of coffee and drank some. I could see that Sarah was blushing slightly.

"Not much," I told Linda as I tried not to laugh. I was pretty sure she got the hint, and she changed the subject.

"Well some of us worked hard today, at least," she said to me. "Meetings all day long. Speaking of meetings, Caleb, I have papers for you to sign."

"What papers?"

"We negotiated a settlement in Ella's case. I can't believe it took this long. It's been almost two years to the day since the accident..." Linda looked up from her coffee and saw the look on my face. "Oh, God, I'm sorry, Caleb," she said to me as she put her mug down. I could see Sarah looking over at me with a look of concern as well. "I didn't even think about it," Linda said, trying to apologize. "We can talk about it another time."

"No, it's okay," I said to her, trying to hold myself together. With all that had been going on recently, and with feeling so good, it had slipped my mind that the accident had happened two years ago this coming Thursday. I could feel the sense of dread and guilt creeping back into my mind. It didn't seem right that I was enjoying life as much as I had been when this anniversary of sorts was right around the corner.

"Maybe you can come down to the office tomorrow and sign them there," Linda said as she tried to move the conversation along.

"Sure, that's fine," I answered.

The three of us sat at the table quietly for a moment before Sarah broke the silence.

"Linda, could you direct me to your bathroom?" she asked, getting up from the table.

"Sure," Linda said. "It's just down the hall on the right. It's the second door."

Sarah rubbed my back lightly as she walked passed me and headed down the hall. Linda turned to me right away as soon as she heard the door close.

"Caleb, I'm sorry," Linda said quietly. "I didn't mean to bring that up with Sarah here. My head was just going, and it came out."

"It's fine, Linda," I said to her. "I'm the one who feels like a jerk. I had completely forgotten that... that the day was so close. I can't believe I did that."

"Hey," Linda said to me. "It's okay that you did. Ella wouldn't want you moping around all the time thinking about her. "

"I get that, Linda, but I should at least respect her enough to remember a day like that. I've been so caught up with..." My voice trailed off, and I didn't finish the sentence.

"With what?" Linda asked. "With living your life? Enjoying time with someone? Caleb, you have denied yourself the right to enjoy your life for so long. I am so happy for you that you are breaking out of that and have someone that makes you smile and feel good. Don't shut that off just because you forgot about Ella for a moment."

Sarah came back down the hall and into the kitchen and stood next to me.

"Everything okay?" she asked as she looked at us.

"Everything's fine," Linda said, standing up from the table. "I am going up to my office to do some work. Sarah, thank you so much for dinner tonight. It was wonderful."

"You're welcome," Sarah said to her.

Linda came over and gave Sarah a hug, and I could see her whispering something into Sarah's ear. Sarah smiled at her and nodded.

"What are you two conspiring about?" I asked.

"Don't you worry about it, little brother. It's just girl talk, something I haven't had the chance to do with someone for far too long." Linda bent down and gave me a hug and then went off down the hall to go up the stairs.

I stood up from the table and took Sarah's hand and led her out the back door. I started to walk back towards my apartment, but Sarah tugged on my hand and stopped me.

"Can we sit out here for a little bit?" she said, pointing to a couple of chairs Linda had set up on the patio that looked out over the backyard. "I could use a little fresh air."

I pulled the two chairs closer to each other, and we each sat down in one of the wooden deck chairs. The sun had long since set, and the sounds of nature were in all their glory tonight. The air had just a hint of coolness to it, enough to make it perfectly comfortable and enjoyable.

"Your family is wonderful, Caleb," Sarah said to me as she reached over and took my hand.

"They are pretty good, I agree," I told her. "They are both smart alecks, but they're lovable."

Sarah laughed and squeezed my hand. She could see that my mind was wandering.

"You know," Sarah said, standing up from her chair and coming over and sitting in my lap, putting her arms around my neck, "It's okay if you want to think about her, or even talk about her. It's only right that you would want to. I'm... I'm not hurt by it."

I held Sarah close to me, and she put her head on my shoulder.

"Thank you," I said to her softly.

"For what?"

"For everything," I said to her. "For this last week, for what you have brought into my life, for helping me to see what living should be like again. I had lost that along the way, and you have given that back to me."

"I think you knew you needed something before I came along," she said modestly.

"I knew it, but I didn't want to do anything about it," I told her. "You have made me want to make myself better, to be the man that I used to be and need to be again."

Sarah kissed me lightly and smiled.

We sat in the chair together and held each other, taking in all the night had to offer and spread out for us.

"This is living," I said quietly as Sarah nuzzled into me.

Chapter 24

Sarah

2^4

I didn't want these last three days to have to come to an end. The time I had spent with Caleb, either just us or with his family, made me see just how much I had been missing out on in life. To have someone that cares about me, who I am, and what I do is something that I have lacked for such a long time, and now that I had it I didn't want to give it up.

Even though I was waking up Wednesday morning still in Caleb's bed and in his arms, I knew it was back to the "real world" for me today. I had needed the last three days as an ideal escape from the problems I was having at James' house, but I was going to have to confront all those issues at some point. I had no idea what I was going to do once I got home, what I would say to Denise, or what I should say to James. I asked Caleb for some advice about it as we sat at the kitchen counter and had breakfast.

"He's your brother, Sarah," Caleb said to me as he took a bite of his eggs. "He deserves to know the truth. I know if it was me and Linda knew something like that, I would have wanted her to tell me about it. Yes, it will be painful for him, but you're his family. Tell him what you know, comfort him, and let him decide what path is best for him to take after that. That's all you can do."

"I guess you're right," I replied, not completely thrilled with the answer. I knew it was the right thing to do, but I was already getting a knot in my stomach just at the thought of having this conversation.

"And what about Denise?" I asked Caleb.

"What about her?" he said. "You don't owe her anything. She hasn't exactly gone out of her way to make your life pleasant. If you ask me, she gets what she deserves out of this."

"That doesn't make it any easier for me, Caleb," I told him. I toyed with the eggs on my plate more than I ate them, worrying about what waited ahead for me at some point over the next day or so. "I hate the idea of tearing the family apart like that. James and Lizzie will be devastated, and I feel like it will be my fault."

"It's not your fault," Caleb said to me, putting his fork down and taking my hand. "She did this to the family, not you. You have nothing to feel guilty about. I know it won't be easy for you, Sarah. Do you want me to be there with you?"

"No," I said to him. "I think this is something I will have to do on my own, as much as I don't like it."

"If something goes wrong, or if you feel uncomfortable, you know you can always come back here. Just go to work, and I can meet you in the morning and walk you back here. I wouldn't mind that all."

Caleb came over and hugged me close to him, and I felt safe and secure in his arms. I knew I could count on him to help me and that I could come back here if I needed to, but I really wanted things to work out well at home. If I were lucky, maybe Denise would have packed up and left before I even got there today, and I wouldn't have to be the one to break the bad news or confront her at all.

I spent the rest of the morning going over some homework assignments I had to do for school. It was nice to be able to sit in the comfort of Caleb's apartment and feel relaxed while I worked. He gave me my space and sat in his chair reading a book and then answering some emails of his own while I worked. I had done enough work so that I had gotten far ahead now in most of my classes, but it was good to go on and get assignments and message with professors about things I would need to do before the end of the semester in just a few more weeks.

By the time I had finished everything, it was getting into the afternoon, and I knew I should head back to the house. Caleb had planned to go to Linda's office to sign his paperwork, and he offered to drive me back to the house so I could get settled and get ready for work tonight. I felt nervous from the time we got in the car, and the anxious feelings were rattling me as we got closer and closer to the house.

When we were coming up to the driveway, Caleb stopped the Jeep in the middle of the street.

"What are you doing?" I asked him, looking around to make sure nothing was wrong or no one was behind us.

"If you don't want to do this, don't do it," Caleb told me. "I am sure you can go to your brother's workplace, talk to him, and arrange to get your stuff if you don't want to be there. Don't feel like you must step into that house. If her car is in the driveway, we can just go on our way, okay?"

I nodded in agreement and felt my stomach tense up as we crept closer to the house. Caleb turned into the driveway and the only car there was mine, parked in the same spot it always was. I felt some of the gut-wrenching ease.

I bent over and gave Caleb a long kiss.

"I'm going to go in, go up to my room, get back into my routine, and we'll see where things go from there," I said to him.

"Okay, you have my cell number if you need to message or call me," he told me. "You will be fine. I'll come by the diner tonight, okay?"

"Okay," I said. "Thank you, Caleb, for everything." I went over and kissed him deeply again. I then took a deep breath, grabbed my backpack, and got out of the car.

I made the long, slow walk down the driveway towards the front door of the house. I turned the handle lightly and felt the front door was locked. I looked back and saw Caleb was still waiting in the driveway to make sure I was okay. I waved to him that it was okay to go, and he backed out of the driveway and left.

I turned the handle again just to make sure it was really locked, and it didn't budge.

Well, that's a good sign, I said to myself and fished my keys out of my purse and unlocked the door.

I opened the door quietly, even though I knew no one was home. I shut the door, hearing it make its usually creaking sound, and then quickly went up the stairs. My sneakers squeaked on the wood steps as I went up. All I had to do was get to my room, go in, and lock the door and stay there until it was time for me to leave. I tapped out a quick message to James to let him know I was at the house and I would see him tonight at dinner before I opened the door to my room.

I pushed the door open as I was looking down at my phone, seeing the reply from James as a simple "Ok." When I looked up, Denise was sitting at my desk. I gasped loudly and dropped my phone on the floor.

"Welcome home," she said to me with a smile. She stood up from my desk and came over to me and picked up my phone, holding it in her hands.

"What... what are you doing here? Why are you in my room?" I said shakily, feeling fear pounding through my body.

"Oh, I brought my car in for an oil change and tune-up today. The man at the shop was nice enough to give me a ride back home, so I've just been relaxing. As for why I am in your room, why I was just waiting for you to get back. I heard the car in the driveway and saw you out there kissing your friend quite passionately, so I knew you were here."

"Please, get out of my room," I said, trying to control my temper and gain control of my thoughts. My body felt frozen in place just inside the door while Denise fiddled with my phone in her hands. She glanced down at the screen to see I had sent a message to James.

"Oh, it was nice of you to send a message to James like that. He has been so worried about you," Denise said sharply. She scrolled through my messages on my phone.

"What are you doing?" I asked her, trying to grab my phone back, but she just snatched it away at the last second.

"I was just checking to see if you had said anything else to James lately," she told me. "No phone calls to him either, I see. That's good." She then took my phone and pushed into her pants pocket.

"Give me my phone back," I said to her, trying to sound strong, but I could hear my voice quivering.

"I don't think so," she snapped. "Have a seat," Denise said pointing towards the bed. "You and I need to have a little talk first."

I slowly moved over to the bed and sat down as Denise stood in front of me.

"You were the last person I expected to run into at the restaurant," she said in a huff. "We've been going there for months, hiding out in the corner, and never saw anyone I knew, and then you come walking into the place. At first, I was worried that you would go running right to James and tell him what you saw, but when nothing happened that night, I knew you weren't strong enough to do anything about it."

"I'm going to tell him," I shot back. "I'm telling him tonight when he gets home."

"No, you're not," Denise said with a smirk. "Even if you think that your boyfriend has somehow given you a backbone, you won't do it. "You know why? Because of these." Denise turned and picked up a folder off the desk and waved it in front of me. She opened the folder and showed me the pictures inside. The pictures that were all too familiar to me from back then.

"I already told Caleb about those pictures," I said to her. "He doesn't care about that."

"Yes, I figured you probably did talk to him about that, letting him know how broken you are. But the great thing about technology today is that you can make pictures look any way you want them to look if you have the right skills. Thankfully, Jared does know the right people to do things like that. He was able to take your pictures and your face and create a whole new set of photos that I think your boyfriend might want to see."

Denise flashed a few of the pictures towards me, flipping through them, and I was aghast at what I saw. Pictures of me, or at least pictures that had my face on them, doing all kinds of lewd things, things I would never even think about it. They had even doctored up some of the pictures that were of me from the past, making them seem much more profane than they really were.

"I am sure your Caleb would love to see these, along with everyone down at the diner, like your boss and your friends. Maybe your professors might like them too. Oh, and of course your parents, I would never leave them out of this."

Hot tears were bursting down my face. I couldn't believe what was happening, that I might have to relive this again, but only a hundred times worse this time.

"Why... why are you doing this?" I said as I sobbed.

"Because I'm leading a great life and I'm tired of you messing things up, Sarah. I have a nice house, a great job, a husband who thinks I'm great and a rich lover to boot. It was perfect for a long time, but then you started messing things up with your Sarah the perfect sister, aunt, homemaker, worker and person routine. Lizzie doesn't even look twice to me when she needs or wants something. It's always "Sarah can help with that," or "I'll talk to Sarah." Well, I'm tired of it. So, from now on, Sarah does what I want. You don't say a thing to anyone about anything you saw, and I won't show these pictures to the world. You just go about your sad little life working at the diner and going to school and taking care of the house. You should probably stop seeing that man you see too. I believe that is going to be a problem."

I was stunned into silence. I didn't know what to say or do or how to react. I could feel my fist clenching and unclenching the blanket covering my bed as I cried.

"Are we in agreement, Sarah, or should I get to work with these?" Denise said to me.

I just nodded without saying anything.

We both heard my phone beep with a message coming in. I looked up and saw Denise take the phone out of her pocket.

"Oh, it's from Caleb," she said smugly.

"Everything okay?" she read aloud. "See you later. I love you," she said in a mocking tone.

"Everything's fine," Denise said out loud as she typed a message back to him and sent it. She then turned the phone off and shoved it into her pocket.

"I think we're all done for now," Denise said to me as she walked towards the door. "You can come down and start dinner any time you're ready. Don't forget to get your clothes ready for work today either."

Denise shut the door, and I heard her walk down the hall. I got up off the bed and locked the door and then slumped back onto my bed.

All the good feelings I had built up over the last few days were dashed inside of the last ten minutes or so. I was a prisoner now, with no way out, nowhere to turn for help, and Denise hanging over my head ready to stomp down on me whenever she wanted to.

I walked over to the closet and got my clothing out for work tonight, knowing I had nothing to look forward to anymore.

Chapter 25

Caleb

For the entire ride over to Sarah's house, I could see how nervous she was. It was a difficult situation she found herself in, and I wanted to help her more, but she insisted that this was something that she needed to handle on her own. I respected her for wanting to face her sister-in-law on her own and defend her brother, but it was not going to be easy for her. Even after I dropped her off, I was still worried about her, though her message to me assured me that everything was okay. I would have to wait to find out more details later tonight when I saw her.

I got over to Linda's office and parked the car in the small lot next to her building. She shared the building with some other businesses, but through smart investing on her part, she had managed to buy the building along the way and earned income from renting out the other spaces. My sister was one smart cookie.

I walked into the building and down the hall to the area where her office was and entered the space. I realized that it had been a very long time since I had been in the office, and I hardly recognized the space at all. She had certainly put money back into her practice and made the office look good, with new plush carpeting and a large reception desk where her assistant Kendra sat. Kendra had been with her for several years now and handled all day-to-day stuff for the office that Linda might not have time for herself. Like Linda, she was a strong, self-assured woman who was someone you didn't want to cross, but who would bend over backward to help you if you needed it. She and Ella had become friends over the years and Linda, Kendra, and Ella would often get together for dinners or just a girls' night out.

"Well hello there, stranger," Kendra said to me as I walked through the door. She came out from around her desk and gave me a big hug.

"I was wondering when you were going to come in so I could see you," Kendra said to me. "It's been way too long."

"About two years," I said to her soberly. I realized I hadn't seen her since Ella's funeral.

"My god, it's been two years already," Kendra said quietly. "I think about her every day, Caleb. I still keep expecting her to come walking through that door so we could go out for dinner."

"I know how you feel, Kendra," I said as we hugged again.

Kendra wiped her eyes and then walked behind her desk. "I'll let Linda know you're here. She's got someone in the office with her right now."

"No problem," I said as I took a seat in one of the comfy, high back leather chairs that were in the waiting room.

I glanced down at my phone to see if I had any other messages from Sarah, but there was nothing.

I hope that means things are going smoothly, I thought to myself.

I sat back, mindlessly flipping through one of the magazines Linda had in the waiting room. All the magazines seemed the same, with the same posed figure or celebrity on the front with a headline telling me how much better my life could be if I followed whatever plan it was that they were endorsing. Finally, I heard Linda's office door open and looked up and saw her walking out with a familiar face right beside her.

"So, we'll get together tomorrow night then?" Linda asked Doug, the owner of the Moonlight Diner.

"Absolutely. I'm looking forward to it," Doug said as he took Linda's hand and shook it, though it seemed like they both lingered with their hands a bit longer than was necessary. Doug turned from Linda and spotted me sitting there.

"Hey there," he said to me with a big smile. I got up and walked over to shake his hand. I could see over his shoulder that Linda was turning three shades of red because she realized I must have seen them together.

"Nice to see you, Doug," I said as we broke our handshake.

"Nice to see you, too," he said to me. "I've got to run back to the diner. Thanks again for your help, Linda," he said as he looked back at Linda. "I'll see you tomorrow."

"Goodbye, Doug," she said, trying to sound more professional for my benefit. Doug walked out of the office and no sooner had the door closed behind him, and I broke out into a big grin.

"What are you smiling at?" Linda said as she put her hand on her hip.

"Nothing at all," I said to her. "I'm sure you're just as friendly with all your clients. Isn't she like that with everyone, Kendra?"

Kendra was smiling as well when my question broke her concentration.

"Oh, yes, definitely," Kendra said, trying to be serious as she stifled a laugh.

Just then the phone started ringing.

"Don't you need to get that, Kendra?" Linda said, trying to change the subject.

Kendra smiled and picked up the phone and Linda waved me to follow her into her office.

I sat in one of the equally plush leather chairs in Linda's office as she got behind her desk to grab some files.

"So, you're getting together with Doug tomorrow night, huh?" I said to her.

"Yes, I am," she said as she shuffled her papers. "Doug wanted some advice about his business and future planning, so I told him I would be happy to help him out."

"Oh, so you're meeting him here at the office then," I remarked.

"Well, no not quite," she said, seeming flustered now. "I'm meeting Doug at his place. He's going to cook dinner for us, and we'll talk over dinner."

"Seems kind of cozy for a meeting with your potential attorney," I said, loving that I could give her a hard time right now.

"Don't you worry about it, little brother," she shot back to me. "I can take care of myself."

"I never doubted that for a minute," I said with a laugh. "I think it's great for you. You haven't had a date in what, fifteen years or so?"

"Shut up, Caleb," she said. "It hasn't been that long."

"How long has it been?" I challenged.

I saw Linda's eyes shift as she tried to think about it.

"About seven years," she said quietly as she grabbed a stack of papers and brought them over to the table on the other side of the room.

I got up from the chair and followed her over to the table, sitting next to her.

"Okay, let's get down to business," she said, trying to get everything back on track. She slid a paper in front of me to read.

"This is the basic settlement," Linda said. "Read it over and let me know if you have any questions."

"You know I don't really care about this," I told her in a serious tone.

"I know you don't, Caleb, but I do, and it's important that some sense of justice is done on Ella's behalf. They can't just get away with it. I know it's just money, but it's something."

I looked over the agreement, which basically said that they were willing to settle the case without any admission of guilt on the part of Brandon Sterling or the Sterling family. The settlement would be sealed, and that would be the end of it. I fumbled my way through the rest of the legal jargon of the document and got to the end, where the finances of the settlement were explained. I looked at the paper, looked up at Linda, and then looked at the paper again.

"Is this right?" I said to her in disbelief.

"Yep," she said proudly. "They knew I had them over a barrel. Even though there was no criminal charge or conviction against Brandon, there was evidence that they had somehow got suppressed. Of course, when you're friends with nearly everyone in this town, including people in the police department and the town attorney's office, information has a way of coming your way. I had enough where I could press the state's DA to step in and open a case up and make things very uncomfortable for the Sterling family."

I looked down at the paperwork again, and Linda could see I was stunned.

"Here's how it breaks down. They agree to pay up to $500,000 to cover Adam's school tuition, wherever he decides to go, including if he goes to law school, grad, school, med school or anything else. They also agree to pay an additional $500,000 to a charity of your choice in Ella's name. Then the rest is for you."

I looked at the papers one more time.

"Linda, that's 3 million dollars."

"Damn right it is. I actually started at seven and only agreed to accept the three if the Sterling family went for the agreement for the additional payments for tuition and donation."

Linda put her hand on my shoulder and looked at me.

"Caleb, nothing can ever replace Ella in your life, Adam's life, my life, or anyone else's. It's a horrible thing that happened, and I would love to have that worm rot in jail for twenty-five years for what he did. Since that isn't going to happen, this is the best I could do for you and Adam. I wish I could do more, or that things could be different."

"I wanted to see him in jail too, Linda. I know how these things go sometimes. This just seems like... like it's too much," I said to her.

"Screw that!" she said, raising her voice. "It's not too much at all, Caleb. If anything, it will never be enough. At least that man can live every day for the rest of his life knowing he did have to pay in some way for what he did. Old man Sterling banished Brandon from the state. They shipped him off to run one of their offices out in Kansas somewhere. Sterling's lawyer made it sound like he was invited to never come back. Good riddance to that trash."

"What do we do now?" I asked her.

"You sign the agreement, I send it over to Sterling's lawyer, and it gets filed with the court. They cut three checks – one for you, one for Adam, and one for the charity you want. Adam's goes into a trust for him. You can do whatever you want with yours. As your lawyer, I can take care of it for you if you want. We can invest it, put some in the bank, or do what you wish. You just let me know, and I'll do it for you."

Linda flipped the pages of the document over to the signature page and handed me a pen. I sat and thought about it for a second, but I realized that this was the only outcome that was viable. I signed my name on the document and handed it back to Linda.

"You okay?" Linda said to me.

"I think so," I said to her. "I don't know... this whole process, everything about it coming to an end, and everything else going on right now... it just seems like... like it's me putting Ella behind me for good. I don't want that to be true, but it feels like it."

"She's never behind us, Caleb. Even if the case is over, or if you are with Sarah, or when Adam goes away to school or gets married... she's always a part of us."

Linda gave me a hug and then sat back in her chair.

"Thank you," I said to her. "I know this was a lot of long hours and hard work for you. Even though I never wanted you to start it in the first place, I'm glad you saw it through."

"It was my pleasure, little brother," Linda said to me. "Now you need to think about what charity you want to donate to. You can give it some consideration and see what you can come up with. We can hold that money in trust too until you come up with something."

"I'll think about it," I said to her. "I'll talk to Adam about it and see if he has any ideas. He may know of something that is perfect for this, that Ella would have loved."

"Good idea," she said to me as she stood up. Linda's phone buzzed, and she walked over to pick it up. I heard her say "okay" and then she hung up.

"My next appointment is here," she said to me. I stood up and walked towards her office door. "I'll see you at home tonight. What are you cooking for dinner tonight?" she said to me with a smile.

"Sorry," I told her, "Sarah is working tonight. If you want me to cook, we might be limited to pancakes. My cooking lessons haven't progressed very far just yet. I can pick up sandwiches if you want. Or maybe you want a cozy dinner with Doug tonight, too."

"Get out, Caleb," Linda said to me, opening her office door.

I walked out into the office and saw Kendra talking to a young couple that was the next appointment. I gave her a wave as I left and she waved back to me and blew me a kiss.

I got out to my car and just sat behind the wheel for a few minutes without starting up the car at all. I still had a hard time processing that the Sterling family would just turn over all that money to make this all go away. Part of me started to feel a little angry about it, and part of me was still sad about it as well, especially since it was so close to the anniversary of the accident. It was all a lot to process.

I turned on the car and headed back home, determined to talk to Adam about all of this and explain it all to him to see if he had any ideas. After that, I would look forward to going to see Sarah late tonight at the diner. She would certainly be the bright spot of a day of mixed emotions for me.

Chapter 26

Sarah

2⁶

The rest of the day was one of the most uncomfortable and unhappy of my existence. After my confrontation with Denise, where she basically decided to blackmail me into not revealing her affair to James, I was backed into a corner. I found myself with no choice but to go along with her or have her ruin the rest of my life with the phony pictures she and Jared Sterling had doctored together. Worst of all, she was trying to put a halt to my relationship with Caleb, and I had to try to find a way around him and dealing with him until I could figure everything out.

After I put my things away and got my work clothing out, I resigned myself to going downstairs and starting dinner. I went into the kitchen and took out some chicken pieces that were in there and put together a simple roasted chicken dinner with rice and vegetables. My heart was hardly in doing any of this, but with Denise keeping a watchful eye over me from her perch just outside the kitchen on the deck, I had to at least try to put on a good front. At least when Lizzie came in it did brighten my day to see her.

"Sarah!" she yelled when she saw me and came in and gave me a big hug.

"Hi, Lizzie," I said, hugging her back.

"I'm so glad you're home," she said to me. "I was getting worried you weren't coming back."

"I wouldn't just leave you like that," I said to her quietly.

"Good!" she said happily. "How was your time with your boyfriend? I want to hear all about it."

Just then, Denise came walking in the back door.

"Lizzie, do you have homework to do?" she asked.

"I do have some, but I can do it after dinner," Lizzie told her mother, looking back to me.

"No, you can go do it now," Denise ordered. "Besides, Sarah is trying to get dinner together before your father gets home, right Sarah?"

I looked over at Lizzie with a resigned look on my face.

"I do have to get dinner going," I said to her. "We can talk later."

Lizzie sighed, picked up her backpack and trudged up the stairs to go do her homework.

"Be careful about your conversations with her," Denise hissed in my ear. "And don't put anything weird on the chicken. I want a nice simple dinner from now on."

Denise brushed passed me and went towards her bedroom, and I set back to working on dinner. I kept things simple, just using salt and pepper, and made basic white rice and some broccoli and cauliflower for dinner. While everything was cooking, I went ahead and set the table and looked to see if the dishwasher needed emptying. It looked like since I hadn't been home the family had been eating takeout every night and there was nothing in the dishwasher but some coffee mugs and bowls used for cereal in the morning.

I had just got everything out of the oven and started to put everything out on the table when James walked through the door. He came over and smiled at me and gave me a hug.

"Nice to have you home," he said to me.

I did all I could to keep from breaking into tears right then and there.

"Thanks," I said simply. "Dinner is ready if you want to gather everyone."

James called out for Lizzie and Denise, and both came to the kitchen so we could sit down and eat. It was mostly quiet at dinner, With Lizzie and James asking me questions about the last few days and me giving simple, one or two-word answers to try and keep conversations short. Denise sat at the end of the table opposite James with a sly grin on her face with each bite she took of dinner. Through the whole meal, my mind was churning about how I could extract myself from this predicament.

While I no longer had my phone to communicate with Caleb or anyone else, I did still have my computer upstairs. I could easily send him a message that way. He was the one person who would understand what was going on and knew the truth. I decided after dinner I would go up and change for work and then get him a message.

I couldn't wait for dinner to end, and when everyone was finally finished, I started clearing the table. James and Lizzie both offered to help, but the look I got from Denise let me know I should decline the help and do it myself.

"Sarah can handle it alone, right Sarah?" Denise said loudly. "I'm sure you have more homework or studying you could do Lizzie, and James, you worked hard all day, you can relax."

Both James and Lizzie looked at Denise and couldn't quite figure out what was going on. When James got up to help me with the dishes, I had to intervene.

"I've got it, James, it's fine," I said to him, trying to smile through it.

I worked hard to get the dishes done, the dishwasher loaded, the leftovers put away, and the counters cleaned. When it was finally all done, I rushed up the stairs. I got into my room and locked the door and went straight to my backpack to get my computer. When I opened the backpack, I saw my computer was gone. Denise must have come up here at some point and taken it. I sat back on my bed and felt crushed. I quickly changed for work and decided I may as well go to work early and maybe I could work something out that I could do.

I came downstairs after getting dressed and saw James and Denise sitting in the living room.

"Has anyone seen my laptop?" I asked, pretty much knowing what had happened to it.

"I thought it was always in your room," James said to me.

"It is... I mean it was, but it's not there. I need it for my school work," I said to him.

"Maybe you left it at your friend's house while you were there this week," Denise chimed in. "You should probably ask him for it back."

"Did you leave it there?" James asked, looking at me.

"I... I didn't think I did, but I must have," I said, looking at Denise the whole time.

"Well just ask him for it back," James said. "I'm sure he would bring it to you."

"Sarah told me they had something of a falling out, James," Denise said to him. "That's why she came back today so early, right Sarah?" Denise shot me another look.

I just nodded, feeling myself choking up.

"Oh, I'm sorry Sarah," James said to me. "That's too bad. He seemed like a nice guy. Do you want me to get the computer back for you?"

"No, it's fine," I said, fighting back the tears. "I'll... I'll figure it out and get it back. I'm going to work." I rushed out the door so James wouldn't see me crying.

I was nearly to the top of the driveway when Denise called to me. She sauntered up to meet me.

"I'm not messing around Sarah," she said to me sternly. "Don't even think about doing anything. There's no room for mistakes on your part. Steer clear of trouble and Caleb, don't say anything to anyone, and everything will work out fine."

"How am I supposed to do my schoolwork without my computer?" I said to her.

"I guess you'll have to figure that out. You're a smart girl. I'm sure you can come up with a solution. Enjoy your night at work," she told me as she walked away.

I walked to work in a complete haze. I don't even remember anything about the walk there and found myself in front of the diner, just standing there, staring at the front doors from the bottom step. Doug finally saw me standing out there and came out to meet me.

"Sarah?" he asked as he stood in front of me. "Are you okay? You've just been standing here."

I snapped out of my fog to answer him.

"I'm sorry," I said to Doug. "I'm just a little out of it tonight."

I walked up the steps with Doug next to me and into the diner. Even though it was still not quite nine, the place was not very busy at all. I went to the back and to the break room to put my things away, still lost in my thoughts about how I was going to handle tonight and every day after this.

I walked into the kitchen and saw Justin doing some prep work.

"Howdy," Justin said to me. "How was your time off?"

"It was fine," I said to him, though it had been awesome up until this afternoon.

"Justin, do you think I can work back here with you tonight?" I asked him.

"It's okay with me," he said to me. "As long as it's okay with Doug... and Fran. She'll be covering all the tables."

"I'll check with Doug," I said and walked out to talk with Doug.

Doug was manning the register, ringing up a customer, so I waited until he was done. He looked up at me and smiled.

"Is it okay if I work in the kitchen with Justin tonight?" I asked him.

Doug looked around the diner. "I don't see it as a problem. It looks like it will be a typical Wednesday. Fran will probably love getting all the tips anyway. Is everything okay with you?"

"Yeah, I'm fine. I just feel like doing some cooking tonight."

I started walking back to the kitchen, glad I wouldn't have to deal with the public, and specifically with Caleb.

"Oh, Sarah," Doug said to me, getting my attention. I turned back towards him.

"I ran into Caleb today," he told me. "I was at his sister's law office for... for some business and he stopped in. He's such a nice man."

"Yes... yes, he is," I said, trying to move on from the subject. "I'll see you tomorrow, Doug."

I went back into the kitchen and headed straight over to Justin. I grabbed a white apron and put it on and was ready for work.

"Okay boss," I said to him, "what do you need?"

I spent the next several hours doing a little bit of everything, from peeling potatoes and other vegetables to making chicken stock, carving turkey and ham into slices, cleaning workstations and grease traps, and countless other jobs. Fran was thrilled to take on the diner herself so she could get the tips for the night, and it never seemed to get so busy that she couldn't take care of it all on her own. It wasn't until later in the night that she came back into the kitchen with a question.

"Hey Sarah," Fran called out to me.

"What do you need?" I yelled to her as I was cleaning out one of the refrigerators.

"Caleb's here looking for you," she said to me with a smile.

I froze and turned to her with a scared look on my face.

"What's wrong?" she said to me.

"Can you just tell him I'm working in the kitchen tonight and can't come out?" I said to Fran.

"Sarah, you can take five minutes to go see the guy, I'm fine back here," Justin said to me.

"No," I said firmly.

Justin just looked at me and went back to his work at the flat top.

"Fran, please, just tell him that for me?" I said, trying to remain calm.

"Sure, no problem," she said to me, shaking her head and backing out of the kitchen.

I went back to work on the refrigerator, scrubbing the shelves. I backed off from the fridge and saw Justin standing next to me.

"What's going on?" Justin said to me.

I am sure he could see that I had tears in my eyes, and I put my head on his shoulder and cried. I finally pulled back from Justin and looked at him.

"It's... it's just not going to work out is all," I told him, regaining my composure. "You were right, Justin. There's just too much baggage."

"I'm sorry, Sarah," he said to me.

"It's okay," I said to him, straightening up. "I'm just trying to get my mind off it."

"No problem," he said, leaving me to my work.

I exhausted myself doing every chore and job that came along, getting myself caught up in a frenzy to help the time go by faster. When it got to be about five-thirty, I had pretty much reached my breaking point. Justin could see that my face was red and I was sweaty, and he told me to just stop for the day.

"I think you did more than your fair share tonight," he said to me, looking around at everything that was cleaned and prepared. "Thanks for the help. You probably saved me about two days' worth of work back here."

"Not a problem," I said as I took a deep breath and exhaled. "It was good for me, too."

I went into the breakroom and sat for a few minutes before I grabbed my stuff and figured I would try to get out of here before Caleb might show up to walk me home. I still wasn't quite sure how to deal with all of that.

I walked out into the diner just as Fran was finishing up with a customer.

"Thanks for letting me take the room tonight," she said to me with a smile. "it wasn't super busy, but there were some really good tippers out here tonight. I did pretty well."

"I'm glad Franny," I said to her. I was starting to feel the physical and mental exhaustion and was ready to get out of here.

"If you want to wait around, I'll give you a ride home," she said to me. "You look beat."

"Thanks, but I'll walk," I told Fran. "The fresh air will do me good. See you tonight."

I made my way outside and could see just the hint of the sunrise beginning off in the distance. Some of the street lights had already shut off, and the morning traffic in town was just getting started as my day was ending. I took a quick look around to make sure Caleb was nowhere to be seen and started my walk home.

Even though the walk itself was never that long, it seemed quite a distance this morning. My legs were achy and tired, and my mind was spent. I felt myself shuffling along the sidewalk, barely lifting my feet up to move along. I had turned off Oak Street and was headed down the street towards home when I heard a voice call out to me. I stood straight up because I knew it was Caleb.

I turned slowly to see him dressed in his t-shirt and running shorts, running towards me.

"Hey," he said, a bit out of breath. "How come you didn't wait for me at the diner? Fran said you already left when I stopped there."

"I just want to get home, Caleb," I said to him, starting up my walk again.

"Are you okay? What happened last night? How come you wouldn't come out to see me? Or return any of my messages? How did things go with your sister-in-law?"

"Caleb, please," I shouted. "Enough with the interrogation. I left my phone at home. I just... just didn't want to deal with... with everything." I looked over at him and then kept walking.

"Did I do something wrong?" he said to me. "Because when I left you yesterday, I thought we were in a pretty good place and now today..."

"Caleb, my life is... very complicated right now. I am trying to sort out everything with school, my family, my parents... and then everything with you just happened so fast. Maybe it was happening too fast. I think I just need to take a step back and figure things out." I wanted to get to my house faster, but my legs didn't want to cooperate with me.

"What do you mean take a step back?" Caleb said, sounding concerned. I just tried to keep walking, getting closer to my driveway.

"Sarah!" Caleb yelled, grabbing my arm. "What the hell is going on?" I looked at Caleb and was already crying again.

"Caleb, it's just not the right time for this. I'm... I'm sorry if I gave you the wrong impression. You have things you need to straighten out with your son, feelings you still have for your wife, and I'm just a complication for you, just like you are for me. We each need to solve our own lives first."

"Sarah," Caleb said to me sincerely, "Don't do this. If something is wrong, we can work it out together, please. You... you told me you loved me. You don't just give that up in a day."

"Caleb, just let me go, please. Please don't come to the diner to see me again. It's... it's too hard for me."

I broke free from Caleb and ran down the driveway and into the house, closing the door quickly behind me. I took a quick peek out the window from behind the curtains and could see he was still standing there, stunned. He stood there for a minute before he started walking off in the direction of his house.

I wept as I started walking up the steps, my head down. When I got to the top of the steps, I saw Denise standing there in her nightshirt.

"That seemed quite dramatic from my window," Denise said to me. "I hope everything is okay."

"I ended it with him," I said curtly. "That's what you wanted, isn't it?" I brushed past her and went towards my room, by Denise came up from behind me and grabbed me.

"Don't get testy with me," Denise whispered strongly. "You're already treading a fine line with me. Just keep listening to me, and you will still have a place to live, a job, and a good reputation."

Denise let go of me, and I stepped back towards my room, fumbling for the doorknob.

"Sleep well," she said to me snidely and walked back towards her room.

I slipped into my room and locked the door quickly behind me. I was so drained from today that all I did was kick my shoes off and climb onto my bed and under the covers. I hoped that sleep would come quickly to me so that maybe I could wake up later and this would all have turned out to be a nightmare.

Chapter 27

Caleb

2 ^{7}

The whole walk home from Sarah's place I kept trying to go over and over in my mind what was happening. Less than twenty-four hours before, everything was fine. It was all even better than fine – it was great. Now she didn't want to see me anymore. All I could figure is that something had happened with her sister-in-law, something unpleasant, and Sarah was unsure of how to deal with it.

I wracked my brain trying to figure it out and was completely distracted, once so distracted that I almost got hit by a car backing out of a driveway. By the time I got back to the house, I had found myself walking into the main house rather than going up to my apartment. I needed to talk to someone that might give me some insight into what was going on.

Adam and Linda were both still upstairs, so I made a pot of coffee and found myself unconsciously making bacon and eggs. I put some English muffins in the toaster, lightly toasted everything, and made breakfast sandwiches for everyone, nicely wrapped in aluminum foil before Linda showed her face downstairs.

"Good morning," she said to me, seeming quite chipper. "Wow, coffee all made, and what's this?" she said, picking up one of the wrapped sandwiches.

"Bacon, egg, and cheese on an English muffin," I said to her as I sat down at the table.

"What got into you this morning? It must have been a really good run and walk home with Sarah."

"Actually, it was the opposite," I told Linda soberly as I bit into the sandwich I made for myself. "She said she doesn't want to see me or have me come to the diner."

Linda sat down at the table next to me in shock.

"Why? What happened?" she said with surprise.

"I don't know. I went to the diner last night, and she was busy working in the kitchen and couldn't see me. When I went to meet her this morning, she had already left and was walking home. By the time I caught up with her and got to her place, she was telling me how she couldn't see me anymore."

"Something must have happened yesterday," Linda answered.

"No kidding," I said, realizing it sounded like a wisecrack.

"I'm sorry, Caleb, I'm just trying to help," Linda said.

"I know. It has to be something with her sister-in-law," I said, trying to decipher it all.

"What's up with her?" Linda asked me.

I went through the whole story of what had happened to Sarah in the past with the pictures at school and her parents, and what happened recently between her and Denise, including spotting them at the restaurant the other day. I told her how Sarah was planning to talk to her brother or confront Denise yesterday when she got home.

"Some time between yesterday afternoon and this morning something went down, I just don't know what. If Sarah won't talk to me or see me, there's no way I can help her. I tried sending her messages or calling her, but she doesn't respond. I don't know what to do, Linda."

"I wish I could help you figure it out, Caleb. I need to get to the office. I have an early court appearance this morning. I can call you after that and maybe we can come up with an idea of what you can do."

"Thanks, Linda, but I'm not sure there's much to do right now."

Just then, Adam came walking into the room with his backpack.

"What's going on?" Adam said. He could see the concern on our faces.

"Just something with Sarah," I said to him. "I made some breakfast for you," I said to him, handing him a sandwich.

"Hey, thanks Dad," he said with a smile. "I have practice and then a game tonight at 7. Are you guys coming?"

"I can't tonight," Linda told him. "I have a... a business meeting tonight," Linda caught herself and didn't say it was a 'date.'

"Okay, how about you, Dad?"

"I'll try, Adam," I told him. "I have an appointment with Dr. Weber tonight. I'm not sure how long I'll be there."

"It's okay if you don't make it over," Adam told me. "Is it alright if I go out with friends tonight after the game."

"What about school tomorrow?" I said to him.

"Tomorrow's a day off," he told me. "Teacher's conference day or something like that. So, is it okay?"

"Sure, I guess so."

I heard a horn honking outside.

"That's my ride," Adam said as he picked up his sandwich and bag. "See you guys later."

Adam went down the hall and out the front door. Linda got up from her seat and grabbed her bag as she got ready to go.

"Are you going to be okay?" she asked me with concern. "I can cancel tonight if you want and be with you."

"No, don't do that," I said to her. "I'll be alright. I just have to work through things. You can't cancel with Doug. It might take you another fifteen years for someone else to ask you out."

"Very funny," Linda said, slapping my shoulder. "I'll talk to you later. Call me if you need anything."

With that, Linda left the house, leaving me alone in the quiet. I tried to busy myself with cleaning up after breakfast and putting things away. I even thought about straightening up the house a bit but then realized Linda had a cleaning service that came in twice a week keeping everything looking spotless.

I trudged back up to my apartment, trying to find things to occupy my mind – mindless TV, reading email, surfing the Internet – but none of it seemed to work well for me. All my thoughts kept turning back to Sarah. Part of me thought I should just storm over there, knock on the door and find out what was going on. I quickly realized that wasn't going to be the solution and might cause bigger problems for Sarah or worse, make her want to stay away from me for good.

I went into the bedroom, hoping that maybe I could try to fall asleep and get some rest, but all I did was toss and turn. Everywhere I looked in the apartment seem to have something that reminded me of Sarah, from the t-shirts of mine she wore to bed each night in the bedroom, to the toothbrush she left in the bathroom, to the groceries we bought together in the kitchen.

I didn't know how much more of this I could take and I could feel anxiety building up inside me and no way to let it out. It was then I picked up the phone and tried to call Sarah again. It went straight to her voicemail, but her mailbox was full, and it wouldn't let me leave a message. I hung up with her and decided to make another call – this time to Dr. Weber's office. I knew it was still early in the morning, but I had to talk to someone.

The phone call to Dr. Weber went to his answering service. I let the lady know on the other end that I was a patient of Dr. Weber's and needed to speak with him, so if he could call me as soon as he could, I would appreciate it. It was less than five minutes later that I got a phone call from Dr. Weber.

"Caleb, I was surprised to get a message from you. Is everything okay?" Dr. Weber asked with concern.

"I'm sorry to bother you this early Doc, but do you think... do you think I could come in earlier to see you today? I think I need to talk to someone."

"Are you at home right now?" Dr. Weber asked me.

"Yes."

"Okay, meet me at my office in ten minutes. I'll be there."

"Thanks," I told him as I hung up.

Normally I would just walk over to his office, but the urgency I was suddenly feeling made me decide to take my Jeep and drive over. I hopped in the car and was at his office in a matter of minutes. I parked on the street near his office, got out of my car, and waited out near the front of the building. I paced back and forth for minutes, alternately looking at my watch and then up and down the street to see if there was any sign of Dr. Weber. The last time I looked up, I could see Dr. Weber hustling down the street. He caught a glimpse of me and double-timed it over to the front of the building.

"You been here long?" he asked me as he unlocked the door.

"I drove over," I admitted as we went in and Dr. Weber turned off the alarm for the building. He then opened the door to his office, and we walked in. He quickly switched on the lights and had me follow him in so we could sit down.

I sat down in one of the chairs while Dr. Weber pulled another chair over, so it was nearer to me.

"So, what's going on?" he said to me as he wiped his glasses on his shirt.

"I feel like my anxiety level is suddenly at a fifteen," I told him as I rubbed the palms of my hands on my legs.

I went on to let me know everything that had happened over the last few days, with Sarah coming over and spending days with me, to the resolution of the lawsuit and the upcoming anniversary of Ella's accident, to what happened this morning with Sarah, and how it all led me to call him.

"That's a lot on your plate in just a few days, Caleb," Dr. Weber said to me. "Anyone would feel anxiety dealing with all that. Let's talk some of it out. What do you think happened with Sarah?"

"I can only assume it has to do with seeing her sister-in-law at the restaurant and how she confronted her about it. There's no way for me to know for sure though. Maybe she just got scared off by things moving so quickly. I mean, suddenly, she's in a physical relationship with me, and I'm telling her I'm falling in love with her. That could be scary, I guess."

"Is it scary for you?" Dr. Weber asked me.

"No, I don't feel scared about it. I never would have said it to her if I was unsure. And she didn't seem to have a problem saying it to me. It has to be something else."

"Caleb, I don't know Sarah, and I'm not going to pretend to be able to figure out what she was thinking, but from what you have explained to me, it sounds like that are a lot of moving parts going on in her life. She may be afraid and confused about a lot of things right now. Traumatic experiences like what she experienced don't just go away easily. Past emotions can get triggered easily by current circumstances. It's very similar to what you go through with your experiences with your wife and with your military career. She may be going through a period where she feels powerless to do anything."

"What am I supposed to do? Just let her keep feeling that way? I can't just sit here and let that happen to her. I have to do something to help. She needs someone right now, and it doesn't sound like she has anyone but me that she can count on."

I stood up and started pacing around Dr. Weber's office. He just looked at me from his chair, watching me walk back and forth.

"Don't you have any suggestions? I thought you were supposed to be the expert here," I barked at him.

"Caleb, I can't tell you what to do. You must make that decision for yourself. I would suggest you not do anything rash that can cause problems or upset her further so that she pushes you further away, but Sarah's not my patient. You are. I'm here to help you."

"You can help me by giving me some advice about what I should do."

"You called me because you told me you were feeling anxious and needed to talk to someone. What is it you are feeling most anxious about?"

I sat back down on the couch and thought about the question for a moment.

"I guess I'm anxious about... about losing her. It just seems like when I have someone I love in my life that I lose..." I ended my thought because I knew where it was going.

"So you worry about losing Sarah just like you lost Ella, and like you have lost people you served with."

"Yes, I do. Is there something wrong with the fact that I don't like losing people I am close to?" I yelled. I could feel myself tensing up the more the conversation carried on.

"No, there's nothing wrong with that," Dr. Weber told me calmly. "None of us like to have something like that happen, and when it happens to us once we always have the fear that it could happen again. Of course, you don't want to get hurt and relive that pain, but you must know Caleb that you're not going to go through the rest of your life never experiencing loss again. You have to learn how to deal with these feelings. Loss doesn't just come in the form of the death of a loved one. Relationships, jobs, friendships, nearly everything we experience in life can end with a loss."

"But this doesn't have to end. This is something I can change. I couldn't change what happened to Ella, but I can change this."

"Sometimes we tell ourselves that just because it makes us feel better, and so that we don't have to deal with the reality of the situation," Dr. Weber said to me.

"If you're trying to help me out, this doesn't seem to be working."

"Caleb, I'm not telling you that you should just give up on Sarah without trying to find out what happened and why. All I'm saying to you is that you have bigger issues that you need to deal with, ones that have to do more with how you see yourself and identify yourself beyond the different relationships you have in your life. Your relationships are very important to you, as they are to all of us, but they are not the only things that define who you are."

"I get that Doc, I really do, and I know that's something I need to work on. I have always found my identity that way – first through Ella, and then through the Army. When both of those were gone, I don't think I knew who I was or what to do. When Sarah came along, it made me see something more about myself. She wasn't just filling a hole for me with a relationship. She brought out something in me that I needed to come out. I can't give that up, not this easily."

"Just promise me one thing, Caleb," Dr. Weber said to me as he saw I was getting ready to leave.

"What's that?"

"That you and I will spend some more time talking about this, about talking about loss, and grieving, and coping. I think we still have a lot of ground to cover."

"I promise, I'll be back. How about Monday?" I said to him.

"Fine, give me a call and let me know when you want to meet. I'll clear some time for you. Good luck with Sarah."

"Thanks, Doc."

I left Dr. Weber's office and went back to my car. I sat behind the wheel for a moment trying to decide what to do. Going to Sarah's house wasn't going to be the answer for me. Maybe even going to the diner wouldn't be the answer. I didn't want to upset her at work and throw everything into a frenzy. I needed to give her today and a chance to sort things out better before I approached her again, and I had to have an answer, a way to help her and let her see that I would be there for her, no matter what.

Chapter 28

Sarah

2^8

The day at home couldn't pass fast enough for me. While I slept most of the morning into the early afternoon, I knew that the later part of the day was going to be unpleasant. As great as it was to see Lizzie, I found it tough to be with her as well, especially because she kept asking me what was wrong and why I looked so down. I felt so torn inside, with part of me feeling miserable because of the circumstances, and the other part of me boiling inside and wanting to do something to break free of all this. Summoning up the strength to make something happen was proving to be impossible. Without having a phone or computer I felt isolated, and even when I went to work, I didn't feel like there was much I could do to help myself. Telling people at work that my sister-in-law was trying to blackmail me might bring me sympathy and support, and I am sure they would do what they could to help me, but what trouble might that bring to them? Denise had proven to have more power than I thought, and if she was linked to Jared Sterling, there was no telling what problems they could cause for everyone.

I went through the motions at home, getting housework done and trying to figure out ways that would buy me a little time with school work until I could figure everything out. The last thing I wanted was to fall behind with all my schoolwork as well and delay finishing up school once again.

I spent the rest of the day helping Lizzie with homework and cooking dinner and doing my best to avoid Denise completely when she got home from work. James was working late, so I really felt like I had no ally at home. Dinner passed along quietly, with Lizzie trying to open up the conversation more than once, but I would give short, terse answers to her questions because Denise seemed to be watching every word that came out of my mouth.

When dinner ended, and I was cleaning up, Denise retired to her bedroom, leaving Lizzie alone with me. She came up to me as I was washing the dishes and started drying to help.

"Are you mad at me for something?" she asked me quietly.

I gave her a quick glance and went back to paying attention to the dishes.

"I'm not mad at you, Lizzie," I said, hoping the sound of the water and dishes would drown us out from anyone that might be listening.

"Then what is going on? I know things between you and my Mom are always a little tense, but you would have needed a chainsaw to cut through all that tension at dinner tonight. If there's something wrong, maybe I can help."

I turned the water pressure up a little higher, so it was louder and continued to talk softly. Maybe this would be my chance to get some help.

"I can't really get into it with you Lizzie, not here at least, but maybe... maybe you can help me."

"We can go up to my room after this to talk if you want," she suggested.

"No," I answered quickly. "Your Mom might... might notice that. I wish you could get to the diner tonight."

"I think I can," she said quietly. "There's a basketball game at the school tonight that my friends are going to, and there's no school tomorrow. I can ask Dad if I can go and then meet you at the diner so we could talk."

"That might work," I said hopefully to her as I washed the same pot for the third time as we talked.

Just then, Denise walked back out into the kitchen and Lizzie jumped back and started drying another dish.

"You aren't done with those dishes yet?" Denise asked.

"Just finishing up," I said to her without looking over at her.

"Lizzie, don't you have homework?" Denise said, turning to her daughter, hoping to get her away from me.

"There's no school tomorrow," Lizzie said respectfully.

"Well, I'm sure you could be cleaning your room or something instead of keeping Sarah from finishing the dishes." Denise's cell phone buzzed, and she looked down at it, and then quickly moved away from us and back towards her room.

I turned the faucet off and looked at Lizzie.

"I need to go get ready for work," I said to her. We both walked quietly towards the stairs.

"I'll send you a message to let you know if I'm coming," Lizzie said to me as we reached the steps.

"No, don't," I said in a hushed tone. "I... I don't have my phone. Just come if you can. I'll keep an eye out for you."

"Sarah, I'm scared for you. Maybe I should talk to Dad."

"Please don't Lizzie. That might make things worse right now. This has to be just between you and me. I'm really counting on you for help."

"Okay," Lizzie said. "Let me get in touch with my friends to see who is going to the game. I'll see you tonight."

"Thank you, Lizzie," I said to her and gave her a hug. I then raced up the stairs to get ready for work.

I put my work clothing on as fast as I could, gathered up my purse, and went down the stairs to get out of the house as fast as I could. Just as I got to the front door, Denise, stopped me.

"Leaving kind of early tonight, aren't you?" Denise questioned as she stood by the front door.

"We're going to be busy tonight, "I told her. "There's a basketball game at the school, and no school tomorrow. The place will be flooded with kids, so they need me early tonight."

Denise was looking me over to see if she could spot anything that might be out of the ordinary with me, making sure I wasn't going to try anything.

"Denise, I really need to go," I said to her, wanting to get passed her.

Denise stepped off to the side of the door, and I reached for the doorknob. Just as I was starting to turn it, she grabbed onto my hand, holding it tightly.

"Just remember our deal," Denise said with authority, making sure Lizzie was not within earshot. Denise's phone buzzed with another message, and then another before she let go of my hand and picked up her phone, walking away so she could answer her text messages.

I bolted out the front door and away from the house, wanting to get away from her quickly. The entire walk to the diner I kept thinking about what Lizzie could do to help me. If she could get to the diner, I could explain to her what was going on. I would have to tell her about her mother's affair, but that would have to be one of the consequences. Perhaps Lizzie could figure out a way to get my phone or let me use hers or her computer, so I could figure things out, or get a message to Caleb. Maybe Lizzie could message Caleb for me. At least it might let him know what the trouble is, and then we could figure something out together.

The big problem was going to be finding a way to prevent Denise or Jared from sending out those pictures. Caleb might not care that much if he got the pictures. I know he would understand about them, even if they were the profane ones Denise and Jared had doctored. The real problem would be if the pictures got to people at work, professors at school, or my family... again. I could protest as much as I wanted, saying they were fake, but there would still be talk or people that wouldn't believe me, and I don't know if I could live through that again. There had to be a way to get those pictures, find where they were kept, and get rid of them, or at least expose who made them.

I got the diner early once again, and Doug could see I was preoccupied once again. He was just getting ready to leave for the day when I walked in.

"Sarah, you're early again," he said with surprise.

"Yeah, I needed to get out of the house, and then Lizzie told me there was a game at the school tonight and no school tomorrow, so I thought we might be busy."

"Damn, I forgot about that," Doug said. "I could cancel my plans and stay to help out."

"Doug, it's fine, we can handle it. Maybe I can ask a couple of the girls if they want to stay and get some extra hours to help out? Even if we just had one on the register as hostess and an extra person to help serve, we would be fine. Fran and I can take care of the rest."

"Good idea," Doug said to me, seeming relieved he wouldn't have to cancel his plans. "I'll ask Victoria and Trina if they can stay and work. They are always looking for extra hours anyway. Thanks, Sarah."

"No problem," I said to Doug as I walked back to the break room. With extra help at the diner tonight, it would be easier for me to work and find time to talk to Lizzie if she could get here. I put my things away and said a quick hello to Justin in the kitchen.

"You seem a little better today," he said to me as I tied my apron on.

"More determined, I think," I said to him with a smile.

"That's a good thing, I think," he said with a laugh. I went out into the diner and saw that it was still the end of the dinner crowd, so we were not quite busy just yet. Victoria and Trina had both agreed to stay, ecstatic that they would get to work with a good crowd to make some extra tip money. I talked with them, formulating a plan for now and later in the night, and let them know that once things died down at around one or so if they wanted to leave it would be okay. Victoria agreed to take the hostess duty while Trina would work the dining room with Fran, and I would take the counter and smaller dining area myself.

I found ways to busy myself until it got to be about ten, and then we started to see a stream of teenagers flow into the diner. By their reactions coming in, I could tell that Swanson High had won the game, and all the kids seem to be full of energy. It wasn't long before the two main dining areas were full. It was shortly after that I saw Lizzie come in with her group of friends, including Aaron, the boy she had a crush on. She looked over at me quickly and smiled, and I moved from behind the counter over near the front where Trina was standing, trying to figure out where to seat them.

"I have two big booths open in my area, Trina if you want to put them over there," I said to her as she gathered the menus.

"Oh, great, thanks, Sarah," Trina said to me. "I didn't think I would have room for them."

Trina led them over to my section and seated them, and Lizzie made sure to sit next to Aaron but grab a seat on the outside, so she could get out easily.

"Hey guys," I said to the group with a smile. I knew Lizzie's girlfriends already, but I was not familiar with the boys. "What can I get you to drink?"

Not surprisingly, the girls all ordered diet soda and the boys regular soda.

As I was walking away to go get the sodas, I saw Trina seat another group in the booth right next to Lizzie's. In that group, I saw Adam,

Caleb's son, with his friends. They were all smiling and laughing, enjoying the fact that their school and team had won once again.

I delivered the sodas to Lizzie's table and took their orders for food, and then moved to my right over to Adam's booth.

"Hi guys," I said with a smile. "Nice to see you all tonight."

"Hi, Sarah," Adam offered, his arm around a girl still in her cheerleader uniform.

"Hi, Adam," I said, trying not to show any signs of nervousness or being upset. I didn't know what, if anything, Caleb had said to Adam, so playing it cool was my best bet.

"I take it you guys won tonight," I said to him.

"We slaughtered them," one of the other boys said. "Our boy Adam here scored thirty-two points."

"Excellent," I said, giving Adam a high-five. "What can I get you guys to drink?"

Each person placed their orders, getting mainly iced teas, and I went off to get drinks and put Lizzie's table's order in as well. I tried to concentrate on the work I was doing, moving from place to place and customer to customer, and didn't know how I would find time to talk to Lizzie at all. The counter was just as busy as the booths and juggling everything was going to be tricky tonight. On top of that, I had no idea what time James would show up to get Lizzie. I carried the drinks over to Adam's table and took their order for food. I walked behind the counter and started entering their order into the computer when I heard Lizzie say loudly that she was going to the bathroom. I turned, and my eyes followed her to the restroom, and she was nodding to me to follow her if I could.

Good girl, Lizzie, I thought to myself.

After my order was entered, I took a quick scan of the counter and saw everyone was okay, and that Fran had come behind the counter to get a pot of coffee.

"Fran," Can you cover the counter for a minute? I have to run to the ladies' room," I whispered to her.

"You got it," she said to me.

I went to the end of the counter and made the left to the short hallway that led to the restrooms. I darted into the ladies' room and found Lizzie standing by the sink waiting for me.

"We have to hurry," Lizzie said to me. "Dad said he would be here by around eleven. I asked him privately if I could come after the game, but I am sure Mom will find out. What's going on?"

I went on to explain the situation to Lizzie, including the unfortunate details about seeing her mother with another man at the restaurant, how she took my phone and computer and was blackmailing me.

"I can't believe she would do all this," Lizzie said to me. "I mean, I know you two don't get along, but I didn't think she would stoop to something like that. And what about Dad and me?"

"I know it's hard to understand Lizzie, and I wish it weren't the case, but it is. Now I need your help. We need to find a way to get a message to Caleb so that he knows the truth, and maybe he can help me."

"I can try calling him, or sending him a message, but Mom checks my phone all the time to see who I am chatting with. If she sees it, she'll know right away."

It was then that the idea dawned on me.

"Do you know Adam Wilson?" I asked Lizzie.

"The basketball player at my school? I know who he is, but we're not really friends or anything. He's a senior."

"Well he's Caleb's son, and he's sitting in the booth right next to yours. Maybe you could get him a message to give to his father."

"Sure, I can do that," Lizzie said.

"Just let him know that I have no way to get in touch with him, but that I need his help. Maybe he can meet me someplace."

"Okay," Lizzie said. "I'll let him know."

"Thanks, Lizzie," I said to her, giving her a hug again. Lizzie then walked out of the bathroom ahead of me, and I waited a few seconds before walking out myself. When I walked out of the restroom and back to the counter, I saw Lizzie standing there outside her booth with James standing next to her.

I walked over, ignoring my customers for the moment, to see what was going on.

"James, what's going on?" I asked him. I looked at Lizzie and could see she was crestfallen.

"I'm here to pick Lizzie up," James said to me.

"I can watch her for a while if you want to give her more time. It's not a problem," I said to James, hoping to buy her some time.

"I can't Sarah," James said to me. He took a step closer to me and whispered. "Denise is having a cow because she is here in the first place and only asked me if she could come. I have to get her home before she explodes."

"Come on, Lizzie," James said to her as she gathered her purse.

"This is ridiculous, Dad, and completely embarrassing!" Lizzie yelled.

James put his arm around her and started to lead her out of the diner. Lizzie turned back to me and mouthed "I'm sorry," before she walked out.

I knew now that things would likely get worse at home, not just for Lizzie but for me. Denise would automatically think something was up between the two of us and have those pictures sent out. I had to do something, and only had one last chance to do something fast.

I took out my order pad and pen and scribbled a note down on the pad. I then walked over to the booth where Adam and his friends were sitting. All eyes turned to me when I came over to the table.

"Your food should be done in a little bit," I said to the table. "Does anyone need any refills on their drinks?"

A couple of the guys asked for refills, and I took their glasses. I then proceeded to rip the note off my order pad and handed it to Adam. He seemed puzzled at first before he looked at it.

"I don't think we're done yet," one of the girls remarked to me, but I walked away from the table to get the refills, leaving the note with Adam.

I got behind the counter and filled the glasses with refills of iced tea and turned back towards the counter before bringing the drinks over. It was then I noticed that Jared was now sitting right in front of me at the diner counter.

I had to do all I could to keep from dropping the glasses on the floor.

"Hello Sarah," he said with a grin.

"I'll... I'll be with you in a moment," I said to him, hurrying over to bring the iced tea to Adam's table. I put the glasses down on the table and looked at Adam.

"Sarah..." He started to say something when I put my finger up to my lips to quiet him. Adam took the hint, nodded, and slipped the note into the inside pocket of his varsity jacket.

I went back behind the counter to try to deal with Jared.

"What can I get you?" I asked him, trying to stay professional. His body and his breath reeked of alcohol.

"Not much in the way of booze here, huh?" he said, looking at the back of the menu where the drinks were listed.

"It's a diner, Jared, not a bar," I said to him, hoping to rush him along.

"Don't get sassy with me," he said rather loudly, loud enough so that other customers at the counter a few seats away noticed.

"Just give me a beer," he said curtly. I walked over to where the cold beer was and grabbed a pilsner glass from the shelf and brought it back. I went to pour the beer into the glass when Jared just grabbed the bottle from my hand and took a swig.

"I don't need a glass," he said to me as he drank from the bottle again, draining almost half of it quickly.

"Can I get you anything to eat," I said, trying to get better control of the situation and keep things normal.

I saw Jared's eyes peer over my body up and down and his tongue gave a long lick on his top lip.

"Oh, you mean off the menu," he said with a laugh. "I wouldn't eat any swill from here," he said crudely. "I just stopped by to give you a message. I heard from Denise tonight, and she thought you might be up to something, so I told her I would come over and talk to you. I'll be glad to send those pictures out tonight."

"Jared, please, you don't have to do that," I said to him, trying to stay calm.

"Well, maybe you can convince me to not do it," he said ogling me again. "Maybe you can start by unbuttoning one of those buttons on your blouse. You're buttoned up like a nun."

"I don't think so," I said to him quietly.

"Oh, come on," he said to me. "You have never let me have a peek, even back in college." Jared leaned over the counter, reaching with his hands towards me. Within seconds, I saw him go flying back off his seat onto the floor.

"I don't think you should be doing that," Adam yelled to him as he stood over Jared.

Jared laughed from his position on the floor.

"Go take a seat, junior. This doesn't concern you."

Jared went to stand back up, and Adam pushed him down again. All eyes were now on what was going on, and I could see already that Trina had picked up the phone and was dialing 911 from the front register station.

"Adam, don't," I said to him. Adam had turned to look at me as I spoke, and two seconds later Jared was up, throwing a punch that landed hard on Adam's midsection, doubling him over. Jared laughed, but Adam rebounded quickly and jumped on Jared, locking his head in a headlock and wrestling him to the floor.

Within seconds, the police were bursting through the front door and grabbed Jared and Adam, separating them. One officer had turned Adam around, cuffing him quickly, while the other did the same to Jared. They whisked both out the door and into their respective police cars while another officer came in to get details about what happened. Half the diner was looking out the windows at the police cars while the other officer was speaking with Trina about what happened.

I tried to contain myself, hoping to calm myself down and figure out what to do. The officer, Officer Hernandez, who had come to the diner often, came to speak with me. He was a kind man who brought me into the back break room so he could speak with me.

I gave him the details of what had happened, explaining that Jared had come in, obviously drunk, and was making inappropriate remarks and threateningly moved towards me. It was then that Adam jumped in and moved him away and the fight broke out.

"Well, we'll have to take them both in and sort it out. Do you want to press charges against him?" Officer Hernandez asked me.

I thought about it for a minute, considering the consequences of what I would do.

"Yes," I said strongly.

"Okay," he said to me. "We'll be in touch with you. You may want to think about getting a restraining order against him to keep him away from you. At least then if he shows up again, we can have a good reason to hold him. You know how it goes with the Sterling family. Their lawyer will probably have him out in a few hours."

"Thank you," I said to Officer Hernandez as he walked out of the break room. I followed him out, so I was back behind the counter. I tried to shake off what had happened and not worry too much about how I had just sealed my fate.

The booth where Adam's friends were had cleared out, no doubt to go home or find out more about what was going on. I went over to the booth where Lizzie's friends were sitting and asked them if they were okay.

"That was kind of scary," one of the girls said to me.

"Yeah, it was, but thankfully, that's over," I said to them. "Let me get you guys some refills and find out about getting you some food."

I turned and went back to get refill sodas behind the counter. I was refilling glasses when I heard a voice behind me.

"Sarah?" the voice asked quietly. I turned around Aaron was standing there.

"What's up?" I said to him as I kept filling glasses.

"What should I do with this?" he said to me.

I turned around to look at him. Aaron was there holding a cell phone.

"What is that?" I asked him.

"It fell out of that drunk guy's pocket when he hit the floor," Aaron said to me. "It had slid under our table. I didn't pick it up until after all the commotion."

It was Jared's cell phone that Aaron was holding in his hand.

"I'll take care of it," I said to Aaron as I took the phone and slipped it into my pants pocket.

Chapter 29

Caleb

2 [9]

After my visit with Dr. Weber, I went back to my apartment and crashed. The last day or so had been draining on me and I knew I needed some rest, especially if I was going to need my wits about me to figure out what the next best step was to take with Sarah.

By the time I pried my eyes open, it was well past six, and I had slept the day away. I rolled out of bed, barely even having the energy to go into the bathroom to shave and shower. I decided I needed to do it anyway, thinking it might make me feel better, but it did little to boost my spirits. Once I was done with everything and got dressed, I decided to make myself a sandwich to tide me over since I had slept so long.

While I munched away on a chicken salad on rye, I checked my phone to see if there was anything at all from Sarah. Once again, no calls and no messages showed up. I did see a text message from Adam, reminding me of his game tonight if I wanted to go. Going to the game seemed like a good distraction for me, and I decided I would go over and cheer him on.

I arrived at the school just in time for the tipoff and got myself a good seat to watch the action. Swanson completely overmatched their opponent tonight, the high school from Garrett High School not too far away. Adam was a real star tonight, racking up over thirty points and making nearly every shot he took. Winning this game clinched their conference title for them, and the crowd went nuts as the final buzzer sounded and Swanson had won the game handily.

I waited outside the school for Adam, making sure to send him a text message that I was here if he was looking for me. Adam came walking out with his friends, including his cheerleader girlfriend. I waved to him when I saw him, and instead of walking over to me by himself, he waved me over to him.

I walked over and stood in front of his friends, two other guys and what I assume were their girlfriends. They all got quiet when I arrived over there, watching to see what I would say and do.

"Great game tonight," I said to Adam proudly.

"Thanks, Dad," Adam replied. "Dad, this is my girlfriend, Ashley." The girl politely extended her hand to me to shake.

"It's nice to meet you, Mr. Wilson," she said with a smile.

"It's nice to meet you too," I replied.

"And this is Jack, and Felicity, and Preston, and Lisa," Adam said, pointing out the rest of his friends.

They all said hellos and seemed like nice kids. They stood around looking at each other, waiting for someone to decide what to do next.

"We're going to head over to the diner to celebrate," Adam said to me. "Are you going over there?"

As much as I wanted to say yes, I knew that I couldn't.

"No, why don't you guys go ahead and celebrate. I think I am going to just head home and crash, maybe watch some TV," I said to Adam. I started to walk away when Adam came over to me.

"Dad, is everything okay?" he asked me. "How come you aren't going to see Sarah? She should be there."

"Sarah and I... she just wanted a little space right now, I guess," I said to Adam.

"I'm sorry Dad," Adam said. He took a quick look back at his friends and then at me. "If you want, I can just come and hang out with you if you don't want to be by yourself."

"No, you go hang out with your friends and have fun. I'll be okay Adam, really."

"Okay," Adam replied, not really believing me. "I'll send you a text when I'm on my way home."

"Thanks, bud," I said to him. "Have fun."

Adam jogged back over to his friends and then walked over to where their cars were parked. I went back to my Jeep, got behind the wheel and headed back home, taking my time to get there since I had nothing really to do for the night. I even took a slow drive passed the Moonlight, and I could see the place was crowded with cars and teenagers everywhere.

I resisted the temptation to go in and see Sarah and instead worked my way back to the house.

I went up to the apartment, opened a bag of corn chips that I probably never should have bought and flipped on the sports channel to see what was going on today. They had a game on that I didn't really pay much attention to. When I was overseas, it was a big thrill to get to listen to a ball game on the radio or, even more rarely see one on TV someplace. Now it didn't seem nearly as special as it used to be to me.

It was a little after eleven when I thought about switching the TV off and calling it a night. No sooner had I turned off the TV than my cell phone was ringing. I thought maybe it would be Adam letting me know he was on his way home, but the number came up as an Unknown Name.

"Hello?" I answered, wondering who it could be.

"Dad?" I heard Adam's voice, but he sounded different.

"What's up? Why aren't you calling from your phone?"

"Dad, I'm at the police station," Adam said with a slight crack in his voice.

"What's wrong?" I asked with a panic. "Are you okay?"

"Sort of," he said to me. "There was a fight at the diner, and, well, the police took me in."

"You got arrested?" I said in disbelief.

"Well... no... I mean, I don't know what's going on. They told me I could call you though."

"Alright, I'll be down there in a few minutes. Just hold on."

"Thanks, Dad," Adam answered, and then I heard the phone disconnect.

I pulled my sneakers on, grabbed my keys and was out the door fast. On my way down to the Jeep, I pushed dial on my phone and called Linda.

"Are you checking up on me?" Linda said jokingly.

"Linda, I need your help," I said urgently.

"What's the matter?" she said, sensing my panic.

"Adam is down at the police station. He said there was a fight at the diner and they brought him in. That's all I know. I'm on my way there now."

"I'm leaving right now," Linda said to me. "I'll make a call over there and see what I can find out before I get there. Caleb, just keep calm and don't lose your temper, okay?"

"I'll be fine," I said to her as I backed out of the driveway. "See you there."

I hung up and swung the jeep down the street. I hadn't gotten very far before I realized I wasn't even sure where the police station was in Swanson. I pulled over to the side of the road to look it up on my phone and then let my GPS guide me the rest of the way there. It was further up towards where the college was located, so it took me a little longer to get there than I would have liked. I finally found it and pulled into the parking lot to park my car. I raced into the building, and up to the front desk, and said I was Adam's father and wanted to see him.

"He's in with his attorney now, Mr. Wilson," the desk sergeant said to me. "They should be done shortly, and then you can see him."

I took a seat on one of the benches located just beyond the front desk and tried to wait patiently. I had hoped Adam wasn't hurt, and I pitied the person that may have been involved that hurt him. All kinds of scenarios ran through my head about what I would like to do, and none of them were very pleasant. Most were properly illegal in some way.

It took about ten minutes of impatient waiting before I asked again and was told to just have a seat. More than two hours later, the door opened, and I saw Linda walking out with her arm around Adam. I ran over to them and met them as they were coming down the hallway.

"Adam, are you okay?" I said quickly.

"I'm fine Dad, there's nothing wrong. I just have a scratch on my head from when I hit the floor." Adam reached up and rubbed the scratch that marked his forehead.

"What the hell happened?" I asked as we walked out of the building.

"He got into a fight with one of the other patrons of the diner," Linda said before Adam could say anything.

"Why would you get into a fight?" I asked, feeling a bit upset now.

"Dad, let me explain. The guy was more than rude to Sarah. He was saying nasty things and tried to put his hands on her, so I pulled him away and then he hit me. After that, we ended up on the floor before the cops came."

I was trying to process everything that was happening, and then Linda added more to it.

"I talked to everyone involved, including the other guy's attorney, and they aren't going to press any charges if we don't press any charges. Adam walks away with a clean record," Linda said.

"So, this guy gets away with assaulting Sarah and Adam? That doesn't seem right. Who was it?"

"Caleb, promise me you are not going to fly off the handle about this. Adam is a lot easier to get out of trouble than you will be," Linda said as she tried to calm me down.

"Who was it, Linda?"

"It was Jordan Sterling."

"The same Sterling family? Are you serious?" I couldn't believe we were dealing with this family yet again.

"Yes, he's Brandon's cousin. The cops cut him loose too, but he had to get released on a bond. I guess Sarah wants to press charges against him. Good for her," Linda said to me.

"Jordan Sterling? A weasely looking guy with blond hair?"

"That's him," Adam said to me.

"I saw him when we went to Peter's for dinner. He was outside hassling Sarah. She told me to just leave it alone." I thought back to when I confronted him the parking lot.

"Well I guess they know each other," Linda said to me. "Are you two all settled here now that you both ruined my date tonight?"

"I'm sorry Aunt Linda," Adam said to her, giving her a hug. When they broke the hug, Adam turned to me as he reached into his jacket pocket.

"Dad, I forgot, Sarah gave me this. I'm supposed to give it to you."

Adam handed me a folded piece of paper. I unfolded it and saw it was a sheet from her order pad, and I began to read what she wrote:

Caleb,

Know that I would never leave things that way with you without a good reason. I've run into some trouble here and at home and can use your help. This is the only way I can get in touch with you. Please come to see me at the Moonlight when you can.

Love,

Sarah

I folded the note and stuffed it into my jeans pocket.

"Linda," I said turning to her, "Can you give Adam a ride home?"

"I guess so since my date is over now," she said to me with a huff. "Where are you going?"

"I need to get over to the Moonlight, now."

Chapter 30

Sarah

I t wasn't much longer after all the hubbub at the diner that Doug showed up to see what had happened. He had an immediate concern about the staff and me, making sure that we were okay. He spent some time talking with me to find just what occurred, and I felt I had to be honest with him and give him all the details, past and present, so he wouldn't be surprised by anything. After I finished telling him everything in the privacy of the small office he had behind the kitchen, I didn't quite know what to expect.

"Doug," I said to him, "I'll understand if you want me to leave. I don't want to bring problems or bad publicity to you and your business with all this mess. Tonight will probably be in the newspaper somewhere, and if those pictures get out, well it might get worse for you."

"Sarah," Doug told me, looking straight into my eyes, "I don't want you to leave. None of this is your fault or doing. If we get some bad press from it, so what. If there are people that care about nonsense like that instead of the truth, well they can go somewhere else. You're one of the best people I know, not just one of the best employees I have ever had. You'll always have a place here if you want it as long as I own the Moonlight."

"Thank you," I told him, feeling deeply touched by what he had said to me.

I sat back in the chair I was in and let out a big sigh, resting my head back on the top of the chair.

Doug looked at the clock and saw it was two-thirty in the morning.

"Why don't you go home?" Doug said to me. "It's been a tough night for you. You look like you could use a break."

I wasn't sure if going home was really going to be the best answer for me since I knew that Denise was likely waiting for me at this point. Once she found out that Jared had been arrested and I was willing to press charges against him, she would push him to send out the pictures, and I would have to deal with the fallout from all of it. Even with all of that, I did feel spent from everything that had happened, and I knew I wouldn't be able to concentrate much on work. I still had hope that Adam would give Caleb my message and he would show up, but there is no way to know when or if he would be here.

"Thanks, Doug," I said to him as I stood up from the chair. "I think I will knock off early if it's okay with you. I'm pretty drained by everything."

"Not a problem," he said to me. "Things have quieted down enough where I think Fran could handle it for the rest of the night. Give me a call tomorrow and let me know how you are and if you think you can make it in. I want to make sure you are okay. If you need anything, you just let me know."

I left Doug's office, went to the breakroom to gather my things, and got ready to leave. I walked out into the diner and saw there were just a few patrons in here now, and Fran was taking care of it all like a pro. I saw her waiting on the tables and gave her a quick wave to let her know I was leaving and she smiled and winked at me.

I stepped out into the night and the quiet of Swanson. Nothing was going on in the town at this time of the night/morning, making my footsteps on the sidewalk the only sound I could hear as I went along Oak Street. My mind kept flashing back to what had happened, and then I remembered that I had Jared's phone in my pocket. That phone was probably my ace card since it more than likely had texts between Jared and Denise on it. I had to make sure I could get a look at what was on the phone to see if there was anything I could use to help myself.

I patted my pants pocket to make sure I had still had the phone in there and felt a little better about things as soon as I knew it was there. I turned off Oak Street and made my way down the darker streets towards the house. The street lights were few and far between on these blocks, and the residences that were here were all dark for the night, making the only light available the slim glimmer from the moonlight.

I could see the shadows of my house looming down the street not too far away, and I picked up my pace to try to get there quicker. Suddenly, out of nowhere, a car came up the street, blinding me with its headlights.

I put my hand up to shade my eyes from the glaring light on my face, as the car came to a stop at the curb right near me. All I could see was a brief shadow moving towards me, and once my vision cleared, I could see that the shadow was Jared's.

I turned in the other direction and started to run, and I could hear his footsteps moving faster behind me as he was gaining on me. Within seconds, he was on me, tackling me and pushing me onto the lawn of one of the nearby homes. Jared turned me over and immediately clamped a hand over my mouth so I couldn't scream for help.

"You're really making me have a bad night, Sarah," Jared said to me. I could see his face clearly, with a menacing look on it framed by the halo of the streetlight across the street. He had clearly been drinking more than before, and he had a wild look in his eyes that sent fear coursing through my body.

I struggled beneath him as he pressed himself against me tightly to keep me from moving away or fighting back.

"Where's my phone, Sarah?" he asked me. "I noticed I didn't have it when I got to the police station, and I was just back at the diner looking for it, and no one there had it. I know you must have it."

I shook my head no, telling him I didn't have it and hoping he would just get up and go.

"Is it in your bag?" he asked, getting louder and more demanding. "Or do you have it on you?"

Again, I shook my head, more frantically this time, because I knew he was likely to start looking for it himself.

I saw Jared reach into his back pocket and he then revealed, in his right hand, a long, thin-bladed knife. The steel blade of the knife reflected in the street light.

Jared pressed his body tightly against me again, this time bringing the blade up to just beneath my chin. I could feel the cold blade pressing on my throat, causing me to freeze the wriggling I had been doing to try to get away from him.

"If you don't admit you have it, I guess I'm going to have to look for it," he said with a sinister smile. While his right hand held the blade against my throat, I felt him reach down and pat the pocket of my pants. Luckily for me, the phone was in my pocket on the other side, but it would just be a matter of time before he switched.

"You know, you probably could have avoided all this long ago if you had just agreed to go out with me back in college," he said as he pawed up and down my right leg. "Maybe then I wouldn't have to put those cameras in your room in the first place. It was the only way I was ever going to get to see you I guess. I had to settle for your sister-in-law instead, but I never thought I would get the chance to do more pictures of you. That was quite a treat for me, almost as much fun as this is now. Nothing in this pocket here. I guess I need to check somewhere else."

I could feel Jared's left hand start to unbutton my blouse. He had gotten the first button undone and was working on the second when I knew I had to do something. Instinctively, I moved my right knee up as fast as I could, catching him right in the groin and causing him to scream out in pain. I was able to push him off me, and I tried to scramble up from the ground and run. I had only taken one step when I felt Jared's hand reach out and trip me, causing me to hit the ground. I felt my head hit the soft, damp grass with a thud.

My head was spinning and ringing as I tried to focus, but Jared was back on top of me again.

"You bitch!" He hissed at me. "It's time to show you who's boss."

I wanted to scream out, but I couldn't get a clear focus on what to do or how to make my mouth work right. I squirmed to try to get away from Jared as I felt him kneel on top of me, trying to get more clothing from me. I looked up at him and could see him smiling at me as he stood up over me, working to undo his pants. Everything was moving in slow motion and was almost dreamlike. At one moment Jared was wrestling with his belt, and then there was a shadow behind him that tossed him away.

I closed my eyes and opened them again and looked to my left. Jared was scrambling to his feet, and Caleb was standing over me to protect me. I moved back, shuffling my body with the palms of my hands, to move away from them.

Jared stood there, unsteady on his feet, wielding his knife while Caleb watched his every movement.

"You again," Jared spat at Caleb. "You always seem to be spoiling my fun lately. I think it's time to end that."

Jared lunged towards Caleb with the knife, and I finally heard a scream leave my throat. The next sound I heard was an ungodly crunching sound. Caleb had ducked under the move by Jared and swept his leg so that it struck Jared's hard. The crunching sound was bone breaking in and around Jared's right knee as he crumpled to the ground. Jared let a loud wail out as he lay on the grass, clutching his knee that was now bent well out of its natural position.

Even in all his pain, Jared still went to grab the knife that was next to his hand. He reached for the knife, and Caleb quickly kicked it away and then stomped hard on his hand, sending another piercing scream through the air as Jared's fingers broke. I saw Caleb walk over and pick up the knife and he knelt next to Jared's quivering body. I could hear Jared crying now, and it sounded like he was pleading for his life.

I could see that Caleb was remaining calm and collected, not even breathing heavy, but I could also see something in his eyes – a look that let Jared know he was willing to do whatever he had to so that this ended. I saw Caleb shift the knife in his hands, bringing it closer to Jared's throat now.

"Caleb, don't," I whispered out, and he looked back towards me and into my eyes. Caleb stood up and folded up the knife, tucking it into his sock. He then came over to me and hugged me, holding me tight.

"Are you alright?" he said into my ear. Caleb moved back to get a look at me, moving the hair out my face and wiping some dirt off me.

"I'm okay," I said, tears in my eyes and caught in my throat as I tried to hold back the emotions I was feeling.

Two police cars had come screaming up the street and came to screeching halt, flashing their lights all around us. Obviously, someone had heard the screams and called 911 for help. I was able to make out Officer Hernandez as he came over to Caleb and me, making sure I was okay. Two other officers were over by Jared, calling for an ambulance.

It took several officers some time to sort everything out as they inter-viewed Caleb, me, and the resident who had called the police and lived in the house that had the lawn where all of this took place. The police tried to get some sort of statement from Jared, and through all his crying and wailing from the pain he was in they were not able to get much. However, they had enough from me that they were planning on arresting Jared on several charges, not the least of which was the assault he had done to me.

The EMTs on the scene checked me out to make sure there was nothing wrong with me. I had some bumps, bruises, and scrapes, mainly the one on my head from where I had hit the ground, but it was nothing severe. Still, as a precaution, they decided to take me to the hospital to make sure I didn't have a concussion, and I was okay.

Caleb followed along in his car and waited for me while doctors examined me and police interviewed me more to get more details about what had happened. I let them know what Jared had said and done, including his admission that he was the one that had placed the cameras in my dorm room years ago and distributed the pictures of me. While the officers weren't sure about that statute of limitations on something like that, the police felt they had more than enough evidence to convict him on a variety of charges now that not even his family's high-priced lawyer could talk his way out of.

It was hours before I was cleared by the doctors so that I could leave, and Caleb was finally allowed to come to see me so that he could take me home. Without saying a word, he put his arm around me and led me out of the hospital and to his Jeep. We went straight to his apartment, where he led me up the stairs and into his apartment.

Caleb took me to his bedroom, handing me one of his t-shirts to wear as I stripped out of the work clothes I had on that were stained and slightly torn. Once I had the t-shirt on, Caleb had me lay down on his bed, and he pulled the blankets over me. My body felt relaxed for the first time in a while. I felt Caleb lean down and kiss me on the head, letting his kiss linger there for a while.

Caleb got up from the bed and went to walk out of the room. I peeked my eyes open to look at him.

"Where are you going?" I asked softly.

"I was going to lay down on the couch," Caleb said to me. "I thought maybe you wanted some space after the night you had."

"Please," I said to him. "Please stay with me."

Caleb came back into the room and crawled into bed with me, wrapping his arms around me and holding me close to him.

I pressed myself even closer to him, not wanting him to let go of me again.

"Thank you, Caleb," I whispered, no longer able to choke back the tears. "Thank you for coming back for me."

Caleb just kissed me lightly on the head again, and we lay there with each other. I felt safe, being back where I knew I belonged.

Chapter 31

Caleb

After spending hours at the police station getting Adam out of there, and then spending hours with the police again, on the scene and at the hospital, I just wanted all the interrogation to be over with. I get that the police were concerned about how much damage I did to Jordan Sterling in a short amount of time, but he was a physically assaulting Sarah when I got to the scene and was threatening me as well. I reacted the way I had to so that I could make sure Sarah was safe. If Sarah had not been there, I am not sure what the outcome would have been.

There was a lot of rage building up inside me, not just for what he had done to Sarah and what he might have done had I not arrived when I did, but I was angry for what he had done to my family. He had assaulted Adam and essentially walked away without any consequences. And then there was the family connection to Ella's death and what they had gotten away with there, simply throwing money at it to make it go away. I wanted revenge in some way, even if it seemed petty and wrong.

I stayed with Sarah all night, doing whatever I could to comfort her and make her feel better. She slept soundly in my arms, and I awoke well before she did in the morning. I made sure to send a message to Linda and Adam to let them know we were safe. I gave Linda some of the details of what had occurred in case the need arose for me to have a lawyer. The police indicated that there wouldn't be any charges against me since I was protecting myself and Sarah, and there was overwhelming evidence against Jared Sterling, but I wanted to cover my bases.

After sending my messages and speaking with Linda on my phone, I went back into the bedroom to see Sarah stretching out on the bed. She was yawning and flexing her muscles, apparently feeling a little sore from the experience of last night.

"How are you feeling?" I said to her as I sat down on the bed next to her.

"I'm pretty achy, and my head hurts some, but other than that, I think I am okay," Sarah said to me. She reached over and took my hand in hers, running her fingers over mine.

"Maybe you want to take a nice, hot shower," I suggested to her as I brushed some hair from her eyes with my free hand.

"That sounds perfect," she said to me with a smile.

"I'll get it started for you," I told her, rising from the bed and going into the bathroom to get the water started. I went in and turned on the water, making it as hot as I could so it was tolerable and came back to the bedroom. Sarah was standing up by then, still dressed in just a t-shirt and pair of pale blue panties.

"Shower's going whenever you are ready," I said to her.

I watched as she reached for the hem of the t-shirt and grimaced a bit as she tried to lift it. I walked over to her and slowly lifted the shirt over her head. She did grunt slightly as she straightened her arms over her head to get the shirt off.

I tossed the shirt to the floor and took a quick look at her back and shoulder. She had a sizeable dark purple bruise running from her shoulder down towards the middle of her back.

"That's going to hurt for a while," I said to Sarah, trying not to touch it to hurt her.

Sarah went into the bathroom so she could look at her back in the mirror. I could see her tracing the bruise with her fingertips, wincing when she pressed on it. She looked back at me from the bathroom, Covering up her breasts lightly with her one hand.

"I'm going to shower," she said as she went to close the door.

"Just holler if you need anything," I said to her. She gave me a shy smile before closing the door.

I went out into the kitchen and started the coffee pot to make some coffee, and then realized Sarah might want something to change into. All the clothes I had would be too big for her, and Adam was much taller than her as well. I figured Linda would be close and shot her another message asking if she had a pair of sweats that Sarah could borrow to change into. Linda gave me the direction of where to find them in the house, and I ran over and grabbed a pair of sweats and a pair of black shorts so that Sarah could have the choice of what she might want to wear.

When I got back to the apartment, the shower was still going. I am sure Sarah was hoping to relax some and let the hot water help with some of the aches in her muscles. I folded the clothes I got from Sarah and a couple of t-shirts for her to choose from on the chair and laid them there. Sarah walked out of the bathroom with one of the towels wrapped around her body, over her chest.

"That shower helped a lot," she said to me. "My body feels much better." She walked right up to me, standing in front of me in her towel.

"I borrowed some sweats and shorts from Linda if you want to change into them," I said to her, pointing to the clothes on the chair but finding it hard to take my eyes off her.

"Thank you," she told me. Sarah lifted her right hand and gently ran it across the stubble on my chin.

"Oh, it's no big deal, I just thought you'd be more comfortable..." Sarah placed her index finger on my lips.

"Not just for the clothes," she said to me. "For everything. For watching out for me, for helping me, for caring about me even after the way I left things, for saving my life. I've never had someone in my life like that before, or that I've felt this way about before."

Sarah stood up on her tiptoes and gave me a soft kiss on the lips. As she started to pull away from me. I bent closer to her to kiss her again.

"Sarah," I said to her, "I know what it's like to be in a relationship that is special, and I know when it feels right to me. This, what we have had, even in just this short period of time, is right. I didn't think I could feel this way about anyone else in my life, but I was wrong. I know how I felt before you came into my life, and just the thought of you being out of it, even for just a day or two, made me miserable. You've made my life better in more ways than I can express."

Sarah threw her arms around my neck and kissed me deeply once again, this time letting the kiss linger. I could feel her moving my body closer to the bed until I couldn't maintain my balance anymore and fell back onto the bed, with Sarah on top of me. We both laughed and went back to kissing, and Sarah's towel had fallen open, leaving her damp body pressing against my clothed one.

"Someone is a little overdressed," Sarah remarked.

She began to slide her body down mine, coming to rest between my legs and pulling my shorts down all the way. She twirled the shorts on her index finger, smiling at me as she did before she flung them across the room. Sarah then dragged her fingernails up my legs, starting at my calves and going all the way up to the tops of my thighs, giving me chills. She then stretched her arms up, pushing her hands under my t-shirt and gliding her palms over my chest, feeling my muscles beneath her while letting her breasts move over my rock-hard erection. I put my head back on the pillow beneath me and groaned.

Sarah had also tossed her towel onto the floor by now, and I could feel her body slowly sliding up and down against mine. She knelt between my legs, looking down at me, and I looked up to see just how beautiful she looked to me. Everything from the way her wet hair curled and hung down to her shoulders, to the small dimple she had in her right cheek as she smiled at me, to every curve and contour of her body drew me to her.

I felt Sarah slowly draw her index finger from my waist up and over my shaft, sending a surge of electricity through my body. I could feel myself draw in my breath through my teeth as she teased me this way over and over until I couldn't take it anymore.

"Sarah," I growled to her, "I don't how much more I can take."

"I guess I should stop teasing then," she cooed.

Sarah shifted her body closer to me, slowly lowering herself down on top of me and enveloping me easily. I could hear her let out a slight moan as I slipped deeper into her, and she began to rock her hips gently on me. I moved my hands to her hips, feeling each movement she took on me so that I could move with her perfectly. I quick glance up at her revealed her eyes were closed and she seemed to be relishing each motion as much as I was.

Sarah's movements became faster, and her hands clawed their way back and forth over my body while my grip on her hips became tighter and more controlled. I was barely holding on at this point and was thrusting to meet her as she moved, rotating her hips, squeezing down on me, until both of our movements and breathing reached a fevered pitch. Sarah pushed down on me and gasped loudly, and the surge caused me to thrust one last time upward before I felt her orgasm roll through her body. The sensation was all I needed to cause me to go over the edge myself, and I heard myself moan as I pulled Sarah closer to me, holding her body flush against mine.

We kissed over and over as the delight slowly subsided, and it seemed I could not get close enough to her, wanting to hold her there with me forever. After the endless kisses, Sarah peered down at me with a smile on her face.

"That is how every day should begin," she said to me with a laugh.

"You'll get no arguments from me," I replied to her.

Sarah slid off to my side so that she could lay next to me and rested her head on my shoulder.

"Can we just stay here and not deal with the rest of what's going on?" she said to me, planting a kiss on my shoulder.

"We can stay here," I told her, "but that's not going to make the other stuff go away."

I turned to look at her, and I could see she had a pained look on her face just at the thought of dealing with all the trouble brought on by Jared Sterling and her sister-in-law.

"I know," she said. "I'm just not sure how to take care of all of this now."

I heard a distinct beep come from somewhere in the room.

"Was that your phone?" I asked her, picking up mine and seeing that I had no messages.

"I don't have my phone," Sarah said to me. "Denise swiped it and my computer when all this started." She then bolted up in the bed.

"Where are my pants from last night?" she said to me as she hopped out of bed.

"Over there on the chair," I said as I pointed to the chair in the corner of my room.

Sarah went over and reached into the pants pocket and pulled out a cell phone.

"Whose phone is that?" I asked her.

"It's Jared's," she said to me as she looked at the phone. "He dropped it at the diner when he was fighting with Adam. One of the kids picked it up and gave it to me. It was what he was looking for when he came after me last night."

Sarah sat down on the bed next to me and looked at the screen. She swiped up to access the phone, and it asked for the passcode to sign in. I could see her brain kick into high gear as she tried to think about how to get into the phone.

She typed in a simple 123456, and it allowed her to get in easily. Sarah smiled and laughed as she looked over at me.

"Jared's not so smart, and pretty lazy," she said as she scanned for where his messages were. Once Sarah found them, she showed the screen to me. There was a message to him from Denise:

Where the hell are you? I know something's up & I need you to send out those pictures ASAP!!

Sarah started scanning back through the message history between Jared and Denise.

"I'm sure Denise has been much more discreet and makes sure to erase her messages," Sarah said to me. "Jared, I guess, doesn't care nearly as much. There are messages between the two of them on here going back for months, and pictures of Denise and of the two of them together."

"Well, that's all you should need to show to your brother," I told her. "He can see the evidence for himself."

Sarah started looking at other parts of Jared's phone to see what else was on there.

"What are you looking for?" I asked her as she started pacing around the room as she looked at his phone.

"If Jared's not smart enough to lock his phone or delete his messages, I'm betting he has access to the pictures of me on his phone somewhere."

After a few seconds of flipping around from screen to screen, Sarah stopped pacing and looked up at me.

"He has them all on the cloud here on his phone," she told me. "He must have put them there so he could access them fast if he wanted to. Based on the message Denise sent, she doesn't have access to them. It's just him."

Sarah sat back down next to me, holding the phone.

"I could just delete them from the cloud right now, and they'll be gone," she said as she turned to look at me.

I could see her hand hovering over the screen. With just one push she could send them all to the trash.

"Sarah," I said to her, taking her hand, "You may not want to do that. That's evidence that the police can use against him, and against Denise. I know you don't want anyone else to see them, and you worry about it, but deleting them will weaken your case against him. We have to give this to the police."

"Caleb, these pictures have caused me nothing but grief for years now," Sarah said, her voice trembling.

"I know," I told her, putting my arm around her.

"I don't know if I could deal with... with more people seeing them, with a court case where they are used as evidence for even more people to see. It's too much."

"Listen to me," I said to her gently, "You are strong enough to do this. Think about all you have done just in the last twenty-four hours compared to how scared you were in the past. You've left that other person behind now, Sarah. You know those pictures are faked, and the old ones were taken illegally. You have nothing to be ashamed or embarrassed about, and if people don't want to believe you, then fuck them, who cares. And I'm here with you, no matter what. Do the right thing."

Sarah stared at the phone for a minute, trying to decide what to do, before looking back at me. She placed the phone down on the nightstand and hugged me, holding me close to her.

"Before we bring it to the police," she said to me, "We have something to do with it."

"What do you want to do?" I asked her.

Sarah stood up from the bed.

"Get dressed," she said to me as she walked over to the chair.

Sarah picked up her clothing and began to dress herself.

"We're going back to my house," she said with conviction.

Chapter 32

Sarah

I didn't want to waste any time on getting over to the house. Denise was more than likely there since I couldn't believe she would try to contact Jared Sterling while she was in her office and risk someone seeing or asking about it. It was still early in the afternoon, but Lizzie was going to be home, and I wasn't sure I wanted her to be there when all hell broke loose, because that was what more than likely was going to happen.

We got into Caleb's Jeep to drive over to the house, but before we pulled away, I asked Caleb if I could borrow his phone. I knew it would only take us a few minutes to get to the house, but I wanted to try to get in touch with James and see if I could get him to come home sooner than he normally would so he could be there as well.

I called James' cell phone, but it went to voicemail after just a few rings, so I left him a message.

"James," I said to him, trying to have a controlled voice, "It's Sarah. I don't have my cell, but as soon as you get this can you come to the house or give me a call at this cell number? It's Caleb's phone, but we'll know it's you if you call. I'll be at the house to meet you. Thanks."

I passed the phone back to Caleb, and he nodded and smiled at me as he began the drive over. I clutched Jared's cell phone in my hand like it was the most important thing in my life right now. My mind raced, trying to figure out the best way to confront Denise about all this and get her to see that this was all over.

As we got closer to the house, I took out Jared's phone and looked at the messages again. I decided to see if I could give Denise a false sense of security and answered the last message she sent to Jared about sending out the pictures:

I'm on it.

I sent the message to Denise, and she sent back a message that was simply an evil grin emoji.

"What a bitch," I said out loud as we pulled into the driveway.

"What?" Caleb said to me as he parked the car.

"Never mind," I told him as I climbed out of the car and slammed the door shut. "You'll see for yourself in a minute."

I strode up the walkway and as we arrived at the front door, I grabbed Caleb's hand and held it tightly, and then took a deep breath before opening the door. I marched down the hall, figuring Denise was either in the kitchen or sunning herself on the back porch. Sure enough, she was laying out on the porch in a lounge chair, wearing the gaudy floral bathing suit she bought before traveling to a conference in the Bahamas last year. In hindsight, maybe there was no conference at all, and she was with Jared.

I opened the door to the back porch and stepped out. Denise peered at me from over her sunglasses and then sat up in the lounge chair.

"Well look what the cat dragged in?" she said to me. "That was sly of you to try to get Lizzie to come to your aid last night, but as soon as I found out she was going there, I put a stop to it. So now, you are screwed. Get ready to have your pictures splashed all over the place."

"What are you talking about?" I said to her calmly, clutching the cell phone in my shorts pocket.

"As we speak, Jared is sending out the pictures to everyone you know, and maybe to a lot of people you don't. I'm sure those pictures will turn up in all sorts of places. You may as well start packing now to find a place to go. You'll never be able to show your face around here again. In fact, pack anyway, I'm tired of having you in this house."

Denise sat back in her chair and smugly sipped her iced tea.

"How do you know Jared is sending out the pictures?" I asked her.

"I sent him a message asking him to send them out, and he said he would," she told me. "For a college girl, you're not so bright. No wonder you're only a waitress."

I pulled the cell phone out of my pocket and looked at the screen and started reading aloud.

Where the hell are you? I know something's up & I need you to send out those pictures ASAP!!

I'm on it.

Denise took her sunglasses off and tossed them on the table next to her.

"How did you know that?" she asked, now wondering what was going on. I saw her look over my shoulder and turned to see what she was looking at. I could see Caleb standing in the doorway to the porch.

"What's he doing here?" Denise said, raising her voice. "How did you know about that message?"

"Jared stopped by the diner last night," I said to her as I held the phone up to her. "He forgot to take his phone with him when he left. I don't think he'll be needing it for a while anyway. He'll be in the hospital for a while before they take him to jail for assault, attempted rape, extortion, DWI, and probably a half-dozen other charges."

Denise sat there staring at me, unsure whether to believe me or what she should do next. I decided to make the next move myself.

"Funny thing about Jared's phone," I said to her as I looked down at the screen. "He doesn't seem to care too much about phone security, and he sure likes to save things – like messages and pictures."

I held up the phone to Denise so she could see the picture displayed of her and Jared, barely dressed, together in a bed somewhere.

"You two certainly have some racy conversations," I told her. "And some not very nice things to say about me, your daughter, and your husband."

Denise stood up and tried to snatch the phone from my hand, but I pulled it away and put it in my pocket. Caleb came over to stand by me while I faced Denise now.

"What do you plan to do with that?" Denise said, suddenly sounding meeker than she had before.

"Well, I do have one thing in mind to do with it before I turn it over to the police," I said to her.

"I'm sure we can work something out," Denise said, now trying to bargain with me.

"There's nothing to work out, Denise," I said to her.

Just then, I heard James' voice calling out from inside the house.

"Sarah? Are you here?"

Denise looked at me with terror in her eyes.

"Out here, James," I yelled.

"What's going on?" James said as he walked out onto the porch with us. He saw Caleb standing there, and Denise looking frantically back and forth between James and me.

"We're getting everything out in the open," I said to James.

"James," Denise said in a panic, "Don't listen to her. You know how she is when it comes to me."

Denise tried to put her arm around James' waist, but he took a step back to look at me. He saw me standing there with the cell phone in my hand.

"You found your phone?" James asked me.

"No, this isn't my phone," I said to him. "It belongs to Jared Sterling. He and Denise have been threatening and blackmailing me."

"What?" James stated, looking confused. He looked at Denise, then back at me, unsure what to think. "Why... why would Denise do that? And how do you know Jared Sterling?" James said as he turned to Denise.

"They were doing it because they have been having an affair together," I stated.

"James, it's not true," Denise said, trying to pull James towards her. James pulled his arm free again, and I handed him the phone, showing him all the messages and pictures that were on the phone.

"This... this goes back for months..." James said as he looked at the evidence before him. "Why would you do this... and say those things about my sister... and me... and our daughter?" James kept looking down at the phone and then back at Denise.

Denise was completely flustered at this point, not knowing what to do. She turned away from all of this, looking out over the backyard for a minute, before turning back to face us.

"Denise?" James said to her again, handing the phone back to me.

"I said all those things because it's how I feel, James!" she shouted. "How long did you expect me to live like this? Stuck living the life married to a plumber with an ungrateful daughter and her," she said pointing at me, "here in this house? Jared is younger, more attractive, and a lot richer than you will ever be and gave me a chance to get out of this. Did you really think I was happy with this? How blind are you? I've been sleeping with him for a long time, James, and you never had a clue.

Everything would have been fine if this bitch and her boyfriend didn't come along and fuck everything up..."

Denise let out a yell and lunged towards me. Caleb pulled me to the side and out of the way of her clutches, so she missed me and tumbled to the floor, landing flat on the wood porch. She turned over and scowled at me as she looked up at the three of us standing there.

"I think you should leave," James said to Denise, staring down at her.

"Leave? Where am I supposed to go?" Denise answered.

"Anywhere but here," James replied, turning away from her stare.

"I wouldn't go too far, Denise," I told her. "I am sure between whatever Jared is telling the police, and what they will see on this phone, they are going to want to talk to you."

Denise brushed the hair from her face and boosted herself up off the porch floor. She marched over to her lounge chair, grabbing her purse and sliding into her sandals hurriedly, before brushing past me and giving me a glare as she walked into the house. We could hear the front door slam as she went out, presumably to get in her car and try to go somewhere.

"Should we have stopped her?" I said to Caleb.

"Let her go," James said quietly.

"I am sure the police can track her down, wherever she goes or tries to run to," Caleb said to me.

I walked over to James and put my hand on his shoulder.

"I'm sorry, James," I said to him. "You needed to know the truth."

Just then, Lizzie appeared at the back door and slowly walked out onto the porch.

"What happened?" she asked. "I saw Mom heading out and tried to talk to her, but she wouldn't say anything to me. She just got in her car and took off."

I walked over to Lizzie and faced her.

"I confronted your Mom," I said to her, "and told your Dad everything."

Lizzie moved over closer to her father and put her arm around him. James hugged her close to him and held her.

"It'll be okay," James said to Lizzie, kissing her on top of her head.

"I know it will, Dad," Lizzie said to him.

I went over and stood by Caleb again, and he took my hand in his. James walked over to us and looked at Caleb.

"I'm guessing you had something to do with resolving all this," James said to him.

"Not really," Caleb said modestly. "Sarah is the one that had the strength to do it."

James looked at me and came over and hugged me.

"I'm sorry you've had to go through all this, Sarah," James said to me. "I wish I could have done more to help you. If had known you were in trouble..."

"It's not your fault, James," I interrupted. "Hopefully, things will be better for all of us now."

I broke our hug and looked back to Caleb.

"We should get this to the police station," I said to Caleb, holding up the phone.

Caleb nodded to me as I looked back to Lizzie and James. I went to them and hugged them simultaneously before Caleb and I went back out to the car.

I sat in the passenger seat of the Jeep and let out a big sigh of relief. I could feel my hands shaking a little bit as I looked down at the phone, and then looked over at Caleb. I could see him glance at me out of the corner of his eye.

"You were amazing," he said to me as he reached over and held my hand on my knee.

"I was a nervous wreck," I said to him honestly. "I kept expecting something to go wrong, or for me to break down."

"You were calm and cool through the whole thing," Caleb told me. "You did everything perfectly."

"Thank you," I told him as I sat back in the seat. I was feeling proud of myself and had more confidence than I had ever had in my life.

"And you were right," Caleb said to me as he turned the Jeep up Oak Street to go towards the police station.

"About what?"" I asked him.

"She is a bitch," he said to me with a wry smile.

Chapter 33

Caleb

The next few days all passed by as something of a blur. I spent a lot of time with Sarah, trying to help her through the mess she had experienced, and providing her with the comfort and support that helped to build her back up. We spent countless hours talking to police detectives, law enforcement officials, people from the DA's office and others, all asking question after question to her about what happened, how it happened, and why it happened.

The police did talk to me several times about what I did to Jared. It was to be expected I guess, and they wanted to make sure of all the facts. I know at one point he was considering filing charges against me for assault, but his lawyers apparently talked him out of it, knowing that he was already facing jail time and that a case like that may make it worse for him.

When all was said and done, Jared Sterling realized he had little leeway and wasn't going to get bailed out by his rich relatives this time. The evidence found on Jared's phone was more than enough to keep him in hot water. The Sterling family didn't want more of a spotlight shone on them more than this had already brought about and strongly suggested to him that he take a deal and face his prison time. He ended up pleading guilty to multiple charges and accepting a ten to twenty-year sentence instead of leaving things up to a jury, where he could have ended up with a lot more. In my opinion, he got off too easy, but the justice system doesn't always work the way we want it to.

As for Denise, after Jared sang about her involvement in the extortion attempt and the evidence found on the phone, the police had more than a passing interest in speaking with her. The problem was tracking her down at that point. Apparently, after she left the house, she went straight over to the bank and cashed out an account she had been using to squirrel away money she got from James, Jared, and her work. The pictures of her on camera at the bank are last ones anyone saw of her as the police searched around for her. The police extended their search to surrounding states, but as of yet, she hadn't turned up.

Doug gladly gave Sarah time off from the diner so that she could recover from her injuries and the trauma and deal with everything that was coming along with the case. This gave her a chance to clear her head and try to get settled more with her life. It also gave her more time to spend with James and Lizzie as they tried to pick up the pieces of what had happened and learn to work together as a family again.

During those few days, I also worked on putting the pieces of my life back together. After all that had happened, I knew how important it was to give my family and those I love the time and attention that is important. It had taken me two long years to see clearly that things can change in an instant, just as they had for me when Ella died, and I did not want to waste the time I had with everyone.

My first step was to try to find greater closure in dealing with Ella's death. I had made another visit to Dr. Weber, as I had promised him, and we talked at length about Ella, how important she was to my life and to Adam's, what her loss meant to me, and how I was working to understand and accept the grief. The meeting was very cathartic for me, and it also made me realize that Adam and I needed to deal with this together, something we had never done in the two years since she had passed.

Since it was near the time of the anniversary of her death, I decided now was the time to visit Ella's grave at the cemetery. I had not been out here since here funeral, trying to avoid coming here for all this time because I thought it would be too painful for me. When I first brought up the idea to Adam, he was genuinely surprised that I would want to go. He and Linda had been out to the gravesite several times over the years, and Adam was more than happy to go with me.

I told Sarah about what we were planning, and how we had planned to go on Saturday morning.

"I can come with you if you want," she said to me as we sat on the couch together. "Unless you're not comfortable with that, which I completely understand."

"Actually," I said to her, "I think it would help me if you were there. It's going to be tough for me, even with Adam there. It would mean a lot to me if you did come for support."

"Of course," Sarah said to me.

When Saturday morning came around, Adam, Sarah and I piled into my Jeep and drove out to the cemetery located just on the outskirts of Swanson. It was a warm, sunny day and the weather made it seem more comfortable and pleasant. I parked in the parking area just outside the graveyard, and we began the walk along the paved pathway that mazed its way through the cemetery in different directions. I had a hard time remembering exactly where Ella's grave was located, so Adam led the way, with Sarah and I following behind. Sarah held my hand the entire walk, glancing over at me as she could see I was getting nervous as we got closer.

"You okay?" she said to me, giving my hand a tug.

I gave her a quick smile and nod and looked up to see Adam make a sharp left and head down a row towards where I assumed the grave was located. He slowed as he reached the end of the row and stood before one grave.

I took a deep breath as we stood before the headstone. When we were here for the funeral, the headstone had not been put into place yet, so I had never seen it myself. All I knew of it was what Linda had described to me, and at the time I was agreeable to anything.

"Aunt Linda makes sure they take care of it and keep it clean and looking nice," Adam said to me.

The three of us stood silently for a minute or two before Adam stepped forward and laid the bouquet of flowers he had brought in front of the headstone.

"Hi, Mom," he said quietly. "I brought you daisies, just like we always picked together. Everything is going great. School is almost over, and I'll be graduating soon, so there's exams, the prom, graduation and all that. I'll be going to Duke in the fall on a partial scholarship, and I promise not to just focus on basketball and parties and get schoolwork done. I'll be sure to come and see you a bunch before I leave for school. I love you and miss you."

Adam patted the headstone with his left hand and walked over to Sarah and me. I put my arm around Adam and gave him a hug. Sarah then looked at me to see if I wanted to say anything. I was hesitant at first.

"Adam, come walk with me," Sarah said to him, and Adam patted me on the back and walked over to Sarah. Sarah put her arm around his waist, and they walked down the row, back towards the pathway that led out of the cemetery.

I slowly approached the gravestone and ran my hand over the top, feeling the cold, smooth marble beneath my hand.

"Hi, sweetie," I said out loud quietly. "I know I haven't been out here, but you should know that not a day goes by where you aren't in my thoughts. It's hard for me to see or do anything that doesn't remind me in some way about you, and I can't tell you how difficult it has been for me these last two years without you. It's taken me a long time- too long, probably – to start learning how to face life without having you here to help guide me along. We were partners for so long that I didn't think I could do it by myself. But then I realized that I'm not by myself. I have Adam, who you would be super proud of now that he is a young man, and Linda, who is the best sister ever and who misses you terribly, and... well, now I have Sarah."

"I know you and I always talked about what would happen if something happened to me overseas, and how I wanted you to be happy and live a full life and be with someone else if that is what you wanted. You always said you wanted the same for me, even though I never wanted to believe something would happen to you. When it did, I didn't know how to handle it, and I never wanted to think about anyone else but you. I didn't think I ever could be with someone again, but Sarah brings out something in me... something I thought I had lost forever when I lost you."

"I just want you to know that you are always a part of me and that I will always love you. I'll keep thinking about you, and I know somewhere you're watching me, making sure I keep doing things the right way. I love you."

I kissed the fingertips on my right hand and touched them to the top of the headstone before walking away. I was feeling choked up and sad and shed some tears on my walk back to where Sarah and Adam were waiting for me. I gave Adam another hug, and then gave one to Sarah, and then the three of us walked back to the car. I walked in the middle with one arm around each of them.

We got back to the Jeep and got inside and started driving back towards Swanson. Adam peeked his head up from the back of the Jeep in between the two of us in front.

"It's still early," Adam said to us. "How about we stop somewhere for breakfast?"

"I guess we could," I said to him. "Where would you like to go?"

"Well the diner has the best breakfast in town," Adam said without thinking.

"Really?" Sarah said to him. "The diner? I agree they have the best breakfast, but I already spend a lot of time there."

I kept driving along while the two of them tried to decide where to go before I took a turn from Oak Street and headed in a different direction.

"Dad, the diner is back in the other direction," Adam said to me.

"I know where the diner is, trust me," I said to Adam, giving Sarah a wink. "I just wanted to take a little drive first."

After a couple of turns, we were coming up the back end of Munson Lane. I slowed down and pulled into one of the driveways. Sarah turned instantly and looked at me, and I just smiled at her.

"What are we doing here?" Adam asked.

I climbed out of the car with Sarah getting out on her side. Adam finally got out and stood there with us.

"Who lives here?" Adam asked.

"Well, no one at the moment," I told him as we walked up the pathway and got near the front door. I turned the handle of the front door, and it was locked.

"Caleb, what are you doing?" Sarah said to me, worrying if I had lost my mind.

I reached up over the door to the top ledge and felt around and found the small black box I was looking for. I opened the box and took out the key I knew would be in there and held it up.

"Are we breaking into this house?" Adam asked, feeling a little concerned now himself.

"Caleb, we can't just go in there..." Sarah said to me as I put the key in the lock and opened the door.

We walked through the front door to see that the home was now completely furnished.

"Caleb, someone lives here now, we have to go," Sarah insisted.

"You guys have been here before?" Adam asked Sarah.

"Your Dad and I looked at this place a couple of weeks ago, just to see it," Sarah said to Adam. "Caleb, come on, this isn't funny. This is someone's home and furniture."

"Wait a minute," I said to Sarah as Adam was looking around.

"Hey... I recognize some of this... some of this is our old furniture, from the old house we rented," Adam said as he ran his hand over the couch in front of the fireplace.

"Yes," I said to him, closing the front door. "It is our old furniture. This is my house... well, our house really. I closed on it two days ago."

Sarah spun around and looked at me.

"How did you manage to pull that off?" Sarah asked me.

"Well I had been talking to Adrianne, the real estate agent, all along, since we looked at it, and I put an offer in. They had another offer already, but I sweetened the pot and offered them cash on the spot if they closed right away. They jumped at it, so I had a moving company bring the stuff over yesterday."

"So, where's my room," Adam said with a laugh.

"Upstairs," I said to him. "There's not much in there right now. I figured you would want some of your own stuff from Linda's house."

Adam went upstairs to have a look around while I led Sarah through the kitchen, which was now complete with a table and chairs and everything else needed.

"I figured we could have breakfast here this morning," I told her with a smile. I took her by the hand and led her outside, where I had some furniture set up around a fire pit out there.

"That's so nice for you two, Caleb," Sarah said to me. "It's just what you wanted."

"It doesn't have to be for just Adam and me," I said to Sarah. "I know it's only been a few weeks Sarah, and a lot has gone on in that time, but I can't imagine a day going by where I don't want to see you, and more than just seeing you while you're working or walking you home. I want to spend my days and nights with you. I love you, Sarah, and I would love it if you would come and live here with me and make this place your home... our home."

I was watching her face to see if I could read a reaction from Sarah. I didn't want her to feel overwhelmed or forced into making a decision she wasn't ready to make, and when she didn't answer right away, I wasn't sure what to make of the situation. She took two steps away from me and was looking out over the yard.

"Sarah?" I said to her.

Sarah turned back to me with a smile on her face.

"When we first looked at this place, I thought... I mean I could envision myself, here with you, making this our home," she said to me. "I just never thought it would really happen. I would love to come and live here with you, Caleb."

I walked over to where Sarah was standing and kissed her deeply.

"I love you, Caleb," Sarah whispered to me.

"I love you, too," I answered, and kissed her again.

"Hey lovebirds," Adam called from the back door. "Are we going to have breakfast or what? I'm starving."

"Get the coffee started," I told Adam. "We'll be inside in a second."

Adam just shook his head and went back into the house. I took Sarah's hand and walked her a bit further back into the yard where there was a small clearing surrounded by a few trees.

"I hung a hammock back here for us," I told her, leading her onto the hammock so we could lay together. "And I thought maybe we could put another fire pit back here for us."

I put my arm around her as we gently rocked in the hammock. Looking up, there was a clear pathway straight up into the sky.

"This will give us a perfect view of the moon and stars at night, and the moonlight will be beautiful, Caleb," Sarah said to me as she looked up.

Yes, perfect and beautiful, I thought. *Just how it should be.*